Extinction

To Dear Sheila.

Thanks for your support!

Love
Paul x

AN ANVIL PUBLICATIONS PAPERBACK

© Copyright 2006
Paul McKenzie

The right of Paul Mckenzie to be identified as the author of this work has been asserted by him in accordance with the Copyright, Designs and Patents Act 1988

All Rights Reserved

No reproduction, copy or transmission of this publication may be made without written permission.
No paragraph of this publication may be reproduced, copied or transmitted save with the written permission or in accordance with the provisions of the Copyright Act 1956 (as amended).
Any person who does any unauthorised act in relation to this publication may be liable to criminal prosecution and civil claims for damage.

A CIP catalogue record for this title is available from the British Library

ISBN 0-9551679-4-9
ISBN 978-0-9551679-4-2

Published by
Anvil Publications
187 Ware Road
Hertford
Herts
SG13 7EQ
HERTS SG14 1PX

Cover design by Paul Mckenzie

EXTINCTION

by

Paul Mckenzie

http://www.myspace.com/extinction_novel

M-Y BOOKS

1   THE ATTACK

The perimeter fence around the complex was scarcely illuminated by the moonlight. Careless guards smoked and their eyes had no time to adjust to the extreme light of the explosion that tore them from their sockets.

The enemy was already within the secondary defences and fast approaching the main structure that loomed in their path as the remnants of the dead guards fell to the flame-scorched earth. This was the first time that the attacking force had hit such a high profile target. In fact, it was the first time that they had launched a major offensive operation and apart from the stealth of their approach, there was little finesse in the attack. Skilled delicate hands worked furiously, placing explosives around the solid steel door that barred the way into the main building. Like most high security doors, this one was fitted with sturdy locks, but frail hinges, and with the charges positioned on the frame and directed towards the hinges, the door would be opened more easily than the cover on a paint pot. A soft fizz followed by a resonant pop was all that could be heard and in an instant the vast doors were levered out of place with an almighty crash as they slammed into the slate grey walkway.

The attacking force raced down numerous corridors carrying heavy steel cryogenic chambers. Each one was carried between two soldiers with another riding shotgun: five chambers in all. None of them was any bigger than five-six and appeared heavily built under their black and green fatigues. Their faces were not visible under their night fighting helmets. However, the soldiers could see perfectly without the benefit of light, even though they had cut the site's electricity precisely at the moment when the first guards had died. Lack of power gave the soldiers one headache; it meant that they had little time to liberate their intended quarry and make good their escape. The lateness of the hour ensured that only essential personnel were on duty - and although the soldiers had no time to hunt them down, they summarily executed any that crossed their path.

The military unit arrived breathlessly at the womb of the building. Two guards appeared from the control room, confused in the darkness and groping their way forwards with weapons slung uselessly over their shoulders. Rapid and precise hand signals from the commanding soldier quickly passed orders to the rest of the following squad. Silence swarmed the corridor while two members of the unit crept forward as ordered, vision assured from their helmet visors. The leading soldier raised his pistol almost mechanically, within touching distance of the guards, until the icy barrel caressed the forehead of the one closest. Realising that the pressure he felt meant only one thing, he stopped suddenly and his comrade behind blindly stumbled into the back of him. Bang! The single shot dropped the stationary guard just as the other was seized from behind. The attackers held him so tight that he could hardly catch his breath, as they wrenched one arm up behind his back and twisted his wrist ready to break it. The restrained guard was forced back into the control room and, even in his panic, he managed to focus on the warm sweet flavours in his mouth, which came from the blood sliding down over the contours of his face. The soldiers began to work on the next stage of the operation and he knew that, in all probability, he would not get the opportunity to wash his dead companion's blood from his face.

The complex was dull and grey, as were most buildings now; as were most lives lived now. The main structure had been partially built into the side of a sheer rock face with various other smaller buildings remotely connected by long glazed walkways that snaked their way across the finely manicured lawns. It was an easy target for the attacking soldiers, because those in power thought it not to be one.

The break away group of soldiers sent to destroy the power plant were now waiting tensely for the signal to reconnect their portable power units to the control circuits. The main generators, and also the back up ones, had been destroyed during the first attack, providing essential cover for the intruders. It was also a pathetic attempt to slow down the manufacturing process when normality returned. Any embryos and the more mature but not fully developed livestock would perish as a result of the power being severed for more than a couple of precious hours. It would take maybe a month or two to get the livestock farm back up to full production, but the soldiers knew that every obstacle they could put in the way of the normal breeding programme, however small, was worthwhile.

The radio crackled into life next to the soldiers waiting to re-connect the power, making more than a few of them flinch from their silent pause in proceedings.

'Tango-Charlotte-Four-Zero to Alpha-Rachel-Three-Zero are you receiving? Over,' asked the ranking soldier waiting in the cryo-womb, which was housed within the main complex.

The senior officer who stood lazily by the main circuit breakers replied, 'Alpha-Rachel-Three-Zero to Tango-Charlotte-Four-Zero, receiving you loud and clear. Please advise on reconnection status, over.'

Before the request to reconnect the power to the control circuits arrived, desperate screams leapt fearfully from the radio.

'Alpha-Rachel-Three-Zero to Tango-Charlotte-Four-Zero are you in need of assistance? Repeat. Are you in need of assistance? Over,' the officer repeated with renewed urgency.

Preceded simply by a single shot, the reply finally came as the screaming terminated.

'Tango-Charlotte-Four-Zero to Alpha Rachel-Three-Zero. Assistance not required. We were just being brought up to speed with the control panel operations, but as you know I never liked male instructors much,' replied the soldier at the cryo-womb doors.

The guard had divulged what little knowledge he had been entrusted with and was now dead, bundled into the corner like a discarded piece of information. The information that he'd given was not essential to the operation, but it had saved precious minutes in completing the final stage of the plan. Moreover, it had put a little entertainment into what was otherwise turning out to be a quiet night.

Two soldiers sat intently in the control room at the two mother panel desks while the rest of the unit moved into the entrance of the Cryo-womb. The soldier at the desk closest to the entrance entered the code 4398 followed by the word *Amazon* into the worn keyboard. The doors opened quietly and the waiting unit advanced eagerly into the defenceless room. The soldiers at the desks began throwing switches and entering further codes while they surveyed the chamber before them. It reminded them more of a mortuary than a place of creation. Located all around the walls of the Cryo-womb were silver coloured doors of varying sizes. A false ceiling concealed the pipes and control valves that fed the development chambers and the seductive lighting made for an extremely peaceful atmosphere. There was a low hum, much like that of a refrigerator. This soothed the soldiers' volatile tensions; but they still leapt for cover as the soft *whoosh* of seals opening on five of the wall-mounted cryogenic chambers broke the pervading peace. The soldiers pulled the trays of black flasks, now drained of fluid, from their frozen sanctuary. No orders were passed; they all knew the drill. They transferred flasks from their trays to the portable cryogenic chambers that they had been carrying and, once full, sealed them. On each chamber there was a small chrome keypad used to input a start-up code; upon the 'enter' button being pressed they purred into life. Finally, with the portable chambers now waiting in the corridor, the soldiers returned to set the charges in the Cryo-womb leaving themselves a ten-minute window in which to evacuate the area. 'This is going to be the biggest bang this womb's ever gonna get' thought the soldier as he triggered the timer and then they were gone into the night, taking with them both guards' testicles, which they had neatly placed in sterilised containers.

2 HISTORY

No one could recollect exactly when, where, or who had instigated the unthinkable attempt at the extermination of the female half of the human race. Over thousands of years of human existence women had been persecuted and denied basic human rights by a male society seeking to maintain the grip on power. Women had fought every step of the way to be treated as equals, they had suffered many setbacks, particularly when dealing with the primitive and draconian philosophies of certain religions and antiquated cultures. Nevertheless, their very existence had never been in doubt despite the never ending battle between equality and supremacy.

Had it all started in 2035 with the love drug, so called because when injected it removed a person's desire for love and companionship, allowing them to live their lives alone and independent of all the pain and joy that relationships bring? People had become accustomed to living alone and by the year 2050 an irreversible operation was being administered in place of the love drug. This was at first by choice, but with the population booming out of control, by the year 2150 the surgical procedure had become compulsory on the specific orders of the Eurostate Government. Human breeding farms were created to control the new population influx, releasing into society strictly controlled numbers of fully matured livestock. The farms used human eggs, secretly harvested from ovaries removed from exterminated women. The ovaries were kept alive and functioning in specially developed laboratory cylinders. Harvested eggs were fertilised using a perfected cloning process that had been first developed in the last few years of the twentieth century. DNA-altered cells were injected into the eggs, which fooled them into believing that they had been fertilised by more traditional methods. Ultimately, this meant that a new human race had been selectively bred with no need or longing for companionship. Cloning had now not just become a reality; it had become the norm - and real human reproduction was nothing more than a pleasure left in the past like a discarded condom.

By the year 2350, male-controlled farms produced only male livestock and female existence was no longer seen as an essential part of everyday life in any capacity. Grades of male livestock were being produced specifically for various workplace functions. Genes were genetically altered in livestock so that they could be reared for the profession for which they had been earmarked. Any abnormalities were strictly controlled and eradicated by the quality control units that worked within the breeding regime. Marginalised, groups of females began to band together and sought sanctuary in the more remote parts of Europe, defending their very existence and defiantly resisting the single gender breeding programme. The renegade women soon realised that without new females to replenish their numbers their gender's days on Earth would end. So they started to recruit from the remaining female population in an effort to stop the male-dominated society from claiming the final victory in a battle that had never before come this perilously close to the extinction of women.

At the first signs of female resistance, male society seemed unconcerned and showed complete apathy to the token displays of defiance. After all, what could a bunch of women who were so dependent on centuries of male dominance achieve? Before long, male complacency had turned to anger and then to complete fear of an enemy that society had tolerated. All attempts to exterminate the renegade groups failed completely. Subsequently, the battle progressed to a higher level; if only the male security forces could prevent all forms of female breeding, then they could extinguish the flame forever. The renegade females' initial attempts at reproduction were extremely unsophisticated. They did not have access to their male counterparts' cloning techniques and technology, and so they resorted to a more basic reproduction method. They began by imprisoning men that they had caught and extracting their semen, keeping them like chickens jailed in a battery farm. In time, they perfected the process so that they could do away with the roosters, artificially keeping alive the amputated testicles using antiquated laboratory equipment, just as the males had done with the ovaries of countless discarded women. Using their own eggs to produce new livestock the women would live to fight on, but for how long? The need for testicles led to the wonderful female pastime of removing them from any male who had the misfortune to be captured - and the practice was, understandably, much maligned by a terrified male population.

The abhorrent abuse of the human form and procreation then took further steps along the road of amorality. The Feman was initially an accident of nature; of mixed genitalia it was shunned and all but eradicated by male society. A no more caring, but more desperate female community harboured the few Femen that survived the male intolerance for mutation. The renegade female communities trained them to spy on their behalf because they could operate undetected in strictly male conurbations. Finally, society sank to new depths: perfect male and female livestock had their chemical balances altered to reverse their gender mentally and, with a small amount of brainwashing, the switch was complete, providing the ultimate disguise. Gender was no longer born of nature - but cynically manipulated by a human race bereft of basic morality.

3 MORNING AFTER

The soldiers removed their night-fighting helmets now that they had arrived safely back at their base - a defunct nuclear bunker, forgotten in post-cold war euphoria, hidden in wasteland and discovered by chance. Rachel McDowell, the most senior of the group, left the dormitory to report to the leader of the female community. The darkened musty corridors were cold, so cold she thought that her sweat-drenched hair would freeze to her scalp. McDowell was drawn and pale from the previous evening's efforts, but warm with the thought that they had procured enough pre-fertilised eggs to supply their crude and makeshift cloning laboratory for many years to come.

Stopping in front of the shabby steel door, she sighed and took a deep breath. As she knocked the door creaked ajar and warm aromas of food and perfume exhausted through the gap.

'Come in,' a deep voice boomed.

McDowell entered the sumptuous office, only to see Jane Langton, her Commanding Officer, deep in conversation with Commune Leader Kefelnikov. The dry heat in the room scraped at McDowell's face and made her skin feel taut and desiccated. She stood to attention and waited silently in front of the vast dining table where her superiors sat, still conversing. Without consideration for their subordinate, the two women talked at length, before Kefelnikov finally deigned to address McDowell in her harsh strain of European English.

'Shut that fucking door, it's cold enough to freeze the balls off a chauvinist,' barked Kefelnikov.

McDowell knew Kefelnikov occasionally liked to use her acquired bar room slang, ironically just to be one of the 'boys', but it did not provoke even the slightest amount of respect within the soldiers in the commune. No one liked her, the infantile attempt to ingratiate herself with her subordinates through the use of basic language lasted only as long as she thought it prudent, before she reverted to her usual pretentious ways. Also, Kefelnikov seemed far too tolerant of the desperate situation in which they had found themselves, choosing not to go on the offensive when all the girls wanted to do was attack the egotistical and self-righteous enemy. After all, Kefelnikov was only the commune leader because it had been she who had inadvertently discovered the nuclear fallout shelter and now she sat on her fat arse in her warm office while others risked their lives.

Kefelnikov looked up as McDowell returned to the table after closing the ill-fitting door.

'Well? Your report. Did you complete the task you were set?' Kefelnikov asked.

'Sir, mission completed Sir. No casualties and the target has been acquired. We have now delivered it safely to the laboratory. Sir,' McDowell replied obediently.

That was the bizarre thing about Kefelnikov. She insisted on being called 'Sir'. She said that 'Miss' did not convey the appropriate amount of respect for her position. Fat and blonde, she was disliked by the troops but this had never seemed to undermine her authority.

McDowell now focused on Commander Langton, a dark handsome woman. Langton had that inane, mediocre, wind-filled smile, the type you get when you are drunk as a skunk.

'What the fuck was that all about?' McDowell thought, as Commander Langton began to speak in her soft annoying tones.

'So, no problems then. Great, yes, good. Well I bet you would like a nice hot bath and bed Corporal McDowell?' Langton said voicing her own feelings rather than her subordinate's.

'A fucking beer would be a start,' McDowell thought immediately.

As she left, McDowell was convinced that the room, with its subtle lighting and sweet fragrance, looked and smelled more like a tart's boudoir than a Commune Leader's office. She did not know that for a fact but had read electronic books about tarts and prostitutes and the thought made her feel sick.

McDowell somehow found herself back at the door to her barracks after walking the squalid corridors for longer than she had intended. She felt the container nestling in her pocket and remembered the testicles that she had placed there during the attack. McDowell smiled - what fun they had had in getting them! But who the hell had the other pair?

'Well,' she thought, 'I'd better take these to the lab now. They'll be no good in a few hours.'

4   THE INVESTIGATION

The dawn rose before any of the attacking military unit from the previous night had woken; they slept soundly, whilst groups of bureaucratic military men arrived at the breeding farm to survey and assess the damage. Major Robert Kellor, the most senior military intelligence officer available, had been assigned the complicated task of sorting out the disaster. At six-foot-three and 100 kilograms Kellor had an imposing frame, piercing blue eyes and dark brown cropped hair. As he peered through the murk of first morning light, Kellor could see the carnage below from his vantage point above the farm. Assorted shades of grey rubble and red brick lay in neat piles next to undamaged parts of the complex. Kellor began to trace in his mind the precise route that the enemy had taken through the fence and into the main building. He made his way down to the first point of contact to track the route for real on foot. During this time of investigation he could not believe what he saw. Kellor knew that the enemy had never been so brazen with their attacks in the past. As the minutes ticked by, one thought filled his head: *neat and tidy job!*. There was nothing extravagant about it; maximum damage and minimum fuss. *Impressive* and depressing.

  Kellor entered the main building, carefully avoiding the destroyed security doors and intermittently stopping and hunting for evidence until he eventually stumbled upon the first dead guard. Kellor looked down at his boots and in the gloom found that they were squarely placed in a pool of thickly congealed blood. The deceased guard was laid face down in what was almost the recovery position. Sliding his blood-tainted boot under the bruised hips of the stiffened guard, Kellor rolled him over with a swift flick. He winced as his torchlight revealed the guard's bloodied trousers, which had been torn down to his ankles. His shorts were cut away and there, where this fine specimen's testicles had been, was a gaping and gory wound. Closing his eyes, he smiled at the thought of some meathead muscle-bound grunt walking around with this guy's balls in her pocket. He would wager that she had always wanted a pair of them for her very own. Moving on, Kellor approached the cryo-womb and was abruptly halted by one of the many junior soldiers now guarding the base.

'Excuse me Sir. I need to see some ID,' the soldier ventured politely, recognising Major Kellor's rank.

Kellor glared at the young private. He did not have a problem with the request in the slightest, but he liked to keep his subordinates guessing about his disposition. As Kellor passed his Eurostate ID over he smiled.

'Will this do for you Private?'

'Yes Sir, fine, thank you Sir,'

Kellor immediately dropped his smile, huffed and looked over the soldier's shoulder into the blackened room.

'Sir, I have orders that nobody is to enter the Cryo-womb at this moment in time. Too many hazardous chemicals about, Sir'

'Let me be the judge of that private,' Kellor overruled.

Kellor strode forward, pushed past the soldier and entered the previously sealed Cryo-womb. While he stood there inspecting the surrounding damage, Kellor took a handkerchief from his pocket and held it over his nose and mouth. The sharp acrid air stabbed at his eyes. He felt the bile surge into his throat as the fumes seeped through the improvised cotton mask and down into his lungs. All manner of twisted metal bounded Kellor. There were cables and pipes hanging from the ceiling like vines in a jungle. In fact, as he negotiated his way through the room, he had to crouch down to avoid them as he manoeuvred around the spoilt embryos that covered the floor. Before very long, Kellor's eyes were smarting and he thought that maybe the soldier was right about the chemical hazards within the cryo-womb. Kellor decided that it was best to leave, but as he attempted to do so a twisted embryonic chamber caught his eye in a darkened corner of the room. Upon closer inspection, Kellor was sure something was amiss - or more amiss than had been immediately obvious.

'Probably around sixteen fertilised egg flasks,' he thought to himself with a wry smile. By now his eyes were burning and tears ran down into his makeshift mask. Kellor left the room in a hurry; he had seen all he had needed to see.

The soldier relaxed as the Major walked past him and, without turning to speak, Kellor passed an order to the Private in a mildly choking voice, 'Don't let anyone in there Private, not without clearing it with me first and this time do it or *I'll* have your balls!'

With tears still streaming from his eyes, Kellor set out for the Incident Command Centre that had been hastily set up in the site canteen.

The heavily scuffed double doors swung gently back into position after Kellor had barged through them and found himself in the harsh fluorescent-lit, windowless canteen. The bright unnatural light bounced off the plastic surfaces that covered the whole room and his eyes began to sting once more, as if lulled into complacency after the relief of the cool, damp morning air. Squinting as he looked around and his gaze finally settled on the gaggle of men fussing around maps of the local area. Directly between them and Kellor sat none other than the top man himself. His back was facing Kellor, but he knew the outline very well indeed from the incessant state television broadcasts. European President James T. Wells was a small dark-skinned man of immense power and stature, the driving force behind male dominance. Sitting to his left at a respectful distance was his so called 'Hatchet Man', the boyishly good-looking Callum Daniels, dressed in an expensive suit.

'A more complete pair of gangsters you could not hope to find,' thought Kellor.

The clock on the wall read 06:50 hours and Kellor knew from experience that it would be a very long day. He took a seat nearby and waited for the panic in front of him to die down. Closing his eyes, Kellor rested the back of his head against the canteen wall.

'A very long day indeed,' he thought once again and finally began to relax after his morning's efforts.

Kellor opened his eyes with a start as he sensed the presence of another close by. He quickly glanced back at the clock on the wall. The time now was only 06:57. As he got shakily to his feet, Kellor felt decidedly sick and he knew that he was not totally clear of the chemical fumes that he had inhaled in the cryo-womb. He faced the man in front of him, trying hard to regain his composure.

'You're the best we've got?' sneered Daniels as Kellor's drowning senses struggled slowly to the surface.

Kellor's teeth clenched in anger but somehow he managed to pull his lips into a pathetic smile.

'I'm afraid so Sir. Well the best that's available at this moment in time Sir,' he replied a little too sarcastically.

Looking around, Kellor now saw that the general panic had subsided and that President Wells was on his own, apart from some boffin in the standard issue white coat.

'Major Kellor, would you be so kind as to give President Wells some of your very valuable time. We are under the impression that you're here to do a job!'

Furious at being spoken to in such a demeaning manner Kellor began to think of a suitable riposte, but eventually decided just to nod submissively. He followed Daniels without further deliberation and, as they approached James Wells, he was introduced to the President and Professor Alexander Chenenko.

President Wells immediately began to speak, as if addressing the nation on state television.

'We have a critical situation here Major. But we must prevail in the face of overwhelming odds,' he explained dramatically.

Kellor found it an extreme turn-off to hear President Wells recite his on-message information in the stereotypical language of a politician, but listened all the same.

5 THE STATE OF AFFAIRS

President Wells had come to power under a cloud of scandal. Vote-rigging, murder and blackmail were all on his increasingly less hidden agenda. As a multi-billionaire media and software tycoon, he had been ideally placed to arrange for the electronic vote casting system to be routed through his empire's vast computer networks. Hence, Wells had been voted in as the head of the ruling Eurostate Government by a landslide majority and his company, Medware IT, went from strength to strength with Eurostate contracts.

Europe, now under one banner and one leader since 2090, was the most powerful state in the world. Borders were long forgotten; English was now a common language, if a little broken in places. A common goal had been decided upon between the men of Europe, who were born of a tyrannical male ethos that drove them to unite and dominate what had previously been a second-rate and splintered continent. The USA and the Far East, for the most part, had shunned the fanatical wave of male dominance that had prevailed in Europe, choosing to breed livestock of both sexes equally. For this reason they were perceived as weak and untrustworthy by the ruling Eurostate party. The Eurostate politicians were sure that the female terrorists, or Femorists as they were known, who operated in their continent, were funded and supplied to a large extent by a sympathetic American population. Diplomatic relations between the two continents were at an all-time low and war seemed a distinct possibility. The Far East however, did everything possible to avoid being drawn into a pointless conflict.

The Eurostate had grown all-powerful, initially on welfare cuts made possible by the new breeding programmes. When the second-generation of cloned livestock reached their twilight years, normal family groups had died out almost completely. Those families who had survived to see the transformation in society were interned and then erased from history. Thus, state benefits paid out, or not, to be more specific, saved billions of Euros. There were no single parent families, no divorce courts with legal aid bills. Gone were the days of unemployment, for the state controlled the breeding programme to meet exactly their manpower needs. Everybody had a job to do and for the most part they were stuck for the rest of their unnatural life with what they had been specifically bred for. Nobody retired; a biological clock inbred into all livestock meant that they ceased to function long before they were physically worn out. Any livestock that malfunctioned during its predetermined lifetime was disposed of without hesitation or argument. State pensions no longer had to be provided, nor child benefit, expensive vaccination programmes or free child health and dental care. There were no schools to fund and finally traffic gridlocks had been eased through the complete lack of mothers having to run their spoilt brats around to and from school. The welfare system had completely disappeared, because there were no customers left and state funds grew beyond all imagination. The Eurostate had been able to invest heavily in advanced technology for the breeding of new livestock and was far in advance of any other state in the world. The livestock was grown at an accelerated rate; from cloned egg to a fully trained indoctrinated man took around two weeks. The manufactured man was then ready to perform his role in life in the capacity for which he had been reared. Recently however, Eurostate scientists had developed an extraordinary strain of livestock. The new breed was superior in strength, intelligence and exhibited limited forms of psychic power. They were able to communicate with fellow livestock of the same breeding strain and, it appeared, with no one else. The psychic powers had come about by pure chance, whereas the other enhancements were made possible by altering the genes that made up the MkII livestock's DNA string. Only one prototype of this improved livestock had ever been brought to full term, or so everybody believed, and currently it was incarcerated under evaluation. A flask of fertilised MkII eggs had been prepared for production purposes and had then been stored, ready and waiting for endorsement of the prototype. Once the lead scientists working on the project had given approval, the 16,000 fertilised eggs were to be brought to full term and unleashed on the unsuspecting Femorists.

President Wells swiped the beads of perspiration from his forehead but the persistent sweat still ran down into his tired dark brown eyes. His voice was still calm and assured as before, but his body language conveyed that he was not at ease. His small athletic frame did not seem to match the round flabby face and greying hair. Wells finally held eye contact with Kellor and began to furnish him with the exact details of the 'critical situation' that had been mentioned just a few moments before.

'Major Kellor, last night at 02:00 hours this breeding institute was attacked by Femorists conspiring to bring the very fabric of our civilisation to its knees. They must be stopped at all costs,'

President Wells was breathing heavily and looked like a man under severe strain. Still he continued in his calm and assured manner, 'During the course of the attack a large quantity of fertilized eggs was taken from the cryo-womb centre.'

Kellor knew all of this - he had seen it for himself - but he dare not interject. The President now sat down at one of the plastic covered canteen tables and gestured to the Major to do the same.

'We know for a fact that somewhere in the region of one hundred flasks of eggs was taken. That equates to around eighty thousand fertilized eggs, give or take a few. Unfortunately, one of the cryogenic chambers that was raided contained eggs of a very special nature,' Wells continued.

Until now Kellor had been only half listening to the tedious facts, of which he was already aware, but now his attention sharpened and focused.

'Now Major Kellor, the following information I am about to impart is strictly for your ears only. Under no circumstances must it be repeated to anyone - and that would include your mother if you had one,'

Kellor smiled at the President's antiquated expression. He had not heard it for a long time - it seemed that only older men used it because they had been thoroughly educated in historical reproduction and parenting. However, education in this area had long since been forbidden, because the ruling party felt that to continue would risk undermining - or rather might reactivate - the hearts and minds of a new generation of livestock. President Wells leant forward, placed both elbows on the table and brought his clasped hands to his chin. His eyes narrowed as he continued with his simulated broadcast.

'The twenty of the flasks that came from this chamber, which equates to around 16,000 eggs, are quite unique. A small team of genetic scientists working in isolation and in secret at this very institute had developed those enhanced eggs. They are the only ones of their kind in existence and would have...' President Wells stopped and rephrased his last statement, 'And will give the Eurostate the edge in our battle against the Femorists.'

Kellor could contain his questions no longer and interjected without another thought for the consequences.

'What's so special about this batch of eggs exactly?'

'Well, let's just say they have enhanced physical and intellectual capabilities, but I will leave the exact details to Professor Chenenko,' replied Wells, raising his eyes casually in the Professor's general direction.

Kellor looked up at the Professor and then returned his gaze sharply to the President.

'So, what you are saying is that you are not interested in the ordinary eggs that were stolen. It's just the enhanced batch you want retrieved?'

'Retrieved or destroyed. But you're right; I care less about the ordinary eggs than for the welfare of the Femorists that perpetrated this despicable act. If you manage to retrieve all of the flasks then you will be doing the State a great service, beyond the call of duty some would say. At the very least as I said before, the special batch of eggs must be destroyed and I emphasize the MUST!' replied Wells as he stood up and peered down at Kellor, who disrespectfully remained seated.

'Now, if you'll excuse me Major, unfortunately I have to return to report to the State Council in Berlin, but Daniels and Professor Chenenko will provide you with the rest of the details. Good luck and, if you are successful, I am sure you will find that the benefits will make the effort worthwhile,' said Wells as he turned to speak to Daniels.

'Right. I should have been long gone by now. Take it from here Daniels and anything Major Kellor requires, provide it, post haste,'

With his last statement the President swirled around and walked briskly towards the exit. His trailing hand grabbed a long black leather overcoat from an unused chair. He swung the coat around his bony shoulders, crashed through the swinging doors and was gone. The remaining men glanced at each other while the doors swung rapidly back and forth in the background.

'Let's get on shall we. Professor, if you'd take us to the prototype nursery - while we walk I can acquaint Major Kellor with the finer details of our situation,' said Daniels as his domineering side resurfaced with the president's absence.

'Okay, but I'm afraid we will have to get there via the farm grounds. The lab leading to the nursery is inaccessible to say the least,' Professor Chenenko replied.

The three men left the building; Daniels walked next to the Major with the Professor taking the lead. Outside, the scene had changed dramatically from that when they had all first arrived. Kellor looked at his watch; it was now 07:45 and the morning had dawned splendidly. Though still cold, the day was very bright indeed and the rubble around them, the ruins randomly interspersed with apparently untouched buildings, looked far less sinister in the daylight.

'Let me continue Major,' said Daniels as they walked on past the homogeneous groups of workers robotically clearing up the surrounding mess.

'These special eggs: they produce mature livestock that's faster, stronger and more intelligent than you. They've been produced with gene modifications to give twice the Special Forces' aggression level. Hell, they could walk through brick walls if so ordered,' enthused Daniels.

They began to walk down a steep grassy embankment, damp from the morning dew, and in between trying not to slip in his beautiful Italian antique leather shoes and vainly attempting not to get them wet, Daniels resumed his briefing.

'We were just about to embark on a massive breeding programme of this new strain of livestock. In fact, we were just waiting for Professor Blaine, who was lead scientist on the project, to give the all clear with the prototype. As you can imagine, with genetic weapons such as these we have to be very careful that they are fully functional and disciplined before we release them into service. We wouldn't want them turned against us now would we!'

Just as he finished his sentence, he lost his footing and weakly grabbed Kellor's arm to avoid any possibility of him crashing to the ground.

'Sorry. Thanks. I mean... Well anyway,' Daniels said uncomfortably as he struggled to regain his composure. He did not like to rely on anyone or anything and to be shown up in such a manner was almost his worst nightmare.

'Picture if you will a 16,000 strong army made up of this enhanced livestock on the march, incubated and indoctrinated with Femorist allegiance! It could spell the end of the male gender forever; at the very least the end of male domination,' he paused, 'Oh and I forgot to mention, the MkII livestock seem to have some psychic ability as well, but only between other livestock of the same strain,' Daniels added nonchalantly as if he were describing an optional extra on a new car.

The three men were now fast approaching the specialist research centre where the prototype nursery was located. Standing silently in front of a pile of charred, blackened rubble, they could just make out a secure route through to a smoke-tarnished steel door, which was clearly visible at the back of what had been the research lab. Eventually, the three contrasting men concluded their silent assessment and looked at each other for reassurance.

'Why don't you just rear another batch of MkIIs to cancel out the ones that we've lost?' Kellor asked, confused, while delaying their foray into the bombsite.

'It's not as easy as that. Apart from the devastation that such a large conflict would undoubtedly cause - don't forget we're effectively talking about an army of supermen - it may be, er, a little while before we are able to produce any more of them,' Daniels replied in a mildly embarrassed manner.

'Why the delay?' Kellor asked, not wanting to let Daniels hide his thoughts so easily.

'Unfortunately, it seems that the development of the MkII had been done completely in isolation in this very laboratory and all information relating to the project was kept in this room that you see before you. And last night a series of unfortunate coincidences meant that the whole of the development team were in the room when the Femorists attacked - every last one of 'em! Usually at that time of the morning the lab would be closed down for the night, but they were just about to complete the last phase of the prototype MkII's education and training. The project staff that weren't killed in the blast were burnt to death in the ensuing fire. The records and technical data relating to the project were either stolen or destroyed; so far we've no way of knowing which. So, all things considered, it's been a monumental disaster. All we know is that the whole project went up in smoke last night and the eggs are the only things, apart from the prototype, that remain intact.'

'How did the prototype survive the attack?' Kellor asked, as he looked between Daniels and the Professor for his answer. The Professor was the first to reply.

'The room where it's receiving the condensed data and image input is behind that Kevanium door back there. Luckily, because of the enhanced features of the MkII prototype, we decided that a stronghold room would be the safest place for it till it had been thoroughly tested and trained - there's no way even that thing could break out. And of course, the room was strong enough to withstand the blast and the fire. It's also powered and air conditioned completely independently from the rest of the complex, so we could be sure the equipment wouldn't crash during the condensed data and image input whatever happened elsewhere in the farm. As you're probably aware, we've had some difficulties with livestock that have had interruptions during this final stage of their indoctrination. Consequently, they have to be taken out of service because of emotional and mental problems that have manifested themselves later in life,'

Meanwhile, Daniels began to move cautiously through the shattered building. He beckoned Kellor to follow and he did so, with the Professor taking up the rear.

'Now, in there is the new MkII prototype, but we're not sure how ready it is. It would seem that programming had completed its full cycle - but we're not a hundred percent. Unfortunately, without any records or staff to confirm this Major you will have to be very, very careful with it.'

While Daniels finished his sentence he wiped a fist-sized patch of black smoke dust from the six-inch thick window that looked in upon the MkII's secure room. He used his white silk handkerchief and Kellor noticed the initials delicately stitched into the material: 'C.A.D'.

'Hold on one moment, my brief is not to act as mentor for this MkII but to retrieve the enhanced eggs. I really don't think it is...' Kellor verbally exploded, astounded that he was going to have to baby-sit this MkII.

'This is not up for negotiation Major Kellor. You will take this MkII and use it to retrieve those eggs, period. Now if you wish you may take a look inside. Then I want you to return to the canteen and provide me with a complete list of the equipment that you need to accomplish this mission,' Daniels said, cutting Kellor dead in mid-sentence.

Rebuked, Kellor moved closer to the window and his rapid angry breath misted the thick glass. Despite the pounding of blood in his temples, he managed to control his breathing. The moisture on the glass dissipated and he finally managed to focus on the impassive MkII that lay within the darkened strong room. Eventually, the creature's form became apparent, just discernible in the gloom, and Kellor's jaw plunged into a bewildered gape.

Marching purposefully through the doors to the canteen, closely followed by Daniels, Kellor was unable to hide his increasing resentment and violently kicked the chairs and tables from his path with his hefty size tens. The once-highly polished combat boots were no longer shiny; mud had worked its way up from the sole during their little excursion and the impact with the chairs and tables had covered the polished surface with streaks of brown dirt. Finally, reaching the area of the canteen where the maps of the surrounding region stood, he turned fiercely as Daniels calmly approached.

'Now, before you say anything you may regret Major Kellor I'd consider your position very carefully. You may think that you have no need for this cross breed, MkII or whatever you may want to call it but, it's as good as any weapon we have in our armoury right now and will give you the edge when dealing with these Femorists,' Daniels stated, clearly brooking no argument.

Kellor glared more intently now and for a time forgot with whom exactly it was that he was dealing.

'That fucking cross breed or abomination, whatever YOU want to call it, is a time bomb waiting to go off! You don't even know if it's ready for combat. What if she turns out for the opposition team instead, just when I'm ready for the kill. No, you have no authority over me, I take orders from one man only and that's not you!'

Daniels smirked. He was surprisingly unconcerned by Kellor's outburst and turned to his laptop, which sat on the table next to him. After punching in various numbers, the words 'uplink established', followed by the flashing word 'Connecting' blazed upon the computer display. A few seconds later, the original screen was replaced with the benign-looking face of Colonel Martin Johnson. Johnson was a military veteran: early forties, blonde hair and baby blues. In fact he had everything needed to be the archetypal Californian surfing god, except he was not from California and had no surfing ability whatsoever. Daniels grinned and began to look directly into Kellor's eyes as he conversed with the Colonel.

'Martin, how the devil are you?' he asked like an old friend, which he most definitely was not.

'Fine Callum, what can I do for you?' replied the submissive Colonel.

Kellor got that sinking feeling as his thoughts entered panic mode. The bastard had called his Commanding Officer and he knew the outcome was not going to be to his satisfaction. Kellor began to feel Daniels' grip over him tightening.

'Martin, I have one of your fine young officers here - a certain Major Kellor. Anyway, to cut a long story short, we just need a bit of clarification about the lines of authority concerning the situation here in Stablinka. Now, Major Kellor would like your approval for him to take his orders directly from me; you don't have a problem with that now? Do you Martin?'

'No, no. Not at all Callum, do as you see fit. All I would ask is for a quick word with Major Kellor before you assume authority. If there's nothing else you need Callum?'

Kellor moved into the view of the laptop camera without daring to return Daniels' constant stare. He knew the Colonel well and was convinced that he would not have sold him out to the politicians without good reason. Observing the Colonel carefully as he spoke, Kellor sensed the unease in his Commanding Officer's demeanour.

'Ah, there you are Major, I trust everything's fine your end?'

Kellor knew something was amiss and he began to focus on calming his furious body. The Colonel was a man he could trust, he was sure of that, so he would have to go along with whatever the Colonel had in mind.

'Yes Colonel, I'm okay. But we have a situation here,' Kellor advised before the Colonel interrupted.

'Yes Major, I fully understand the situation there, but I have full confidence in Mr Daniels to direct you in a manner conducive to rectifying this situation. I would remind you of the Greenland siege that we served on together and ask you to employ some of the tactics and application that you used to resolve that situation. That's an order Major. Well, must be going now. We have a situation here as well, lunch. Good luck chaps!'

Without delay, the Colonel's image was replaced with the 3-D Eurostate logo revolving around the otherwise empty screen.

Silent deliberate looks passed between Daniels and Kellor, both now believing that they were in control of the personal battle between them.

6 MUTATION

Rachel McDowell had been awake for hours on the morning after the raid but, uncharacteristically, she was still not dressed. She lay quietly on her bunk, eyes closed, far from asleep, far from at peace. The previous night's attack was running repeatedly through her mind; she was always looking for improvement. Although she had not lost any soldiers during the mission, McDowell still felt somehow flat inside, but she could not put her finger on exactly what it was that was eating at her. A junior officer entered the dormitory where she lay and peered up towards her bunk.

'Corporal McDowell, Commander Langton and Commune Leader Kefelnikov would like to see you down in the IVF Lab straight away,' ordered the junior officer.

McDowell gritted her teeth and sat bolt upright before speaking, 'Yes Miss. Right away Miss!'

The officer reached the door, ready to leave the barracks, half turned and smiled at McDowell.

'Bloody good job last night McDowell. Well done. Had some fun as well by all accounts!'

'Too fucking right Miss! Two more sets for the trophy cabinet,' she replied, returning the smile and, with that gesture, she felt some of the usual warmth return to her spirits.

McDowell climbed down off her bunk and began to put her uniform on over her khaki boxers and vest. Her breasts were small but she was still as shapely as any female in the commune. Men had bred smaller-chested women when the female form was still in production. Other than this minor change, they had left the female form alone, choosing to discontinue production rather than alter the physical and biological differences any further.

For some bizarre reason, commune leader Kefelnikov had also ordered the lab to produce small-breasted women. Sure, a small bust had its advantages in combat - and anyway women were conditioned to frown upon large bosoms - but it seemed strangely as though the male regime still had their influence, even inside this female bastion. McDowell did up the last few buttons on her tunic, covering the tattoo on her left shoulder, which could be seen just above the vest and depicted a female grim reaper carrying severed testicles over her scythe. McDowell smiled as she saw it disappear from sight before setting off to the cloning laboratory.

The corridors were as cold as the previous night; in fact, the temperature changed very little because they were so deep underground. Stark and unsanitary, the passageway led to rooms that were heated, bright and basically comfortable. The 'IVF Lab', as everyone called it, was held within the deepest point of the shelter. McDowell entered the stairwell and descended at a brisk pace. Most females would have taken the service elevators but not her; she preferred the dark, dank stairwell with its rats and all. When she reached the bottom, McDowell punched a well-used code into the tarnished keypad next to the double doors. The light on the keypad flashed from red to green and with a painful whine the doors shuffled open. McDowell walked into the lab. It wasn't slick or imposing; it was more functional than state-of-the-art, but at least it meant they held the future in their own hands. Either side of her, undersized rooms full of assorted breeding paraphernalia lined the route to the end of the hallway where she entered the substantial main laboratory. The blue walls and white false ceiling evinced an air of calm efficiency, but that was where the similarities between the male cryo-womb and the IVF Lab ended. All of the livestock production equipment here was either home-made or stolen from male livestock farms. It worked after a fashion, but most of it was definitely on the verge of retirement. Despite the age and condition of this equipment, the team of female livestock scientists were performing miracles. Their reproduction technique did not include cloning but instead artificial fertilisation of any healthy eggs that they could get their hands on, just like the IVF treatment in the twentieth century but without the hosting mother. Unfortunately, this simulated IVF process meant that they still required the sperm from their male oppressors. Nevertheless, all other processes matched the male breeding program even if they were a little unsophisticated.

McDowell observed the neatly stacked cryo-chambers in the corner of the room, which still contained the liberated flasks. The chambers were running from an external power supply and around them stood Commune Leader Kefelnikov, Commander Langton and the Head Scientist, Dr Margaret Oliver.

'What the fuck is up now?' she thought, approaching the three solemn-looking women. She stood to attention in front of them. Langton looked up with that smile again and she cringed.

'At ease McDowell,' ordered Commander Langton.

McDowell relaxed a little and then noticed the portable DNA scanner situated nearby.

'Last night, Corporal, when you liberated these eggs, did you notice anything strange about any of the flasks or chambers? In fact did you notice anything strange at all?' Kefelnikov asked in a concerned tone.

'No, nothing that I can think of Sir. Is there a problem Sir?'

'Well it seems that there is Corporal. Most of the eggs that were retrieved were of normal DNA structure. However, there are around 16,000 eggs with gene alterations, the like of which we've not seen before,' Kefelnikov replied, with surprising candour.

'Is that going to cause a problem Sir?

'No, not on its own, but if the male authorities were aware that we were going to raid the livestock farm, then they could have doctored the eggs; doctored them in such a way that however we incubated them they would come out fighting for the male species,' explained Kefelnikov, seeking confirmation from Dr Oliver with a nod of the head.

'That would also explain why you had such an easy time of it last night,' Langton added dismissively.

'Fuck you and the incubation bag you were raised in!' thought McDowell, annoyed at Langton's belittling statement. The jumped up bitch had never been on an active field assault; in fact she had only had limited field-training full stop. Now she was too old for any serious action. In fact, Langton was only in a position of authority because, out of the breeding batch of Commanders' eggs, she had been the only one to reach full term in any sort of fit state to lead. The eggs from which she had been reared had been stolen from breeding farms, taken in ones and twos by female orderlies working at the complexes. But that was before the Eurostate ruled that only males were to work in the livestock centres. This decree coincided with the official halt to female production.

There was also a twenty-year age gap between McDowell and Langton and this did not help their relationship. Times had changed and Langton was of the old school, bred of a time when women were only passively resisting male dominance; a wet blanket to McDowell's firebrand in fact.

'Can't you work out what status the livestock will acquire?' McDowell asked in a frustrated tone.

Dr Oliver then spoke for the first time, 'Theoretically we could, but the only way to really tell is to bring one of the eggs to full term and evaluate its character. But that could be catastrophic. We don't have the time or facilities to predict the outcome precisely otherwise. They all seem to have the same cocktail of mutated genes, but we can't tell for sure if that's the case. We simply do not have the equipment for the job. Our best guess right now is that they're some sort of physically improved livestock and that could have very serious consequences for us as a community.'

Kefelnikov spoke again, 'Yes, if we can only harness these special livestock to further our cause, but only after we are sure of exactly what we've got. So McDowell, what we've decided is to send you on a little fact-finding mission to the nearest town to the Stablinka complex: Shenka.' Kefelnikov looked at Commander Langton and nodded for her to finish the order.

'Yes, that's right Corporal. We want you to go to Shenka and acquire any information that you can on the street. Tie up with our Feman contact there and see what it knows. If need be, kidnap one of the farm workers or something. There must be some rumblings, but whatever you do, find out what's going on,'

McDowell had heard of the Feman breed before but had never met one in the flesh - mainly because when they were identified during rearing the male livestock farms disposed of them. Against all odds, though, some had still been brought to full term and were taken in by an increasingly desperate but no more sympathetic female society. The Feman, at first glance, was a man for all to see, but with a full set of working male and female genitals. A chemical imbalance in the brain could be exploited and cause the breed to side with its female tendencies. The Eurostate was acutely aware that the Feman breed could be made undetectable to many of their gender tests and so used to aid the female fight for existence. A handful of Femen over time had slipped through the system and then had been delivered into female training facilities, before eventually being released into the outside world to spy on the so-called 'male civilization'.

'How will I locate this Feman in Shenka?' asked McDowell, trying hard to conceal her excitement at the prospect of escaping the commune's tedium.

'You will make your way to the only drug store in Shenka, of which the Feman is the owner. We'll arrange for the exact location to be given to you in coded form before you leave. Anyway, it, the Feman, will show you around, point out targets and sources of information and such like. Find out what you need to know and return as soon as possible. Do not use any form of communication link to the commune unless the Feman tells you that it is safe to do so - as you know the security forces have satellites covering this whole region looking for us twenty-four hours a day. Other than that, get your stuff together and be ready to leave at 06:00 hours tomorrow,' Langton smiled as she finished the last sentence and McDowell frowned in her mind.

7 DELIVERANCE

Professor Chenenko entered the canteen, closely followed by the MkII who was flanked by two young soldiers. Kellor continued methodically checking the delivered kit he had requested for his mission. The MkII had short brown cropped hair and very dark, almost black eyes, which seemed to watch everything intently as if soaking up the surrounding information. It had small delicate wrists, which were held tightly by the bright silver electronic handcuffs. The MkII's combat uniform was most at odds with its physical appearance, considering the female form and feminine facial features. At five foot eleven it was almost as tall as the Major but very much leaner and Kellor was sceptical about this thing's strength, allegedly so hugely superior to that of the standard livestock. Daniels stood adjacent to Kellor, quietly admiring the MkII as they faced the Professor and the two soldiers.

'Well here it is Major, your final piece of equipment. Look after it - you may find it more useful than you think,' Daniels said with pride.

'Why the cuffs?' Kellor asked the Professor.

'Well, up until now we have had no problems with the MkII but, until it bonds with you, I would suggest that you keep them on. Two or three days should be enough but you must interact with it as much as possible to create a relationship. We think that this is the only way at this moment in time to control where it directs its aggression. Don't worry though Major, I'll give you some Impatromine just in case it fails to submit to your authority; the drug will just keep the chemicals in its brain in a passive state. I've administered the first dose but it'll take a few hours to work. Unfortunately, a dose that would work immediately would more than likely kill the MkII outright. Keep giving it a shot every day then, when you think that the MkII is ready, stop giving the drug for 24 hours and see how you get on. The MkII should then be ready to fight, but not with you - hopefully.'

Kellor detested the idea of spending time with the MkII, let alone trying to bond with it. He abhorred the female form and he was now being asked to work with what was, to all intents and purposes, a woman.

'Now, I believe you have here all that you have requested Major Kellor, so may I suggest that you start your mission in Shenka. We know of a Feman spy there who supplies the Femorists in the surrounding region with drugs, food and information. If you use some 'persuasion', you might get some useful leads. Till now we've had the Feman under surveillance only, but I think this situation calls for some direct action,' Daniels said smiling.

Kellor had calmed down sufficiently to return the smile and was now thinking much more clearly. There was no use in going head to head with Daniels; he was sure that he would be crushed. There was also the Greenland Siege that the Colonel had mentioned to consider. He had never been dispatched to the Greenland Siege, despite being on standby for weeks. In fact, he had never been anywhere near that region of the Eurostate. He would have to look into it; for he knew that there was something to be gained from doing so. Kellor bent down, breaking the eye contact with Daniels, to pick up his rucksack and multi-purpose firearm from the floor.

'Yep, I think then its time for us to leave, little lady,' Kellor said imitating his hero John Wayne. He used to watch Westerns avidly during every moment of free time that came his way; that was until the Eurostate had banned dual gender films from being broadcast or even copies being kept for that matter.

As Kellor grasped his newly supplied weapon, he heard the unforgettable sound of Daniels' arm being snapped by the MkII's accurate kick. Daniels squealed like a stuck pig as he involuntarily crashed backwards across the unused tables and chairs behind him. Kellor instinctively rolled backwards, rifle firmly held in both hands. Then, with the same boot that had struck Daniels, the MkII aimed the heel at Kellor's temple, only to see it miss its target by mere millimetres. Kellor rolled backwards a second time and as he did so, he caught a glimpse of the MkII forcefully swivelling to face the soldier on the left. The head butt was placed higher than normal, above the bridge of the nose, but the powerful blow devastated the forehead of the soldier. Blood now ran down the MkII's face as, still facing to left, it pressed both palms together making one long extension and with lightening speed smashed its right elbow into the throat of the soldier behind. Kellor loosed off a shot as he rolled for a third time, just to ensure that he was completely out of range of the MkII's lethal aggression. The shot blasted a pointless hole through one of the maps behind the Professor, who now fell to the floor as if he had been hit.

'Don't kill it, stun her,' Daniels yelled, still writhing in pain and cradling his arm as if he were in a freezing room.

Obediently, Kellor flicked the switch on the firearm to stun and looked up. Twenty metres away, the MkII had torn the pistol from the side of the isolated rucksack and now pointed the weapon in his direction. Kellor leapt to his left, not once but twice, as the MkII proficiently squeezed the pistol trigger. The laser bolt grazed Kellor's backside as he gracelessly disappeared over the canteen's stainless steel serving counter. He hit the tiled floor far way too hard for his liking and rolled immediately onto his back. Wincing from the pain in his rear, Kellor acrobatically rocked forward onto his backside and then onto his feet without using his hands. Another laser bolt strafed the top of the counter and blazed a hole straight through the electronic chef machines that towered behind him, then another and then a third. His mind raced, it had only taken seconds for it all to go fatally wrong, but now Kellor could see the power of the MkII in all its menacing glory. Still handcuffed, the MkII seemed to hold just one focus, to eliminate any source of perceived danger to itself.

While the MkII had been focused on Kellor, the Professor had naively crawled to the corner of the room and was now sitting with his back to the wall. His head was bowed and he had placed his hands firmly over his ears trying to block out the surrounding anarchy. The MkII moved swiftly across the room, trying to gain a better angle to one side of the main map stand, before rapidly firing two shots. The first shot was intercepted before it reached its intended target. It shattered the front leg of the main map stand before the unsupported frame crashed almost casually to the floor. The second shot ripped into the Professor's chest leaving a neatly burnt hole about a foot in diameter.

Kellor used the short distraction to get his head above the counter; he saw the Professor's chest light up like a flaring match and the MkII turning around to look for Daniels. Somehow Daniels had managed to escape from the canteen, so the MkII turned full circle to face Kellor. Kellor pulled the trigger on his laser rifle and multiple shots darted towards his target. The stunning laser bolts crashed into their target and lit up the MkII with a blue aurora quite unlike the flesh burning shots that had been previously fired. The MkII stood erect as the lightning voltage bolted through its body. Kellor relaxed a little and uncurled from his crouched position. The MkII keeled over to one side, muscles locked, sending tables and chairs flying, before collapsing on the floor convulsing. Kellor knew that in normal livestock one stun bolt was enough to render the target completely useless for around two or three hours but with this freak he was unsure what exactly the outcome would be. Furtively, Kellor re-entered the dining area through the door to the right of him. As the door swung back behind him, the MkII merely raised its head and the pistol it held in its left hand, before firing without hesitation. The laser bolt struck Kellor's rifle, saving him from instant death and he dropped the weapon instantaneously as it flared and burnt his trembling hands. Now he was unarmed. All the other weapons were thirty feet away, just beyond the head of the cross breed and he knew that he would have to act quickly to save himself. Meanwhile, the MkII had sat upright and raised the pistol higher, trying hard to track Kellor's evasive movements as he ran like a man possessed towards the canteen exit. He could see the asylum of the doors a few feet away, but by now the MkII was on its feet and in deadly pursuit. Various shots fizzed their way past and above Kellor's head, blasting holes in the walls surrounding the exit. Kellor observed the troops approaching through the glass in the exit doors, just in advance of the shot that ripped into the back of his clothing, launching him headfirst through the exit in front of him and knocking him semi-conscious to the floor. The last thing that he saw was the soldier's boot standing level with his rapidly flickering eyelids - and he was sure that he could distinguish his own dim reflection in their black polished surface.

8   REVELATION

McDowell had not slept at all. The night had taken an eternity to pass but now there was no time left for dreaming. She rose quickly on the stroke of five, having completed all of her packing the night before. From her locker she took the civilian outfit that had been liberated from some unfortunate male amputee. The blue suit and polo-neck sweater fitted McDowell perfectly, but she chose her own army boots over the fragile suede shoes that had been supplied. She knew that they would not last five minutes during any conflict or, for that matter, the severe weather conditions that she would most definitely encounter on her mission. One last look in the mirror was all that was needed. McDowell studied her cropped hair, no longer blonde but jet-black and thought that maybe she would keep it that way when she returned. The electronic documents in her possession, obviously, had been stolen; they had specified black hair and although the team of forgers at the commune had managed to insert McDowell's picture, her underlying appearance would not fool anybody for long. She hoped that the DNA data held on the card would solve any problems the she might encounter. The original owner's data was still programmed on the card as gender was immediately apparent from this information. However, the previous male owner had also been a donor and hence McDowell had enough biopsy material to provide and exact DNA match.

McDowell set out for the dispatch area where her power bike was waiting. Airborne vehicles were held in reserve at the base, as they could be easily tracked and targeted by the male authorities. It was for this reason that all journeys to and from the base were kept strictly to ground level, mostly on bikes, as the terrain in the surrounding area was rough and obstacle-strewn. Nearby skulked the carcass of a nuclear reactor that had gone into meltdown, contaminating the whole area. In the fierce explosions that followed the initial reactor incident, the landscape had changed dramatically, but this had occurred long before the current troubles, in fact over 300 years ago just after the complete breakdown of functioning society in Russia. Because of the crumbling financial state of the nation, the reactor had become unstable, the male staff abandoned the site at the first sign of danger and the inevitable had occurred. The Eurostate had been created just in time to prevent further reactors suffering the same fate as the one at Chernobyl by injections of cash and expertise from the more affluent member states. Unfortunately, the area surrounding the Chernobyl reactor was considered far too dangerous to visit or colonize. This provided the ideal haven for the female commune; homeless at the time, they had set up a fighting base in the wasted region. All was well at first and the discovery of the redundant nuclear fallout shelter provided a welcome release from the elements and, of course, the lethal levels of radiation. In the shelter, Geiger counters registered a bearable level, but not without its adverse effects; the eighteen months spent living in the wilderness had many far-reaching implications. Women in the commune were now becoming less and less fertile and livestock produced from these diminishing supplies of eggs were maturing with such appalling abnormalities that immediate termination was the only option. The only course of action left open to the Femorists was to source a supply of uncontaminated eggs. Even the short journeys in and out of the fallout shelter had caused fresh livestock to go the same way as their predecessors. Hence the struggle to re-generate and grow the commune population - which became a never-ending battle with this deadly environment.

McDowell entered the dispatch area at 05:45 hours and was greeted by Commander Langton. She thought this somehow strange; Langton was normally a nine-to-five sort of girl.

Commander Langton was sitting side-saddle on the power bike that McDowell was about to set off on, surrounded by boxes of supplies and ammunition ready for just such missions. The dispatch area was at the highest point of the shelter and hence in wintertime became very cold indeed. The few bright spotlights hid from view the surrounding area's vast expanse of emptiness and served only to highlight the vapour streaming from breath and speech.

'Good morning Rachel. Just thought I would come down and see you off.'

'Very good of you Miss, but that really wasn't necessary. I'd prefer to go quietly if it's all the same with you.'

'You know if we had...' Langton choked on her words. '...If we had children then you would be one to me,' she continued. Her eyes seemed to look through Rachel in a grotesquely loving fashion.

Stunned, Rachel stammered, 'what do you mean Miss? I ... I...'

Commander Langton leaned forward and placed a gloved hand on her shoulder.

'You see, in the early days, as you know, we were all producing eggs for the good of the commune. Apparently you...' Langton stifled her tears, placed her other hand on Rachel's free shoulder and continued. 'What I mean to say is, that I was in a privileged position because of my breeding line. Before I became completely sterile, Dr Oliver concentrated on providing the commune with a second-generation military leader. And you are it,' she smiled.

'If you will excuse me Miss I must be leaving now. Thank you for the send-off but I am not sure what the fuck I am supposed to do with that information.'

Without respect for rank, McDowell wrenched Langton's hands from her shoulders, pushed past her and mounted her bike. Gone was the smile from Langton's face that had annoyed her so much, replaced by an expression full of uncertainty. McDowell slammed the bike helmet onto her dismayed head and switched on the guidance and night sight systems. She held eye contact until the visor eventually severed it, before placing both hands on the handlebars and firing the bike's power pack into mechanical life. The same eyes, fixed a moment ago on Langton, were now fixed on the scroll-down menu displayed on the inside of the visor. McDowell picked *manual speed control* and *auto-guidance* literally in the blink of an eye. With a gentle twist of the wrist, she sped from Langton's grasp, out of the bright light that showered from the spotlights and into the elevator to make the short trip to the surface.

The groaning of antique gears and cables ceased as she reached the bleak surface. Ahead of her the doors rumbled slowly apart and she was greeted with flurries of the first snow of winter. All around it was dark and the moon shone sparingly through the trees, casting shards of light onto the snow-dusted forest floor. McDowell reflected that if the frozen downpour stopped, her tracks would pose a problem, but she was now in no mood to delay. All she wanted to do was get the hell out of there - maybe never to return.

The bike moved forward silently and the crunch of snow under the hard arctic tyres was all that could be heard, until, with the snap of her wrist the power pack lit up the rear wheel. The auto guidance system now had to work at full capacity as the bike careered around trees and boulders. Auto speed was always too slow for McDowell, especially when she had some place to be.

At around ten in the morning, the sun began to rise and McDowell knew that she had just enough time to reach the transit camp they had set up for just this purpose. Travelling during daylight in such a region was hazardous as outlaws and thieves frequented the area. After many years in the wasteland most were unspeakably disfigured by the residual radiation but this did not stop other men from civilised society joining them.

The new livestock came here to escape termination for some criminal or political misdemeanour - a life marred by disfigurement, after all, was infinitely preferable to death. Normally well organised, the outcasts known as Orgers, set up lucrative drug production plants hidden in the surrounding forests. The drug, for there was only one, had far exceeded the popularity of the obsolete 20th century substances. Heroin, cocaine and the rest paled into insignificance when compared to what Orgasma could do for the male population. Genetic modification had ostensibly eradicated the libido of every male yet, with one shot of Orgasma, a man could climax for up to twenty minutes. Due to his conditioning, he still did not focus this desire for fulfilment on the female form, but he ejaculated none-the-less. Orgasma undermined all the ideals of the ruling Eurostate party, and as such became highly sought after by the male population in an effort to bring some enjoyment and focus into their sterile lives, despite the sanction of death if caught in possession of the drug.

The bike slithered to a halt in the leaf-strewn gully from which the transit camp had been hewn. By now it was light and the gully hid the bike and McDowell alike from the surrounding area. It was not a good place to defend - high banks on three sides looking down on the gully below - but it was out of sight and that was half the battle. The snow had not penetrated to the muddy subterranean floor, but was drifting dangerously high on one of the looming banks. She dismounted and wheeled the bike to the opposite side of the gully from where the snowdrift was overhanging before turning the bike to face the exit, just in case her position was compromised and she needed to get out in a hurry. From the back of the bike McDowell removed the perimeter guard unit and placed it where she thought it would be most effective while she was sleeping. Taking some rocks and fallen tree debris, she initialised the perimeter guard unit and then camouflaged it before returning to the bike. At intervals along the gully's sunken walls there were hollowed-out bunks. To the untrained eye, they looked just like natural formations, but they had been manufactured during numerous stopovers on journeys to and from the commune. Removing the weapons and the heated sleeping bag from the bike's panniers, McDowell slid into the nearest bunk. Even with all the revelations that she had heard earlier, she was still exhausted and began to sleep soundly, albeit with Langton's smile invading her dreams.

9 THE FEMAN

Shenka was as cold as any place on earth, in more ways than one. The town supported the sizeable workforce of the livestock farm nearby and many workers from the encircling mineral mining industry. New faces came and went all the time and no man ever really got to know any other; an ideal situation for a female partisan infiltrate and obtain the information that the commune needed. A light grey dust fell unseen every minute of the day, caused by the vast surrounding mining operations. This gave the town, even in summer, the look of a well-used ashtray. It was made up of mostly prefabricated buildings, scattered amongst the ash, like extinguished cigarette butts, all clinically built on the twenty-five square miles of concrete base that had been laid many years before.

The drug store on the corner of Valeri Legasov Street seemed deliberately greyer than most, in an effort to prevent any unwanted interest in the goings on within. Nicola, or Nicolas Timosina, depending on whom she was talking to, was one of only a handful of Feman spies located around the Eurostate. She had tried living a normal life within various female communes, but the weight of prejudice had finally forced her into a life of espionage. In the male world, she had been accepted as a man, which was ironic - for if they had known better her death would have been immediate.

The store was now closed. It was earlier than usual, but with the snow falling harder now Nicola knew that there would be no more customers today. Besides, she had things to do. There was the amputee to dispose of and the imminent arrival of the Corporal to prepare for. Removing the genitalia from one of her unfortunate customers was an extremely dangerous business, one that could lead to the Feman's discovery, but occasionally an ideal donor came through the door and the opportunity was too good to pass up.

Nicola looked at the large digital clock hung above the door that led to the rear accommodation: 14:35.The stores' shopping area was bright and well-stocked and holographic product adverts played continuously while she instructed the building management system to close the shutters at the front of the store. If things had been simpler she would have made a damn fine pharmacist, she thought. The business was making a healthy profit and she lived a comfortable life. The shutters fell silent as they locked in place and she went purposefully through into the storeroom just behind the shop. She paused before the large wall-mounted drug storage unit at the very back of the room and flicked a switch behind one of the many bottles of pills located upon it. The powerful sound of the heavy mechanical latch disengaging always made her jump, no matter how often she activated it. The unit itself was beautifully balanced and glided back upon the hidden runners that were visible only when it was pulled to one side. The fluorescent tube lit automatically over the stairs and the Feman descended heavily downwards on the worn metal steps. At the bottom of the stairs the she scratched her groin and adjusted her ill-fitting underpants. She had never felt comfortable having two sets of genitalia and had inherited the male habit of adjusting herself at every opportunity. This had the benefit of helping her blend in amongst the unskilled men of Shenka, who were bred with a basic education, and her large overweight body meant that the small breasts fitted in satisfactorily with her figure. Nicola had a full round face, which was devoid of any facial hair, but this did not pose any problems and with a reasonably deep voice, altered surgically, the deception was complete.

The Feman now opened the dark wooden door in front of her and walked into the basement workshop hidden beneath the drug store and sat in the corner there was a small testicle incubator, humming tunefully to itself, as if pleased with its amputated contents. Searching her pocket as she straddled the naked male corpse, Nicola grinned, showing it a mouthful of decaying teeth. She bent down and ran the laser scalpel across its bare shoulder. The arm severed cleanly like a carved slice of prime pork and the Feman walked to the raging furnace below the stairs and cast the limb into the fiery tomb. The process was always the same: the man came in looking for Orgasma and Nicola provided the fix in the rear of the shop. In the victim's desperation to reach fulfilment he would eagerly ingested the drug and then collapse as the poison with which she'd laced it took hold. After a small trip downstairs, Nicola would drain his blood to keep things clean and then surgically remove the testicles to a donor incubator. The liberated blood provided a nice little sideline; being sold on the black market for various weirdoes to do with as they pleased. Unfortunately, the sale of body organs was far too risky, so after a few further cuts with the laser scalpel the remaining body parts blazed away to insignificant ash.

    Following the efforts of disposing of the body, Nicola washed her hands and wiped the perspiration wearily from her forehead. Patches of sweat had also formed around her armpits and only served to highlight the stains of previous sweat patches that had gone unwashed. The Feman walked over to the computer terminal in the corner and sat on the stolen bar stool placed in front. She pressed one of her stubby, fat nicotine-stained fingers on the screen where it displayed 'Eurostate mainframe connection'. The screen whirled with the 3D Eurostate logo as the Feman lit a large roll-up and then the terminal spoke to her in a hard robotic voice.

    'Connection completed. Ten minutes until location tracked. Please terminate link before tracking complete. Please enter mainframe function required.'

Working quickly, Nicolas was soon at the screen that listed the breeding farms located within the Eurostate. Pressing the 'Stablinka' button, then the button marked 'Employees', she watched as the screen whirled with the 3D Eurostate logo before the voice spoke again.

'Retrieving data from mainframe. Eight minutes till tracking complete.'

Nicolas was painfully aware that there was no time to waste. With the roll up stuffed into one side of her mouth and squinting from the smoke that was now pouring into her eyes, she placed the micro disk into the open slot in the computer. The screen changed suddenly without warning and displayed fruitfully a list of names and addresses of the Stablinka farm employees.

'Six minutes till tracking complete.'

There were one hundred-and-twenty-nine names in total, from cleaners to the Facility Manager. The Feman rapidly scanned through them to identify any obvious targets or any man to whom she had sold Orgasma without taking his life afterwards. While concentrating on the countless names she was oblivious to the next warning countdown.

'Two minutes till tracking complete,' spoke the robotic voice again, surprising Nicola and now there was also an audible beep every ten seconds, then five and finally every second as the search for a suitable source of information continued.

'Thirty seconds till tracking complete,' the computer reported, now louder than ever.

Nicola relished the thrill of cutting things fine. She knew that she would save the file to review it later at her leisure. However, the vision of male government employees running around at the other end of the mainframe, thinking that they had her by the 'short and curlies', bolstered her ego beyond measure.

'Twenty-one seconds, twenty seconds, nineteen,' the computer exclaimed.

Nicola pressed the save button, waited for the beep and then pressed hard on the 'purge connection' icon located on the touch screen.

'Five seconds, four seconds, connection severed.'

The room fell silent.

Nicola stubbed out the spent roll-up and began to load the saved file. While it was doing so, she waddled over to the cabinet marked 'liquid drugs only'. Opening the steel shutter, Nicolas took out a bottle of vintage Morgan rum and poured a large glass. As she sat back down the sweat dribbled down her temples, soaking the collar of her grey shirt. Sipping at the rum methodically as if imbibing a calculated dosage, her eyes again scanned the employee list and settled upon the name of a junior lab technician who might possibly have the information that they needed and who would be far enough down the chain of command not to be missed after they had obtained what they needed to know. While the Feman wrote down the name and address of Andrew Tilbury from 164 Yeltsin Heights, she thought of the fun that she would have in extracting the information, if indeed Mr Tilbury had any to be extracted.

10 THE REUNION

Kellor's eyes opened expectantly, but for a while he could see nothing. Distorted shapes swam around him and there was an annoying beeping sound, which caused him to try even harder to focus. He tried to sit up in the bed but any strength in his shoulders had long since departed. 'Must've been one hell of a night!' he thought to himself, wincing and shivering.

He coughed and pain sliced through his body. His back felt like it was on fire and he cursed his discomfort. He heard the door open, the shuffle of feet and then fluid, blurred outlines began to move over him. Hearing the blinds being lifted, Kellor squinted as the light held behind them flooded through into and over the room. He began to cough uncontrollably and felt himself being lifted gently by someone who cradled his head and back into their upper body. They gave him water in an effort to subdue his coughing and he then managed to take a deep breath - which was when he noticed the strangely sweet smell of deodorant wafting around him.

Much to Kellor's relief, his sight began to clear bit by bit and, with the aid of some eye drops, all around him finally swam into focus. The first thing he recognised was Daniels, who stood in the corner of the room with his broken arm in a fibrecast and his jacket slung over his shoulders. A nurse and a doctor stood in front of Kellor busy checking his stats and, next to Daniels, he noticed another white-coated boffin. 'A Professor,' he thought correctly. When the doctor had completed his checks and left the room, Daniels sat down next to Kellor's bed.

'Major Kellor! How nice to see you! Glad you could rejoin us. We had the impression that you didn't want to regain consciousness and complete your mission. Oh! By the way, this is Professor Timms. He's now in charge of the indoctrination facility at the breeding farm,' Daniels said, radiating an aura of friendship and warmth that was too good to be true in Kellor's view. He was becoming seriously worried as to what had happened to bring about this spookily perpetual smile.

Kellor's voice croaked, as he spoke for the first time since the fracas in the canteen.

'What the hell is going on? I should be dead; I was dead and now I'm in hell.'

'Well Major you were dead, so we cloned you; you now have a healthy female body,'

'You've done what? You bastards! I'll fucking kill you,' Kellor shouted as he tried to raise himself from his bed.

By now Daniels was laughing quietly, even the Professor behind him had begun to smirk and before Kellor could work his anger up any more Daniels spoke.

'Now Major, would I really do that to you? I would have let you die before putting you through that ordeal. Tell me what you can remember. I'll fill in the gaps for you... So calm yourself. You are going to be fine,'

'Some fucking joke,' thought Kellor, who by now could almost see normally as he began to talk as calmly as humanly possible about what he could remember from the incident in the canteen.

'I remember the dining hall, you, the guards and the Professor,' stated Kellor.

Before he could go any further, Daniels interjected, 'Ah yes the Professor - unfortunately he's dead and the guards too, but the main thing is I survived; and of course you,' he added as an afterthought.

Kellor continued recounting his memories of the incident, 'I can remember trying to save your sad arse, but you'd already gone. Then I was running for the door. The laser bolt. I *am* dead. I *must* be dead.'

'Yes that's about it. I couldn't wait all day for you to bring the MkII under control so I went for some help. Yes, the MkII shot you right between the shoulder blades. Fortunately, you were wearing one of those new advanced laser proof vests that I'd just procured for the mission. By a stroke of luck you must've put it on straightaway but thought it too early to switch it on to full power. That's why, you didn't escape totally unscathed... But at least you got away with your life,' said Daniels, elaborately filling in the missing details.

'But I shot it three or four times with stun bolts. The fucker should have stayed down,' Kellor said as the extent of the MkII's awesome resilience dawned on him.

'All part of the learning and evaluation curve for the MkII my dear boy,' came Daniels' unctuous reply as he moved closer.

'Now Major Kellor, unfortunately time is of the essence and I was just wondering what plans you had for embarking on your mission. The doctors say that you should be fully recovered in a couple of days. But you've already been unconscious for twenty-four hours and that's more than enough precious time to have lost!'

'Well, the one good thing to come out of this is that I don't have to take that cross breed with me now. How did you kill it in the end?'

'Kill it! Kill it? I wouldn't let that happen to your new partner. No, we did nothing of the sort; let's just say we pointed out the error of her ways. The Professor here came down here at short notice and has worked wonders with Beta 666 as we now call her. So unfortunately, Beta will still be making the trip with you,' Daniels replied smoothly as he leant back in the chair and stretched his one good arm in the air and yawned.

Kellor wondered if Daniels had lost his mind completely during the last twenty-four hours. He was stunned to think that after all that had happened he was still to take the cross breed with him to reclaim or destroy the eggs. And growing at the back of his mind was the concern at the complete transformation of Daniels' persona since their first meeting. He looked directly into Daniels' eyes, but did not speak. He had learned this trick in his interrogation training, leaving long silences so the interviewees felt compelled to fill the silence with their own words - and often they were the words Kellor needed to hear. Many prisoners had sealed their own fate when he had used this method.

'What?' was all that Daniels offered.

'Why are you so bloody cheerful and where is that God-forsaken cross breed now?' Kellor asked nervously.

Daniels' smile returned once more and it did not take him long to fill the painfully extended silence with information.

'Let me allay your fears Major. Beta has exceeded all expectations and when you retrieve the eggs from the terrorists, I will then have the army that I promised myself before this whole sordid mess started. So everything's looking good for the future. I'm also very close to identifying who the Feman spy is in the Eurostate organisation. Just a few more pieces to put in place and one less thing to worry about.'

'All very interesting, but where did you put that cross breed?'

'Who do you think is behind you holding you up?'

Kellor felt suddenly cold and rolled his eyes upwards so that he could see above and slightly behind him. There, looking down, was Beta's impassive face, its black eyes deeply probing his own. Shuddering, he tried to move, but with the pain in his shoulders and the Beta's unyielding grip, it was all he could do to move his head.

Kellor looked sharply at Daniels.

'What do you think you're doing, you fucking people you, he gagged on the torrent of abuse in his flash of fury, eyes bulging and the veins in his temples throbbing fit to burst. Meanwhile, the Professor began to look sadly awkward in the corner of the room until at last Daniels abandoned his superficially affable posture.

'Look Kellor, this isn't about you or me. It's about keeping the Eurostate ideals in safe hands. No man's bigger than the continued success of the Eurostate and if you can't work to the male doctrine then you're of no use whatsoever. Never underestimate what I'll do to safeguard those principles Major. Yesterday, when you were taken out so efficiently by Beta here, we weren't sure if you'd make it, so we had nothing to lose. We put you and it in the secure ward on-site and the Professor arrived to oversee the little experiment.'

Daniels paused for a moment and took Kellor's unopened drink from his bedside cabinet. While continuing to talk, he held the drink behind him so that the Professor could open the carton. After studiously reading the instructions on the back of the orange juice, Timms removed the seal and handed the drink back to Daniels. Taking small sips, Daniels continued with a seriousness that could not have contrasted more deeply from his earlier jovial mood.

'You see, we managed to get your so-called cross breed to care for you. A case of Orgasma or bust if you'll pardon my expression. If your injury killed you, then so be it. If she nursed you back to health then what a fantastic bonus for us all. But if you survived and Beta finished off the job she'd started earlier then well, let's just say we are all expendable - some more than others I might add,' Daniels said clinically.

Kellor could not believe the arrogance of the man. Nevertheless he could not help but admire Daniels' focus and single minded determination to get the job done.

Kellor yawned spectacularly, adding sarcastically, 'I'm tired now. If you want me to get up and out as soon as possible you'd better let me get some rest. And when you leave take the frigging Beta with you,'

'Unfortunately Major, where you go, she goes now. She thinks of you as her little pet and will do anything for you! Inseparable, that's what you two are. You never know, she may find you useful at some stage,' Daniels said as he stood up and started to walk towards the open door closely followed by Professor Timms. Stopping in the doorway Daniels turned to speak.

'Oh, and from now on, puppy dog, your mission is to be known as Operation 'Alpha Male',' Daniels advised and with an accepting nod from Kellor, he left.

Physically, Kellor was not tired in the slightest; he had just had his fill of Daniels' superciliousness. Also, remembering his conversation with the Colonel, he knew that before he did anything else he needed find out exactly what he'd meant by that obscure - and false - reference to the Greenland Siege. Obviously, the Colonel was trying to convey something of importance, maybe even warn him, but he knew it was something that the Colonel did not want Daniels to know about. Inexplicably and with a start, Kellor remembered Beta, who was holding him somewhat gently now, and he felt somehow comfortable even in his panic. He took two deep breaths and spoke to the cross breed nervously.

'Mark t....,' Kellor started, stopped and thought again.

'Beta,' he corrected himself, 'can you sit me up in bed and then bring me over the hand-held terminal from the rucksack over there,' Kellor said gently.

Just as he finished the sentence, Kellor noticed the laser pistol with which he'd been shot, tucked into the holster on the side of the rucksack. Under his breath he began to mutter, 'Oh shit, shit I'm dead...'

The MkII marched over to the rucksack and bent over. Its hand passed over the holster without hesitation and Kellor sank back into his pillows with relief. A few moments later, Beta returned with the terminal and stood obediently by the bed waiting for her next order. Kellor began to concentrate on entering his personal identification number and afterwards brushed the transponder chip, which was implanted in his right index finger, against the sensor on the terminal. This gave him the authority to enter the Eurostate's confidential military database. While waiting for the terminal screen to proceed to the main menu, Kellor glanced up and he was sure that the MkII smiled at him before speaking to him in a soft and somehow innocent voice.

'Major, is there anything else you require Sir,'

He'd had enough surprises for today and could not hide his shock at the words. After a moment's hesitation he replied, 'Not at this moment Beta, but when I do you will be the first one I call for.'

Kellor still did not trust this creature, but even he was impressed at the transformation they'd achieved. The terminal beeped and he looked down to see the database menu. Scrolling through various pages of historical conflicts Kellor settled upon the 'Greenland Siege' and hit the 'enter' button with a flourish. Instantaneously, the details of the operation littered the screen and he began to read with escalating interest. He knew that there must be some relevant evidence in amongst all of the information at his disposal and he was optimistic that it would help him understand why the Colonel had cut him loose.

An hour later, Kellor had read the military file from front to back and digested every piece of information that he thought pertinent and some that was not. It transpired that many years earlier, before Daniels took up his current position, President Wells had appointed his vice president to take charge of the Greenland Siege. A group of women had broken out of their ghetto in a bid to escape certain extermination. The group had the dubious honour of being the last remaining females alive within the male infrastructure. Realising that their fate had been preordained when they had been confined to the ghetto, they managed to arm themselves with weapons taken from their dead guards. Once out of the ghetto, the women had scarcely managed to cover safely the distance to the nearby breeding farm, before the local male militia attacked. Besieged in the farm, the women seized the male staff and livestock and held them hostage for two months.

The Vice President, Nigel Lock, took the decision to deal with and placate the Femorists who were resisting the power of the Eurostate Government somewhat successfully. The unconstitutional management of the crisis was vehemently opposed by the military attaché tasked with helping resolve the situation, a certain Colonel Martin Johnson. The Colonel had remonstrated with Lock, advising that they should attack the farm with Special Forces without delay, reckoning that the longer the siege went on, the bolder the Femorists would become. His superiors had forsaken the Colonel, namely General Cohen, Commander in Chief of the Eurostate armed forces and he was now to take his orders directly from the Vice President.

It became apparent to the Colonel that the authorities were trying to flush out a high ranking Feman spy who had been undermining the last stages of male domination. Lock was thought to be the prime candidate. Johnson had argued that by insisting on dealing with the Femorists and blocking any immediate attacks on the farm, Lock had exposed his true allegiance. Ultimately, Lock was arrested and the inevitable attack went ahead without delay. All of the livestock was lost, since the women had systematically destroyed it over the course of the two-month siege. Nearly all of the male staff and some fifteen Special Forces soldiers were killed. The disastrous attack was blamed on the delaying tactics of the Vice President and consequently he faced trial for treason. Lock's only defence centred upon the fact that, at the time of the siege, there had only been one other breeding farm in the Eurostate. To lose the livestock, over a million eggs and 10,000 in incubation, would have been catastrophic. Since the siege highlighted the vulnerability of the breeding programme, the ruling party decided to scatter livestock production all over the Eurostate and produce livestock in smaller batches to prevent the same disaster striking again.

Colonel Johnson interrogated the few surviving Femorists and provided irrefutable evidence that Lock was indeed a Feman spy. The State spent hours on medical tests trying to prove that both sets of genitalia had existed on the Vice President at one time or another. Nevertheless, after all their efforts, they were unable to find any trace of female organs. Although they thought this strange, the doctors did not rule out the possibility of re-engineering a Feman's genitals to leave only testicles and a penis, while leaving no traces of the alterations. Unfortunately, by the time the physicians had finished their investigations, Lock was dead and a damaging trial was avoided.

11 THE AMBUSH

McDowell woke with a start at the thunderous sound of the snowdrift crashing to the gully floor from the bank above. She looked at her watch through sleep-ridden eyes and saw that although it was two in the afternoon it was almost as dark as night. The snow was falling harder than ever now, driving almost horizontally with the razor-like wind but despite this McDowell decided to push on rather than risk being stranded out in the wilderness. Inside the heated sleeping bag she was warm and relaxed and it was with some foreboding that she managed to muster the will to slide out of her artificial haven and expose herself to the glacial afternoon air. The ice-laden atmosphere did nothing to revive her senses. In fact, it made her more lethargic and she was unable to hold back the flood of yawns that came in constant waves, overriding all her efforts to pack up and push on. Emerging from what little shelter she had enjoyed in the sleepy hollow, she packed her sleeping bag neatly away, walked over to the perimeter guard unit and began removing the camouflage that covered the device. As she cleared away the foliage from over the display, she noticed that the unit had been reset to 'standby mode'. This meant it was of no use whatsoever if attacked. McDowell was sure she had set the device to 'silent warning' mode and she felt for the alarm receiver still nestling in her freezing ear. Nervously, she stood up, listened for any sound that might cut through the wind's mournful dirge, but she heard nothing. Still unsure, McDowell picked up the unit and loaded it back onto the bike; it was then she heard a crack above her.

Instinctively, she looked upwards and was struck squarely in the face by the soiled boot of an Orger rapidly abseiling into the gully. She landed heavily on her back and felt the icy snow melt into her clothes as her vision drifted out of focus and time slowed to a halt. Then, as suddenly as they'd been lost, she regained her senses. She could taste blood in her mouth and with her rapidly swelling tongue she felt for her front teeth. They were gone. Nothing left but a bloody hole. Now she was really incensed. Her weapon was just in reach and she groped for it frantically. Finally, gripping the wet and muddy stock, McDowell pulled it in close, loving the safety that it brought. Then, before the mutant could remove his harness from the tangle of ropes; he lost his head. Literally, she noted to herself with grim satisfaction. The laser bolt caused his skull to disintegrate into strands of flesh and shards of bone. The body stood there, without its head like an empty spacesuit, held up only by the harness ropes and she thought how strange it looked before springing to her feet. Quickly evaluating the situation, McDowell saw that there must have been at least twelve more mutants abseiling into the culvert and immediately decided to make a break for open country.

McDowell now ran to the bike, mounted and started the power pack in one swift movement. Slipping the helmet on, she activated 'auto speed, auto direction'. Then, holding the handle bar with her left hand only, she began to move off, firing her laser rifle with her free right hand, strafing from left to right and blasting molten holes in the repugnant Orgers sliding down the gully walls. Rounding a small awkward bend in the muddy path, she saw that there, some way in front of her, was another abseiling freak and she automatically fired. The shot hit the mutant in the groin, tearing one leg from the torso and leaving the other held by only a thread of muscle. The body slammed down to the ground below, strewn across the small path that the bike was negotiating. With no time to stop, McDowell took aim at the smouldering corpse before her. Ten feet away she fired a burst of laser bolts and as she passed the place, a gory shower of blood and sinew engulfed her visor. She smelt the burnt flesh in her nostrils and choked back the rising vomit. Riding on, less rapidly than she would have normally chosen, she emerged from the clutches of the gully and out into the relative safety of open country. She placed the weapon in the secure holster on the side of the bike and picked out the 'manual speed' icon with a flick of her retina. The sudden increase in speed caused her to take flight at the slightest bump in her path and she began to relax a little as she rapidly put distance between herself and the Orgers.

Before long, complete darkness descended about her and she looked at the digital clock displayed on the inside of her visor - it glowed 15:05: one-hour since waking and thirty minutes since the start of the attack. The surrounding landscape had closed in once more, as had the weather. Through the snowstorm she could only just make out the lights that sporadically illuminated the main road into Shenka, all of fifteen long kilometres away. The track dipped precariously in front of McDowell on a rock-blemished hillside that sheered away steeply to the right. Steadily, she began winding her way down the rocky decline, hoping that soon the treacherous track would meet up with the relative comfort and safety of the main road. Feeling vulnerable again and struggling to see further than ten yards ahead of the front wheel, McDowell slowed the bike to a crawl.

It was this decrease in speed that saved her life.

The cheese wire had been tightly strung across the treacherous path by the Orgers who had somehow managed to overtake her. The wire held firm and launched McDowell backwards, slamming her to the ground onto her tension-packed shoulders. Only her snail's pace had spared her instant decapitation. The bike continued, riderless, before finally sliding to a halt in bushes to her left. But before she knew what was happening, two attackers leapt from an overhanging tree, landing directly upon her breastplate and legs, knocking what little wind she had left clean out of her. Their faces were covered, but McDowell could still smell their stinking breath as they pinned her down.

The headlights of numerous unseen vehicles instantly flooded the scene and McDowell could hear their engines starting and loudly revving from high up on the hill above. Thinking fast and ignoring the pain of her whiplashed neck, McDowell struggled frantically to extricate the pistol from her hip holster.

'You fucking bitch, think you're smart do you?' said the Orger, now placing his face within licking distance.

'Wait till you see what we got for you. Payback for all those poor bastards you wasted back at the gully,' he growled menacingly.

McDowell placed the tip of the liberated pistol barrel strategically up under the vocal mutant's rib cage.

'I'm smarter than you think motherfucker,' she replied, pulling the trigger.

The surprise on his face was hidden behind the black rags that he used for a weather shield. But McDowell heard his last word quite clearly - 'Shit!', he gurgled a nanosecond before his chest cavity opened up, ribcage splayed like a broken basket and pouring blood and offal all over her torn jacket. Using all of her remaining strength, she struggled to roll from under the dead weight. Seeing this, the isolated Orger at her feet went for his weapon. After a period of inept fumbling, he raised his pistol precisely as she fired; the shot flashed past his right shoulder and engulfed the tree behind him in blue and crimson flames. McDowell, realising her error, violently kicked her right boot into the mutant's unprotected groin with enough power to put him off balance and wrack him with pain. Seizing the opportunity, she finally managed to manoeuvre herself out from underneath the dead Orger. Completely clear of the restrictive weight that had been on top of her; McDowell could now take precise aim at the attacker while he held his excruciatingly painful groin. The laser bolt hit him square in the chest and, dead, he rolled backwards with his legs folded grotesquely underneath his torso as if in a final, desperate, prayer for mercy.

Immediately, McDowell rolled to her left and dropped into a ditch that was almost completely full of snow, as optimistic random shots from the hillside above blasted all around. The bushes, which ran along the length of the snowy retreat, hid her from sight and they were so damp that even the Orgers' incendiary bolts failed to ignite them. After a breathless pause, she managed to steal a look up towards their source, but could see nothing through the glare of headlights. She knew that any attempted escape down the hillside, would result in the Orgers effortlessly picking her off before she managed to get even ten feet from where she was pinned down. Panting hard, she watched the mist rising from her breath and realised that the wind had now ceased to gust completely. The snow was waist-deep in the ditch and her clothes began to absorb the freezing cold liquid as she managed to melt the snow with her ever-dwindling body heat.

McDowell's short hiatus was suddenly and violently interrupted when bolts began to rain down on her once more and she became aware of Orgers trying to take up sniper positions below her. Still hidden, she waded closer to her bike, praying that the covering fire was just that. The bike was resting on its side and the shadows cast from the adjoining bushes, covered the vehicle and the snow-covered path with dappled shade, which the strobing headlights turned to a kaleidoscope of serpents hunting her down in the night. On the opposite side of the path, she suddenly saw the light that showered down around her reflected in the retinas of a solitary Orger. Putting his head above the parapet of the opposing ditch, the cat-eyed mutant smiled malevolently at McDowell. He was asking for it. She fired blindly at his mocking image. But the laser bolt fell short and hit the ground in front of him, peppering his smug, grinning face with nothing more harmful than mud and snow. The hunters above McDowell had been waiting for just that moment. Now they had an exact fix on her location, on which they could unleash their sizable firepower. All around bolts ripped into the soft ground; she sank below the snow that filled the ditch and pressed her back hard against one side of the improvised retreat. Even with the solid wall of earth behind her, McDowell could feel the shots punching hard into permafrost beneath the mud and slush. The heat generated from those shots was melting the snow's crust and tepid water began to dribble onto her forehead and neck. In her mind, McDowell could hear what she thought was her heart pounding. But then suddenly it stopped. Either she was dead, or it had been the sound of the bolts ripping into the earth that had ceased. Tentatively, she lifted her head from what had almost been her snowy tomb to see which was true. And then all hell broke loose.

A colossal explosion cascaded fire and shrapnel down upon her. 'Fuck this. I'm history,' she grated, cursing her apparently sealed fate. Suddenly, though, the searchlights were extinguished as suddenly as they had appeared and to McDowell's pleasant surprise, survivors of the blast began to flee desperately past, ignoring her and hurtling down the scorched and blasted hill, where a second explosion from a well-aimed laser missile caught them unawares. McDowell picked up the somehow undamaged rifle and laser bolt tracer raced after the fleeing Orgers through the black night air. Eventually, it dawned on her that by some miracle she now had an ally. Deciding to secure her position before any initiative was lost, McDowell turned, just in time to see an injured mutant trying to make off with her bike. She fired without hesitation and was relieved to see the Orger punched from his feet. The rags that covered his face flew off as his body sailed through the air and he eventually bounced to a standstill face up. On the floor, dying, he searched his killer's stare for some solace; some mercy. He found none. McDowell could only gasp at the hideous features illuminated in the moonlight. The flesh on the man's nose had been completely consumed by his radiation-induced cancer and the receding lips barely hid the black stumps that were once teeth. The pathetic eyes were only just visible through tumour-laden eyelids and his matted hair crawled with lice. McDowell swung her rifle towards the bony bridge of his nose, fired again without hesitation and the gruesome head disappeared from her soured sight. Hearing the nuclear-powered vortex engine descending from the hill above, she assumed a defensive position with practised rapidity. Soon, the piercing lights hovered steadily at chest height above the opposite ditch and she could just make out the profile of the air catamaran that was normally grounded at the commune. The catamaran consisted of two separate but parallel black hulls joined only by thin aerodynamic struts. The hulls were in the shape of arrowheads but appeared as a fulsome 'W' shape with the single points to the fore. Ostensibly a civilian aircraft, it had been fitted with discreet military hardware, ideal for such occasions. Continuously firing her rifle, McDowell moved towards the nearest hull as the thick black cockpit hatch slowly opened. Commander Langton, grinning as usual, poked her head clear of the hatch into the smoke-filled air.

'Fancy a lift soldier?' Langton asked.

For as long as she could remember McDowell had hated that smile and right now was no exception.

'Don't mind if I do, Miss,' replied McDowell, returning the smile mockingly.

Returning hurriedly to her bike, McDowell punched in the termination code through the keypad located on the power pack. The bike spoke in a harsh electronic voice and began counting down from sixty seconds. The vacant cockpit opened invitingly and she scampered back to the empty hull and eagerly vaulted into the warm cradle-like seat before placing the VR helmet on her battered and bloodied head. Although they were in separate hulls, she was instantly transported onto the virtual reality flight deck where Langton sat at the helm.

'Let's get the fuck out of here - bike's going to blow any second now,' said McDowell.

Langton manoeuvred the craft nose up and, with one small movement of her left hand, they accelerated away at great speed. McDowell noticed that she was also grinning on the virtual reality flight deck, just before Langton said to her, 'First stop Shenka, I think my dear.'

12 THE GAME BEGINS

After a day's rest and a night spent in the muscle repair chamber, Kellor was feeling a great deal better and was by now well enough to shower without assistance. Still residing in the sumptuous hospital wing of the breeding farm, but tiring of the constant attention from all around him, he longed to be on his way. He stood in the darkened room with his back to the mirror, looking over his shoulder while drying himself. There were scorch marks all around the point where the laser bolt had hit him and the place of impact was mildly burnt, but he felt no pain. Having seen enough of his dwindling injury Kellor began to dress just as the MkII walked into the room without knocking.

'Major Kellor; are we leaving soon?' Beta asked politely.

'It looks very likely that we will be leaving in the next two to three hours. So get your equipment together please Beta. Oh and can you try to look more like a man, we don't want to arouse any more suspicion than we have to in Shenka,' Kellor replied, starting to re-organize the equipment in his rucksack while still naked and completely indifferent to her quasi-female presence.

Kellor began thinking about the MkII and how she had made amazing progress in her development over the last forty-eight hours. She had gone from being out of control and deadly to lovingly caring for him and now she was respectful, organized and eager to please. Maybe Daniels was right he thought; perhaps the MkII *would* be an asset to the mission.

The MkII walked purposefully out of the room after acknowledging the Major's observations. Kellor only noticed that Beta had gone when the door slammed shut behind her, leaving him to his thoughts once more. He began to work over in his mind the puzzle of facts surrounding the Greenland

Siege, the Colonel, Daniels and the deceased Vice President, Nigel Lock. He knew that Feman spies had been known to have surgery to remove or mask their female genitalia, but this would only fool a physician who was not looking for any alterations. Any thorough investigation would have revealed Lock's true sexual identity had there been anything to hide, but in this case it had turned up nothing. Then there was the corroborating evidence from the Femorists who had been interviewed by the Colonel and his men. Kellor still had the feeling that the Colonel was trying to warn him about something to do with Daniels, but how much deeper it went from there was anybody's guess. All he was sure of was that he'd known the Colonel for as long as he could remember and that he could trust him with his life. Kellor finished re-packing his rucksack with the precision and organisation of a military clone. He dressed and went outside to the main desk where he used the idle internal communications terminal to contact Daniels, who was still on-site.

'Mr. Daniels, I'll be ready to leave here in around two hours. Can you arrange for an airborne vehicle with two power bikes to be made available for my exclusive use?'

Daniels replied in an over friendly tone, 'Good. I'm pleased to hear you're feeling better. What sort of airborne vehicle would you like Major Kellor?'

'The fastest one that you can lay your hands on!'

'I'll see what I can do. It'll be ready in two hours in the transport compound, whatever it is. See you down there at around 18:00 hours Major Kellor,' Daniels hung up without saying goodbye.

Back in his room, Kellor logged on to the Eurostate mainframe using his hand-held terminal and downloaded the files on all the Feman spies who were known to be operating within the Eurostate. Many of these spies were allowed to remain operational amongst the mainstream male society, just so that the security forces could keep tabs on them, feed them false information and hopefully trace their specific female colony. The Shenka spy was a relatively new discovery who had only been under surveillance for three months or so and Kellor studiously worked his way through the file making mental notes.

The Feman in question was called Nicolas Timosina: around forty-five years old and obese. He operated from a drug store in Shenka, which provided wholesale and private medication to the surrounding mining camps and their workers. Timosina had been identified as a spy during an undercover investigation into the illegal sale of the drug 'Orgasma'. During the surveillance operation, men had been seen to leave the store with 'Orgasma'; they were then followed and picked up later by the state police. Nearly all were arrested in possession of 'Orgasma' or, they had been arrested while still enjoying the powerful effects of the drug. The planned raid on the store had been about to take place when someone noticed that a visiting customer had not re-emerged after acquiring his fix. The drug team had decided to break into the premises when the Feman ventured out on one of its rare business trips. They had found a pair of human testicles in a donor incubator and drawn their own conclusions. By the time the Feman returned, the drug store was as Timosina had left it and blissfully unaware of the intrusion she went about her business as usual.

The Feman still naively assumed that her hacking into the Eurostate computer was going untracked - but in fact the team had begun to monitor the connection from the drug store to the information superhighway. The last entry in the file was a report that the Feman had hacked into the personnel records of the Stablinka breeding farm and downloaded the file, but for what purpose it did not disclose. Kellor had some ideas on why the Feman had an interest in the breeding farm. Maybe the Feman intended to kidnap an employee to obtain process details or possibly she just wanted the name for assassination purposes.

In any case he thought, it would be a good idea to get to Shenka as soon as possible and monitor exactly what the Feman did with this information.

Until Kellor could reach Shenka, he would have to rely on the security police to keep watching Timosina's every move and report these back to him. He knew the man in charge of special security operations, Alec McGeady, and his reputation for being difficult to deal with.

Logging out of the mainframe, he entered the communications menu. Kellor typed in the name 'McGeady. A' and pressed the 'connect' button on the screen. After a few short moments, Alec appeared on the screen with an overcast grimace on his face.

'Yes, McGeady here,' he said abruptly and looked away from the screen, uninterested in the caller.

'Director McGeady, Major Kellor, just calling you with regard to an operation your guys are conducting down in Shenka,' he said trying to sound as authoritative as possible.

'What operation? And who the hell are you?' McGeady replied distractedly while searching his desk drawers for something or other.

'We met at the state security convention last year and I'm interested in the surveillance of an alleged Feman spy, Nicolas Timosina.'

'Robert Kellor you mean? Yes, I remember you now. You work for those bloody sneaks in military intelligence don't you?' he replied, continuing his fruitless search.

'That's one way of putting it Alec! But moving to the business in hand, we've had a security breach here in Stablinka. We believe that your spy might have some useful information that will help us plug the leak.'

'What sort of breach are we talking about then Major Kellor?' McGeady was now smiling, enjoying the petty mind games that he was renowned for.

'Unfortunately I am not at liberty to expand Alec, but needless to say your help would be gratefully appreciated with respect to this matter,' he replied guardedly.

Kellor had no authority over McGeady. In fact, McGeady had a higher professional and social rank than he and they both knew it.

'See what I mean? Fucking sneaks the lot of you. Not at liberty to say, bullshit! You call me expecting me to spill my guts after three months of painstaking surveillance! And for what?'

'I don't mean to be so evasive, but I've taken a direct order from Callum Daniels to maintain a complete blackout on the situation here.'

Immediately the colour drained from McGeady's tanned face and he stuttered, 'Callum Daniels you say. You're reporting directly to him?'

'Yes that's what I said, didn't I,' Kellor replied confidently, seeing that he now had inadvertently got the upper hand.

'Oh right, I guess that means that whatever I can do for you I will. Now let me see, Nicolas Timosina is still being covered by two of my men. We've hard evidence from a visit we paid to his premises, while he was out of course, that he is a Feman spy. Also he's been hacking into the Eurostate computer and downloading a variety of restricted files,' McGeady said, his earlier antagonistic tone now noticeable by its absence.

Kellor butted in, 'That's all well and good, but I'll be arriving in Shenka in a few hours and I'd like to join your officers if I may. Can you get them to inform me if Timosina makes a move from the premises before I get there? I'd be very grateful.'

'Yes, I can do that for you Major Kellor, no problem. In fact I'll contact them right away and get them to meet you when you arrive at the park and ride station. They have a mobile surveillance unit so they don't need to be near the target to keep watch on him.'

'That would be appreciated Alec,' said Kellor, smiling broadly.

'And if there's anything else I can do for you Major don't hesitate to let me know,' said McGeady, just as Kellor cut the link without formally concluding the conversation.

Kellor sat contemplating why so many top officials were terrified of Daniels. It was probably to do with the security breach in the Eurostate organisation, he thought. Daniels had immense unstated power right now and could condemn any man to death without trial. It was rumoured that Daniels was also looking to rid himself of any man that caused him concern, whether authentic or imaginary. Kellor involuntarily shivered, as he contemplated the way in which he had talked to Daniels in the hospital room the previous day. The fear passed quickly and he looked at his wristwatch. *Time to go*, he thought. Picking up his rucksack, Kellor left the room and met Beta entering.

'We're pulling out Beta - have you all of your equipment?' Kellor asked.

'Yes Sir,' replied Beta, who by some means had now achieved a distinctly masculine appearance.

As they both began to walk along the access road down towards the transport depot, Kellor surveyed the changes in Beta. She now wore full body armour from head to toe. This had veiled all those indiscreet feminine curves and she appeared heavily built, even upon closer inspection. Her hair was closely cropped, which made her look even more like a well-built young man, albeit one with a vaguely feminine face. The afternoon had slipped into darkness by now, but intense road lights lit their way to the transport hangar. A thick blanket of snow covered the ground even though the sky was as clear as any Kellor had ever seen. Entering the pitch-black hangar, he called out tentatively, but there was no answer. He moved forward cautiously and collided with a large mobile toolbox. There was a loud crash as the loose tools scattered on the top of the toolbox fell to the hard and unforgiving concrete floor.

'Ouch! Shit! Where the fuck are you Beta?' said Kellor, continuing to mutter aloud.

'I'm over here by the light switches. Watch out Major, don't...' replied Beta, wincing.

Before she could finish her sentence, he had walked into a compressor unit to his left, stumbled backwards and then knocked over a container full of oil, dispersing it across the previously spotless floor. Kellor moved again, trying to rub his painful shin as he went. Managing only a few steps, he slipped in the thick black lubricant and fell with an almighty thump on to the meat of his back. With the wind knocked out of him he rocked in agony, mouthing silent curses like a fish out of water. Beta began to laugh.

'What's so fucking funny?' Kellor finally managed to gasp between breaths.

'You! I've never seen anything so funny in my life,' Beta said as she walked carefully over to the Major to help him out of his predicament.

'Who taught you about humour? You've never seen anything funny in your life at all! What are you doing now?' Kellor asked as he felt her strong grip upon him.

'Just helping you up.'

'Why don't you just turn the bloody lights on?' Kellor said, showing his frustration.

'I don't see any point in doing that, I can see perfectly clearly without them,' she stated, still smiling and giggling to herself.

Beta now straddled Kellor's floundering body. She had bent over him, grabbed the lapels of his combat jacket and with one swift movement pulled Kellor up and onto his feet. From this position she then swung him upwards and over her shoulders before carrying him to safety.

'Whoa... What do you think you are doing?' Kellor said in his surprise.

'I don't think it's safe for you in the dark Major. I just thought I'd put you somewhere where you won't hurt yourself,' replied Beta innocently.

'Just put me down and turn the fucking lights on!' screamed Kellor as he floundered across her muscular shoulders.

'Okay Sir, but personally I don't think that's such a good idea. Perhaps you should stand still while I go and turn the lights on,' she replied, not intending to make him feel inadequate, but inadvertently doing so all the same.

Beta made her way over to the plain grey wall near to where they were standing and flicked the bank of silver light switches to on. The hangar blinked into life as the lights came on, one by one, seemingly racing each other down the two banks of fittings that ran the length of the roof and Kellor breathed a sigh of relief at the return of his deprived sense. He looked down at himself, saw that he was covered in oil and muck from his fall and he began to shake his head in disbelief. Not only had he made a complete mess of himself, he was also trying to come to terms with the revelation that Beta showed all the signs of being completely at home in the pitch-black hangar. Still contemplating the revelation, Kellor looked up, while she stood silently by the light switches smiling at him. Not a mocking smile, but one of concern, as if looking upon a silly child who had been the innocent victim of a messy accident. Seeing the smile for what it was, Kellor too began to grin at the surreal situation, just as Beta first heard the aircraft approaching. She turned her head sharply towards the noise, a noise that Kellor was a long way from even faintly hearing, and moved quickly outside without any explanation.

'Where are you going now?' he asked as he began to follow her.

'I can hear an aircraft heading this way. Sounds like a Cobra AFVE Mk12, two miles east of here I would guess,' Beta said, now craning her head in the direction of the noise that Kellor had only just begun to hear.

'Seems you got all the tricks,' stated Kellor suspiciously.

After what seemed like only seconds, a uniform array of lights appeared from the east, skimming the trees and hills as it came. Kellor looked down at his watch and saw it was almost exactly 18:00 hours, the time previously agreed with Daniels for their rendezvous. The craft approached the massive hangar and began to hover at a safe distance from the structure, before eventually setting down without actually making contact with the tarmac, just as if it were suspended by strings above the grey magnetic surface. The advanced funnel vortex engines in due course whistled to a stop and Kellor rushed towards the craft like an excited boy on Christmas morning. The ship was an elegant 'V' shape with two engines at the rear and a large cockpit that was big enough for four men. The aircraft was as fast as anything currently flying and Kellor was quietly impressed that Daniels had managed to lay his hands on something so state-of-the-art at such short notice. The aircraft's body was made from an advanced liquid crystal based organic-ceramic, which meant that it was hard to track using even the most up to date microwave radar. Reflecting the colour and general pattern of its surroundings almost perfectly, the ceramics also made it extremely difficult to identify visually. Just behind the cockpit, in the thickest part of the hull, was the equipment pod, where he assumed the power bikes were stored. Suddenly, there was a hiss of air and the cockpit hatch lifted and slid sharply backwards up to the rear of the craft. Kellor observed the plaster cast sooner than he managed to recognise Daniels while the pilot came into view once the hatch had retracted fully.

'Major Kellor, how nice to see you up and about, even if you are a little grubby - and on time as well!' said Daniels just before climbing delicately from the cockpit.

'Who does this dream belong to?' Kellor said, now hanging half in and half out of the spacious cockpit and scanning every nook and cranny with excited anticipation.

'It belongs to a friend of mine. He's in charge of AMARA (Advanced Military Aircraft Research Agency) and it seems he had this ship to spare. And please, don't get oil on it!' replied Daniels smugly.

'And the bikes? They're in the equipment pod I take it?'

'Of course! Would I let you down Major Kellor? Oh by the way, how is the MkII coming along?'

'You mean Beta. She's doing fine,'

'Sounds like you're getting on famously and if that's the case Major I'll leave you now. Mark here will take you through the finer points of the aircraft - all pretty standard stuff. By all accounts, even I could fly her! One last thing though, don't bend it or you'll have me to answer to,' Daniels called over his shoulder, already strolling down the service road back to his accommodation suite. While Daniels walked, he felt at ease with himself like never before. He breathed in deeply, looked up at the stars and thought that all his problems would be over very soon.

Before Daniels was out of sight, Kellor was deeply engrossed in conversation with Mark Grace, the pilot. Beta was busy bringing the kit out from the hangar, just as she had been ordered, and then loading it neatly into the equipment pod that had been lowered from under the hull.

'It's quite easy to operate Sir,' began Mark in a respectful tone. 'You've flown the Cobra VE Mk5 I take it?' he continued.

'Yes and the Cobra VE Mk10,' replied Kellor impatiently.

'Okay, good. Well it's very similar, just a few things to note. The AFVE has thirty percent more acceleration and is twice as fast top end. So gently does it when accelerating - things tend to get close very quickly. It has the same virtual reality flight deck as the VE Mk5 but with a modified weapons index. Basically, you tell the computerized weapons officer what you wish to shoot at and what results you would like to achieve and then he does the rest for you. Autopilot and navigation systems are the same as on the Mk5 and Mk10. The major difference is on the outside. It has a skin made of crystal ceramics that means it is almost undetectable to any tracking device and in Chameleon mode it mimics its environment, so it can't be seen by the naked eye either!' Mark fell silent, inhaled deeply and smiled proudly.

Kellor smiled right back, 'If that's all I'd like to set off.'

'Yes that's all Sir, but remember to take into account the acceleration and top speed. Oh I nearly forgot. If you crash land then just before impact the cockpit area will fill with a spongy fluid. This will absorb your body impact, but you must keep your respirator masks on at all times or you'll drown,' Mark warned seriously.

Ten minutes later, Kellor had cleaned himself up and the cockpit hatch hissed closed with both safely inside. Mark watched intently as the engines fired up and the magnetic undercarriage disappeared into the hull, before the craft raced out of sight in the general direction of Shenka.

13 THE KIDNAP

'What happened to your mouth?' inquired Langton.

McDowell responded by thrusting her tongue into the toothless gap, suddenly self-conscious about her missing two front teeth.

'Had a little argument with an Orger's boot before I forced him to chew on a bolt,' she answered with great difficulty.

'When we get back to the commune you should get that fixed up.'

'Why? Don't you think it goes with my new image?' said McDowell, grinning broadly.

'Let's just say I've seen you look better. Still it does add something to the male disguise,' added Langton, but by now McDowell had lost interest in the conversation and was busy investigating the deep laceration on the inside of her mouth. The cut had long since stopped bleeding and was swelling out of all proportion. All in all, McDowell was in a bad way, but she was still alive. Apart from the facial injury, she was also soaking wet and covered with spots of mud and dead foliage. The heat in her cockpit was turned up to full power and, beginning to feel her muscles relax with the intense warmth, she closed her eyes and sank back in her seat.

'No time for sleeping - we're nearly there,' said Langton softly.

They were now only a few short minutes away from the park-and-ride station in Shenka. No airborne craft was permitted to over fly any town within the Eurostate; crashes had killed many men in the past, on the ground as well as in the air. Instead, large areas were set aside just outside of the towns and cities for craft to set down and road vehicles took their passengers into the heart of the conurbation. It was not advisable for the two women to hang around the station for too long and Langton hoped that the Feman would be there to meet and greet them as soon as they arrived, as agreed. In the remaining time before they landed, Langton explained how she had come to the rescue of McDowell.

'When you left the commune, we saw the weather set in and were extremely worried. There was a break in the satellite surveillance coverage of the area because of a random solar storm, so we managed to get the catamaran out before it could be re-established. Commune leader Kefelnikov tried to talk me out of going myself, but I explained the need for experience on this particular mission and she accepted my argument. It didn't take me long to track the passive beacon on your bike. I could see the fire fight from a few miles away and I knew that it must have been something to do with you,' Langton paused.

'I'm very glad you came along when you did, thanks,' said McDowell.

Before she could get too sentimental she was distracted by the slowing of the aircraft and the pitch of the engines lowering as they came to a standstill and then gently set down.

Langton smiled, looked McDowell in the eye and finally spoke after a painful pause, 'Lets say no more about it and get on with the task in hand. Okay?'

'Okay,' she concurred.

Langton pulled a small lever on the virtual reality flight deck and the two cockpit hatches opened simultaneously. The craft looked as though it was suspended above the tarmac by invisible wires; but this was no trick. A female scientist some seventy-five years before had revolutionised road travel and vehicle parking. Using a highly magnetic synthetic material mixed in with concrete or tarmac that provided a strong, but benign, magnetic field just above and around the laid surface.

The vehicle was fitted with magnetic landing gear in the case of aircraft and road-based vehicles lost their wheels and inherited four magnetic power packs in each corner, each of whose field was of the same polarity as that projected from the surface below. Because like poles repel, these packs not only kept the vehicle at a safe distance above the road but also provided the propulsion. Roads were then free from the wear of tyres and hardly, if ever, had to be resurfaced. Many accidents were prevented because rain, ice and snow did not affect the vehicles' grip on the road surface - since they never actually came into contact with each other. Of course, the female inventor went unrecognised for her brilliant innovation and many years later the Eurostate replaced her name in the annals of history with that of a failed male inventor who had existed at the same time.

Both women jumped gracefully down onto the tarmac, but with a certain machismo consistent with their male appearance. It was dark and Langton scanned the surrounding area frantically for the Feman contact, but all she could see was row upon row of civilian aircraft. Abandoning her visual search, Langton quickly went to the back of the catamaran and unloaded her equipment and luggage from the storage pod. McDowell stood there empty handed; she was wearing all that was left of her clothes and by now was looking anything but the professional fighting woman that she undoubtedly was.

Langton glanced up and spoke, 'Plenty of spare clothes in here for you - and the Feman should have weapons to replace the ones you lost back there.'

McDowell huffed. She looked like a child who had lost her favourite toy and she shuffled along after Langton as they set out to find the Feman. Langton knew that they should avoid the main reception area and the pick-up point. So they skirted around the perimeter fence until, after what seemed an age, they came across the Feman idling on the other side of the fence. Nicola stood smoking, looking up at the sky and wishing she were somewhere else - another time, another place and in some other body. Langton had encountered the Feman a number of years before in the commune, before she had been forced out. Nicola had changed and those years had not been kind thought Langton. She had put on more than a few pounds and the fat hung unflatteringly over her trouser belt. McDowell could not take her eyes off the Feman, whose bulging outline was clearly visible in the bright moonshine. She was quietly disgusted by its appearance but she managed to hide it skilfully. As they casually approached, the Feman turned with a smile that lit up her face, showing two beautiful rows of black stumps that doubled as teeth. The air was almost freezing, but the Feman wore only a lightweight pair of trousers with a slate grey sweatshirt tucked inside them. Behind her was a cab that she had borrowed for the evening and by now its owner was probably enjoying the full effects of the free Orgasma she had given to him in exchange for the use of the vehicle. Langton had told McDowell to wait for the Feman to speak first because, as good as their disguises were, their vocal tones would have almost certainly condemned them before they had even started out on their mission.

'Good evening gentlemen, do you need a taxi to the drug store?' said the Feman.

Langton recognised the first part of the arranged conversation and responded by pressing the vocal deepener chip implanted in her throat against her voice box, 'Is that the drug store in Commune Street?'

'No it's the drug store on Langton Street,' replied the Feman.

By now McDowell was shivering uncontrollably and was getting increasingly impatient with the whole situation

'Well that's the introduction over. Now, how about we get the fuck out of here to somewhere warm!' she said, ignoring Langton's orders completely.

Langton glared at McDowell and shook her head in disgust. She then turned back towards the Feman and found it was gone. Peering through the chain link fence as it started to snow she set eyes on the Feman rummaging through the boot of the cab. Nicola gleefully returned with a substantial pair of bolt cutters, leaving small heavy footprints in the virgin snow as she went.

'Sounds like your sister has a plan - somewhere warm right away!' said Nicolas as the clunk of the wire cutters made short work of the fence.

They squeezed through the small hole made by the Feman and as they sat in the cab with the heat turned up Nicolas proceeded with a cosmetic repair so that anyone passing the fence would not notice the intrusion. Putting the last metal tie in place, the Feman struggled up off her knees and waddled back to the cab with damp muddy circles etched on her trousers. Nicola threw the tools into the boot with a crash that made Langton and McDowell jump almost out of their skins. McDowell was curled up in the rear of the cab and had been drifting off to sleep, finally warm enough once again to relax. When the cutters hit the spare magnetic power pack in the boot, the loud metallic clank forced open her reluctant eyes.

'Shit, what the hell was that?' she asked, bleary eye and confused.

'Don't you worry your pretty little head about it. Go to sleep, but remember, if you ever disobey an order of mine again you'll be up on a charge. Understand?' said Langton half turning around in the front seat. McDowell had never seen her so forthright.

'Yes Miss. Sorry. I didn't mean to undermine your authority Miss.'

McDowell began to think that maybe there was more to Langton than met the eye. In future, she was going to have to be a little more careful with any outward show of contempt for authority, a crime of which she had been guilty of many times in the past. The driver's door opened, breaking the awkward silence and the Feman dropped heavily onto the front seat. McDowell settled back, finally taking the opportunity to sleep while Langton's attention was diverted towards Nicola.

'You must arrange for some permanent secure communications to be installed between the commune and the drug store. It's not safe waiting around the station for you like that, for you or for me,' said the Feman who, after all the rigours of the last ten minutes, was now sweating liberally.

'What can I say Nicola? It's the best we can do for now. I do realise that we need something more manageable, but it was as much as we can do to let you know when we'll be arriving full stop.'

'Yeah, well that's the other thing. The pager you use to beep me with when you are near to landing - it's playing up. I've been down here three times tonight before I got your second confirmation by the fence. The blasted thing kept picking up stray signals or something like that. It's more trouble than its worth.'

'But we know the pager is safe. There is no way the authorities would be monitoring the airwaves for old communication systems like that. Even if they did intercept the signal it tells them nothing!'

They both fell silent, waiting for the other to continue the argument, but neither did and as they smoothly travelled back into town, McDowell began to snore rhythmically from the back of the cab.

The snow was getting deeper, but that did not slow the vehicle; there was no risk of skidding and the Feman's pace accelerated as her boredom with the journey grew. The cab sped past groups of drunken men spilling out onto the previously dusty grey streets after spending their hard-earned wages on their solitary remaining comfort. The neon signs above the bars flickered intentionally in the cold night air, in the vain hope of attracting any passing soulless men in the need of some inner warmth. However, by now the weather had made prisoners of all but the most desperate.

The cab eventually pulled into the rear courtyard of the drug store while the surveillance vehicle drove on past the entrance and stopped some way down the street. Ray Travis and his partner, Simon Chapel, were sick and tired of the surveillance job that they had been covering without backup over the last three months. The only saving grace was that they had been left alone to operate as they pleased, but now they had a third party taking an interest in the Feman. They were still unsure of their intentions and the conversation with their boss, Alec McGeady, had not shed any light on exactly what that interest was. All they knew was that they were to provide any assistance and information that this Major Kellor wanted. If they did not, McGeady had assured them that they would be digging mineral ore with a very blunt spoon in the nearest mine.

'We'd better get back to the P and R station and pick up this Major Kellor and his sidekick,' said Chapel unenthusiastically.

'Yeah, we wouldn't want to be late now. McGready has *"plans"* for us if we screw up,' replied Travis sarcastically.

'When we gonna call this Major and tell him the target has been out moonlighting tonight?' continued Travis, while from the safety of the surveillance vehicle he scanned the pictures received from the hidden cameras in the drug store.

Ignoring the question, Chapel turned the volume up on the audio feed from the store and leaned back gracefully in his chair. They both sat silently in the rear of the large blacked out surveillance vehicle transfixed by the covert activity being played out on the monitors. The armchairs in which they sat had been customised so that they could do almost anything in them, sleep, drink, eat and, of course, observe.

Suddenly, remembering McGeady's orders, Chapel began to type efficiently on the communications laptop in front of him, until it finally made contact with Major Kellor's aircraft.

'Yes, Kellor here,' the Major said, sounding startled as the holographic image of Simon Chapel's dour face invaded the virtual reality flight deck.

'We understand that you have an interest in our target here in Shenka. In addition, we're to afford you any assistance that you may require,' Chapel said frostily without introduction.

'I wouldn't quite put it in those words. Nevertheless, you could say that,' replied Kellor, trying to take the pressure out of the situation. He was going to have to work closely with the two special agents and wanted them to be as open as they possibly could. No point in alienating them and failing to obtain the information needed to complete his mission.

'You wanted to know if the target made any moves at all before you arrived,' Chapel continued frostily.

'Yes. I did ask Director McGeady if you could make me aware of the Feman's movements tonight, if any,' continued the awkward conversation.

'Here it is then Major. The target has moved four times tonight. It looks like three false alarms and one genuine pickup. Between 17.00 hours and 18:04 hours, the target made three visits to the Shenka park and ride station only to come away empty handed after spending five minutes standing around at a deserted corner of the station,' reported Chapel, giving as little information as he needed to, while still appearing informative.

'What happened on the fourth excursion?' asked Kellor, impatient at an unnecessary pause.

'The target arrived at the station and waited in the same location as on the previous visits. At around 18:30 hours the target received another bleep on its pager,' Chapel answered before being abruptly interrupted.

'A what?' Kellor inquired

'A bleep. On a pager? You know that primitive twentieth century device they used to contact each other on?'

'I've heard of them, vaguely, but I didn't know that there were any still in service,' Kellor stated, belying the fact that he was supposed to be one of the top military intelligence officers.

Travis shook his head in disbelief, disguising his hilarity by nestling his face in his hands while Chapel desperately tried to keep a straight face.

'Well that's the point sir. They're not! The target uses it because she thinks it can't be monitored,' Chapel exclaimed.

'Right. I see. So who did the Feman pick up on this fourth visit?' said Kellor now on the approach flight path to the park and ride station.

'There were two associate targets. Both were probably female. One looked to have been in a bit of a scrap. All three returned to the Feman's residence at 18:45 hours and are currently inside the dwelling,' Chapel explained elaborately.

Then Chapel was distracted by Travis, who had picked up on a conversation that the targets were having in the basement quarter of the Feman's lair.

'Hold on one moment sir. It seems we have some new developments coming through,' said Chapel looking away from the communications camera and then directly at Travis. Travis was craning his head to one side, desperately trying to decipher the ongoing conversation.

'I have identified an ideal source of information. Tilbury is his name and if we don't get what we want from him then I have more for the pot,' Nicola advised, sipping leisurely at her favourite rum drink.

'What happens when he doesn't appear for work the next day?' asked Langton, aware that the extraction of what they needed to know would lead to the death of its source.

McDowell was surprised by the Commander's statement and she gulped the alcoholic concoction that the Feman had mixed for her.

'That's a chance we'll have to take. He's been at the farm for about a year and looks to be in a position to give us what we want, but who can tell. If we need to, we can go right to the top!' added the Feman exuberantly.

'I think we should go tonight. The longer we wait the more risk we run of being exposed,' Langton offered, visibly pumped up and eager for the night's events to unfold.

'Whatever you say. No problem, let's finish our drinks and we'll get off,' said Nicola, smiling and licking her lips in anticipation.

McDowell now spoke for the first time since her verbal misdemeanour at the Park and Ride station, 'I'll need some tools for tonight - run a bit short during the trip here.'

The Feman immediately crossed the inhospitable but functional room, before reaching the cabinet located behind the donor incubators and then slid open the grey metal shutter on the front.

'These do for you?' asked the Feman, taking the latest laser automatics from the cabinet. Separately, Nicola threw the rifle and pistol the last few yards between McDowell and herself, sat back down, and downed her drink in one. She wiped her face and smiled with an exaggerated toothless grin.

'All set?' was the last thing Travis heard before the targets left the building.

After an extended pause, he swiped an index finger across his throat, gesturing to Chapel that audio-visual contact had been lost with the targets. They exited the store via the back door and once again nervously checked their equipment as they made their way across the enclosed courtyard to the waiting cab.

'Targets are on the move Major. Looks like they are going after some employee from the farm,' said Chapel excitedly.

Travis leapt into the driving seat of the surveillance vehicle and started the power packs instantly. They whined into life and the vehicle resettled, shifting gently on its invisible magnetic cushion like a bird getting comfortable on a nest.

'What is your current position Major?' Chapel inquired urgently.

'Just about to land, but don't let the targets out of your sight. I want them alive if I don't get there in time. Give me your destination and we'll meet you there.'

'Please bear with me Major,' he replied, while logging onto the Eurostate employee database.

'Just one more minute sir and I'll have the employee's address for you,' continued Chapel and without a word of warning Travis fiercely swung the vehicle around in the road to face the drug store's exit.

Chapel gripped the armrest on his chair tightly to stop himself being slung down to the floor of the automobile.

'Whoa, take it easy Travis!' he shouted.

'Excuse me?' Kellor said, now setting the Cobra down at the Park and Ride station.

'Nothing Sir, just trying to keep upright,' Chapel replied as he directed a fierce but impotent glance at Travis as the vehicle stopped dead in its tracks.

The battered cab pulled out of the courtyard and, surprisingly, turned towards them. Travis hit the deck before its laser headlights caught him in their intrusive beam. Chapel could hear his partner swearing quietly as he nestled down on the floor of the vehicle with three months' accumulation of fast food rubbish and cigarette ash for company.

'What's going on up there Travis?' asked a disgruntled Chapel.

'Look at your bloody monitors! They're heading straight for us!'

'Why the hell did you turn around?' Chapel asked and then fell silent, needlessly waiting for the cab to pass harmlessly.

'You can get up now - they've gone. Turn this bloody thing around, but not too quickly. Let them get around the corner first. Finally, got it: Tilbury,' Chapel said as the terminal beeped with the information that he had been waiting for.

'Gentlemen, what's happening? Speak to me!' Kellor enquired anxiously.

'Okay Major, I have it. The employee they're after is one Andrew Tilbury, Junior Lab Technician at the Stablinka farm. He lives at 164 Yeltsin Heights. That's in the south-west corner of Shenka,' Chapel explained as once again he had to hold on for dear life while Travis turned the vehicle around at speed.

'Chapel, how long's it going to take me to get there from the station?' Kellor asked hurriedly.

'About twenty-five minutes Sir. That's if you drive like Travis,'

'Like who?' Kellor asked confused.

'My partner Sir, that's who. Drives like a maniac!' replied Chapel, grinning at Travis in the front, who was now putting the vehicle through its paces.

'No time for jokes. I'll see you in twenty minutes and don't make a move until I get there, unless you have to of course,' said Kellor, shutting down the communications system on the Cobra.

Beta was already out of the aircraft and had readied the bikes for an immediate departure. Kellor bounded out of the cockpit and ran to the back of the craft.

'Are we leaving now Major?' Beta asked as she powered up both bikes and ran them through their diagnostic set-up procedure.

'Yes. We're going right now. Set the auto route-finder on the bikes for Yeltsin Heights,' replied Kellor as he sorted through the equipment pod for two laser rifles and two pistols.

'Here take these - you may need them,' said Kellor, handing Beta her weapons as nonchalantly as if he were handing her a pack of cigarettes.

Turning to their respective vehicles they each placed their rifles in the secure holsters located on the side of the bikes. Kellor rammed the matt black pistol into his waist holster and Beta placed hers in the one strapped over her shoulder. Kellor liked the waist type; it made him feel like a cowboy, and if it was good enough for John Wayne, it was good enough for him. Beta was already on her bike when Kellor quickly put on his crash and control helmet and mounted up. Both picked 'auto-route' and 'manual speed' from the scroll-down menu in their visors and then with a squeal of tyres they set off. Kellor had asked Daniels for conventionally driven bikes; he thought that they might have to use them in the surrounding countryside, far away from the magnetic roads that crossed the built-up areas. He preferred the wheeled kind of bike, it gave him a greater sensation of speed, but in these circumstances he was terrified, for although the snow had stopped falling, it had settled to quite a depth and was beginning to freeze. Together, they pulled out onto the main road leading into Shenka, but Kellor had neglected to activate his magnetic stabilizers. He pulled across the road with full throttle and made a right turn. The rear wheel went from under him; Kellor shot out his right leg, gently adjusting his weight and held the skid perfectly, gently fishtailing the rear end as the wheels began to bite into the freezing snow. There were no such extravagances from Beta; she followed without drama and maintained a safe three-second gap that she had calculated before they had left the P & R station. Suddenly, quiet synthesized commands were emitted through the speaker in Kellor's active helmet. The soft voice kept up a dialogue with him, telling him which turns to take and where. The two bikes raced along the icy roadways, spraying plumes of snow from their rear wheels as they went and Kellor desperately hoped that they would get to their destination in good time.

Andrew Tilbury was at home feeling very ill and a little sorry for himself. After all of the genetic and medical advances during the last three hundred years they had yet to find the cure for the common cold. 'How ironic!' he thought. His apartment was on the first floor of twenty. It was small and functional - as much as any man could hope for in this day and age. Tilbury was lying on the sofa, covered with a heated blanket, watching the state television channel. He had missed all the fun at the breeding farm, having been at home for over a week now and he wondered how much longer he could stretch out his illness without the incurring the wrath of a State Doctor. Sickness was frowned upon and too much down-time brought about the threat of termination if the State Doctor decided you were particularly susceptible to illness and unlikely to improve. Sipping at a cup of steaming lemon tea, he was startled to see the Stablinka breeding farm appear on the news broadcast. He grabbed the handset and turned the volume up loud, despite the violent banging upon the ceiling from an irritated neighbour.

'A Eurostate facility situated in Stablinka was attacked two days ago in an apparently motiveless raid. The attack took place in the early hours of Wednesday morning and was repelled successfully by the security forces based on site. Seven terrorists were reported to have been killed and four taken prisoner. There were no security force casualties. And now the weather. It will snow all...' Tilbury abruptly turned the volume down on the newsreader; it was the fifth time he had heard the weather report in the last hour.

He gulped down the dregs of his tea and wondered about the accuracy of the news report. He knew there was some funny stuff going on at the farm until all hours of the night and then there was the special flask of eggs that had been rushed through the cloning section where he worked. Tilbury would normally perform the cloning procedure on all the eggs that passed through his small department. Strangely though, on this occasion, a professor whom he had never seen before had visited and completed the task. Tilbury closed his eyes and drifted off into sleep, wondering if it had anything to do with the failed raid.

The Feman pulled into the underground car park below Yeltsin Heights, parked and switched off the power packs. The windows began to mist as the three occupants sat there contemplating the next crucial hour or so. They had parked in the darkest corner of the car park, so all that could be seen from the outside were the outlines of the three women as they continued to sit there in apprehensive silence. McDowell's mouth was dry, so dry that she was unable to swallow back the acid bile rising from her gullet and she began to regret consuming the alcoholic cocktail back at the drug store. The bile was now burning her throat and she thought she was going to be sick at any moment. This was the first time McDowell had been on a mission in such small numbers and she was uncontrollably nervous.

'It's time ladies, let's do it,' said Langton, after noisily expelling air through her mouth in an exaggerated sigh.

Nicola was quietly pleased at being called a 'lady' and as they all emerged from the cab, she began to feel good about herself for the first time in months. Opening the boot, she took out a pistol, checked the charge and ensured that the safety was activated, before sliding it ungraciously between the rolls of fat and the stressed trouser belt that tightly bound her waist. She slammed the cab boot with aplomb and the sound echoed ominously around the concrete walls. The three women began to walk to the elevator, spreading out across the car park in the hope of escaping the clutches of any ambush, however unlikely. McDowell used the butt of her rifle to smash the lamps that lit her path towards to the elevator. If there were any action on the way out then they would have a safe unlit route back to the cab she planned.

Langton was the first to arrive at the elevator doors and without hesitation she pressed the call button. She stood back, turned to one side, raised the pistol in her left hand and cradled the butt with the palm of her right, just in case the lift arrived with some unfortunate male on board. The floor countdown drifted from the speaker to the left of the elevator and she braced herself as the voice eventually proclaimed, 'Elevator now at basement level car park.'

The defaced elevator doors began to hum as they started to withdraw and the janitor within initially smiled as he exchanged a respectful glance with the waiting passenger. The shot threw him backwards and slammed him into the rear of the cramped metal lift. He fell into a sitting position with his head slumped onto his chest. Before Langton could react, Nicola was down on her knees in the elevator and, with great distaste, undoing the dead janitor's trousers.

'Leave him alone, we haven't got time for that,' shouted Langton.

'We've always got time for this,' the Feman said rubbing her hands together in mock anticipation.

Langton raised her pistol again.

'What the f...' Nicola shouted, diving for some non-existent cover.

Langton fired straight into the dead man's genitalia and the material around his groin flared and caught fire. Langton moved forward and stamped the flames out with her boot, causing the body to pitch over to one side.

'Let's get things straight right now. I'm in charge of this mission. You may be a field operative but you still take your orders from me. Don't try my patience or I'll shoot you now and save myself the grief later on, okay!'

'Whatever you say boss,' said the Feman pulling herself up on to her feet, resigned to the fact that her wish would not be granted.

'McDowell! Get your arse in here now!' screamed Langton in an uncharacteristically aggressive manner.

'Yes boss,' McDowell replied, mimicking the Feman.

'You can shut the fuck up too! Now take our dead friend here and hide his body somewhere. We'll meet you on the first floor. And take the stairs just in case we meet trouble on the way,' Langton ordered before pressing the first floor button just after McDowell dragged the janitor's smouldering body clear of the doors.

'First floor, next stop,' announced the elevator.

Langton was now comfortable with the fact that there was going to be no ambush to speak of and she relaxed a little after the earlier problems. The lift slowed to a stop and they prepared to exit in a hurry. The lift doors could not open fast enough for Langton - she thrust them impatiently aside and leapt out, sweeping her pistol from left to right, ready to gun down anything that moved in the hallway. The door opposite the elevator proudly displayed the number 134; the one to the left of it 132. Langton spun to her right and began to jog. Nicola wobbled along some way behind carrying her boss's rifle, her fat cheeks puffing in and out as she went. Langton approached the end of the landing and slowed to a quiet walk. Under her breath she read the door numbers as she stalked warily forward, 158, 160, 162, 164 and then quickly backed into the wall on the far side of the door to wait for Nicola to arrive.

The landing was gloomy rather than dark and they could see clearly the blood smears on the grey tiled floor. Langton had imprinted them down the hallway as she made her way towards the target's apartment. The footprints began to die out halfway along the passageway when the supply of blood on the soles of her boots had finally been exhausted. Langton raised a smile as the Feman eventually arrived at the target's door wheezing from her efforts and placed both hands on her knees, gasping for air.

'Are you enjoying the evening so far Nicola,' she asked sarcastically.

'Yeah, sure, fucking marvellous,'

'Right, no time like the present,' Langton said as she reached across and pressed the intercom button on the left-hand side of the apartment door.

'What about McDowell, aren't you gonna wait for her?

The intercom button beeped before Langton could answer and Tilbury's voice boomed from the overzealous speaker.

'Yes?'.

'Pizza delivery,' Langton lied using the vocal chip.

'I didn't order one, sorry,'

Unconcerned, Tilbury walked back to his sofa, sat back down and yawned. He looked at his watch and realised that he had been asleep for only a short while. He scratched his head and yawned again as a well-placed kick sent the front door crashing open and splinters of door frame spraying across the plain hallway.

'What the hell?' Tilbury cried out, now on his feet and cowering away from the living room entrance that led to the hall.

Langton charged down the hallway, through the living room door and into the lounge and thrust the pistol right between Tilbury's terrified eyes.

'What do you want? I didn't order any pizza. Please don't hurt me,' he babbled.

'On your knees Orger breath,' she rasped, ignoring Tilbury's plea and battering him with the pistol butt until he succumbed.

McDowell ran into the room, only to be greeted by Langton's pistol pointing defensively towards her. When she realised that it was only McDowell, she swivelled back around towards Tilbury.

'Thanks for waiting.'

'Stop with the wisecracks and tape his hands and mouth,' Langton ordered as she threw the reel of packing tape at her subordinate.

McDowell did as she was ordered and, with the Feman keeping watch in the hallway, they dragged Tilbury to his feet.

'Right Mr. Tilbury we're going for a little ride. If you co-operate you won't be hurt, but any nonsense and you're dead. Okay? Do you understand?' menaced Langton without bothering to disguise her voice as male and looking fiercely into his eyes, which were open wide in abject terror.

Dumbstruck, Tilbury nodded vigorously and with that the two women escorted him out of the apartment. When they reached the living room door Langton shouted ahead to the Feman.

'Nicola, get down to the lift and call it. You'll take Mr. Tilbury here down in the lift with McDowell. I'll take the stairs and meet you at the bottom. I want to check the area out before we head for the cab,'

Nicola ran as fast as her body would allow, still breathing heavily from the journey there. Her comrades followed, frogmarching their prisoner at a fast walking pace. Ominously, Tilbury saw the janitor's blood on the tiles as they approached door 148 and it began to open. In a heartbeat, they stopped in their tracks. Tilbury took his chance and shoulder barged Langton into the wall on the right. Winded, she fell to the floor. He spun to face McDowell and she punched him full in the face, knocking him backwards on top of Langton. The apartment door opened fully and a large weathered man entered the hall carrying a scarred aluminium baseball bat, which he instantly swung hard across McDowell's shoulders. Fortunately, the rifle slung over her back absorbed most of the impact. Nevertheless, she fell instantly to her knees, then onto all fours, and the vigilante quickly raised the baseball bat above his head ready to administer a deadly blow with all his might - until the laser bolt removed the handle of the bat along with his hands. He continued with the swing, followed through and stood up sharply, puzzled when his attack made contact with nothing but air. Bewilderment clouded his face as he held up the bloodied and charred stumps at the end of his forearms. The second shot lifted him off his feet and sent his crashing through his own closed front door. McDowell sucked in her breath, stood up painfully and looked down at Langton. It was she who had fired the shots that had saved her from getting her skull crushed.

'Get him up; we've got to get out of here fast. It'll be crawling with state police in no time,' Langton shouted.

McDowell dragged Tilbury up onto his feet and he wobbled as if his bones had turned to jelly.

'Try that again and it's goodnight Mr Tilbury,' said McDowell, pushing hard under his chin with the barrel of her pistol.

Langton got to her feet quickly and they set off down the landing once more, but this time with two laser pistols jammed securely into Tilbury's ribs.

'Shit, what kept you?' said Nicola.

'Nothing to worry about, but the sooner we're out of here the better,' replied Langton.

Arriving at the elevator, McDowell pushed Tilbury violently in the back and he fell headfirst into the lift. With no free hands to save himself, his head took the full force of the fall and the skin split open like a half-peeled orange from his hairline down to his right eyebrow. Tilbury screamed in pain, until the Feman followed up with a kick to his solar plexus.

'Give me two minutes to get downstairs and then come down when I bleep you. If anybody comes out of their apartment set off straight away. If I don't bleep you after five minutes kill him and get the hell out of here,' Langton ordered, disappearing through the stairwell doors.

Waiting for what seemed like ages, the odd couple scanned opposite ends of the hallway from the refuge of the lift, while behind them their hostage noisily fought for every gulp of air entering his lungs.

'What the fuck is taking her so long?' lamented McDowell.

'I'll have a look in my fucking crystal ball shall I!' retorted the Feman, showing her tension just a little.

McDowell instantly heard the threatening noise behind her, but before evaluating the situation she kicked Tilbury until he keeled over once more. Innocently, he had only tried to sit up, but McDowell's adrenaline-pumped hair-trigger reactions assumed any move as aggressive.

'Four minutes and thirty seconds!' the Feman announced agitatedly.

'What we gonna do?' asked McDowell, once more surveying the hallway.

'I dunno about you but I'm about to shoot the fucker!' replied the Feman, straddling Tilbury and waving her gun beneath his nose.

Tilbury's eyes fluttered in anticipation of his impending execution, but with ten seconds to go, the Feman's pager bleeped into life.

'I hope this ain't no false alarm,' said the Feman, awkwardly reaching around her hapless victim to press the button that would take the lift to the basement.

McDowell, now relieved of her duties as hall monitor, looked down and noticed the expanding wet patch sprawling across the front of Tilbury's light blue trousers.

'You dirty bastard, not so full of it now, are you?' McDowell said before delivering another swift kick as she tried in vain to vent the pent-up tension that still riveted her body.

The surveillance vehicle pulled up serenely outside Yeltsin heights some five minutes after the targets had arrived. Travis had already managed to contact the local police and advised them not to respond too rapidly to any calls from concerned residents inside the apartment block. The two agents had resisted the temptation of going on inside to take a closer look at the clandestine operation and were now impatiently watching the car park exit for any sign of activity. The laser shots fired by Langton could not be heard from any great distance, but the agents knew that there had been some activity because they were monitoring the emergency calls made to the state police from the alarmed residents. Chapel scanned the display monitors and physically flinched as Kellor's voice leapt from the radio speakers without warning.

'What's happening Chapel?' Kellor asked urgently.

'Just waiting for the women to come out of the building Major. They went in around fifteen minutes ago and by all accounts shots have been fired. We've told the state police to delay their response to any emergency calls they get, but if the targets don't get a move on they will end up being intercepted anyway,' replied Chapel.

'Tell the police to send in two officers. Advise them that we don't want any heroes. Let the targets escape, albeit under fire. Tilbury's expendable, but I must capture the Femorists alive and interrogate them,' Kellor instructed unhappily.

'How long before you get here?' asked Chapel after a lengthy pause.

'Fuck knows. We're going as fast as we can, and it's...' replied Kellor, riding by the seat of his pants.

'One moment Major, targets are on the move. Repeat, targets are on the move. It seems that they are heading west, back to the drug store I bet,' Chapel interjected.

Chapel waited for Kellor's reply but before it came he saw the two bikes heading towards the surveillance vehicle from the direction in which the cab had turned. The snow made it difficult to be sure that it was indeed the Major and his sidekick. 'But what other fools would be crazy enough to go out riding in this weather?' he thought.

The Feman pulled out onto the main road at a sensible speed, not wishing to draw any unwanted attention. Tilbury sat in the back seat, flanked by her two associates. McDowell was the first to notice the bikes and commented that it was a strange sight on such a filthy night. Fortunately for Kellor, at the precise moment he and Beta were spotted by the women, a wheeled State Police vehicle careered around the corner ahead of the cab, sirens wailing and lights flashing manically. McDowell forcibly dragged Tilbury down out of sight, so the cab looked as though it only carried one passenger.

'Shit that was close,' exclaimed a nervous Nicolas.

'Strangely slow aren't they?' said McDowell, sounding muffled from the rear foot well.

'Probably the weather,' Langton answered.

The police vehicle sped past the Femorists before sliding its way down the ramp that led into the underground car park from where they had come. At the end of the road, Nicola calmly stopped and then turned gently left, heading for the safe haven of the drug store.

'Why are there so many Medware vehicles about?' Langton randomly queried, as they passed three parked in a row.

'They do everything from delivering your groceries and livestock surveillance to rat catching. Every neighbourhood has their fair share of Medware employees - you can't get away from them I'm afraid,' replied Nicola.

'Things have certainly changed since I was last...' Langton fell silent as painful memories began to haunt her.

'Major Kellor, come in, Major Kellor!' Chapel shouted frantically.

Kellor could hear the frenetic calls but he had been distracted by the warning from the helmet visor informing him that they had reached their intended destination: 164 Yeltsin Heights.

'Yes! I can hear you Chapel.'

'Sir! You have just passed the targets and are heading straight for us,' Chapel reported, shaking his head in genuine disgust.

'Right, er. I don't think they made us. Where are the targets now?'

'They are out of visual contact sir. If you pull up on your right, about 150 metres in front of you... We're in the white Medware vehicle, the middle one of three,'

Covering the 150 metres at breakneck speed, he expertly slid the bike to a stop by the side of the surveillance vehicle. Activating the magnetic stand, he jumped off the bike, ran to the rear doors and hammered on them hysterically. After the anarchic performance, Travis could no longer contain his laughter and Chapel smiled as he opened the doors for the bemused Major.

'Major Kellor, what a thrill to meet you in person,' Chapel said in a leisurely tone, while laughter spilled from the front of the vehicle.

'Okay, let's cut the crap and get on with the business in hand. There'll be plenty of time for joking around later.'

Chapel instantly returned to his usual professional manner, but Travis was much more cynical and continued to snigger resolutely.

'May I propose, Major, that you follow us at some distance while we return to the drug store? We can then work out how to proceed from there,' suggested Chapel.

'Sounds like a plan; let's go.'

The drive back to the store was carried out in complete radio silence. Not for any tactical reason, but because their thoughts had begun to focus on the task ahead. Before Travis pulled up near the drug store, Chapel had managed to re-establish visual and audio contact with the targets. The ladies had bundled their hostage through the back door and immediately took him down into the basement workshop, ready for interrogation.

Kellor entered the surveillance vehicle and shut the door heavily behind him. He took a seat next to Chapel who was transfixed by the violent preamble being administered to Tilbury. Kellor listened with growing fascination as the interrogation deepened into his own worst nightmare and he knew that he would have to act, despite his earlier careless statement.

14 POKER TIME

It was late in the evening and Daniels presided at the head of the large mahogany conference table. He was flanked by Colonel Johnson and Alec McGeady, and at the opposite end of the room sat a silent individual whom no one knew except for Daniels. McGeady looked at the young blond haired, blue-eyed man and from somewhere he conjured up a smile. It was not returned.

Daniels was busy looking through a pile of official reports, deliberately keeping the rival intelligence officers waiting. The atmosphere was saturated with nervous tension, to an extent where McGeady was uncharacteristically smiling at everyone. Both men had been summoned to Berlin for a review of Operation 'Alpha Male', or so McGeady thought. The Colonel however, believed that this was a cover for something much more sinister. The large digital clock above Daniels' head silently marked the passing of every second and looked strangely at odds with the exquisite mahogany furniture that filled the large state room. McGeady's mind began to wander as he watched dust particles gently rise in the columns of light towards the ceiling spotlights. The room was extravagantly spacious, used as it was for major Eurostate conferences, but the islands of intense brightness were claustrophobic; like cells barred by their own illumination.

Minutes ticked by and Daniels continued reviewing the paperwork strewn across the table. He coughed, looked at the clock behind him and then at his wristwatch. The blond man continued to scrutinize Johnson and McGeady and both felt they were being singled out for some unknown reason. The Colonel held his clenched hands below the table and could feel the throb of the blood pulsing through them. He was just about to stand and pour some water from the distant drinks tray when Daniels finally looked up and spoke,

'Gentlemen. Thank you for coming here at such short notice. I thought it would be a good idea for us all to get together at this crucial time.'

Noticing that Daniels seemed only to be addressing McGeady and himself, he once again began to speculate about the role of the blond man.

'I understand Major Kellor has made contact with your men and they are currently tracking the terrorists,' said Daniels, now looking solely at McGeady.

'That's correct Sir. It would seem that the terrorists have taken, by force, one of the Stablinka employees and are now in the process of interrogating him.'

'Colonel Johnson; you've had no direct contact with Major Kellor since our brief conversation the other day I take it?' asked Daniels, looking down at the papers in front of him.

'No, none at all Callum,' the Colonel replied and Daniels shot him a rebuking look. The Colonel did not know whether the look was for using Daniels' Christian name during official business, or because he thought that just maybe the Colonel was lying.

'So who did the Feman pick up at the Shenka P & R station Alec?' Daniels carried on impassively.

'Two targets, both normal females. Femorists it would seem,' replied McGeady, keeping his answers as short as possible.

'And then?' Daniels asked impatiently.

'They returned to the Feman's drug store and were monitored by my men until they set out to kidnap the farm employee Andrew Tilbury,'

'And where was Major Kellor while all this was going on?' Daniels said, looking across towards the Colonel, hoping to see if there had indeed been any contact between them.

Before the Colonel could reply, McGeady began to speak again, 'He was travelling directly from the station to Tilbury's home address, where the targets were heading.'

'What were your agents doing?' Daniels asked McGeady.

'Following the Femorists of course sir,'

'Either of you have any ideas about who the Feman operative is in the Eurostate hierarchy?' asked Daniels completely out of the blue.

Daniels again looked down at the reports in front of him. McGeady looked at the Colonel and they began to speak at the same time as the pressure to fill the silence became overwhelming.

'Sorry Colonel, you first,' said McGeady, feeling the bite of his shirt collar and trying to loosen its grip with his left index finger. McGeady was pleased to be able to defer the first reply to the Colonel but he knew his moment would come.

'Intelligence reports indicate that we are looking for a new strain of Feman, one that has none of the characteristic dual genitalia. It could have been prematurely aged to hide the fact that they, the Femorists, have only had this technology for approximately the last five to ten years. As you are aware, the female livestock are the equivalent of around eighteen years old when they are brought to full term. So previously, we were looking for any livestock between the ages of twenty-three and twenty-eight. If the latest reports are true, then we do not even have this parameter to go on,' the Colonel reported.

'Is it true that most are left handed Colonel?' asked Daniels, watching McGeady taking notes with his left hand.

McGeady swallowed hard, placed his pen down upon the defaced pad, smiled at Daniels and coughed.

'No, that has not been confirmed. There seems to be no way of identifying this new strain, especially since we've never got our hands on one to dissect and run tests on,'

'Alec! What information do you have on this new breed of Feman?' asked Daniels before shuffling through the insignificant paperwork yet again.

'Well sir, not as much as Colonel Johnson, but my department's looking through the breeding data of all Eurostate employees to see if we can turn something up. As you can imagine though, it's a major task - and it's not going to be done any time soon' McGeady replied ruefully.

'How long?'

'It's hard to say,'

'Ball park figure?'

McGeady looked skywards and began to mumble. Counting in his head but also out loud, he looked back towards Daniels and answered, wincing as he replied at its probable inaccuracy and broad range.

'About another four years, give or take a year.'

'Fine. Keep up the good work.'

McGeady nearly fell from his chair. To his complete surprise, Daniels did not have a single query after such a non-specific reply and he looked to the Colonel for some form of reassurance.

'Martin, would you excuse us? There's something I want to discuss in private with Alec. If you could make sure you're available until Operation 'Alpha male' is completed, I would be grateful,' Daniels said. He then pressed the button located under the arm of his high-backed leather chair, which was infinitely more comfortable than the hard tubular seats upon which his guests sat.

The grand double mahogany doors unlocked automatically and Johnson left without further deliberation while Daniels yet again turned his attention to the papers in front of him. The door closed gently behind the exiting Colonel as Daniels pensively placed his clasped hands beneath his chin.

'I'd like you to undertake a personal surveillance job for me Alec - and I mean personal. I want you to look into the Colonel's past and watch his current movements, unofficially of course. Report back to me as soon as you have anything,' Daniels ordered.

'What am I looking for sir?'

'Anything and nothing. Just look and, as I stressed before, I want only you to conduct this investigation. Don't delegate this, if you need help then make sure the men you choose are from another region, out of the Colonel's reach so to speak.'

McGeady began to relax for the first time during the meeting and thought perhaps there was nothing to worry about after all. The Colonel was obviously under suspicion and that could only relieve the pressure on everyone else involved.

'Now I have some urgent things to do. So if you could leave me now... I'll look forward to your findings Alec,' Daniels said, pressing the button on his chair once more.

After McGeady had left, Daniels turned to the silent blond man and spoke to him for the first time in the proceedings.

'You're to watch McGeady like a hawk, night and day. I want to know every move he makes, when he shits, sleeps and eats! And, don't forget to monitor the operation at the same time. When Kellor moves out of Shenka, follow him. Let me know you are going and I'll assign another to watch over our friend McGeady,'

The blond haired man nodded He left without having to be asked and without speaking. Daniels sat back in his chair and smiled. Someone would break soon and he would be there to pick up the pieces and make something out of them.

15 ASSAULT

From a distance, the white surveillance vehicle sporadically disappeared from view as the storm intensified. The snow fell heavily and the wind swirled wildly as if it were trying to steal the snow's thunder.

'Your partner, is he going to be all right outside in this weather?' Travis asked from the front seat of the deliciously warm vehicle.

'Yes, he's fine,' said Kellor, peering out through the one-way glass fitted in the rear doors.

Beta was sitting side-saddle and she felt relatively warm in the heated over suit that she was wearing. The streetlights struggled to illuminate the ground through the heavy snow and Kellor was quietly pleased that, for the time being at least, he was not outside facing the elements.

'He doesn't seem to know much does he?' said Chapel, transfixed by the interrogation being played out before them on the monitors.

'I think if he knew anything worthwhile he would have told them by now,' replied Kellor, feeling guilty about not intervening in the current events.

'Do we know where the two Femorists are from?' he continued.

'No sir. All satellite coverage has been down for the last twelve hours. Some sort of solar electrical storm, coupled with the bad weather, well it's caused a surveillance blackout for many of our key systems. They could have arrived from anywhere for all we know,' Chapel replied unhelpfully.

'How long have they been questioning him for now?' Kellor asked, deliberately not using the word 'torturing', which was a more accurate description of the Femans' 'interrogation technique'.

Chapel looked at the clock on the visual data storage unit that was recording the whole distasteful event and replied, 'Forty-six minutes exactly sir.'

'Drop the "sir", it's not needed here,'.

'When we gonna go and get this guy out sir?' asked Chapel, ignoring Kellor's request.

'Soon, very soon,' he replied, looking backwards over his shoulder towards Beta, who had not moved an inch since the last time he had looked.

Langton hurriedly left the basement room where the Feman was still trying to extract information from their hostage. She leant over the basin in the basement toilet and retched without success. It had been a long time since she had last eaten, she thought, as the neglected stomach bile clawed away painfully at the back of her throat. She had never managed to become inured to cold-blooded torture no matter how long she'd stomached it and benefited from its results. She was saddened to see that McDowell had taken a morbid fascination in the interrogation, although she had not actually participated in the torture... yet. The various implements that Nicola used had been acquired over many years of information-gathering for the commune. She had also become very useful with her fists, used as they were on a male who was unable to defend himself.

'Fancy a little rest Mr Tilbury?' asked Nicola, lifting his forlorn head by the blood-sodden hair.

'Why are you stopping?' McDowell asked, in the mood at this point for more debauchery.

'He'll die if I continue just at this moment. We wouldn't want that right now, now would we Mr Tilbury!'

With her last statement Nicola needlessly struck Tilbury with the palm of her hand. The blow broke his nose, spreading it across his already devastated face, before the force of the punch slammed his head backwards over his shoulders, where it rested. McDowell studied the sadistic scene, leeching every detail into her psyche. Blood began to pour over Tilbury's shallow cheeks and dribbled from his ear lobes onto the highly polished granite floor below. The only thing that held him in this lifeless position was the piano wire that bound him to the steel chair. The wire was pulled tight and in places cut deeply into his naked skin as he faded in and out of consciousness. The use of electrodes clipped to his testicles had failed to secure any worthwhile information. Consequently, the Feman removed one of his nipples and gleefully eaten it in full view of her screaming victim. She then wiped the blood and saliva from her mouth while he cried desperately for the first time during his ordeal.

Nicola left the room to relieve herself and passed Langton, who was on the way back from the toilet. They paused by the furnace and faced each other. Nicola smiled but Langton could not find it within herself to reciprocate the gesture.

'He's taken my best shots and he's still holding out - tough man!' said Nicola admiringly.

'Did it occur to you that maybe, just maybe, he's told us all he knows!'

'Well we'll soon find out. He won't be able to resist my next attempt at getting him to talk. Either that or he'll be dead.'

'Listen. I think he's given us all he has to give. We know that recently there was a special batch of eggs fertilized using the cloning process in his department. And that this cloning was done by a physician unknown to Tilbury. This would seem to tie up with the batch that we have seized. So, why don't we just put him out of his misery now and secure another source of information. One further up the ladder,'

If they took another man, Langton knew that she would have to watch the same painful process of interrogation all over again. Nevertheless, at that precise moment she could not tolerate watching the Feman at work any more; or listen to

Tilbury's isolated screams from the normally quiet parts of the drug store.

'We still don't know what they did to those eggs, and more importantly why they are different. Until we know that, it goes on! That's my part in all this mess,' said Nicola irritated by Langton's weakness.

'And my part is to give the orders on this mission. So let's stop with your personal crusade to torture and kill the men that cross your path as painfully as possible, as often as possible; and regain some female decency and compassion.'

'So what would you suggest Commander? Put his teeth in a bag and send him on home like a good boy? If you want Tilbury out of his misery, *you* kill him!'

With that the Feman turned and walked upstairs to the vacant shop area, forgetting for the moment that she needed to urinate. Langton returned to the basement room where McDowell was sitting, rather bored, now that the stimulation had stopped.

'Enjoy that did you?' asked Langton aggressively.

'Orgasmic! That Nicola really knows how to treat a man!'

'Right, well if you enjoyed that so much you can have the pleasure of finishing him off,' ordered Langton.

'What?'

'Kill him, put him out of his misery, whatever you want to call it, just do it'.

'Surely Nicola will want to finish the job herself?' McDowell said hopefully.

'But I want you to finish him off, NOW!'

McDowell stood up.

'Okay,' she said, taking the pistol from her shoulder holster and pointing it at Tilbury's battered head.

'No not like that, with your hands, or maybe a knife. Yes, take a nice sharp knife and gut the poor fool,' Langton said, handing her a long silver blade she had taken from her boot.

'It doesn't seem right somehow. Why can't I shoot him?' replied McDowell losing her nerve slightly. She had killed a few men in her short military career but all in the context of a combat mission. This was the first time that she'd been involved in a cold blooded torture session. She liked to watch, but that was enough. During the attack on the livestock farm she had preferred to let others take charge of the guard's torture, but even that was relatively humane compared to what she was being asked to do now.

'No, you've got to feel the life you're taking from him, through your hands. When the knife goes in and jolts on the hard bones. Feel his last breath on your cheek as you slice the knife gently through his soft skin and watch his internal organs spill on to the floor covering your lovely shiny boots with his warm red blood.'

'You've gotta be kidding. Why should I want to do that to him?'

'Having fun aren't you? Enjoyed what you've seen? Well it's only one small step to being able to do it yourself. So come on, show me your balls Corporal McDowell! Or at least remove his... Fucking cut him!'

'I can't Miss. I don't want to do it like that and you can't make me,' McDowell said, muted like some sort of spoilt child as they squared up to each other.

'Surely it's not a problem for the commune's number one testicle taker?' Langton quipped.

'That's different; that's in battle and they're always dead. I don't want to kill him in cold blood, not like that,'

Langton thrust the knife into McDowell's hand and held it there, then walked around behind her before pushing her towards the unconscious hostage. McDowell resisted and with one swift movement threw Langton acrobatically over her shoulder. Langton came crashing down on the floor within touching distance of Tilbury's chair and, as she tried to stand quickly, she slipped on the bloody floor. Langton lay where she had fallen, trying to catch her breath along with her thoughts, while McDowell began to fill with remorse for what she had done. She moved around the room to help her prostrate commander get to her feet, but Langton's speed surprised even her. She whirled around on the sticky floor, sweeping McDowell's legs away with her own and before she knew what was happening, Langton was on top of her with the long blade at her throat.

'You little ignorant fucker!' screamed Langton, spitting saliva in her anger not two inches away from McDowell's face. Memories of Greenland flooded her senses and her rage became uncontrollable.

'Don't you ever fuck with me you little shit. I'll kill you! Don't ever start to enjoy seeing the blood because you'll end up seeing your own soon enough,' continued Langton.

McDowell tried to move a little but the blade gently sliced into her skin just above the larynx and she felt a trickle of blood run down to the back of her neck. Mesmerized, she stared into the Commander's eyes in the brief hiatus while booth regained their breath after the exertion of their struggle. Finally, Langton relaxed her limpet like grip and slowly stood up, removing the knife from McDowell's throat at the very last moment. Dazed, she could not believe that Langton had made a small cut into her unblemished young neck, which she now held with both hands as if her life depended on it.

'Get upstairs and help Nicola get ready for the next trip. I'll tidy this mess up,' Langton ordered as she began to cut the wire free from the lacerations on the demolished body.

Still clutching at her throat, McDowell shuffled out of the room without another word and made her way upstairs.

Chapel now looked up with a seriousness that Kellor had not seen before.

'Major, time to move I think, or he's dead. It's your call, but you're on your own from now on if you don't,' an insubordinate Chapel stated.

Kellor was apprehensive. He knew more now than he had twenty-four hours ago but still he had not discovered from where the two Femorists had arrived. He could wait and hope they would give the information away for free - and if he found their base, he was sure he would find the illustrious eggs. However, if he moved now he could save the hostage and hopefully take at least one of the three Femorists alive and make them talk. If he came up empty handed then Daniels would more than likely crucify him. Anyway, he could not watch this hideous cruelty any longer.

'We're going in now. Travis round the back please. Chapel, remain here and call for back up. My partner and I will go in from the front,' ordered Kellor, as he leapt from the back doors of the vehicle before he had even finished his sentence.

'Beta, we're going in now. There are three Femorists inside, one downstairs in the basement with no way out and two upstairs in the shop area. This man here is Travis, he will go in the back at the same time that we go in the front - okay?'

Travis handed the communication earpieces to Kellor and his companion, while Beta removed her crash helmet, revealing her soft feminine features. Travis gawked like an idiot before finally speaking,

'Here, put these in your ears. Just speak normally and Chapel will be able to co-ordinate things from the vehicle. Everybody can hear everybody else, so we shouldn't get in each other's way, okay?'

'Travis, what's the matter? Never seen a lady before?'

'Er, yes Major, well of course I have, but, well, erm,' Travis mumbled, unable to avert his stare.

'Just get around the back and we'll see you soon - hopefully,' Kellor ordered.

Turning on his heels, Travis ran down the side of the building and with an athletic leap mounted the wall surrounding the rear courtyard.

'I'm in, Major. The courtyard's about fifty-foot square: a couple of small outbuildings and the cab. No sign of life,' Travis reported immediately as he touched down on the other side of the defensive wall.

Travis jogged to the rear entrance of the shop, crouched down low, so as not to make too big a target if the people inside were watching. He held the pistol in his right hand and covered the door as he approached with characteristic insouciance. Finally, he managed to find sanctuary against the wall to one side of the entrance and he blew hard from his nostrils as he felt its safety press hard against his back.

'Major, I'm in position. Ready when you are,' Travis reported.

By now, Kellor and Beta were directly in front of the store and shielding themselves behind an parked truck. Beta seemed a different person at this particular moment thought Kellor, just as she had in the canteen when they had first met: silent, focused and very calculating. Snow had settled on her dark hair, her face showing no discernible emotion and he shivered from past experience of her aggression levels.

'Travis, Kellor here. We're in position. When I give the order, get inside as fast as you can and hold your position by the rear entrance. I repeat, *do not* try to advance into the store; we don't want a blue on blue. Please acknowledge, over.'

Just at that moment, Chapel noticed movement on the surveillance monitors, the Feman was responding to an internal alarm panel and he suddenly realised that they had somehow tripped a sensor, probably when Travis had climbed the wall he thought. Nicola waddled over to the alarm panel and studied it with some consternation.

'Bloody thing! It's always doing this; especially in this poxy weather,' she moaned.

Patiently Nicola reset the alarm, but after the sensor came back on-line it re-alerted her that a pressure pad, laid by the back door, was still activated.

'Shit! Must be that stupid cat again. Far too temperamental these sensors. When this is all over I'm gonna get them replaced and fix the fucking camera as well,' Nicola said, resigned to the fact that she would still have to check outside, despite her suspicions.

'What's up Nicola?' asked McDowell belatedly taking an interest.

'Not sure yet, it's probably nothing, but you'd better get your rifle while I take a look outside.'

Calmly, McDowell walked down the stairs to the interrogation room where she had left her weapons. Entering the basement workshop, she nervously observed Langton just sitting, staring into space.

'Miss, Miss!' she said, struggling to gain Langton's attention.

'What?' she eventually replied.

'Pressure alarm outside the back door has been triggered. Nicola's going to have a look as she can't seem to clear it,' detailed McDowell, now holstering her pistol and then picking up her rifle before checking its charge.

'Right, better leave this little job until later then,' said Langton miserably.

She stood up as McDowell left the room and headed upstairs. Nicola was already unbolting the back door: four bolts in all and a heavy-duty electronic lock. It would take her a few minutes to enter the security codes into the bolts and then de-activate the lock. Then she would be able to open the steel door and see what all the fuss had been about.

'Travis, are you reading me? Over,' Chapel said, whispering needlessly.

'Loud and clear. What's up Orger breath?' whispered Travis cheerfully, who was feeling more than a little cold and wishing he was back in the warmth of the surveillance vehicle.

'Target one is by the back door and about to exit. Seems you're standing on a pressure sensor fitted by the back door. No! Don't move, stay where you are! Target one thinks you're a nice little pussycat. If they don't open the door there ain't no way you're gonna be able to bust it in with all the bolts and locks on it.'

'Okay Chief, whatever you say.'

'Major Kellor, I think you should wait for Travis and go in on his command instead of yours? If you wait by the front entrance and let him clear the top floor, then you can both take target three alive downstairs, over,' Chapel advised.

'Kellor here. Sounds fine to me. Make the arrangements,' Kellor concurred having heard the previous report.

The very last bolt hummed as it retracted into its housing on the steel door. Travis readied himself to deal with whatever came out and as the door handle moved he froze.

McDowell had returned to the shop area and stood by the opening that separated the front of the store from the rear. Langton's mournful footsteps echoed through the stairwell as she tramped heavily up the spiral stairs.

Indistinctly, McDowell heard the Commander shouting, something about waiting until they were all present and in place before opening the rear entrance. As she arrived at the top of the staircase Travis gave the signal.

'Go, go, go, Kellor hit it! I'm on target one,' Travis whispered as the adrenaline rush swelled within his chilled body.

He watched silently as the Feman leant from the doorway, away from the warmth and safety of the bright store. It took a little while for Nicola to adjust her eyes to the minimal light levels and rampant weather conditions outside. She began to distinguish forms in the gloom but too late to stop Travis bringing his customised riot baton hard down on the back of her skull. Stunned but not unconscious, she collapsed to the ground, so that her rotund body lay half in and half out of the doorway. A large gash unzipped across the back of her head from which blood began to pump freely and she moaned pitifully, her clumsy plump fingers groping for the source of her pain.

Quickly, Travis stepped over the Feman and entered through the rear entrance before speaking, 'I'm in! Target one is down but alive. Visual on target two!'

Standing aimlessly in the doorway at the end of the hall, McDowell had been waiting for Langton to come out of the stairwell so she had not seen the activity taking place down by the back door, while the howl of the wind drowned any tell tale noises. As Travis took another tentative step further inside, he screamed wildly; Chapel thought that his eardrums would burst before he managed to sling the headphones down onto the control panel before him.

'Travis, are you okay?' Chapel bellowed at the top of his voice, fearful for his partner's welfare.

Travis's manic scream reached a bloodcurdling pitch. Nicola had flailingly managed to grab his trailing leg and was now trying to bite a second lump from the muscular calf. McDowell turned, no longer waiting for Langton's entrance. She saw Nicola lovingly wrapped around the intruder's left leg, his arms thrashing wildly as he tried to keep his balance. The pistol in his hand fired involuntarily, spraying laser bolts around and about the hallway and forcing her to take cover as a stray shot thudded and flared into the wooden doorframe next to her.

'Kellor you've gotta get inside now! Travis is in trouble,' Chapel shouted over the radio.

Beta stood ineffectually, recovering from the uncontrolled screams that had been broadcast in her earpiece without warning. While she stood, eyes closed, hands clasped ineffectively over her naked ears, Kellor tried in vain to batter down the front door with his shoulder. Finally, he gave up the impossible task, stood back, and fired desperately at the hidden locks behind the door.

Langton had reached the top of the stairs when she heard the violent cacophony emanating from the rear entrance. She took the final steps in one bound and slid the unlatched drug cabinet to one side, faster and more forcible than it had been designed to take. She emerged into the bright hallway light, oblivious to the crashing of medicine bottles behind her and identified McDowell crouching behind the scorched doorframe. Travis was now on the floor with the Feman and as they fought, McDowell was trying to get a clear shot at the male intruder without hitting her comrade.

'I told you to wait!' Langton shouted, as they both suddenly heard shots being fired rapidly at the front door.

'McDowell! Get down the back and help Nicola out. I'll cover the front. Move! Now!'

Evaluating their fast deteriorating position, she moved in behind the darkened drug counter and prayed that the front door was as strong as it looked. She only had a pistol for company and wished she had brought the rifle as well.

McDowell charged down the hallway, taking the opportunity to close the gap while Travis was otherwise engaged with the Feman. As she approached, the intruder got the upper hand. He rolled over on top of Nicola and punched her hard in the face. The solid floor behind Nicola's head did nothing to absorb the impact and he felt various bones in his hand crack. Travis roared in pain once more, but before he could regain his composure and finish off the Feman, McDowell fired.

Chapel could watch no more and scrambled for his firearm. He jumped from the back of the vehicle and sprinted towards the courtyard doors. He passed Kellor and saw Beta running mindlessly towards the steel shuttered window front. Tracer spewed perpetually from Chapel's weapon as he headed towards the large wooden doors leading to the courtyard, firing until at last, five yards from them, the lock ultimately disintegrated. Dropping his right shoulder, he barged the door at full speed and it swung uncontrollably out of the way, crashing into the side of the building upon which it was hinged. Inside the courtyard, Chapel tried to turn quickly in the direction of the rear doorway, but he slipped on the icy surface and hit the ground with a gentle cushioned thump. Fortunately, the thick snow-covered surface had broken his fall - but he had lost valuable seconds. Chapel got to his feet and began to run towards the back door again, precisely as the Feman emerged dragging Travis' lifeless body. Chapel's shot tore through the Feman's fat upper torso and he fired twice more, causing Nicola to fall majestically dead next to his partner. Nicola had made the fatal mistake of only taking a cursory glance outside to see if the vicinity was clear. When she thought it was safe to do so, she had pulled the body outside, so that the path down the narrow hallway was clear for any further action. McDowell could not easily pass the obstruction to cover her comrade, so Nicola had taken the risk anyway and hastily dragged the body outside. McDowell, barely inside the entrance, screamed out the Feman's name as she saw the lumps of Nicola's obese flesh fragment from the impact of several laser bolts. At that moment, there was an imperious roar of thunder from the front of the store, as if the world was coming to a catastrophic end. Breaking glass and the sound of falling masonry filled all parts of the store and for one moment McDowell was torn between avenging Nicola's death and assisting the Commander.

Langton could hardly believe her eyes when the awesome apparition came storming through the steel shutters that masked the glass shop front. The steel uprights that held the shutters in place had broken in two and shattered glass had spread to every corner of the darkened shop. Beta stood up unsteadily, throwing the steel shutter roll that hung from her right shoulder across the open threshold, which separated the store from the external footpath. Eventually, after her initial disbelief had receded, Langton observed Kellor standing on the sidewalk facing the store, weapon in hand, sweeping it left to right, ready to confront any perceived threats. Prioritising targets, Langton aimed at the armed soldier but as she pulled the trigger a monstrous form leapt to block the shot. The bolt hit Beta square in the chest. But the laser-proof vest absorbed most of the energy, causing her to soar backwards, initially unharmed, through the shards of the window. Seizing the opportunity, Kellor aimed at Langton, who once again had a clear shot, and they both fired at the same indistinguishable moment.

McDowell waited a few seconds before darting from the doorway, hoping to neutralise the most pressing threat. At the exact same moment, Chapel made it half way across the courtyard. Identifying the potential danger from the emerging woman, he fired and missed and McDowell ducked thankfully back inside the building. Chapel was now completely isolated without any cover to speak of, a rare mistake for such an experienced agent. The vision of Travis' dead body being unceremoniously dragged from the rear entrance was still haunting him and anger clouded any thoughts for his personal safety. It was then that the first shot hit him in the shoulder. It was a glancing blow, but it nevertheless impeded his progress towards safety and removed the skin from the top of his arm to the base of his scrawny neck. There was nothing for it but to keep advancing and he fired continuously as he approached the rear entrance in an effort to pin down whoever it was that had unexpectedly winged him.

Despite the torrent of bolts, McDowell lay down on the floor, poking her head and pistol alike around the bottom corner of the doorway before firing again. This time however, Chapel leapt towards the nearby cover and rolled acrobatically, before striking his left temple hard against one of the nondescript piles of junk lying around in the courtyard. Fortuitously, the second shot missed him by mere centimetres and clattered into the passenger door of the taxicab parked in the far corner of the courtyard. The laser bullet flared for a few seconds and then extinguished. After sinking back behind the doorframe, McDowell waited a short time for her fire to be returned. Even the slightest noise from behind her had ceased and she assumed the worst. The wind howled unhindered through the hallway as the return fire failed to materialise. Moving quickly now with the deathly silence fuelling her fear and without any thought for her own safety, she ran into the courtyard and past the unconscious man that she had just shot. Chapel was lying on his side, with a blossoming patch of blood stained snow that seemed to surround the upper torso of his body in a crimson halo. She had no time to check if he was alive and had just one intention, to flee the scene as quickly as possible.

The cab pulled out of the drugstore courtyard, rapidly negotiating the broken and charred wooden doors. Without a glance back, McDowell began to head for the Park and Ride station. Almost immediately, she realised it was more than likely that the authorities would also be watching the catamaran. So she swung the cab slowly around and headed sadly out of town in the opposite direction, still wondering about Langton's fate.

During the cab's erratic escape, Kellor was beginning to regain consciousness, having been saved once again by his trusty laser flack jacket. Upon her violent ejection from the building, Beta had impaled her left leg on the main metal shutter upright, which had broken when she had crashed through the shop front windows. Outside in the settling snow, she lay on her back, deathly pale and in shock. A few small fires smoked harmlessly around the store, started by the stray shots from Travis as he fought with the Feman. Kellor stood up, gathering his scattered thoughts and staggered a little as he walked towards the devastated store before him. Avoiding the large shards of window pane, he climbed slowly into the shattered shell. Kellor knew that he had hit the Femorist with his shot and instantly saw her lying on the floor next to the virgin white serving counter, whimpering in pain from a severe wound to her chest. Cautiously, he advanced, kicking her pistol out of reach as he went and the approaching State Police sirens whined jeeringly into earshot. Pushing on through to the back of the store, he scrutinized the bodies of Travis and the Feman; they lay side by side and looked strangely peaceful as the snow settled over their faces and lifeless remains. Kellor stepped over the two cadavers at his feet and scanned the courtyard for any sign of Chapel. He heard the cries first and, suddenly distraught, scuttled across the yard before lifting him up into his arms. Chapel was shivering fiercely and Kellor's heart sank further at the realisation that he was responsible for this whole sordid mess. Without further consideration, he carried Chapel back into the store to make the most of what little warmth and shelter it had to offer. Chapel opened his eyes as Kellor laid him down in the hallway at the rear of the drug store.

'Major, screwed up didn't we?' he said meekly.

'Don't you worry about that. Take it easy,'

'Still one thing Major, at least Travis won't be stuck down the mines with me and a spoon for company!' the broken man smiled weakly.

Kellor was unsure what he meant exactly, but he smiled back all the same. State Police officers were beginning to pick their way through the ravaged building and he shouted for a medic.

'Stay with me Chapel, damn it, you're going to be fine! Just stay with me! Medic!'

'Don't beat yourself up Major, it's just a graze, but I think I banged my head pretty hard. It hurts like hell...'

'Over here, yeah you, man down here. Look after him, I need to... I need to get some answers,' Kellor said as the medical team eventually arrived with a police escort.

'Who is the senior officer here?' Kellor shouted as he returned to the shop area where several police officers now inhabited the scene.

'I am. Are you agent Chapel?' replied Sergeant Lewis Clark, who stood in a darkened corner sifting through some indistinguishable debris.

'No, Major Robert Kellor, Military Intelligence. Agent Chapel is being cared for out back.'

'Major fuck up you mean!' Clark said offering his unsolicited opinion.

'And you are?'

'Sergeant Clark at your service. This all your own handiwork is it? Or did you have help?'

'Okay Sergeant, save the humour for someone who gives a shit. Now, get this lady patched up - and make sure you keep her alive, whatever it takes,' he ordered as Clark finally emerged from the shadows and stood impassively observing the unconscious Femorist.

'She looks like she is in need of hospital treatment - that's if she's not already dead,'

'No way. She's alive all right. Take her to the room downstairs. It's behind that drug cabinet there. And if she dies I'll hold you personally responsible,' Kellor added, checking her pulse.

'Better get a medical team down there right away, but not before they stabilise her. They interrogated a man down there and he's in a bad way. I'm going to report in to HQ and when I come back I want to get started on this bitch right away!' he continued, remembering that Tilbury was still downstairs in God knows what sort of mess.

'What about the one in the front there? Do you want her downstairs as well?'

'No, she's with me. Get her to a hospital. Oh and make sure you tell her I asked after her and that I'll be with her as soon as I can.'

Clark seemed confused by the presence of these women, nevertheless he began to carry out the Major's orders efficiently, calling for further medical assistance and personally overseeing Langton's treatment. Kellor left the building and returned to the empty surveillance truck. He sat in the warm vehicle in stunned silence, trying to muster the courage to speak to Daniels. Before long, he had talked himself out of reporting the events to Daniels and in frustration kicked the back doors so hard that they flew open. With a full head of steam, Kellor marched back into the store to begin interrogating Langton.

16 SURVEILLANCE

The blond man remotely watched McGeady pacing around his apartment through the microscopic eyes of the nanocam particles he had dusted about the place earlier. The tiny dwelling was filled with fine furniture, a fringe benefit of holding a high rank in the security forces. McGeady was sitting on the huge leather sofa, eyes closed and gently humming to himself when he heard the rustle of paper. He walked into the entrance hall and saw the note pushed under the door. Picking it up, he began to read as he returned to the sofa.

'Please be aware that you are being watched. Go immediately to the virtual reality amusement park in Koblensk and visit the zoological gardens in London. We will find you. Bring your observer with you and we will take care of him,'

The blond man frantically switched between the various cameras that covered the entrance and hallways of the residential building, trying in vain to catch a glimpse of the unknown courier who had left the note. While he sat in the sparsely furnished room on the floor above McGeady, the blond man played around with the surveillance equipment, but it seemed that all the communal area cameras were out of action. By the time his view returned to McGeady's apartment, he was gone.

It was a little after ten and the blond man was glad that darkness had descended as he began to vault down the stairs. He knew McGeady had no transport available to him at the apartment block so, he reasoned, his target must have left on foot. As he neared the stairwell exit to the main foyer, he put on his black woollen balaclava, pulling it just far enough down to cover his short straw-coloured hair. He looked through the small window located in the door, checking that he would not run straight into McGeady.

When he saw that his exit was clear he raced across the marbled lobby and into the cold night air. Stopping on the kerb directly outside the apartment block entrance, he listened intently, staring vacantly down at his boots. The weather was still atrocious and it meant that few had ventured out and he heard the crunch of footsteps clearly on the freezing snow coming from what he guessed was the adjacent street. As he started to run, the blond man hoped that it was indeed McGeady's footsteps that he had heard.

McGeady walked confidently, making sure that he was visible from a long way back. His heart was racing. It was the first time in twenty years of doing the job that he had felt vulnerable. He was being singled out by people more powerful than himself and he knew this would be the case until he could identify and neutralize the threat. He marched on, hoping to pick up a cab, but there was very little traffic due to the weather, so he continued to walk, more slowly now as the snow still fell heavily. Turning into the main road that led towards his destination, McGeady waved down what seemed to be the one and only cab left on the roads that evening. He began to worry that whoever was supposedly following him, would not be able to stay with him - unless another cab happened along immediately after his own had pulled away. This seemed unlikely, so McGeady told the driver to wait, while he tried to identify his pursuer from a distance. Finally, at the far end of the road, he saw the intimidating figure turn the corner.

'Koblensk amusement park, and take it slow please,' McGeady requested as the cab pulled away with a jolt. McGeady watched while the man in black approached the pick up point and miraculously another cab pulled in right on cue.

'Slow you say. I don't know any other way,' replied the driver jovially.

The cab slowed to a crawl and McGeady continued to watch while the man in black began to jog effortlessly towards the junction.

'Ain't you a bit old for the park mister?' asked the juvenile driver.

'Shut the fuck up and drive!'

'You're the boss! Whatever you say man, but I was just pointing out that...' before the cab driver could finish his sentence, McGeady grabbed the young man's long hair from behind and placed his free hand tightly around the exposed throat. He moved forward in the rear seat and now whispered gently in the terrified man's ear. So close that the cabbie could feel the warm breath slide down his stiffened neck.

'I told you to be quiet - and I won't tell you again. Now speed up a little and you'll get a nice little tip when we get to the Park, okay?'

He let the young man go and the cab swerved a little while McGeady sat back, his attention diverted.

The cabbie thought about the tip, and decided to keep his mouth shut as requested. He coughed gently and drove on, anxiously checking the rear view mirror for trouble - but his passenger was busy looking out through the smeared rear window.

McGeady wondered where his would-be assailant had disappeared to. - because the cab tailing him had inexplicably turned off the highway ten minutes earlier. The exit for Koblensk eventually arrived and it was then that he spotted him, running at incredible speed. As the cab turned back on itself, as the slip road passed under the highway McGeady shook his head in disbelief; not only was this man running as fast as the cab, but had been doing so for the last eight miles. Beginning to lose his composure, he quickly felt for the pistol in his shoulder holster.

'Speed up!' McGeady said sharply despite the prior written orders not to lose the observer.

'Whatever you say.'

McGeady watched until his pursuer disappeared into the dark distance as the cab sped out of sight and finally sat back and nervously closed his eyes.

17 RETRIBUTION

Sitting handcuffed to the same chair that Tilbury had recently vacated, Langton heard the clank of footsteps on the stairs that led to the basement. While she waited for the descending man to enter the workshop to begin her inevitable interrogation, Langton thought it somehow ironic that it was she, the one who had shown some modicum of mercy towards their hostage, who had ended up taking his place.

Kellor viciously kicked open the dark wooden door that led to the basement workshop. Sergeant Clark, who stood within, thought it would come off its hinges - and that maybe a guilty conscience was to blame. Walking over to the chair placed directly in front of Langton, Kellor sat down with the back support to the front. He rested his unshaven chin on his hands, which were neatly crossed on the top of the backrest.

'Langton, Commander, No 54372,' she said without being asked.

'Excuse me?' replied Kellor.

'Langton, Commander, No 54372. Name, rank and military number. That's what you want to know and that's all I have to say.'

'If I'm not mistaken, this is not a standard military operation. In fact, I'd go as far to say it was a blatant case of spying. You are wearing civilian clothes and not military ones. I think we can safely say you are on a spying mission. The Eurostate requires the death penalty for spies, as you should well know.'

'And they also execute military prisoners, so I've nothing to lose,' she replied defiantly.

'How's your chest? Causing you any pain?'

Kellor could see that the medics had patched the hole above her left breast, but he did not know how long it would be before she died of her injuries. They were certainly terminal even if they were treated, here or in the best hospital. But his concern was not for the woman's welfare - far from it, he simply wanted to do everything that could be done to prolong the time for interrogation. These matters, after all, could not be rushed.

'Do you need any pain relief for that?' he continued, nodding towards the dressing.

'Why not. I'm not going anywhere for a while I dare say!'

The pain was growing exponentially as the adrenaline in her body subsided and she gratefully accepted the offer. Kellor for his part, knew that without the medication she would go into shock and die sooner rather than later. Looking across to the medic standing quietly by Clark's side, he nodded and the medic went to his bag. Once the painkiller had been administered, Kellor continued.

'I suppose it won't do me any good torturing you now? You won't feel much of anything.'

'Suppose not, but thanks for your concern. I'm deeply touched.'

'Why were you interrogating that man earlier?' Kellor asked quickly.

'I don't like men much and you're no exception,' she spat.

'What did you hope to get out of him?'

'I was interested in finding out why you men are such arrogant bastards,' Langton replied, trying hard to ignore the dulling effect of the painkiller.

'Tell me something I don't know.'

'Like who the Feman spy is in your organization,' Langton replied, trying to fudge the issue.

'What makes you say that?'

'Questions, questions nothing but questions,' she moaned.

By now, Langton was feeling totally engulfed by the painkilling drugs and she wondered what exactly it was that she had been given. She was aware of a Feman spy high up in the Eurostate organization but she did not know the name it went by in the male world. Langton had been involved in various commune meetings to discuss the best way to direct the spy, but recently it had come to her attention that the Feman in question was becoming some sort of maverick. As hard as they tried, the various female hierarchies could not bring it back into line; the spy resisted their pressure and became a loose cannon, independent of any outside female intervention.

'So what shall we talk about now?' Kellor asked, with the feeling that however long he had with this woman it would never be enough.

'Football maybe?' joked Langton, struggling to keep her head upright as her blood pressure dropped dangerously low.

'We have the other woman upstairs you know. She's being very cooperative. She says that you come from a base in...' Kellor paused as her head dropped forward lifelessly.

'Commander Langton? Commander can you hear me?'

Receiving no response, he made eye contact with the medic before speaking, 'Give her the once over - see if she's bluffing.'

The medic gently felt for a pulse below her jaw line before lifting her head. Langton's eyelids flickered, but the eyes behind them seemed to hold no life even though the pupils were still reacting to the stimulus of light.

'So?' Kellor asked the busy medic impatiently.

'She's all but dead. You're wasting your time. If you do anything to her in this state she'll surely die immediately,' the medic said with genuine distaste.

'Damn!' Kellor said and stood up, before launching his chair across the room in a fit of pique.

He looked menacingly at Sergeant Clark as the chair bounced off the wall and smashed a pile of empty pill bottles.

'Any of your officers spotted that fucking cab yet?'

'I'll just check,' Clark replied coolly, before speaking into the microphone that projected from his earpiece. 'Clark to HQ controller, over.'

Kellor could not wait for the answer and walked out. He jogged up the stairs, went outside, sat down and waited for Clark to join him.

Clark finished checking for any information on the cab and then spoke to the medic, 'Leave her. See if they need you upstairs; there's nothing you can do for her now anyway.'

'Suppose you're right. No point in wasting time on her. I'll be off then,' said the medic as he threw his equipment back into his medical bag.

'Close the door behind you, I don't want her to catch a chill,' said Clark smiling.

Waiting for the footsteps on the stairwell to subside, Clark moved in close to Langton. She raised her head unsteadily and managed to focus one last time just as Clark stepped around behind her and snapped her neck in one ferocious movement.

Strolling out of the store, Clark beckoned to two of his men to come over to him. He spoke to them briefly, before they disappeared inside the drug store. Looking around, he spotted the Major, seated on the kerbside, oblivious to the bitter weather even though it had improved slightly.

'She's passed away,' Clark said, almost respectfully.

Kellor lifted his head from his hands and looked up towards the Sergeant, who was now standing over him.

'And I didn't even get a chance to...' he stopped in mid sentence as images of Tilbury's ordeal fractured his thought process.

'What now Major?'

'The cab, any news?'

'No none. But don't worry we'll find the bitch.'

Kellor rubbed his temples and brought his fingers up through his short brown hair.

'Beta!' Kellor said with a start.

'Who?'

'The female injured outside the shop front'

'Oh her. She's down at the Metro ER, just like you wanted,'

'Let's go then, I need her,' Kellor said as he stood wearily.

'I'll drive you myself. I think your injured man has gone to the same ER as well.'

'He's not my man, he works for special-ops' Kellor replied quietly.

'Just as well; by all accounts he's in a bad way.'

Kellor plodded along behind Clark as they walked over to one of the many police vehicles strewn across the road. Clark got into his patrol car and hurriedly switched off the communications console before his passenger had even managed to open his door.

'We'll get information on the cab as soon as they find it won't we?' asked Kellor, labouring the point.

'Not in this squad car - no comms unfortunately. The unit in here is out of action and my personal radio for some reason won't send or receive with all these magnets around. Must be the EMC screen gone faulty. Under-staffed and under-resourced we are. You'll have to wait until we get to the ER and I'll check again, okay?' Clark lied unconvincingly.

'It'll have to be. It'll have to be,' repeated Kellor under his breath, without bothering to question Clark's putative communication problems. After all, he reasoned, the night could hardly get any worse than it already had.

18 ESCAPE AND RESURGENCE

McDowell drove for just a few miles before she realised that every prick cop in the city would be looking for her in the shiny yellow cab. She needed a place to dump it, preferably out of sight. She also assumed that the police would be crawling over the Park and Ride station looking for the ship that had brought them into the city. So, she surmised that she would have to find an alternative means of transport to travel back to the safety of the commune. In the distance shone the lights of an all night diner and as McDowell approached, she saw it was empty apart from the night chef who was sipping coffee at one of the many vacant tables. Without hesitation, she parked the cab in the semi-secluded parking lot to the rear of the restaurant, deciding that this spot would have to do even though the vehicle could be seen from the road. She got out, went to the boot and began rifling through the contents for anything worth taking. The bolt cutters were jammed into one corner, probably dumped there in McDowell's rapid escape in the cab. She hastily shoved them inside her jacket but they seemed to be all that was worth salvaging. Slowly but deliberately, she walked to the restaurant entrance, removing the pistol from her jacket as she went.

McDowell had spotted the power bike nestled in between two large overflowing refuse bins behind the diner. It was not like the bike that she had started her journey on; it was the magnetic power pack type and so had limited functionality. There were no wheels, just two magnetic power pack units, front and rear. That would have to do for now, but she knew once she had cleared the city it would be useless on the non-magnetic natural terrain that she would have to cover to get back to the commune. The restaurant door chimed as it opened but the night chef paid no attention to its reverberation around the previously silent and deserted diner, choosing instead to continue reading his electronic book and sip his strong black coffee. McDowell stood at the counter trying to calm herself. All she wanted to do was kill the guy and get the hell out of there, but she knew she had to be patient and wait till he was behind the counter, out of sight from the main road that looked intrusively into the dining area. She had cried most of the way to the diner, for the first time ever in fact, and she did not enjoy the feeling. Her eyes were red and swollen from the outpouring of emotions and she felt mildly ashamed at her inexplicable show of weakness.

The chef got to his feet at last and, still reading as he walked, returned to his post behind the counter.

'Yes?' the Chef said, without looking up to see the pistol pointing straight at his forehead.

'Your bike please,' McDowell replied softly.

Confused by the request, the Chef looked up immediately and McDowell saw from his face that he was incredibly young. Just before she shot him, she thought that the Eurostate must be really short of livestock to have let this one out into the big wide world so under-developed. But now there was no emotion, no second thought about taking a life in a non-combat situation as there had been earlier. She was cornered and it was a case of kill or be killed. Before collapsing, the chef staggered backwards, knocking a stack of stainless steel bowls clanging onto the hard concrete floor. Motionless, McDowell waited until the cacophony subsided and then dragged the body through the back entrance of the restaurant to where the bike was parked before returning to lock the front door. Turning the lights out, she hoped would buy her some time, as anybody passing now would think that the chef had simply shut up shop on a slow night.

Returning to the brand new red and chrome bike, McDowell got on and tried to start the power packs using the chef's crash helmet from his locker. Each time she picked out the 'engine start' icon from the scroll down menu viewed from inside the visor, the display flashed 'Transponder malfunction'. After several failed attempts, she realised that the elusive transponder had to be implanted somewhere on the chef's lifeless body and guessed that it must be an index finger. Try as she might, McDowell was unable to hold the Chef and swipe his index finger over the sensor without losing her grip so that the dead body crashed to the floor at her feet. McDowell suddenly felt sick with the thought of what she had to do. Taking the bolt cutters from her jacket, she rolled the body so that it was face down. She did not want to see his face as she removed each finger in turn and then tried to unlock the electronic starter system by pressing the finger pad onto the sensor built into the bike's display panel. Eventually, by the time McDowell had tried seven of his fingers, she was beginning to panic. Finally, she placed the pad of the eighth one on the sensor and the bike sprang into life. McDowell breathed a heavy sigh of relief as she disrespectfully tossed the successful finger into the bin to her left along with all the rest; more raw meat for the night's scavengers.

She took off as quickly as the bike would carry her and she could not believe how smooth and safe the ride was without antiquated wheels. She sped to the outskirts of the city and took the main road out; the one on which she had intended to travel into the city before the operation had started so badly. She would go as far as she could on the chef's bike, McDowell thought, and then look for a more appropriate form of transport. As the city lights dwindled to speckles of luminescent dust in the background, she began to cry again.

Clark pulled into the drive-in ER and parked in a restricted zone. Turning to Kellor, he pulled a painful smile and said, 'Go on in and I'll follow on in a moment. I just want to check on the cab and have a smoke.'

Clark took his cigarettes from his breast pocket and lit one without offering them to his passenger. Kellor did not say anything and got out of the vehicle like a man with the weight of the world on his shoulders - or at least the weight of Daniels. Ten feet away from the cab, Kellor stopped and turned back, just as Clark was about to switch on the communications console. Clark tried to look casual as the passenger door opened.

Kellor bent down to speak and received a face full of smoke for his trouble. 'Find out if the team watching the park and ride station have come up with anything?' Kellor instructed.

'Yeah, when I finish this,' came the less than helpful reply.

The squad car door slammed shut unnecessarily and Kellor trudged towards the obtrusive ER. Harsh bright light radiated from every window and he observed how run-down the single storey building was in the gloomy glow of the surrounding streetlights. Apprehensively, Kellor approached the entrance, slowing his pace until the double doors finally rattled apart at the very last moment. Now inside, Kellor scanned the shabby ER as he stood by the registration desk waiting for the receptionist. The floor was streaked with grime. The walls were concrete grey, because no one had bothered to paint them in the forlorn hope of cheering the place up. Chairs lay scattered around, not all were upright and Kellor thought it looked almost like a Wild West saloon after one of those famous bar room brawls that he had seen in his beloved John Wayne movies. He turned and impatiently rang the antique bell that stood quietly on the table behind the counter. Strange, he thought, and very out of place, as probably the oldest man Kellor had ever seen rushed angrily from the office behind the reception desk.

'What?' bleated the greying old man, looking Kellor up and down with distaste.

'I'm looking for a woman - she was brought in about an hour ago?'

'Oh her, cubicle five,' the old man replied, completely uninterested in the fact that a rare female specimen had been brought into the rundown ER.

'There was a man as well, Simon Chapel. Where's he?'

'No he's not here. They took him to the private medical facility just down the block.'

'What?' demanded Kellor in a disgruntled tone.

'The man, Chapel, they took him to a private hospital, down the block. Clear enough for you,' repeated the old man, more sarcastically this time.

Struggling to hold in his anger, Kellor strode through the waiting room to the treatment area and entered cubicle five without ceremony. Beta was on the gurney, lying there still untreated, eyes closed with the metal strut cut short either side of her propped up thigh. She looked like Death personified - and he was startled by the depth of his concern for her well being.

'Beta,' Kellor said as he gently rubbed her arm.

Beta raised her eyelids slowly.

'Sir,' she replied quietly.

'How are you feeling?'

'Not too good Sir. I feel so tired.'

Beta winced with pain as she tried to move to a more comfortable position and that was as much as he could tolerate. After more than an hour, he thought she should have been seen and treated, especially as business in the ER was so slow tonight.

'You rest for a bit and I'll get a doctor to see you.'

He marched from the cubicle straight back to the reception desk, where the old man was busy playing a game of computer chess on his pocket terminal.

'Why has she not been treated?'

'Don't ask me, I'm not a doctor,' replied the old man, looking up at Kellor over his half moon spectacles.

'Well I *am* asking you! So get a doctor down here and we can sort this problem out right now.'

'Can't.'

'Can't or won't?'

'Can't. I'll lose my train of thought - and you're not helping either.'

That was the breaking point. Kellor grabbed the old man by the throat and dragged him over the desk, scattering the antique bell and other personal belongings across the floor. Kellor lifted the helpless receptionist up high, so he could see the surprise in his rheumy eyes.

'It's a woman we're talking about - some old tart, not a man,' the old man choked out, trying pointlessly to reason with the irate Major.

He did not give the old man any more time to speak before he punched him with his free hand. The old man hit the floor, but got up immediately, only to be hit even harder. This time, Kellor pulled him to his feet by his collar before dragging him back behind the reception area.

'Unfortunately your game's over!' explained Kellor, as he dropped the pocket terminal on the floor and stamped on it.

'Now call a doctor. Oh and get one for yourself,' he continued.

After a long and unbearable wait for the battered receptionist, a doctor eventually appeared and Kellor squared up to him as soon as he walked into the reception area.

'Who called me?' the doctor said, yawning.

The old man shot a terrified look upwards, still at his desk and afraid to move.

'It was him!' the old man said quickly.

'What can I do for you? And it had better be fucking urgent!'

'Cubicle five. My partner has been impaled on a metal strut.

If you could sort it straight away, I would appreciate it,' Kellor said in a friendly manner belied by the way he was trying to intimidate the doctor with his physical presence.

The doctor looked at the older man over Kellor's shoulder and saw the streaks of blood down his face and the rapidly swelling nose and eye.

'I'll take a look, but I want to call security in here now.'

Kellor swiftly withdrew his pistol from his holster and rammed it up under the doctor's chin.

'You can call who you fucking well like - after you've seen my partner, right?'

'If you say so,' replied the doctor with his hands nervously raised just as if he were the victim of a stick up, which, in effect, he was.

Kellor spun the doctor around and shoved him hard in the back. The doctor walked to cubicle five, hands still raised and trembling.

Clark smoked his cigarette right down to the filter, then lit another and did the same with that one before he felt it safe to power up the communications console. He adjusted the rear view mirror so that he could see the ER entrance and then began to speak, 'Clark here - over.'

'Sergeant Clark, very nice to hear from you,' came the reply after a few short moments of indecision.

'I'm with Kellor now. Commander Langton is out of the picture, but he is pressing me hard on trying to locate Corporal McDowell,'.

'Whatever you do, let her go. We have McDowell covered. Stall Kellor, I don't want him off in pursuit of our rabbit,' said the voice on the radio.

'Okay, but we have a dead guy from special operations and another on the way out probably. It won't be long before McGeady gets his fucking claws into us and then there will be no way of containing the situation.'

'Don't you worry about McGeady. We have plans for him. Just do your job and call me in the morning.'

'Fine. It's as good as done.'

'One last thing. Make sure you kill that cross breed that Kellor's got with him.'

'How? He's with her now.'

'Just do it. She could upset all our plans if she's anything like as effective as our livestock.'

'Right, whatever you say Colonel.'

Clark got out of the police vehicle and lit another cigarette. He seriously doubted that he could terminate the cross breed without Kellor suspecting something. Clark had hoped that by delaying her treatment he could make sure she croaked of her own accord and saved him the trouble of killing her. But he had not reckoned on Kellor's inexplicable display of loyalty towards Beta. Entering the ER, he spoke to the battered old man, who was now on his knees, gathering up his scattered possessions from the floor.

'Where the fuck are they?' Clark demanded.

'Cubicle five, but he's got a doctor in there now treating the bitch,' the old man whined bitterly.

'I thought you were told to delay her treatment for as long as possible!' Clark barked with intensifying anger.

'That's what I did, but your friend did this to me, so I thought it prudent to call a doctor,' said the old man, clearly fearing Kellor more than he did Clark.

'Right, I suppose I'd better see what's going on then,' Clark said realising that further intimidation of the old man was futile now that Kellor had put the fear of God into him.

Clark swaggered through into the treatment area and was disgusted by the conditions. Not that he was about to say anything about it. He entered cubicle five. Beta was unconscious by now and he observed that between the distraught Major and the terrified doctor, they had somehow managed to remove the intrusive strut from her leg.

'What about infection doctor?' Kellor asked.

'Antibiotics and lots of rest are all that I can offer her.'

'There must be something more we can do for her?' Kellor persisted, unhappy with the primitive 20th century-style treatment on offer.

'Well the only thing I can suggest is the private facility up the block. They have a microwave regeneration unit that'll close the wound in a few hours. She'll probably be laid up for a while, but it'll kill off any risk of infection as it works.'

Clark was only half listening because he was transfixed by Beta's naked body. He had never seen female genitalia before - well at least not in the flesh - and he could not avert his eyes.

'Sergeant, can you take us there?' asked Kellor, who had relaxed a little with Beta's receding pallor.

'Sorry?' Clark replied suddenly coming to his senses and flushed with embarrassment.

'Can you take us to the private medical facility down the block? I want them to treat her.'

'They won't take her! Shit, they wouldn't take *me* if I was dying!' Clark replied, now trying to work through the implications of this course of action in his head.

'They fucking well will! I'll make sure of it. All it will take is one call.'

'Fine, whatever you say. Let's go.'

Clark was not sure he was doing the right thing, but he knew that to antagonize Kellor at right now would be a big mistake. He would have to bide his time, as he was painfully aware that the Colonel wanted Kellor to continue with the mission, albeit with external control and that if all else failed he still could not kill Kellor without the Colonel's express authorisation.

19 ASSASSINS

McGeady stepped warily out of the cab, scanning all around him as he paid the now-relieved driver. The surrounding area was completely deserted, save for a few hardened thrill seekers wandering in and out of the Virtual Reality Park. The Park was open twenty-four hours a day, seven days a week and apart from the bars, this was the only form of entertainment in town. Berlin was not as it used to be, most of the fine 20th century architecture having been removed and replaced with faceless acid rain-proof buildings. There was a massive museum in town and it held the relocated buildings of architectural note. These properties had been saved from being dissolved away in the all pervading acid rain, but there seemed to be little nostalgia for that sort of thing nowadays. McGeady had no great love of historical buildings either, but thought it somehow sad that the very personality of every Eurostate town and city was being eroded, its soul dissolved, with the removal of its unique architecture at street level. But they might as well have left those buildings to dissolve slowly in the rain for all the good the museums had done.

He moved into the shadow of the building and paused for a while, watching, waiting for any warning signs that would help him. He looked at his wristwatch - one-fifteen it read - and he wondered if he would live to see the morning. McGeady had always known that this day would come, when his future would be in the balance, but his foresight made the prospect no more palatable. The silence swarmed around him and he began to hum gently in an effort to calm his nerves. Finally, once he was satisfied that there was going to be no immediate ambush, he went inside. The interior of the single storey building was a mass of colour and light; in fact it was the total opposite of its outward appearance. Inside there was a single corridor that curved in a horseshoe away from the entrance and back again. Hundreds of doors lined both sides of this corridor and these led to the interface equipment that was used to enter the hidden virtual reality world mainframe.

'One twelve-hour pass please,' McGeady said, as he walked up to the cashier and pushed his cash under the gap in the security glass.

The cashier said nothing as he passed back the smartcard used to operate the equipment. He was a little surprised that McGeady had used cash. Most people paid with Eurdits that had been placed onto their personal identity cards. The cashier stared at McGeady, who snatched the card while still keeping his right hand on the pistol tucked safely into his overcoat pocket. Looking down at the smartcard in the palm of his hand he read the gold booth number etched on it and walked swiftly to the designated entrance before sliding the card into the electronic controller to the right of the door. As the door buzzed open, a digitised male voice spoke.

'Welcome. Please enter your booth and follow the instructions on equipment use. Thank you for choosing Medware IT Virtual Reality Parks and we hope you enjoy your experience.'

'Fuck you,' said McGeady as he slithered into what seemed no more than a glorified broom cupboard.

The booth was extremely small - about six feet square - and in the middle of the room hung what looked like a medieval torture contraption, suspended from spring wires upon a tri-directional treadmill. In reality, what faced McGeady was a suit made of a gossamer type material, covered in a multitude of electronic sensors to monitor the precise position of the body within. Around the room were hundreds of infrared beams that criss-crossed like a three-dimensional spider's web and they in turn received data from the suit's sensors. The master computer in the basement worked out the position and speed of the client's body and transferred those measurements into the virtual world. Contained within the suit were also flexi-ribs, pressure pads and environmental actuators to recreate physical sensations such as pain, pleasure and climate changes.

Once inside, McGeady returned to the door and opened it slightly; he looked out into the brightly lit corridor and waited until a young thrill seeker strolled past. The dark haired man jumped backwards as McGeady emerged from the darkened room, his large wire-like frame towering over the small young figure.

'Would you mind if we swap booths? I'm not too keen on this one,' McGeady boomed, deliberately over-friendly.

'Well I not sure, depends,' replied the young man, slightly intimidated just as McGeady had intended.

'I'm sure we can come to an arrangement. I'm a reasonable man. Let's see now. How long is your smart card valid for?'

'Six hours.'

'You can take mine. It's valid for twelve! And I'll throw in two hundred Eurdits. How's that sound? Take it or leave it.'

'Make it three hundred and you've got yourself a deal mister.'

'You drive a hard bargain son,' McGeady replied, rapidly handing over the money and taking the boy's card in return.

'You must really hate that booth!' the boy said, and added, 'Three-hundred! Sucker,' under his breath.

The young man was still counting the cash as he entered his newly acquired booth, so he did not see McGeady walk away with a satisfied smile. Quickly McGeady entered his 'newly acquired' booth before slamming the door shut with relief. There was no way to reinforce the security of the door if whoever it was who had called him there wanted to target him. And anyway, if that were the case, there was no way out. He hoped that the change of booth would throw them off his scent; at least for a while anyway and if trouble flared, in his own selfish way, he wished the young man well if they did indeed attack the one he'd booked.

McGeady ignored the suit and placed just the large bulbous helmet upon his head. He only needed to see where he was and had no need for any of the physical sensations that were available to him. In truth, he was worried that they could use these physical persuasions against him and decided to limit his exposure. Inside the helmet was a three-dimensional liquid crystal display, which listed the park access menu. Scanning the list, he chose the zoological tour with his retina, then London Zoo and finally 'No Crowds'. He did not bother with his choice of clothes and weather, preferring instead to accept the default settings. Now he could feel the blood racing in his body as his senses were transported in the blink of an eye to the 20th century zoo. 'Strange.' he thought, 'the sun's shining and it always rains whenever I'm in London, whatever the time of year!' All around the air was filled with various animal sounds, the whooping and squawks began to deafen him as he approached the entrance. 'Cheap trick!' he thought as he passed through the turnstiles. His virtual reality body moved in a rather ungainly fashion, since he had to use both his hands to move the leg sections of the gossamer suit on the electronic treadmill. He did not want to be trussed up like a Christmas turkey waiting to be slaughtered, if that was indeed what was going to happen to him. Every time he stopped to look around for signs of life, he felt for the weapon, which he had moved to his shoulder holster, and wished that he had acquired a pistol that would work in the virtual world that he now inhabited. Eventually, after scouting around and securing the general area, he walked to the chimpanzee enclosure, took a seat and he began to wonder what all the fuss had been about while the artificial sun warmed his weathered face.

The blond man ran into the real world entrance to the amusement park fifteen minutes after McGeady had gone into his booth. He was sweating heavily and still trying hard to regain his breath when he asked the whereabouts of the tall thin older man.

'He seems very popular tonight,' replied the cashier.

'What do you mean?'

'Oh, a group of men came in about, er, ten minutes ago or so and asked after him.'

'How many men?'

'Six of them. There was one real important looking guy, but he didn't come over to the counter. No, he stood all aloof over there against the wall, waiting for the five of them crowded around little old me... Way I see it is...' he said, before being interrupted.

'What booth is the old guy in?'

'One-hundred and sixteen - originally,' the cashier said as an afterthought.

'What the hell do you mean?'

'Well it seems he swapped with the guy from two-sixty-seven. He, the guy from two-sixty-seven that is, came out complaining that the display in his headset wasn't working and that was probably why the old guy had wanted to change booths. Well I could.'

'Did you tell the other men this?' he interrupted, more urgently this time.

'Well no, not really. You see I didn't know that the old guy had moved when they came in, so I told them he was in one-hundred and sixteen,' the cashier said, enjoying the company as respite from the customary night's boredom.

'Where did they go?'

'They said they were from Medware security services and that this old guy was trying to put some sort of virus on our network,' the cashier said without answering the question.

'Yes but where did they go?'

'They went into the room where the neural mainframe operates from - it runs the software for the park attractions.'

'Where is this mainframe room!'

'In the basement man, chill out. Here, take a card for nothing,' said the cashier as he suddenly saw the array of weapons on the inside of the blond man's jacket when he unzipped it to let out some of the heat generated from his extended run.

'Get the guy out of one-sixteen and then get out of here. Now!'

'Why, what's this all about man?'

The question went unanswered, as the blond man had raced off in the direction of McGeady's booth without a second glance. As he ran, he withdrew two high-powered laser pistols from the armoury attached to his waistcoat and hoped fervently that he would get there in time.

For his part, McGeady sat on the bench, within the zoological gardens, feeling quite relaxed in the summer sunshine. He watched the chimpanzees frolicking in the computerised cage and thought that perhaps this synthetic environment was not such a bad place after all.

Two sharp-looking intellectual men sat at the control monitors in the basement and worked methodically through the code displayed on the screens above. Behind them sat another, in the darkened area of the control room, surveying the computer experts in front of him.

'Have you found him yet?' inquired the observer.

'No sir! He's not in the zoological gardens as ordered. Very strange, it seems he is somewhere in the Alps, snowboarding? We'll find him soon though; I've sent the assassination software out to locate him. It should only be a few minutes before we catch up with him,' replied the senior computer operator, continuing to enter data into the 3D virtual keyboard.

The young man with whom McGeady had exchanged rooms was flying down the virtual ski slopes at great pace when he became aware of a faceless figure effortlessly overtaking at incredible speed. In all the time that he had been using the park, it was the first time he had seen such a featureless body frequenting this virtual place. The face, if you could call it that, turned towards him as it passed and he felt a shudder through his soul. Then without warning, the young man inconceivably lost his balance and wiped out. 'Strange!' he thought. He had never fallen before in the hundreds of hours that he had spent on the slopes and, as he careered out of control, the young man saw the faceless figure melt before him and convert the gentle slope ahead into a deadly crevasse. Still he did not worry, he was certain that there was no way the software would let a paying customer come to any harm. In a curious way, he began to enjoy the experience - that was until he hit the bottom of the crevasse. The pressure pads in the suit contracted violently causing compound fractures of both his legs and arms. The man screamed as he had never screamed before, but his cries of pain could not be heard from outside the soundproof booth. The whole series of events had taken just seconds and he saw McGeady's face flash in his mind before he passed out.

'We've got him Sir. He's just had a very nasty "accident" - he shouldn't give you any trouble now,' reported the junior computer operator who was tracking the assassination code's advance towards the unsuspecting target.

The observer, who still sat in the shadows of the room, glanced at the security monitors hung on the wall to h is left and began to speak into the microphone that hung from his earpiece, 'Target is incapacitated. Go in and finish the job, but be careful - he may still be dangerous. I should also inform you that another one of your breed has just arrived upstairs and is looking to get involved. This man is not on our team. I repeat *not* on our team and he may cause an obstacle for us. Over.'

The three men had been patiently waiting in the dimly lit fire exit stairwell, but now they set off at speed, striding up the stairs towards McGeady's booth with the radioed warning still spilling around in their thoughts.

The senior man at the mainframe computer keyboard spoke again to the observer, this time in an uncomfortable tone.

'Sir, we don't have a match on the physical dimensions and features of the body on the slopes and McGeady's. I am now scanning the park for those particular dimensions.'

'Fucking great. Are you trying to tell me we've busted up the wrong guy and the three wise monkeys are about to terminate him?' the observer moaned, getting to his feet and fuming at the incompetence about him.

The computer suddenly projected a stream of code into the heart of the room, as the assassination software sought a match for McGeady's virtual existence. The lines of data imperceivably rotated and inverted, swarming inexorably towards their victim via the powerful neural mainframe. The innumerable lines began to condense and coalesce into the clear, flashing message: 'Target Found'.

'Sir I've got him. He's in the zoological gardens but he has changed his booth to number two hundred and sixty-seven. We only have a facial dimension match - there seems to be a problem with the rest of the suit measurements. The assassination software is approaching McGeady now Sir,' the senior computer operator reported, instantly forgetting the plight of their first victim in his relief.

The man in the shadows spoke into his radio microphone once more, 'Target is now in two hundred and sixty-seven. He may not be incapacitated upon your arrival. I repeat. He may NOT be incapacitated upon your arrival. Once you've dealt with the target, kill the fool in one hundred and sixteen, he must be involved in some way.'

McGeady saw the faceless figure walking towards him along the gravel path that ran the length of the chimpanzee enclosure. The lack of recognisably human features worried him and he hesitated before turning to face the strange apparition. The spectre lunged towards him without warning and seized his virtual body. Immediately, McGeady felt the suit legs in his hand jerk ferociously and he knew he was in trouble. Before the faceless shape could turn its deathly attention to his virtual head, he ripped the helmet from his face and threw it gratefully to the floor.

'Fucking bastards - they're trying to kill me,' he shouted, lunging for the booth door without really knowing who 'they' were.

McGeady stopped to unholster his weapon and as he did so, the door crashed inwards on top of him. McGeady felt powerful arms drag him from underneath and he swung two or three futile punches at the shadowy figure as he was pulled to his feet. The intruder's punch caught him square on the chin. It was not hard enough to knock him out, but it managed to drain any fight that he had left. He spun McGeady around and bear hugged him from behind. Disoriented, McGeady gasped for his last breath.

'Listen McGeady, if I'd wanted to kill you, you'd already be dead. If you fight me any more, you will be. There are men heading this way and they'll kill us both if you don't stop fucking around. Now stay close to me and I'll get you out of here alive. Okay?'

McGeady nodded enthusiastically. He knew that whoever this guardian angel was, he could have broken his neck at any moment. If he'd wanted to.

'No time for questions now McGeady. I hope you're fitter than you look - you'll need to be to stay alive,' continued the intruder.

Face to face, McGeady saw the blond hair under the balaclava helmet and suddenly realised that this was the same man he had seen on the highway and who'd also been present in Daniels' office at the previous night's meeting.

'What should I call you?'

'Alpha One. Now, follow me!'

Leaving the booth without further delay they turned left, taking the long way back towards the entrance. They ran, both hugging the inside wall, weapons drawn, McGeady all but holding on to Alpha's shirt tails.

The three men entered the entrance area of the park through the stairwell doors. In the bright lights they looked as though they were triplets; all had blond hair, blue eyes and were physically an exact match for one another. The lead man directed one of his companions along the left-hand side of the horseshoe corridor and then told the other to stay put. Both men did as they were told, although no words had been spoken. The lead man then set off down the right side of the corridor. He did not run for he knew that he and his team had both exits covered. Instead he walked, confidently, as if he did not have a care in the world.

The assassin, who had made his way stealthily down the left hand side, heard screaming up ahead and raised his pistol defensively. He could see that the door to McGeady's original booth was wide open and he approached it cautiously. As he reached the room, he peered inside. Within, the cashier was endeavouring to extricate the young man from his suit, but however delicately he tried to remove the gossamer material; his efforts set off screams of agony. The cashier did not see the man in the doorway before the two fatally placed shots were fired almost simultaneously. Both the cashier and the young man were dead before they knew anything about it. The assassin did not stop to pick over the bodies; he knew there was more killing to be done and so he moved on without another thought, other than the one he had passed to his two comrades.

Alpha One came to a rapid halt, causing McGeady to very nearly knock him over. Alpha had seen the lead assassin and had stopped in an instant; unfortunately the assassin had seen him too and as he tried to back up laser bolts began to demolish the wall around him. Alpha fired back without taking aim, but it had the desired effect, making the assassin cease his attack and dive for what little cover there was. McGeady and his companion both turned and began to backtrack rapidly - and it did not take them long to run into the killer, who was closing in on them from the other direction. As the killer stopped to take aim at McGeady, who by now was rolling acrobatically to his right and trying desperately to maintain a shooting position, Alpha took his opportunity. Using the distraction to full effect, he swiftly fired multiple rounds at the killer, who, in his surprise at being hit, dropped his pistol. McGeady started to fire just as his companion stopped. The surprise, and everything else, was obliterated from the killer's face as one of McGeady's shots ploughed into his sharp manufactured features and the charred and bloodied body crashed dead to the floor.

The killer had not let a single cry of agony escape his lips during his final death throes - and his two associates could not have seen his brutal demise. Yet they writhed in agony, as they became aware of his death; as if they could feel his pain. Now fired up with the sense of shared pain and loss, the assassin in the reception area ran down the left-hand side of the corridor to close the trap once again. As he ran, a door to his left opened, the occupant exited and walked straight into the assassin's path causing them both to crash to the floor in a heap.

'Stupid bastard!' the assassin shouted, now on his knees and reaching for his fallen weapon.

The winded customer looked up, terrified, when he saw the two men rounding the bend in the corridor, weapons at the ready. The customer had heard no shooting from his soundproof booth, but he was now painfully aware that he was in the middle of something he would rather not be. He tried to roll back into his booth, back into the safety of virtual danger. But Alpha One's unfailing aim took his innocent life with a single shot The assassin, weapon now in hand, began to fire wildly at McGeady and his companion but all he managed to hit was the false ceiling in front of them. The laser bolt fizzed around the cavity above their heads, causing various pieces of debris to fall to the carpeted floor. The fallen assassin attempted to regain his feet but before he could do so, the two opposing men fired together at the dwarf target in front of them. Both shots hit him in the middle of the upper torso, tearing his body in two, leaving one half still on its knees and the other face down in the pool of blood that instantly saturated the carpet.

'Shit, I killed a punter,' Alpha said apologetically as he and McGeady both ran past the carnage and stepped tentatively over the dead bodies outside of the empty booth.

'He died so that we could be saved!' replied McGeady, preacher-like.

Loneliness consumed the lead assassin in a way that he had never felt before. Confused and panicking, his mind crazed with grief for his lost siblings, he ran. And as he ran, he screamed, the chilling sound of his anguish echoing after the fleeing men, replenishing their terror and driving them on.

The lead assassin swiftly rounded the corner that led into the reception area. As he did so, Alpha shot out his clenched, muscular fist at neck height. The exit doors swung wildly behind McGeady as he saw his chance to escape with his life. The prostrate assassin looked up from his terminally vulnerable position. For a moment, he felt his mental isolation invaded by a new telepathic presence. Alpha looked down at himself as if outside his body and unfamiliar thoughts entered his head. His single-minded focus was compromised for a few brief moments. Both combatants were paralysed by one and the same pain. A flicker of surprise and bafflement crossed both faces before Alpha dropped to his knees. Blood dripped from his groin as the laser bolt ate its way into his abdomen. He fell forwards, still conscious, on top of his biological brother. One sibling exhaled and his mirror image took a final breath, before the assassin was isolated once more - this time permanently.

20 RUN RABBIT, RUN

McDowell decided to discard the bike sixty miles outside the city when she had been approaching the point at which she needed to travel across the surrounding natural terrain. This, coupled with the fact that she stuck out like a sore thumb, as she seemed to be the only living soul travelling on that particular road, had convinced her that it was time to look for an alternative means of transport. She was exhausted by now and had been awake and on the move for more hours than she cared to remember and still there was an extremely long way to go before the safe haven of the commune. Her clothes were not up to the job of spending a night out in the open - and nor was she. Her mouth was throbbing again as her body's adrenaline subsided. McDowell knew she would have to commandeer another all-terrain vehicle. So she laid her discarded bike on its side in the middle of the road to create the impression of a recent accident and moved across to the undergrowth on the shaded part of the verge to rest and wait for some unsuspecting male to take the bait.

McDowell woke with a start when she heard the groan of the large mineral ore lorry labouring to a halt. She tried to move and obtain a better view from her hide. However, her muscles had other ideas and immobilised her with pain as they refused to raise her battered body. Enduring the pain, she eventually sat up as if made of cardboard, unable to move comfortably. She rested there for a while, damp, shivering and yawning, before she felt strong enough to attempt to overpower whoever it was with the vehicle. The hiss of a cab door opening alerted her to the presence of another and then McDowell heard a soft, reassuring voice, 'Go on boys, go find him.'

The undergrowth rustled ominously and McDowell heard the first bark just as the dogs broke through into the small den that she had made for herself. Before she could grab her pistol, the first dog was on top of her, snarling viciously, as the other bit into her right forearm. McDowell tried to struggle but with the weight of the dog on her chest and the pain from the teeth still sunk into her arm she decided that it was best to give it up - for the time being at least.

'What have you got my boys?' said the truck driver, who was now slicing through the undergrowth with a customised machete.

'Heel!' he shouted when he finally saw what it was that the dogs had attacked.

Immediately, the dogs stopped what they were doing and ran back behind their master. They looked like Doberman Pinchers but strangely they still had their tails intact. McDowell nonchalantly reached for her pistol and noticed a trickle of blood running over the veins on the back of her hand as she trained its sight on the luckless driver

'Please don't make me shoot you. I really don't want to hurt you, believe me,' pleaded the truck driver.

The old trucker looked down at McDowell with soft smiling eyes that seemed to be swamped in the mop of grey hair on his head and a beard that you could hide in.

'I don't want you to shoot me either,' McDowell replied, thinking that this man was long past his termination date.

'Well that's a deal then,' the truck driver said, lowering his sawn-off pump action shotgun.

McDowell had never seen a shotgun before, but she knew of their existence - in ancient history - and the respect that she should have for its presence. The old man slid his machete into the sheath on his belt and then thrust out his left hand to help McDowell to her feet. She took it and hauled herself up. Without moving her head, she looked for her pistol. It was just out of reach. Damn.

'My name's William, William Hanner, at your service miss,' said the trucker, bending down and picking up the laser pistol himself.

'Can you tell me what the time is William, please?' McDowell said, suddenly realising that the night had passed.

'Only if you tell me your name!'

'It's Corporal McDowell. I mean Rachel McDowell,'

'It's nine-thirty, Corporal Rachel McDowell and you look like you could do with some food and a nice warm sleep.'

'Why?' McDowell asked, unsure of Hanner's intentions.

'Why what?'

'Why are you so concerned? By rights I should be dead by now or at the very least bound up with your gun at my head,' McDowell explained.

Though neither was pointing a weapon at the other now, the tension was unabated.

'I've no fight with you. I meet all sorts of people...' Hanner began.

'All sorts of *men* you mean,' McDowell interjected.

'Okay. I meet all sorts of *men* on my travels. The good, the bad and the Orgers. If they knew that I was a redundant Feman I would be dead. But I've no argument with them - or you. And what purpose would it serve if I did? One of us would be dead and still nothing would change. So relax a little Corporal McDowell, I want nothing from you. In fact, if you wish, you can go back to your organic bed and I'll leave you alone!'

'Funny that, up until yesterday I'd never met a Feman, now two in two days!'

'You mean Nicola Timosina? I'm on my way to see her - we have a business arrangement.'

'Strange, she never mentioned you or for that matter your impending visit.'

'Why would she? We run a little contraband - not something to shout about, particularly to your handlers.'

'Prove it,' she challenged.

'You want me to expose myself here?'

'Only way I'm afraid.'

'Well, excuse me if I don't feel like humiliating myself just because you say so! I'm the one with the shotgun remember. You'll have to take my word for it and anyway why else would I be prolonging your sad existence if I weren't what I say I am? Besides, what good would it do for me to get my kit off? You know what happens to our breed, surgical procedures to hide the obvious...So my private parts prove nothing - and they're staying private!'

'She's dead,' McDowell stated as if she hadn't heard Hanner's protests.

'Nicola you mean?'

'Yes, the bakery was attacked last night. I managed to escape but I'm sure of it. I saw her taken out...'

'That's a real shame. She was okay, for a Feman that is. Weird though, what was she doing in a bakery?' Hanner paused. 'Oh, I see, your clever way of checking my story...'

'Crude but effective,' she smiled.

'And I was beginning to worry that I'd have to take the Orgasma back and return with some yeast!'

But the moment of levity was lost as McDowell's stomach started to growl and the thought of some hot food and a good sleep became very appealing.

'I wouldn't mind some bread or something - that's if you have some to spare?'

'Bread! We can do better than bread. I have some lamb stew and dumplings in the slow cooker on the rig. There's a bed you can use and even a shower.'

'Since you put it like that, I don't mind if I do William Hanner!' McDowell exclaimed, warming considerably to her good Samaritan.

They started to walk back towards the road and crossed over to where the massive truck, the length of two or three train carriages and twice as wide, sat quietly parked like a sleeping dinosaur. The old-fashioned wheels were lowered, although it had magnetic power packs, because old Hanner liked the sensation of the contact with the road although he had a magnetic surface to travel along. Back at the vehicle, the dogs sat obediently by the front wheel. The snow was starting to thaw in the bright morning sunshine and small delicate streams of water stitched their way along the gullies on either side of the road.

'Here, you'd better have this back. You may need it when you go on your way,' Hanner said, giving McDowell back her laser pistol, handle first.

McDowell gave Hanner a long hard, searching look and then placed the pistol back into her holster with the tiniest nod of gratitude. Together, they then headed towards the large cab, which was more like a small mobile home, with the main driving controls situated within. William opened the door remotely when they reached the far side of the road and turned to face her.

'You go on inside and make yourself at home. I'll retrieve your bike from the road. I assume it's your bike?'

'Sort of, let's just say I borrowed it from a friend of mine and he doesn't seem to want it back,' she replied with a reluctance born of her guilt about the unimportant and innocent chef whom she had killed and then mutilated.

McDowell climbed the steps and stood in the thin blue hallway that ran from one side of the cab to the other. Either side there were doors leading to the driving cockpit, shower, toilet, bedroom and a kitchen-cum-sitting room. She smiled at William as the door closed between them and he walked back to where she had abandoned the bike in the road.

Around thirty minutes later, William entered the cab and called out to his new house guest. There was no answer, so he begun to open various doors to see what she was doing. As he opened the bedroom door, he heard her snoring loudly and stood for a few minutes watching McDowell sleeping soundly, still in her torn and dirty male clothing. When he was sure that she was indeed asleep, he retired to the driver's cockpit and switched on the communications console. Hanner slid his thumb into the security reader and the 3D display leapt from the console. He punched in the code carefully until the live holographic image of a man appeared.

'Hello William. I do hope everything is okay at your end. Do you have the rabbit in your sights?'

'I have made contact and I am in the process of arranging for the rabbit to be tagged and released,' replied Hanner, looking furtively over his shoulder.

'Good. Contact us again when the rabbit is off and running.'

'It may be a day or so. She looks like she's in need of some serious attention.'

'Whatever it takes. Give her what she needs to continue her journey: money, food, weapons…'

'Okay Mr Lock, it will be done. Can you ask the Colonel what he wants me to do with the truck when I'm finished?'

Lock disappeared from the display and William could hear the muffled conversation in the background before the Colonel's 3D image materialized.

'Take it to the processing plant in Trabula. They're expecting you - no questions asked. When you've done that, return to Berlin. We need to see you. McGeady escaped the trap that we set,' explained the clearly discontented Colonel.

'How did you manage that? I thought that your Aryan agents were supposed to be infallible?' Hanner said, pushing his luck just a little.

'Now William, you may be one of our best operatives, but don't think for a minute you can get away with a total lack of respect for our ideals. One more crack like that and you'll be pensioned off, permanently. However, before we do it, I'll kill your beloved fucking dogs before your very eyes and feed them to you for your last meal.'

'Charming,' William muttered to himself. 'And fuck you too!'

Maybe the man was deadly serious. But William hardly cared. This was his last job for them - whether or not it was a success. Lock had recruited William from the State Police - the Undercover Operations Department to be precise - and had told him he was going to improve the security of the Eurostate. It had all changed when Lock and the Colonel had decided that the time had come to fake Lock's death. William was tired of the goals that drove them both and for more years than he cared to remember he had been a slave to their pursuit of a pure European populace. Hanner had been a key member in the underground organisation, carrying out all forms of unsavoury work on their behalf. However, recently he had found out that the Colonel was planning to have him executed once he had delivered the truck to the processing plant. William had friends within the organisation who were equally dismayed at the direction that things were taking and they were only too willing to warn William of his impending 'retirement'. Open criticism of the organisation meant a visit from Lock's Aryan death squads and fear was rife amongst the ordinary men within the regime.

William planned to leave his job before they could get to him and disappear from the sterile Eurostate. He was going to take the large sum of money that he had amassed throughout his years of treachery and travel to the Far East. But first, he planned one last big payday; one last coup before he finally vanished and left the evil bastards and his former life behind.

'I'm sorry you feel that way Colonel,' Hanner finally said calmly and with a smile that said 'fuck you' after the threat against his beloved dogs.

'Now William this is no time for your games. This has to be done correctly. Otherwise we shall all be out of a job,' said the Colonel, growing impatient and uncomfortably aware of his lack of control over William while he was isolated in the field.

The Colonel was showing all the tell tale signs of strain, thought Hanner. It couldn't have been easy planning to take down the Eurostate government and kill off the last major bastion of Femorists in one fell swoop - for William knew that was exactly what Lock and the Colonel were planning.

'Okay Colonel, whatever you say, you know me. I don't mean anything by it. Just trying to get through the day with a smile on my face. I'll be in touch!' Hanner finished, not wishing to prolong the conversation any further. He sat quietly for a while and then fiddled with the comms console once more.

'Eurostate Headquarters,' Hanner requested.

'Hello, you are through to Eurostate HQ. Please say the name of the person you wish to talk to,' asked the automated operator image.

'Callum Daniels please.'

'I am sorry. Mr Daniels is not available at this moment in time. Can I take your name please?'

'He's available to me. Tell him "Doberman" wants to speak to him,' Hanner said, unable to restrict himself to just the key word.

'Override enabled' flashed across the screen, just as Daniels had said it would.

'Mr. Doberman, you should have said earlier. He is expecting your call. Putting you through to his assistant now. Have a nice day,' the automated operator advised.

The image blanked for a moment before another displayed; one more forthright than the operator's.

'Doberman you say?' asked Daniels' PA.

'Yes that's right, for Mr Daniels,' Hanner replied, exasperated now.

'One moment please,'

'Doberman! Finally you call. What do you have for me, something useful I hope?' Daniels said cheerfully.

William had called Daniels forty-eight hours before, advised him of the extent of the treachery within the Eurostate security personnel and promised to call back with more details soon. Daniels had pressed Doberman for more, but William knew he had to hold back the exact details until he was out of harm's way.

'Mr Daniels, I have Corporal McDowell with me and she will be tagged as agreed with the Colonel and Nigel Lock. I'm sure you will find that they will attack the commune shortly after it's located. Once I have confirmed the funds are in place in the Bank of Singapore I will contact you and give you the exact tracking frequency for the bike transmitter. From then on you can do exactly what you wish with the information. Please do not let me down,' Hanner said tersely.

'You *have* been busy! I must say that it's a pleasure to do business with you Doberman and I look forward to hearing from you shortly.'

Daniels disconnected the call, quietly satisfied that everything was going to plan. Okay, he had not got the name of the Feman spy that he so desperately wanted, but it was a start. He knew that he only had enough resources to fight one battle at a time and with the information that he would get from Doberman he could remove two threats to his power base in one devastating action. Daniels would arrange an attack on the commune moments after the Colonel's men had secured the area. Then he would move against the organisation that Lock had built up over the years, claiming that they were all a part of the female conspiracy to bring the Eurostate down. 'Yes, it's all coming together nicely,' Daniels thought, as he continued to ponder the identity of the Feman spy.

As William switched off the comms console he suddenly heard a noise from the corridor behind him. He walked to the door and opened it apprehensively before he realised that it was just the dogs scratching at the cab door, hoping to be brought in from the cold.

'One moment boys, let me just check on our friend,' Hanner said to his canine companions.

Walking back to the bedroom, William placed his ear tentatively against the door. McDowell was snoring loudly. He smiled to himself and began to think of the Far East where he was soon to be, far away from all the lies and sedition that he was so tired of.

21 TRUE COLOURS

Driving towards the Woodlands Medical Facility, Sergeant Clark switched on the supposedly faulty radio and deliberated what exactly he should do next. He had been recruited indirectly into the organisation by his commanding officer - who had now been transferred out of town. The new boss, Smicer, was unaware of the subversive affiliation that most of the officers in Shenka were signed up to and that was just the way Clark wanted it to stay. He was now the top man in Shenka and it afforded him certain privileges he was loth to relinquish.

'Victor-Charlie 397 to HQ?' he finally said into the mic hanging from his earpiece.

'Clark, where are you? It's Honnegan.'

'Can't talk now Kurt, can you patch me through to the Colonel? I need to talk to him urgently.'

'No problem. Keep me informed about your whereabouts though. Smicer's on the prowl and wanting regular updates. I've stalled him - but if you get a chance ask the Colonel if we can make him an offer he can't refuse. It's tiresome having to cover for people all the time,' Honnegan moaned.

'Put me through and I'll see what I can do. I'm not promising anything mind. Last time I asked, the request was denied so don't hold your breath,' he lied.

'Okay, just thought I'd mention it, putting you through now.'

'Johnson speaking.'

'It's Clark again Sir. I have a small problem that you can help me with. Can you arrange for Woodlands to take the cross breed? Kellor won't be satisfied any other way. I can bring

Kellor to you afterwards and you can advise him of the right thing to do. If we can get him away from the cross breed then we can dispose of her and maybe he will join us without too much grief.'

'Maybe we should bring Kellor in? God knows we could do with the manpower. We failed to kill McGeady tonight - and I don't want that traitor messing things up, especially now we're so close to our goal. No, Kellor won't respond well to the whole truth, given time perhaps. If we tailor it to suit his morality then, he just might go for it.'

'We're going to be there in fifteen minutes Sir. Can you speak to the Director at Woodlands and have us met by the medical staff? He's determined to get her treated and the sooner that happens the sooner I can bring Kellor in,' Clark persevered, ignoring the Colonel's rambling thought process.

'Yes, okay. I'll do it straight away. By the way, did Major Kellor get anything out of Langton?' the Colonel asked, changing the subject completely.

'No. She mumbled something about Feman spies, but not a word about the location of the eggs or the fact that she once worked for you.'

'Good. She used to be such an excellent resource. That was before she stopped playing ball of course. Still the bitch is dead now, so we'll have to rely on McDowell to provide us with the commune's whereabouts.'

'Yes Colonel, if that's all?'

'No. Bring Kellor to me after you've run your errand for him and I'll arrange for the cross breed to be taken care of. Now I'm finished!'

'Okay Sir. We'll see you in maybe a couple of hours or so.'

The tree-lined drive gently wound its way towards the private medical facility. The artificially planted wood that surrounded both vehicles masked the hospital from the encircling metropolitan conurbation and as such seemed very indulgent, opulent even, in such a godforsaken town. Clark parked quickly in a space allocated for hospital VIPs and waited impatiently, watching the main entrance. Kellor had been following the patrol car, driving an ambulance borrowed from the state hospital. The ambulance stopped conveniently outside the entrance. Kellor jumped out hurried round to the back doors, ready to open them. The medical staff waiting inside emerged unenthusiastically as they watched the ambulance come to a standstill. A single doctor and three nurses strolled from the haven of the lavish building with the support of a rather humble-looking trolley bed. State ambulances had very little in the way of equipment so Beta had been condemned to lay uncomfortably on the floor of the vehicle, with just a pillow and blanket for comfort.

By the time Clark approached the entrance, the medical team had already placed Beta on the trolley and wheeled her inside. Kellor followed the doctors like an expectant father, demanding attention and directing their efforts. Clark aimlessly caught up with the gaggle of white coats, while they waited for the lift in the ornate marble and teak decorated entrance hall.

'I don't know who you spoke to but thanks. Strange though, it looks more like a five star hotel than a hospital. Not what you'd expect in this town,' Kellor said to Clark.

'We do have *some* wealthy suburbs; it's not all ash and gruesome miners you know.'

'Actually, it was a mutual friend of ours who arranged the clearance for the woman to be treated here,' Clark continued, choosing his words very carefully.

The lift chimed elegantly, the doors slid open and they all entered.

'I don't understand. I don't know you. Who can we possibly know mutually?'

He was now extremely suspicious of Clark and his supposedly good intentions. And that was precisely the attitude he was trying to avoid provoking in the Major.

'Maybe it's better that we go and see him. He'll be able to explain things much better than I can. You'll just have to trust me I'm afraid.'

'Why the mystery? Just tell me who it is!' he demanded, frustrated by Clark's evasive reply but trying to keep his cool in front of the medical staff.

'Colonel Johnson. He arranged all this,' Clark said reluctantly.

'And your comms console. It's not broken. Is it!'

Clark flushed a little with embarrassment at being exposed.

'What makes you say that?'

'I noticed that you never called anyone before we left the ER and we didn't stop on the way here. So you spoke to him from your vehicle, right?

Kellor smiled, he knew he had Clark on the defensive, exactly where he wanted him.

'Fuck. What a fool!' Clark cursed himself aloud. 'It's not what you think though. We just needed some time to get control of the situation again. Really. No offence?'

'None taken, but why? The Colonel has never gone behind my back like this before - and where do you fit into all of this? You're a cop for God's sake not military.'

'I tell you what. Let them look after your partner without you fussing around. I'll take you to see the Colonel and you can ask him all the questions you want.'

'No! Let's just hang around until they've removed the rest of the metal from her leg and started her regeneration treatment. *Then* we'll go,' Kellor insisted, refusing to be swayed by Clark's childlike persuasion.

'Whatever you say Major. I'm sure the Colonel will appreciate you taking time out to see him, whenever that may be,' he replied, trying his best to placate the Major without giving away too much of the detail. He hoped to get Kellor away from Shenka and deliver him into the Colonel's custody where they could control any adverse reaction.

The chime in the elevator played again and Kellor followed the trolley out onto the ward landing while Clark stayed put in the lift.

'I'll see you downstairs Major - when you're ready of course.'

'Fine. See you later Sergeant,' Kellor responded, walking away from the elevator, now immersed in his concern for Beta's welfare.

Remembering Daniels' words about ensuring Beta came to no harm, Kellor thought that if there was one thing he was going to do right today, it was this. The medical staff took Beta to the preparation area to remove any last fragments of metal from her wound and only after this essential procedure had been meticulously carried out would she be able to enter the regeneration unit. Kellor slunk around outside the preparation room and while he waited he began to relive the previous night's catastrophic events until, finally, his thoughts inevitably turned to Chapel. Kellor's guilt swelled painfully and he decided that perhaps he should go and check on the progress of Agent Chapel while he was waiting. Making his way back downstairs to the entrance he asked at the main reception desk the whereabouts of the source of his guilt. After a short walk back up to the third floor, he approached the room where Chapel was being treated and was shocked to see the military guard that had been placed outside the door.

'Agent Chapel, is he in there?' Kellor asked the young military guard.

'Yes Sir!' replied the guard, surprised to see such a senior military officer at that time in the morning.

'Why are you guarding this patient Private?'

'Special Operations has been shut down Sir, with immediate effect.'

'On whose orders soldier?' he said, astonished by the news.

'Colonel Johnson's, Sir,' informed the guard, surprised that the Major was unaware of the fact.

'I'm going in to talk to the patient. Stand at ease.'

'One more thing. When did the order to shut down special operations come through?' Kellor asked, opening the door to Chapel's room.

'06:00 hours, this morning Sir.'

Kellor nodded and entered the hospital room, quietly closing the door behind him. Inside, the drapes were pulled and he stood for a while, trying to adjust his eyes to the lack of light while listening out for Chapel's presence.

'Chapel, are you there? Chapel, you awake?' whispered Kellor.

The reading spotlight by the bed unexpectedly blazed through the black silence and Kellor's dazzled eyes began squinted against the painful glare.

'What the fuck do you want? Come to finish the job?' Chapel said bitterly as Kellor's eyes began to pick out his outline.

'How are you? I just came to see how you are, nothing more. Then I find the soldier at your door.'

'What the hell is going on?' Kellor continued and began to move cautiously forwards.

'Stay where you are! I have a pistol pointed straight at your head. Your fucking jacket won't save you this time,' Chapel replied coldly.

'What's going on? I only came to see how you are?' Kellor pleaded.

'See the chair in the corner? Turn it towards the wall and sit in it. That's right, face it away from me,' Chapel ordered.

Kellor carried out the demand before he spoke again.

'Now what's all this about? The first I heard of a problem was when I asked the guard outside,' asked Kellor, trying to put some authority back into his voice.

'Your lot. McGeady was right - sneaks the lot of you!' Panic ran through Chapel's voice as he spoke.

'Look calm down. Just tell me what you think is going on and maybe then we'll get somewhere,' said Kellor, feeling the uncompromising pressure of the pistol nestle into the back of his head.

'For what it's worth I'll tell you. Then I'm gonna kill you, if you don't have some plausible explanation why I'm under arrest.'

'After I got here, I perked up a bit. Only a flesh wound you see, but I'd been in shock before. What with the concussion on top, it looked a lot worse than it really was. Once I'd started to feel better I thought I'd better contact McGeady and tell him what had happened, if he hadn't already heard about the disaster at the drug store. Anyway, I spent an hour or so trying to track him down. Just when I'm about to give up, he contacts me here. It seems your lot tried to take him out tonight, but failed miserably.'

'How would he know it was military intelligence tried to kill him? We don't wear fucking name badges you know.'

'He escaped your little trap. Kept his head down and hung around, trying to work out where to go. After a while, who should walk out of the building where they tried to kill him, but your Colonel and three of his men.'

'Okay, so the Colonel was at the scene, but what possible motive does he have for killing McGeady?' Kellor replied, treading verbal water while he tried to think of a way out of the difficult situation.

'It transpires that your boss has had a private meeting with President Wells and got a free rein to detain all Special Operations personnel. All because, in his opinion, McGeady's a security risk. Apparently, he's managed to convince Wells that McGeady's a Feman spy and that none of us in Special Operations are to be trusted.'

Silence rested upon the room. Kellor's mind raced wildly, trying to figure out what the hell was going on. He was sure that he could trust the Colonel's judgment, but could he trust his motives?

'What's McGeady doing now?'

'As if I'm gonna tell you. You're probably here to find out exactly that.'

Chapel was obviously still strung out and their conversation so far had done little or nothing to alter his state of mind. Fearfully, Kellor watched fearfully the undefined dancing shadow thrown on the crisp white wall in front of him as Chapel began to pace manically up and down behind him.

'All right, tell me. All the time you were watching Nicolas Timosina, what did you do with all the information you gathered?' asked Kellor, trying to think the problem through logically.

'Forwarded it onto McGeady of course.'

'And what did he do with it - to your knowledge?'

Chapel was nonplussed - then caught Kellor's smug I-told-you-so smile.

'I know what you're trying to suggest. But that proves nothing! Just because he didn't act on most of it does not mean that he's a fucking spy. Your lot will twist the truth to suit yourselves just so you can eliminate your enemies,' Clark babbled, filling in the gaps and reacting angrily to Kellor's unspoken accusation.

'Okay. Is there anything you reported on during your time watching Timosina that you thought should provoke some form of action from McGeady?'

'No, nothing. He called you in when Travis and I told him that the Feman was scouting for farm employees and that there were probably some female terrorists coming along to help out,' Clark replied honestly.

'He didn't call me in,' Kellor said and grimaced as he again felt the influence of the pistol applied to the back of his head.

'Yeah right!' Chapel said, still unconvinced.

'I contacted McGeady. He wanted nothing to do with me till I told him I was acting on direct orders from Callum Daniels.' Kellor continued.

'So what were you working on that would need that prick to get involved?'

'I'm not supposed to say; but I think I can make an exception in the circumstances,' Kellor nodded grimly over his shoulder at the gun. 'A shitload of eggs were nicked from the Stablinka breeding farm.'

'What!' Chapel shouted. 'When did this happen?'.

'Five days ago,' replied Kellor, slightly bemused by the force of his reaction.

'Motherfucker! Travis and I warned him. We fucking told him it was going to happen. We followed the Feman to an area that overlooked the farm and she spent the whole day mapping out the defences. Then we saw her bury what looked like a small amount of that new explosive, Forximite, and then she left. The Feman, Timosina, well, she then goes back to the drug store and we called it in immediately. McGeady said that you guys at military intelligence were on top of it already and that any attack was to go ahead unhindered. Travis and I didn't get out much from that surveillance job. We must have missed the news report. Even when we did get out from that stinking surveillance vehicle the last thing we'd watch would be state fucking television!' Chapel said with the dawning realisation that something was seriously amiss.

'If we'd been on top of the situation they wouldn't have got away with anything - they'd all be dead by now.'

'I know - you don't have to tell me that.'

'So what now?' Kellor asked hopefully, as without explanation the pressure from the pistol relented.

'I'm not involved in this Kellor. I don't deserve your lot pulling me to bits in the hope that you'll find something you shouldn't.'

'After what I've seen tonight I know you're not involved. But you'll have to trust me and I'll get you out of here. You up to it?'

Chapel shuffled across the room and lethargically sat on the end of his bed with the pistol harmlessly pointed at the floor. Kellor got up and faced him with the light still blazing into his squinted eyes.

'You coming?' Kellor reiterated laconically.

'Why not. I'm dead if I don't.'

'Where's McGeady now?' Kellor asked again, more hopeful of an answer this time.

'One of our safe houses. I'm not sure which one, but he's going to see Daniels as soon as he can get hold of him.'

'Right let's get you out of here. Book into the motel near the Park and Ride terminal and wait for me. Okay?' Kellor advised.

'Sure, whatever you say. Funny though, I never thought I'd be envious of Travis. I mean. At least he's in the clear.'

'It'll be fine Chapel, just trust me. Now get your stuff together.'

Minutes later, Kellor opened the door and called out to the bored guard, who turned to find Chapel holding the gun to his hostage's head.

'Get in here now and lock the door or he's dead,' Chapel demanded.

'Do it,' Kellor ordered with an affirmatory nod as the soldier looked to him for reassurance.

Entering the darkened room, the soldier closed the door behind him and began to operate the lock, before being shot with the pistol set to stun.

'Should keep him quiet for a couple of hours. Now, put his uniform on and we'll get out of here. I'll wait outside just in case anyone notices the guard's gone AWOL,' Kellor explained.

They descended the stairs together before Kellor stopped, searched his pockets and withdrew the smartcard used to operate the state ambulance. He opened the exit door just enough to reconnoitre the immediate area. Seeing that the entrance hall was strangely quiet, they strolled unconcerned and unseen to the entrance. Oblivious, Clark sat in his police vehicle and Kellor watched his cigarette smoke aimlessly rising from the driver's window. The two men approached the ambulance and without delay got inside the cab.

'Get in the back, out of sight. I just want to check on my partner before we leave. When I come out, that police vehicle will follow us back to the state ER. Keep out of sight - he's seen you before earlier tonight and it would appear he works indirectly for the Colonel, small world... Anyway, when we get to the ER I'll park and get into his patrol car. Wait until we're long gone and then make your way to the motel,' Kellor explained, handing the smartcard over.

'Where're you going after you leave me at the ER?' Chapel asked, sounding worried.

'The Colonel's summoned me. Maybe I can shed some more light on recent events when I've heard what he's got to say. Whatever you do stay put until I come and get you,' replied Kellor, suddenly very sombre and full of foreboding about this meeting and what it might involve.

'And what if you don't come and get me?' inquired Chapel like a lost child.

'You're on your own... I'll probably be dead; or worse.'

'Why, you're all on the same side. Aren't you?' Chapel asked, confused by Kellor's sudden morbid pessimism - or, worse, realism.

'Seems there are more sides to the Colonel's activities than I've been aware of before. Who knows what other skeletons he's got in his cupboard? You think you know someone and then they start shafting you...'

'Hey, you want to try working for McGeady sometime! Still I suppose that's out of the question now...'

Their conversation seemed to have run its course and Chapel decided that now would be a good time to move to the back of the ambulance. Kellor immediately went back inside. He was exhausted. 'Where the hell is all this going?' he thought. The lift chimed annoyingly as he entered and pressed the button to take him to the floor where Beta was being treated. Kellor stumbled his way towards the regeneration unit; it was all that he could manage. As he arrived at the door, he heard arguing within. Kellor stood to one side, intently listening to the altercation.

'Turn the microwave level down, we're not to kill her until Clark has left with Kellor,' said the doctor.

'No one fucking told me. I don't know. I'm told to get rid of her, but not yet,' moaned the technician sitting at the control desk.

'Just do it or we'll have the Colonel to answer to. He'll have us on permanent Orger patrol if Major Kellor gets wind of this.'

Kellor had not seen these men before, but something told him that they were not just hospital employees who had been recruited into the subversive organisation.

'All right gentlemen, turn the machine off now. My pistol and I would like one of you to get my partner out of the chamber. Doctor, if you would please,' Kellor said, taking the men by surprise after silently entering the room.

The outside of the chamber had a bright stainless steel appearance and harsh light seemed to recoil from every surface. The chamber was dark inside, now that the regeneration process had ceased and Beta was only partially visible through the wire-shielded glass in the large access door. The doctor reluctantly entered the chamber and began to wheel Beta out on her trolley bed.

'That's fine, leave her there. Now if you'd like to go back inside I think it's time for some popcorn,' Kellor said, unsure of where he should place his loyalty, but deciding that the MKII was his priority.

'Wait, the Colonel won't… Aaagh!' The doctor's reply was strangled into a scream.

Kellor had aimed at his head, skilfully removing his left ear. The man held his hand to the scorched wound, trying desperately to staunch the flow of blood.

'Looks like you're in need of some treatment yourself!' Kellor quipped grimly, then barked, 'Now get inside!'

The doctor finally did as ordered and Kellor kicked the door shut, still keeping one eye on the technician.

'Turn it up to full power. Set it to start in five,' Kellor ordered.

'You don't want to do this. We're on the same side. The Colonel thinks she may be spying for Daniels. He's got your best interests at heart Major Kellor,' the technician pleaded.

'Bye bye,' responded Kellor.

Kellor shot him without deliberation, but this time with the pistol set to stun. He dragged the comatose technician from the desk, placed him on a spare trolley and pushed it to the chamber door before opening it. The doctor made a last hysterical attempt to overpower Kellor, but he was too far away to have any real chance of success. Kellor fired before the injured man could close the gap between them and he slumped to the floor unconscious. Moving to the centre of the chamber, Kellor placed one body on top of the other. Returning to the control desk and unsure of what function the controls actually performed, he turned them all to maximum, switched to manual override and pressed the 'start' button on the timer. The chamber window glowed in shades of ultra violet and blue and it did not take long before the bodies began to swell, cooking from inside out in the generated heat.

Within ten minutes, Kellor had made his way outside, carrying Beta down the fire exit staircase, deliberately avoiding the elevator in case of unforeseen problems. While he loaded Beta into the rear of the ambulance, the bodies in the chamber exploded. It would take a while for the authorities to sort through the mess and find out that it was not Beta's flesh that they were sponging from the walls, but the bodies of two junior military intelligence officers.

Chapel was the first to speak from the back of the ambulance as Kellor drove away from the Woodlands facility behind Clark's police vehicle.

'What do you want me to do with her? It seems we're in the same boat now.'

'You'll have to keep her with you in the motel. Do your best for her. She's already started to heal. I guess they screwed it up by trying to kill her too quickly - pathetic really. Anyway, as I said before, she's strong, very strong.'

'How you holding up?'

'Apart from not knowing who to trust and no idea what I'm doing, fine…'

'You can trust me… And, I suppose, her…'

'I suppose so… She took a bolt for me you know, back at the drug store, no questions asked. Just threw herself in front of me, I guess that's the only loyalty I should trust.'

Both men fell silent and the remainder of the trip back to the state ER was completed without another word being spoken. It seemed only too soon before they surreptitiously said their good-byes and went their separate ways. Clark now drove the Major back to the Park and Ride station to pick up the AFVE aircraft, so that they could rendezvous with the Colonel. Kellor feared the worst. He hoped that they would not be able to establish what or who had caused the mess back in the regeneration chamber. The Colonel had always had a soft spot for Kellor - But he could kiss that approval goodbye once the Colonel found out that his golden boy had slaughtered two of their own!

22 THE VIPER'S NEST

After avoiding the assassination attempt, McGeady fled the scene, but not before he had watched the Colonel and his remaining men leave the VR Park. He finally headed for a department safe house in the suburbs, where he spent what was left of the night. By morning, he realised that he was a sitting duck and decided to risk everything and act on his gut reaction. McGeady knew that the city would be flooded with intelligence personnel trying to locate him and that Daniels was the only man who had the authority to save him.

Leaving the safe house, he instinctively returned to his apartment building where he knew there would be someone on surveillance duty awaiting the unlikely event that he would be fool enough to return. After the morning rush hour, the unmarked vehicle was easy to identify; a solitary officer watching the apartment lobby from across the road. McGeady approached from the rear and simply opened the passenger door, before pushing the pistol into the nape of his neck.

The two men had travelled to the parliament building in almost complete silence, apart from directions. The officer tried to make conversation, in an effort to defuse the situation - but McGeady's threats soon shut him up. Thirty minutes later, the surveillance vehicle pulled into the parliament car park entrance.

'Stop here,' McGeady ordered.

The officer stopped the vehicle by the security scanner, and McGeady attempted to use his pass.

'Pass invalid, please wait for assistance,' informed the machine.

McGeady did exactly that, while the security attendant ambled from his small cubicle.

'Mr McGeady, it's you. I er, well it seems, perhaps you should...' stuttered the attendant, beginning to panic.

'Ralph, relax. I'm not going to hurt you, as long as you let me in. Then we'll say no more about it. Otherwise I might have to come back and kill you and I've done too much of that for my liking in the last few hours.'

Ralph strolled back to his office and without protest opened the barrier. McGeady knew that Ralph would not give him any problems, for he was that type of man - no backbone, just as he had been bred.

'Drive!' McGeady ordered.

The officer drove down the ramp and parked in the first available space. McGeady sat patiently in the vehicle, deliberating over his next move. It would be difficult getting to Daniels, especially now that all of his authority had been sequestrated, so there seemed little other option other than to go right on in, by whatever means possible.

'Okay, you're coming with me,' McGeady explained.

The two men exited the vehicle, McGeady pushed the officer in the back as they marched towards the lift.

The elevator doors opened and out stepped Sam Franklin, one of the many Eurostate political media advisors. McGeady immediately recognised the young ambitious man. He disliked all of the E.P.M.A's, as they were known, and he thought that he would enjoy using Franklin to gain access to the building and possibly wasting him if need be.

'Good morning Mr. Franklin, am I glad to see you! ' McGeady said, back in good spirits.

Franklin endeavoured to dive back into the safety of the lift, but before he could do so, McGeady tripped him with a quick flick of his right foot. Franklin crumpled weakly to the floor, rolled over onto his back and looked directly up at the pistol pointing towards his nose. The doors closed behind him and

McGeady turned to the intelligence officer, who was now surplus to requirements.

'Thanks for the ride, I believe I won't be needing you now,' he said and shot the officer with the pistol still on full power.

The officer's body slammed into the solid concrete wall behind, dead before he even hit the ground.

'Ooops, I could have sworn I'd placed the thing on stun,' he continued with a mischievous frown.

'You won't get away with this. They're all over the building just in case you turned up,' Franklin said just before a swift punch from McGeady's weaker left hand stopped the drivel pouring from his mouth.

'Shhsh, I don't want to hear another word from you. Just give me your pass and be quiet; please,' McGeady ordered.

Franklin gave up his pass without any more objections and McGeady swiped it through the adjacent sensor. The doors immediately opened and he dragged his hostage into the lift by his collar.

The elevator computer spoke in almost mechanical tones, 'Good morning Mr. Franklin, which floor do you require? Please speak after the tone.'

The doors closed slowly and McGeady enthusiastically tapped the seriously unenthused Franklin on the head with his pistol to encourage him to speak.

'Floor number thirty-five,' requested Franklin, grimacing from the light but painful blows to his skull.

The voice recognition system Franklin's speech pattern with that on its records and then spoke again; 'If there are any other passengers, please swipe your passes now.'

McGeady knew the parliament's security systems inside and out. The lift sensor located in the floor would measure the total weight as soon as it was satisfied that no more passengers were on board, other than those that had swiped in. The database also held the dressed weights of all government employees with passes and was designed to stop this very occurrence: the hijacking of Eurostate personnel to gain access to the building. All belongings brought in and out of the building had to come and go via a separate lift and if you were lucky you were reunited with your property at your final destination. Fortunately, McGeady knew a way to defeat this basic security measure. As soon as the lift acknowledged that there were no more passengers on board, McGeady hopped around the lift from one leg to the other, ensuring that every other second he was off the floor with both feet.

'What the fuck are you doing McGeady? It really has got to you all this shit!'

'Wouldn't you like to think so,' McGeady grunted with the effort of his strange exertions.

As soon as McGeady thought it was safe, he stopped his idiotic dance, pulled Franklin to his feet and the lift began to ascend.

'Where's Daniels this morning?' McGeady asked menacingly.

Franklin was loath to tell him, but he was aware that a course of non co-operation could be fatal and like all E.P.M.A's he believed in looking after number one.

'I've just left him. We had a press briefing. He'll be back in his office by now I should think.'

'Fantastic, that's sorted then. Would you be so kind as to escort me to his office?'

The lift soon arrived at the thirty-fifth floor and the doors opened. McGeady was behind Franklin with the pistol pushed into his back, unseen by any onlooker. However, in front of them as the doors parted, were half a dozen office staff impeding their progress. It did not take long for the tense atmosphere to migrate from the lift and out to the paper pushers who stood there in stunned silence. Slowly the office staff moved apart to leave a nice tidy path down the middle of the group and McGeady needed no second invitation.

'Thank you gentlemen, normal service will be resumed in just a moment,' McGeady said as he passed through the middle of them.

He knew there were no heroes to be found in the government building, apart from maybe the security staff and they were probably blissfully unaware of the security breach. McGeady forced his way down the nondescript corridor towards Daniels' suite, now waving his pistol in the air energetically, just in case anybody took too much of an interest in the strange rear embrace he had on Franklin. They arrived at the outer office where Daniels' secretary resided and both men were pleased to have reached its comparative safety.

'Good morning Brad, Mr Daniels in?' McGeady asked as if nothing out of the ordinary was happening.

'I'll try him for you Alec, but I'm not sure he'll see you,' replied Brad, unruffled as usual, despite the obvious weapon.

'Well if you could try your best. I'm sure Franklin here would be ecstatic if Mr Daniels could spare us some of his very valuable time.'

The secretary buzzed the intercom, which was connected into Daniels' desk console. McGeady started to hum nervously and, looking around, he realised how bloody bare and depressing the outer office was in complete contrast to the suite where Daniels actually sat. A display of his status thought McGeady, because Daniels seemed to lack a title of any significance.

'Mr. Daniels, I have two gentlemen here to see you if that's possible, Alec McGeady and Sam Franklin.'

Brad looked calmer than the two men stood before him, despite the fear radiating from a strangely quite Franklin.

'McGeady you say? No problem Brad, send them in,' Daniels replied indifferently.

Just at that moment, two burly security guards came into view. Comically, their bulk completely filled the outer office doorway, their weapons drawn and at the ready. Brad looked them in the eyes and defused the situation with a small shake of the head. The guards reluctantly placed their weapons back into their holsters and remained where they were. The door to Daniels office began to open slowly and McGeady backed his way into the opening, watching the two guards' every move - not that they made any. Then, as the door closed in front of Franklin, McGeady felt the disapproving prod of a gun between the blades of his bony shoulders.

'Hello Alec! I do hope we can resolve all this peacefully. Now let Sam go. Give me your weapon and we'll have a chat,' Daniels insisted, holding the gun in his unfamiliar left hand. The right arm had only been in its cast for twenty-four hours and thanks to the state-of-the-art medical equipment it had already healed in that short time. Unfortunately, it was still very painful and bruised and Daniels was trying to rest it as much as possible.

'Since you put it like that,' McGeady said, and at the same time he released Franklin and held his pistol over his right shoulder for Daniels to take.

'Go and get yourself a drink Sam. I'll speak to you later,' said Daniels smiling. His tone betrayed his anger at the fact that Franklin had allowed the whole situation to develop and had then been stupid enough to bring it into his presence. Franklin fled the office with a mixture of pure relief and impending doom, still with his life but no longer a career.

'Sit down Alec. Would you like a drink?'

'Scotch. I don't normally drink this early, but on this occasion I'll make an exception.'

Pouring a large scotch and sitting back behind the large tubular glass desk, he slid the drink across the smoked glass surface and it halted right in front of where McGeady sat. Daniels placed both pistols on the table in front of him and leant back in his chair.

'I take it you've heard then?' Daniels said as McGeady sipped his scotch.

'Heard! They tried to fucking kill me last night. It took your man, the one who sat in on our meeting the other day, to get me out of the shit,' McGeady whined.

'Peter you mean? He's not been with me for long, but he's certainly proved to be an extremely versatile asset.'

'I hate to be the bearer of bad news, but he's not gonna be with you any more after last night.'

'I see. You know that for certain do you?' Daniels said, frowning.

'Well no, not for certain. But he didn't come out before the Colonel and his men and they didn't have "Peter" in their custody. I watched for thirty-five minutes after I escaped. He must be dead or I'd have seen him leave.'

'What's it all coming to Alec? All this internal strife. Men fighting against each other isn't how it's supposed to be,' lamented Daniels in mock distress.

'You're so right. I thought that was the whole reason for eliminating the need for relationships. You know, to cut out the daily toil men had to deal with and to let us get on with our lives without shackles,' McGeady smiled, speaking the language of a politician.

He knew that the male-manufactured fabric of society had solved many of the past's problems, but had also created many contemporary ones. In numerous cases, men had the whole reason for their very existence removed, without their ever perceiving what it was that they were being denied. Strangely enough, this manifested itself clearly in male livestock who had never had any experience of love and companionship.

'Can I trust you Alec? I hope I can,' Daniels finally said after a long pause in the stifled conversation.

'It seems to me you that you have little choice Callum. Martin's gone over your head to bring me and my department down. Leaves you rather toothless doesn't it. He must have convinced Wells that you weren't able to police Special Operations yourself. So I'd say that now puts him level with you on influence and power within the state; maybe even more powerful...' McGeady said, just warming up. Sowing seeds of doubt in Daniels was the only way he could see of saving himself from the Colonel's henchmen.

'How many of your men are being detained at the moment Alec?'

'Around 130 - about a third in total.'

'So by my mathematics you have 260 men still available to you?'

'Give or take a few, but they're scattered all over the continent.'

'Can you assemble a group of the ones you trust? Ones that you know are beyond Martin's extensive reach. Arrange for them to put a round-the-clock surveillance on him and his associates. I'll also need around one hundred mercenaries, experienced ones - no rubbish. They'll earn their money. Ten-thousand Euros a head for probably a day's combat. Payable if they survive of course,' Daniels detailed.

'Are you going to start a war?' asked McGeady unconcerned, knowing he was a little safer than when he had first entered the office because he could see Daniels' priorities lay elsewhere.

'No, I'm going to fucking end one!' Daniels replied. losing his composure for the first time that McGeady could remember.

'I think I'll join you in that drink now,' Daniels added, walking over to the drinks cabinet where he poured himself a glass of wine and then returned to his seat. A few deep breaths later Daniels had regained his usual self-possession.

'Do you remember Nigel Lock?' asked Daniels unexpectedly.

'Yeah... As I remember it, he screwed up in Greenland some years ago and was accused of being a Feman spy. But it was never proved beyond clinical doubt. They executed him - or as good as...'

'Not so. It seems he's alive and well. Johnson and Lock are an item, working together for a brighter future you could say. Unfortunately, if you don't have blond hair and blue eyes that future is not for you.'

'I thought Wells had given express orders for all that Aryan idiocy to be wiped out?'

'He did, but it seems they've taken it upon themselves to resurrect and perpetuate those ideals.'

'It doesn't seem that morally different to what has been done by the Eurostate in the name of mankind, if you know what I mean - breeding a male-only society and all that crap...'

McGeady had never really understood why men should want to remove a key pleasure from lives that were already quite mundane enough. He had always believed that men were worse off, both physically and emotionally, without women being involved in their lives, but he had always kept it to himself. Anything for a quiet life.

'You know they're completely different doctrines Alec. We don't discriminate against any race, colour or creed any more,' Daniels replied passionately with the standard official answer.

'Only if they have vagina and a pair of breasts attached to that, race, colour or creed - *then* we discriminate!' McGeady said, pushing his luck and venting some of his frustration.

'Keep going on like this and I'll start believing you really are the spy that Martin says you are.'

'Would it make any difference to you at this precise moment? I don't see you have any choice. You need me, even if I were the infamous Feman spy.' McGeady spoke as if he did not have a care in the world. A few hours ago he was a dead man. However, he was gambling that Daniels' current needs were way ahead of his need to reassert his dwindling authority on a possible ally.

'I always have choices Alec. You should know that. All I need is some proof of the Colonel's association with a traitor like Lock. Then Wells would give me all the resources I need to take them down, even if we can't expose the Nazi ethos they're promoting,' Daniels shouted with such vehemence that spittle flew from his mouth.

'What's happening with Operation "Alpha male"? My man Chapel told me it was one fuck up after another last night,' said McGeady after a brief pause, attempting to defuse the situation.

'It's of no relevance now anyway. I've found another way to find those bloody eggs and it doesn't involve Major Kellor or the female MKII.'

'Talking of eggs, how did they get away with them when military intelligence were purportedly watching the breeding farm so closely?'

'Beats me. When you spoke to me about the movements of Nicolas Timosina, Martin said he'd handle it. None too well apparently.'

'He's not doing at all well lately, missing his chance to take me out last night, for example.'

'He'd be doing a lot worse if I had my way.'

The room fell silent for a while as McGeady looked to secure his position.

'So how you gonna square this away with Martin and Wells. I'm sure they'll want to know why I'm not available for interrogation - or dead for that matter,' McGeady said, making his next move.

'They'll have to take my word for it that you're in protective custody. I still have some power left, despite what you may think,'

'Why don't you just tell Wells what Martin's been up to?'

'As I said before, I don't have any hard evidence. Martin has covered his tracks well. If we could get Lock into custody, that might do it, but I'd rather wait until Martin has made his next move. He's tracking the female, the one that got away from the drug store, and so am I. Martin will attack the female base once he's located it and we'll be waiting for them to finish the job. Then we'll wipe him out and his fucking Aryan men.'

'You want me to handle that side of it I suppose?' inquired McGeady, quite relaxed with his rapidly solidifying position.

'Of course I do. Why else would I be talking you? I'll let you know what the tracking frequency is and you can be waiting for them once they've finished the Femorists off. I don't want Martin or Lock screwing things up in the meantime though, so watch both of them closely, if you can establish where they are...'

'What if Lock isn't there when they attack?'

'I'm not sure about that just yet. If you happen to locate Lock just keep tabs on him. Otherwise if we arrest him, Martin will know for certain that we're on to them. We can't be sure that Lock would incriminate Martin. If he doesn't, Lock no doubt will be executed - then Martin would bide his time and then we'd have the same problem all over again I'm sure. No, the main thing is they don't know that they have a leak in their camp. I've only known for two days exactly what Martin's been up to and everything makes sense now. He's been acting strangely for months and now I know why. It must've been quite stressful trying to bring his plans to a head and put the final piece of the puzzle into place, bring to a close what he and Lock must have been planning for years... The overthrow of the socialist Eurostate government and its replacement with a fascist state. You know, if he weren't my enemy I'd quite admire his fortitude!'

'So these eggs, what's so special about them?' McGeady asked, bored with the incessant preaching about political ideals and hoping to stop Daniels in his tracks.

'They are far superior to any livestock we have ever managed to produce before: stronger, faster, more intelligent and they can communicate telepathically, to a minimal degree. If our enemies get their hands on them before we manage to, they'll be unstoppable.'

'What were you going to do with them?' McGeady asked pointedly.

'There had been some intense negotiations about that very thing. Martin wanted to produce all males at once, under his command, but President Wells decided to go with my plan. I was arranging for the eggs to be developed into a pseudo female army, ultimately under my control of course and most of those reared would have been placed undercover in the field. I was going to use them to locate and destroy any female facilities that they came across. Can you imagine the confusion in the battlefield? The Femorists not knowing who was fighting for their side and who wasn't. It would have been perfect.'

'You talk as if they're already beyond our grasp. Almost as if they have been developed past the point of no return?' said McGeady in a quizzical manner.

'Figure of speech, I can assure you Alec. I'm sure it wasn't by chance that the Femorists got away with the eggs without hindrance. Martin was about to lose his superior new MkII army for good, the very army that he was depending on to carry out his coup against the Government.'

'The men who tried to kill me last night, they must have been of the same breed as the eggs that were stolen. They were a match for each other and your man Peter as well - blond, blue eyes, very strange indeed,' said McGeady, his eyes betraying the fear that he had felt last night.

'MkII prototypes all of them. I know Martin had some bred for his personal protection squad. I, on the other hand, sneaked Peter from right under his nose no less! Kellor has the first female MkII to be brought to a full term - it's just a shame we don't have more...'

They sat in silence finishing their drinks. With a last sip, McGeady stood purposefully and gently placed his glass down on the table in front of him.

'I need a place to run things from,' he asked.

'There's a cabin. It's belongs to me, clear of any state surveillance, Colonel's or mine. It's in the Black Forest. I'll arrange for my private aircraft to fly you there,' Daniels explained before he pressed the intercom button in front of him.

'Brad, have my aircraft readied. Mr McGeady is leaving now,' he said, smiling and passed one of the pistols back to McGeady.

23 THE SET UP

'Thank you William, I don't know how I can ever repay you. I don't suppose we'll ever meet up for a drink or anything like that,' said McDowell optimistically.

She smiled serenely at the old man standing before her while mounting the all terrain bike that William had given to her in exchange for the one stolen from the dead chef.

'I don't suppose we ever will,' replied William, in his mind picturing the Singapore sunset and tasting the ice-cold beer that he was going to drink all day long.

'William,' she said slowly and then paused glumly. 'Do you suppose there will come a time when women can live normal lives again?'

'Depends on what you call normal.'

'Cooking, cleaning. Maybe even having children, like the good old days?'

'Not in my lifetime Rachel, but there's always hope. You may see it in yours, but I doubt it that too. Make the best of what you have here and now. Just try to be happy.'

There was a long pause and it was clear to William that Rachel had seen a side of life that she had never seen before: a pleasant encounter with a man.

'You must get going now, otherwise you'll get caught out in the open in daylight tomorrow,' William advised in a fatherly tone.

'Can't have too much of a good thing William.'

'You can if it kills you!' he replied forcefully.

The last comment from William concerned McDowell and she felt compelled to go now. William was being cruel to be kind and he sincerely hoped she would fulfil her dreams. Nevertheless he had a job to do and her plight could not get in the way of his retirement plans.

The bike hesitated before it roared into life seconds after McDowell placed the crash helmet on her head and, with a small salute, she pulled away. The bike spun sharply on its axis as the rear wheel skidded on the wet surface. Now facing the opposite side of the road, McDowell eased the throttle down and the tyre bit into the hard magnetic tarmac and she departed through the adjoining bushy terrain. William walked aimlessly back towards to the hulk of the cab, still waving, before finally he turned and disappeared inside, walked into the driver's cockpit, immediately switched on the comms console and connected to HQ.

'Hello William,' Clarke said as his image projected in front of William.

'Where's the Colonel? - or Lock will do...All the same to me,' William asked.

'Both are with Major Kellor. Can I do anything for you?' Clark replied in good spirits. He had completed his tasks to the Colonel's satisfaction and now he had his feet up, eating his meagre lunch.

'Just tell them that the rabbit is on the run again, fully tagged and you can see it for miles and miles. They should be able to track its run from there, once it's up in the hills again of course.'

'Right, you mean "the" rabbit. Okay I got that. Anything else?'

'No, that's all. I'll return the truck to the agreed destination. If you could tell the Colonel I may be a while though - one of the power packs is playing up.'

'No problem Hanner, I'll do that for you. Are you looking forward to our soon-to-be-victory - women all but wiped out and this bloody government overthrown? It's gonna be great!'

'Oh yeah, it's gonna be bloody marvellous. You'll be able to kill who you like then Clark!'

'Maybe? Hadn't really thought about it that much, but yeah I suppose I will. No more speeding fines just BAM! One to the back of the head by the roadside,' Clark said, laughing manically.

'Sounds like Utopia Clark. Just remember to keep your foot off the throttle. Otherwise, it may be you getting the BAM! Instead.'

Clark jumped as William shouted 'BAM!' at the top of his voice and it confused him no end to think that he could conceivably be on the receiving end of a laser bolt.

'I'm signing off now Clark - see if I can't get this power pack fixed,' William lied.

'See you Hanner.'

William shook his head ruefully as he cut Clark off. The guy was a real asshole, thought William. Got his kicks from killing people - and the organisation was full of evil little bastards like Clark. William now contemplated contacting Daniels, as it had been over two days since they had last spoken. McDowell had been asleep for all of the first day and through the night as well. She had woken mid-morning and had eaten as much as she could get inside herself without being sick. Bloated and content, she showered and by early afternoon was yet again fast asleep. The following day she had risen at around ten and readied herself for the late afternoon departure, stocking up on food and weapons for what she knew would be a perilous trip. William and McDowell had agreed to the exchange of the bikes without too much discussion and she was ready to go.

Finally, after much thought, William decided not to bother calling Daniels at this particular juncture. After all, he still had to get out of harm's way before he threw his final and most devastating spanner into the works. Troubled by an unknown emotion, William started the power packs and drove the truck away in the opposite direction to the processing plant in Trabula.

24 BEST LAID PLANS

Two days had passed slowly after Kellor had flown into the Berlin Park and Ride station and then been driven to the Colonel's covert command centre. After several unexplained delays, he was now tired of waiting for his pre-arranged meeting. Kellor had been advised that he was free to go whenever he wanted, but he knew any unauthorised departure would be tantamount to signing his own death warrant. The Colonel, for his part, had been made aware of the two dead junior officers at the private medical facility and he hoped to assemble the sparse facts before he presented himself to the Major. There was also the problem of Agent Chapel and the cross breed, both having gone missing without trace. The Colonel was concerned that Kellor had somehow been less than truthful with Clark when asked about the events before they had left the Woodlands ER.

The command centre was on the outskirts of Berlin and from the outside looked like an innocuous derelict steel factory. Inside there was little evidence of the underground workings and, apart from the rats scurrying around the dirty floors, there was little sign of life. Inside one of the dormant blast furnaces was a set of spiral stairs, rusting and dull, but still in use. They led down to a vividly shiny set of chrome doors, which were quite obviously out of place and completely lacking any form of camouflage. This was where Kellor had entered and walked down the long sloping tunnel to the operation's heart. He had, for most of his time there, been kept in the living quarters, with a few brief visits to the nearby canteen. He had no way of contacting Chapel or Beta. He hoped that they had both fared okay in their effort to find sanctuary amid all the double crossing that seemed to be rife at the moment. The accommodation afforded to him was small and very claustrophobic. The bunk scarcely supported his imposing frame and as tired as he was, he struggled in vain to obtain any genuinely restful sleep. The relentless artificial light seemed to drain his energy at an alarming rate and he yearned to be outside, immersed in daylight and filling his lungs with the cool fresh morning air. There was a constant background hum, which he put down to some form of air-conditioning or generator supplying the centre. It was very strange he thought, that after all his years in the military services he had never before come across this hideaway. The knock at the door scattered Kellor's thoughts and Clark entered without being asked.

'Come in Sergeant why don't you!' Kellor exclaimed sarcastically, without moving from his bed.

'The Colonel will see you now.'

'About time too! Let's go before he changes his mind shall we.'

Without another word, they both vacated the room, walking quickly along the clean bright corridors towards the main control room. Only a handful of men were working in the command centre; the Colonel did not have as many committed staff as he would have liked and most of those he did have were out on active duty. He and Lock had recruited wherever they could; finding sympathetic men who possessed the required skills was always a challenge. There had been some success in acquiring new livestock ready to enter into their very own specialised training centre, where they could be brainwashed into the Fascist mind-set. They had only managed to progress this far because Lock had disappeared from public office by faking his own death and now spent all his time working for the cause. Still, it was a slow process and it was all the fault of President Wells and the totalitarian grip he held over the Eurostate and its breeding policy.

The president's past was murky to say the least. He had been reared from one of many eggs fertilized by a previous

President's sperm and the group of presidential offspring had been left to fight amongst themselves to see who would rise to the top of the political pile. This privileged group of men was conceived by a manner completely at odds with the usual cloning process used for all other livestock. As such, they acquired the nearest thing to a father that there could be in this day and age. Wells held very close to his heart the strained family history that clung to his soul, although he was far removed from the head of his perceived family tree, which had been of Jewish descent. From generation to generation of president, the lessons of what the Nazis had done to the presidents' ancestors during the dark period of the Second World War had never been lost or forgotten. Continuing this honourable tradition, Wells had ensured that the breeding farms produced an ethnically mixed society. Even though there were no individual national identities in Europe from which to breed, colours of skin, eyes and hair of livestock were strictly produced in equal quantities, so that no one breed would dominate. President Wells had been horrified Nigel Lock's suggestion over ten years previously, that the breeding strain should be procured only from 'purer stock'. It was at this moment Lock realised that Wells would have to be removed from power if he was to achieve his goal in his lifetime.

Lock had struck a deal with the Colonel during the infancy of their so-called organisation and they had engineered the whole Greenland Siege with the aid of Commander Langton who was already orchestrating some passive resistance against the male-dominated society. The Colonel had persuaded her to lead the last remaining group of women held within the male infrastructure to break out of their ghetto and head towards the nearby breeding farm. In exchange for her freedom at the end of the siege, Langton was to destroy all stocks of human eggs at the farm and any livestock being nurtured at that time. Once Lock had disappeared from the scene, he had hoped to get his own biologists to introduce vast amounts of blond-haired and blue-eyed males into the breeding programme, but it was not to be. Wells had scattered the breeding of livestock across the Eurostate far and wide and then implemented his strict quotas for hair, eye and skin colours. One year had rolled into the next and ten years down the line it seemed that Lock and the Colonel still had much to do before they would finally achieve their goal and take control of the Eurostate. Wells had been secretly relieved when the Vice President had apparently died during the 'medical' interrogation that took place towards the end of the Greenland Siege. Hanner had been assigned the job of arranging the production of Lock's clone and minding it until the time arrived. Now the Colonel had a body to interrogate and the doctors had an innocent clone to cut up. At the time, Hanner was informed that the programme was all about eliminating disease for the greater good; that the new breeding stock that they hoped to introduce was more tolerant to disease. But it was not long before Hanner had established that Nazi ideology was the real rationale behind the whole sordid operation.

Finally, the Colonel had stormed the livestock farm, when Lock was satisfied that Langton had completed her task. All the Femorists had been either killed or captured, with the exception of Langton of course. The Colonel released her on the understanding that she would work for him covertly. Unfortunately for the Colonel, she betrayed him some years later and he had not forgotten her deceit. Langton had never given the Colonel the exact location of the female commune where she had sought refuge. Instead, she had sent him on fruitless searches across the vast barren landscape, where her snipers picked off a few token soldiers for the sheer sport of it.

Kellor and Clark waited an age before they received the all-clear to enter the main control room. The silver door buzzed open and Clark tentatively entered the circular room first. It was one hundred feet across and dimly lit, apart from the spotlit workstations monitoring various state communication lines.

Dead in the centre of the room there was a large steel table where Lock and the Colonel sat in pensive silence. Formally, Clark led Kellor to the table and pulled a steel chair noisily across the stone floor for him and Kellor silently obliged.

'Sergeant, take over the comms console at the field operations desk. I'm waiting for Hanner to report in. He's got McDowell with him and she's about to move off any moment soon. Once he's called in, you can finish for the day,' ordered the Colonel.

Clark turned instantaneously and marched overzealously across the dimly lit floor towards the exhausted comms operator. Kellor watched him move from one localised area of brilliance to another, until he reached the isolated console. Clark sat down contentedly on the vacated chair and began to eat the lunch that he had brought with him.

'Major Kellor, what can I say? I'm very sorry for keeping you hanging around for the last few days, but the delay was unavoidable,' the Colonel apologised.

'No problem Sir. I needed the rest.'

'How rude of me... I haven't introduced Nigel to you. Major Kellor, this is Nigel Lock, you may have heard of him. Nigel and I, and the small team you see around you of course, are working together on the future advancement of the Eurostate.'

Lock stood and shook hands with the seated Kellor and then re-took his seat immediately. Lock had short blond hair and piercing, preternaturally blue eyes. He had worn well for his age - mid-fifties thought Kellor. The bony face was pulled into a hard smile that seemed more for show than a genuine display of friendliness.

'Under whose direction?' Kellor said quickly in reply to the Colonel's statement, almost verging on insubordination.

'Under our own direction unfortunately, Major. There's been a lack of vision from the current ruling hierarchy for quite some time. Someone had to provide some foresight - and that's the role that Nigel and I have had to fill.'

'I see - and what advancements exactly are we talking about here Colonel?' Kellor continued with his low key interrogation.

Kellor, if truth be told, wanted to inquire how a dead man came to be sat in front of him alive and well. Nevertheless, he knew he would have to bide his time and see how the conversation developed.

'The mission is to purify the livestock we breed, to enhance their performance, reduce failures and provide a national identity: something we've sadly been lacking since the creation of the Eurostate. For instance, what nationality are you Major?' the Colonel asked.

'I suppose you'd call me European, but I'm not sure what region of Europe I would most identify with. I suppose Ireland, where I spent most of my formative years.'

'That's the problem you see Major. You have no passion about your continent. You work and fight for it, but you have no feelings for it. Take our army, led by that Jew General Cohen. When and if they fight, what will spur them on to annihilate the enemy? If we go up against the USA, we would lose every time, because they have a national identity. They can see, feel and breathe what they are fighting for: Uncle Sam and Mom's apple pie and all that shit.'

Clearly the Colonel could hardly contain his passion for the cause. Kellor could see this was not just some pipe dream being laid out before him, but a fervent obsession and that the Colonel would stop at nothing to ensure its accomplishment.

Lock began to speak as the atmosphere finally calmed, 'You see Major, the Colonel and I had a vision a long time ago of the way things should be. Unfortunately, President Wells isn't so forward-thinking. You're probably aware that I'm supposed to be dead. Well it seemed at the time the deception was the only way

I could work towards improving our society, without the government's candy-arsed liberalism getting in my way. The Colonel here was like minded. So, ten years ago I became officially dead. We had hoped by now to be producing the purer livestock, but the controls Wells implemented have made it almost impossible to breed anything that's not tainted with ethnic impurities. We have decided that maybe now's the time to raise the stakes, take issue with the state and begin the long overdue insurrection.'

It was quite apparent that Lock was equally passionate about the cause, but different somehow from the Colonel - and Kellor could only see one way out of his untenable situation.

'Do I fit into this profile, you know, the type of livestock you wish to infest the Eurostate with?'

'I'm not sure "infest" is the ideal word to describe what we're trying to achieve. All the same, that's not the point Major, right now anyway. The point is, are you willing to work to ensure that purer livestock comes to fruition and replaces the mongrels we fill our cities with now?' Lock asked.

Kellor's short brown hair and dark brown eyes were quite obviously at odds with the Aryan profile; but then again so were the features of most of the Nazi party members during the Second World War, especially Adolph Hitler's, thought Kellor.

'You may have done things recently Major... Well let's just say that they were done through ignorance of the situation that you found yourself in. I don't think we should dwell on them too much, in fact not at all. As long as we have your support now we'll say no more about it.'

The demand for commitment from the Colonel had come earlier than Kellor had expected and he was not ready to answer just yet.

'Where does Daniels fit into all this?' Kellor asked, moving the conversation on hastily.

'He doesn't. He's a puppet for Wells and his cabinet. In fact not only is he a mongrel but he's a female-loving one at that,' Lock said, with complete conviction.

'What makes you say that? He seemed extremely keen on getting those eggs back and I know he's desperate to find the Feman spy that's rumoured to be about.'

'The eggs you mention - it seems he wants to turn them into a female army to fight under his control. Confuse the enemy - that's his bright idea. If we can't beat those bitches as men then we don't deserve to beat them at all. Apart from that, now he's gone and placed McGeady in protective custody where we can't get to the spying bastard!' offered the Colonel.

'How do you know that McGeady is the Feman spy?' Kellor quizzed.

'He had forewarning of the attack at the Stablinka breeding farm and he kept the information to himself. Covered his tracks brilliantly - told Daniels that he'd advised me of the potential attack and that I did nothing. Daniels needed an excuse to deplete my power base and seemed unconcerned by the authenticity of McGeady's allegations. But McGeady had nothing to gain from the attack going ahead unhindered, unless he really is the high ranking Feman we are trying to identify. Still, there's one good thing to come out of all this: at least Daniels won't be getting his hands on the MkII eggs now,' replied the Colonel mischievously.

'You'd have let the Femorists get away with the attack even if you'd known,' Kellor stated.

'Maybe, but that's irrelevant now. We need to acquire the MkII eggs and get them under development. You're in a position to help us achieve that goal and in the process secure your future within our new regime!'

'So, what do you have in mind? I've got Daniels breathing down my neck thanks to you Colonel,' Kellor asked, a little more cockily than was wise.

Kellor could by now see that he had very few options open to him if any. To resist would be ineffectual, 'And anyway, just how bad could it be?' he asked himself. Spawning an Aryan population certainly would provide a European national identity after all - and surely it was only one small step on from male domination to the vision that the Colonel and Lock had in mind.

'I'd like you to continue with your mission Major, but from now on you report directly to me. Be very wary of Daniels from now on. I know he's not the spy that we were looking for, but he *is* the enemy within and he has McGeady close to him. We're tracking the female who escaped from your little fire fight the other night and I'm sure it won't be long before we can make a move on the Femorist base. When we do attack, I want you to take a small team inside and retrieve the eggs. Then, on your way out, lay enough explosives to bring the whole place down around them,' the Colonel explained and then paused, looking to Lock for nod of assent.

'Once we have the eggs, the organization has a facility ready to produce the livestock to our specifications. Once they are operational, that's when we move on the government,' he concluded.

'What if Daniels tries to contact me? In fact, I'm supposed to report in any time now; what should I tell him?' Kellor asked, starting to almost feel part of the team. He was starkly aware that the information that the Colonel had imparted sealed his future. Kellor now knew more than he should, more than they would allow him to know and walk away without a firm commitment to join the organisation.

'Just bluff him. He's relying on you to find those eggs for him. Tell him you're following up some leads and that cross breed has gone to convalesce after her unfortunate accident. Daniels hasn't got anyone good enough to track you. The only other MkII that he had was wasted the other night, but that won't stop him trying - so cover your tracks in any case,' the Colonel replied.

All too willingly they appeared satisfied that Kellor had had the good sense to join the organisation. They desperately needed experienced operatives, whatever their ethnic background - and they seemed prepared to take a chance on their loyalty to get them.

'What do you need me to be doing in the meantime - that is until we locate the Femorist base?' Kellor asked enthusiastically.

His affirmed new bosses glanced at each other before Lock spoke gently, 'I would like you to get acquainted with the team you'll be leading in the attack on the Femorist base. Get to know them well; find out their weaknesses - they may be a little raw. We have a mature and reasonably experienced MkII for you to use as you see fit. His name's Raymond and he'll arrange your introduction to the new livestock. They should be delivered here in two or three days hopefully. Then all you have to do is track a target signal and wait for the final location to emerge. It would be a good idea if you contact Daniels proactively. Don't let him agonise about what you're up to.'

The Colonel got to his feet and stared unflinchingly into Kellor's eyes.

'One last thing Major. Forget Chapel and the cross breed. They'll find their way back into the rat's nest they came from. The cross breed was a plant by Daniels, there to keep an eye on your movements and Chapel works for McGeady, so he's not to be trusted under any circumstances. Don't let yourself down by placing your loyalty with a losing team!' he emphasised.

'You've nothing to worry about on that score, Colonel. I just wish you'd taken me into your confidence earlier,' said Kellor, smiling peculiarly as he stood to attention.

The Colonel beckoned to Clark, so that he could escort Kellor back to his quarters. As Clark approached the three men, he spoke, 'Hanner has just been in contact…'

Clark stopped before he said anything he should not in Major Kellor's presence.

'Go on Clark. We have no secrets from Major Kellor. He's on the team,' Lock said impatiently.

'Right. Glad you're mucking in with us Major. Anyway, Hanner has just sent "the" rabbit on its way and we should be able to pick its signal up very soon. He said he's on his way to drop the vehicle off at the processing plant as ordered, but he has a problem with one of the power packs. So it may take him a while to get there,' Clark reported.

'Good. There you go Major. You may not have long to wait to prove yourself to us,' Lock said with new warmth.

'Clark, take Major Kellor back to his quarters now - and before you go back to Shenka, arrange for Raymond to make contact with him,' he continued.

'Right away Sir, and you'll contact me when you need me again?' Clark inquired obsequiously.

'It'll probably be a few days Clark, but be ready. We'll need to move fast if we're to succeed,' said the Colonel, already calculating his next move.

The two subordinates left the control room in an aura of stunted silence. The Colonel and Lock waited for them to exit through the security door, before they spoke once more.

'Can we really trust him?' Lock asked.

'Who knows? Fortunately, with Raymond to keep him in check there should be no problems. I'll speak to him later and tell him to keep a close eye on the Major and that if need be he should kill him at the first sign of any dissent. If Raymond has no concerns, then I'm sure the Major will be a crucial asset to our organisation in the coming months of conflict,' the Colonel replied.

25 SITTING DUCKS

In the ice cold operations room, Kefelnikov sat with four of the most senior officers from the commune's small military force. Panic had spread during the last few days because there had been no contact with the Feman. This had led Kefelnikov to believe that there were serious problems with the operation in Shenka. She really wanted to get the meeting done and over with, so that she could go back to her warm office and get some sleep. She had not a clue whether it was night or day outside because she had not slept much at all recently and was now feeling the cumulative effects. Nevertheless, she knew the current crisis had to be resolved without postponement and so she persevered.

'Ladies, it's four days since Corporal McDowell and Commander Langton arrived in Shenka. I think it's prudent to assume that we have problems heading our way - just to be on the safe side,' Kefelnikov stated.

'It's five days Sir,' Lieutenant Jenny Stroud corrected. The other three women sat around the table were all Lieutenants too: Belinda Numen, Georgia Read and finally Victoria Kalcina.

'Okay five days - even more reason to plan for impending trouble. Any suggestions as to what we might do?' Kefelnikov asked.

'Surely there's only one option. We must evacuate the commune and hide out until this thing blows over or, the male authorities turn up here. Then we'll know they've given us up,' said Kalcina sadly.

'What happens if we stay and the army attacks?' Kefelnikov asked.

'War of attrition. They'll blockade the commune and starve us out. This is no place to try and fight your way out of,' Numen answered.

'Too right, they'd cut us down as we came out. We're sitting ducks,' Kalcina added.

'So we'd better get out of here pretty damn quick!' added Read.

The lights flickered as the noisy generators stuttered and coughed - out of sight but rarely out of mind - and the group fell silent. Finally, the lights died altogether and they held their breath, praying this was not the prophesied attack come earlier than they had expected. The seconds ticked into imaginary minutes, before the desultory lighting flickered and half-heartedly re-lit the dirty and cold operations room just as a rather large rat decided to take advantage of the temporary blackout. It had severely mis-timed its run and Read was quickest to draw her pistol and in one rapid action fired at the scuttling rodent as it desperately tried to cover the ground between its two bolt holes. Once the fur had stopped burning and its corpse smouldered quietly in the corner, they resumed their emergency meeting.

'I thought Langton had a contingency plan for just such an occasion. Had she taken any of you through it?' Kefelnikov asked hopefully.

'Yes, but it'll take twenty-four hours to complete. Is that soon enough?' Kalcina asked.

'It'll have to be. If we can't safely return here I want to take as many home comforts as we possibly can,' Kefelnikov answered.

There was a weary knock at the door and one of the communications operators walked in without ceremony.

'Commune leader, I have a person on hold called Alexandria. He says you will speak to him, that you know him well,' reported the operator.

'Patch him through to my office immediately - could be just the break we need,' Kefelnikov said eagerly.

'Wait here ladies. I'll return in a while with good news I hope. This is a call from our Feman spy in Berlin,' continued Kefelnikov, backing away from the battered conference table.

Kefelnikov left the room and quickly walked the short distance to her office. She opened the door and the warm air rushed past her face in a pleasant welcome. Inside Kefelnikov sat down at the comms console in the corner of the plush private quarters and proceeded to patch into the call.

'Alexandria, I don't hear from you in two years and now you contact me twice in one month. Strange way of operating if I may say so!'

'No time for your cynicism Kefelnikov. I've got two minutes before they track this call and then you'll be fucked!' Alexandria explained and paused as if to emphasise her point.

'Now listen carefully. Langton's dead, but it seems she didn't give the game away during her interrogation. Nicola's dead too. Luckily, she pegged out before they had a chance to get the thumbscrews out. McDowell escaped the raid somehow and is still at large. Maybe she'll inadvertently lead a force of men your way - but I wouldn't count on it. There's all sorts of shit flying around here and I dunno how much more help I can be before it all blows up in our faces,' Alexandria said hurriedly.

'We've done okay without your help for the last two years; this time'll be no different,' Kefelnikov said spitefully.

'I'm sorry you feel that way. May God be with you and I wish you and the commune all the luck in the world,' Alexandria said, ready to finish the conversation there and then.

'Alexandria don't fucking hang up on me now. Alexandria you bastard!' Kefelnikov screamed down the radio mic.

But the line was dead and Kefelnikov began to contemplate what she had been told during the deeply disturbing conversation.

Her mind was made up now, if it had not been previously. They had to get out of there, before they were completely exterminated. Kefelnikov was the only one who knew Alexandria's real identity. She was sad and infuriated to have seen such an effective spy become lazy and complacent. It was clear to her that Alexandria was more concerned with self-preservation than putting her neck on the line for the wellbeing of women everywhere. Morosely, she returned to the operations room, where the group sat eagerly waiting her return.

'Use Langton's contingency plan, but I want to be out of here in twelve hours - less if possible. Kalcina you're now acting commander. Langton's dead. McDowell's on her way back to us but we must try to intercept her before she gets here. It seems she could be leading government forces straight to us. Lieutenant Numen, take a dozen or so soldiers out and scout the surrounding terrain. See if you can locate McDowell before she gets too close. The rest of you get the plan going right away - we have precious little time,' Kefelnikov ordered, resuming her place at the head of the table.

'Sir, I think you and a small force should leave right away and take the eggs that we have. Then even if they attack before we have time to get out completely all won't be lost,' Kalcina said, reflecting her newly appointed position.

'Where would we go?' Kefelnikov asked nervously.

'Two hundred miles south of here is an old missile base. Closed down at the end of the cold war. There are thirty or so empty missile silos and a control centre. It's all underground so it will afford you some protection. It's the best we have at short notice sir,' Kalcina replied.

'Let's do it. I'll be ready in a couple of hours. Let's go ladies. Jump to it!' Kefelnikov roared.

The room cleared in a hail of barked orders and Kefelnikov was left to bear the burden of power alone. She was sad for

Langton but knew it was no time for mourning - there was too much to do. She returned to her office, began to pack a few important items ready for her journey and then rotated the thermostat down as far as it would go. Kefelnikov knew that the place that she was going to would be cold and it filled her with dread. Switching off the office lights, she thought that maybe she would pay a visit to the clothing stores before she left to get some thermal long johns for her journey. She walked without purpose down the corridor with her meagre box of belongings under her arm, wondering if she would ever return to the only comfort that she knew: her extravagantly luxurious office.

26 SUBTERFUGE REIGNS

Daniels entered the Eurostate conference room and took his seat, inwardly anxious. This time the lighting was less sultry than before, when he had met with the Colonel and McGeady. Around the table sat the most powerful men in the Eurostate, with the obvious exception of the Colonel and the spotlight of pressure shone directly upon Daniels. Seated opposite was President Wells; to his left, General Cohen, who commanded the regular army that was more conditioned to sitting in its barracks than actual combat. Next to the General was Air Chief Caulfman, another ethnically mixed breed. Finally, to the right of Daniels sat Admiral Riedler, the only one of the three to have a archetypal Aryan profile. The three military men were in their sixties thanks to their extended biological life clocks, a privilege they enjoyed because they were fiercely loyal to the President. There was a measure of contempt amongst them for Daniels, his progressive outlook and unconventional methods were a cause for concern. Nevertheless, he still had the support of the President and hence was tolerated, if not actually respected.

'Gentlemen, I'm sorry to keep you all waiting. I know it's highly unusual to call you all here at such a late hour. However, I think that you'll find what I have to show you of great interest.' Daniels finished speaking and nervously sipped his steaming coffee.

'I have uncovered...,' he began, but before Daniels could finish his sentence President Wells interrupted him.

'Callum, before you go any further - about Alec McGeady. I'd like an explanation for your actions. I'm told that he is in your protective custody, WHY?'

'That's exactly why I've called you here. If you let me proceed...' Again Wells interrupted Daniels.

'Do not fuck me around boy! I don't employ you to obstruct the people who action my orders. Colonel Johnson has been in touch with me today and it seems he can't interrogate McGeady because you have him. I had you bred as my special assistant to support me. Not to go behind my back and undermine my authority. Answer my question in one sentence now. Then and only then, I just might let you proceed!'

'Lock... Nigel Lock, I'm sure that name's familiar to you. He and the Colonel are planning a coup.'

Daniels surveyed the table warily, but for once no interruption erupted. Now they were listening!

'I asked McGeady to keep the Colonel under surveillance,' he went on.

'Somehow the Colonel found out and tried to assassinate him yesterday at the VR Park. Fortunately, I'd covered such a move and McGeady escaped.'

'How are you so sure it was the Colonel who tried to kill McGeady,' asked Wells, curiosity replacing his earlier rage.

'McGeady identified the Colonel personally. He saw him leave the park with three of his men - but in the attempt two of the Colonel's men, one of mine and three civilians were killed.'

'So where does Lock fit into all of this? He's supposed to be dead,' asked a confused General Cohen.

'Lock wants to make changes in the state's breeding programme. To do this he plans to remove the government and form his own - the Colonel's helping him to achieve this goal.'

'The Colonel tells me that McGeady was told of the MkII eggs' existence, not two weeks before they were taken?' interjected Wells.

'Not true. He new nothing of their existence. But McGeady told the Colonel that Femorists were targeting the Stablinka farm well in advance of the attack and he did nothing.'

'What possible motive would he have for allowing the raid on Stablinka?' Riedler asked.

'He's planning to use the stolen MkII eggs to strengthen their challenge for power. Without them, they have only a handful of Fascist sympathisers to overthrow the government. Surely, it's conceivable the Colonel took those eggs himself and is now preparing them for his own ends.'

Daniels was unsure exactly where the eggs were. What he did know for certain was that the Colonel did not currently have them in his possession. Nevertheless, he knew that a little scaremongering would go a long way towards winning over the four most powerful men in the Eurostate to his way of thinking.

'There were confirmed reports of women on the premises the night Stablinka was attacked. I don't think even the Colonel has an army of women at his disposal,' said General Cohen.

'Maybe the plan was to let the Femorists take the eggs and then to ambush them at a later date. It's not in dispute that the Colonel did absolutely nothing to stop the attack - but maybe he's already repossessed the eggs.'

'What proof have you got?' Wells asked cautiously.

'A few taped conversations, nothing tangible. I have McGeady continuing the surveillance work though.'

'You mentioned fascists earlier. What did you mean by that? Eurostate law prohibits the existence of such a political party,' quizzed Riedler.

'Very true Admiral. Unfortunately, Lock and the Colonel have scant regard for Eurostate law. The whole reason for Lock's staged death was so that he could work on this political and social madness without the President's intervention. The Aryan race he's hoping to introduce is in direct conflict the equality laws as set out by the President himself and his forefathers.'

Wells, in spite of everything, exuded discontentment with the situation, but he was sufficiently concerned by what he had heard to permit Daniels to continue with his masterful performance.

'What you accuse Colonel Johnson of - I want to see some hard evidence, but for the moment you have our full attention,' Wells said calmly.

Daniels began to speak with an authority well-rehearsed at many high powered meetings. He played various recorded conversations that McGeady had procured. The conversations in themselves were by no means incriminating, but the electronic date stamp proved that they were definitely recent exchanges. The voice spectrum analysis when compared with Eurostate records showed beyond doubt that the two voices were indeed those of Nigel Lock and Colonel Johnson. Daniels also demonstrated that these matches were as certain as any fingerprint or DNA match, even when compared against clones. As Daniels retook his seat, the other men in the room sat bewildered.

At long last, Air Chief Caulfman broke the silence, 'I take it there was a clone made of Lock and that is who our military intelligence surgeons cut up?'

'I have it on good authority that this was indeed the case and the Colonel ensured that the clone was never compared one-hundred per cent to Lock's biological structure. As you know, we can normally identify if livestock is subsequently cloned from an original, not sure how, but I am assured by my scientist that they can. However, I think the time for how and why this has happened has long since passed gentlemen. We now need to concern ourselves with the way forward; how best to handle a difficult situation,' Daniels replied sanctimoniously.

'As soon as Colonel Johnson returns to his HQ, have him arrested. Torture him until he tells us where Lock is operating from - and I want to be there. I want him to see me smile as he suffers and I definitely want to see him spill his guts as to who's involved in this betrayal of the Eurostate,' Wells coldly detailed his expectations.

Wells was full of venomous rhetoric now. Daniels though, was far from impressed. He knew that if the President had had more confidence in his ability to run things it would have never come to this. The old man was losing his grip and Daniels would be waiting when the power fell from his grasp.

'I could flood the city with soldiers; shut the whole place down. I'm sure it wouldn't be too long before we apprehended these traitors,' General Cohen offered.

'Gentlemen please, what if I could promise you that, without our raising a finger, the Femorists who attacked the breeding farm would be destroyed. And then, that without official Eurostate intervention, the Colonel, Lock and most of their treacherous consorts were to be wiped out... Unfortunately, we'd have to sacrifice the eggs in order to achieve this outcome,' Daniels fell silent, waiting for some reaction to his offer.

'It seems to me that the eggs are already beyond reclamation and even if they aren't there is no certainty that we will get hold of them before Lock,' Wells paused before speaking again.

'What is it you are proposing Callum?'

'All I need is a single nuclear ICBM brought out of storage. One of those the Americans think we disposed of.'

Daniels talked solidly for another hour before he finally wrapped up his sales pitch, sat down and gulped down the last dregs of his now-cold coffee. Wells looked around the room as the men in front of him unanimously nodded their heads in approval.

'Callum. you shall have what you need. If you fuck this up though I'll personally kill you without a second thought. There are plenty more where you came from,' Wells threatened.

The President stood and the others followed suit. All except for Daniels, who remained seated. The ageing quartet trudged from the room one by one, and had there been anyone to observe, it would have been plain to see that they had somehow lost their collective stomach for bloody conflict.

27 CLONE TIME

Kellor was forced to sit around for another seventy-two hours before Raymond reluctantly came to see him in his quarters. The knock at the door startled him from his disillusioned reverie.

'Come in,' said a subdued Kellor.

The door opened and Raymond entered - and though he was smiling warmly, his expression, and his cold blue eyes as they settled on him, sent a chill through Kellor. Raymond did not speak - and in a reversal of the roles Kellor was used to, he felt the need to fill the silence by blurting out the first thing that came into his head.

'You must be the MkII that Lock was telling me about?'

'I have a name Major Kellor.'

'Yes, you're right. I'm sorry if that sounded rude, but I going a little crazy stuck in this room.'

'Raymond, isn't it?' Kellor added, as the room again fell silent.

'What?' Raymond replied pedantically.

'Your name. It's Raymond isn't it?'

'You're quite right Major Kellor. Raymond is the name that I go by. They haven't seen fit to bestow upon me a surname, as yet. I'll know I've made it when they do though.'

The MkII spoke without any feeling, as if there was no depth to him. Kellor knew for a fact that there was more to Raymond than just his fearsome blue eyes and he wondered if the MkII in front of him could read his private thoughts.

'What do you know Raymond? What's happening?' Kellor said in an upbeat manner, trying to lighten the atmosphere.

'The livestock for our unit will be arriving in around twenty minutes. I've just returned from an assignment and thought it was about time that we met and then we can take a walk down to Goods In and receive the MkIIs for your inspection.'

Raymond, other than opening his mouth, had not moved an inch since setting foot inside Kellor's room. The rest of his body had remained completely motionless.

'Shall we go then and talk on the way?' Kellor said getting up from his single armchair.

Kellor pulled on his boots and begun to lace them up skilfully. He wore new combat fatigues supplied by the Colonel and looked as if he were in a position of authority although his gut feeling told him otherwise. Raymond held the door open impassively for Kellor while he finished lacing his boots.

The walk down towards Goods In was a slow and painful experience, as the conversation, stifled and guarded, failed to blossom. Raymond offered little insight into the hierarchy that was to mould their relationship and so Kellor was unsure of how to behave with him. Beta had been much easier to deal with, as after the initial problems she had settled into a fairly submissive role and looked to Kellor for leadership. This however was a completely different MkII - a whole new personality. Raymond had been operational for at least two years and had developed a persona to suit his clinical creation - one in which Kellor had detected a serious lack of humour. He wondered if this was a genetic flaw in the Aryan MkIIs or whether it was just because Raymond was a miserable bastard by design. Either way, he realised that it had to be strictly business when dealing with this MkII and that he would have to start taking the task at hand seriously or more than likely he would be forced out.

The underground base kept the organisation safe from prying eyes and that was essential since the Eurostate seemed to have informants everywhere. The Goods In area, located at the highest point of the base, was not much bigger than thirty feet square. There were no doors at the entrance from the internal access point. Instead, the corridor came to an abrupt end and the storeroom opened out into a luminescent expanse. A severe-looking man of immense proportions strode around, moving from delivery to delivery with an officious-looking electronic clipboard clasped in his baseball glove-sized hand. Kellor and Raymond stopped behind the gleaming yellow line that sliced through their immediate path. The yellow line acted as an almost invisible fence that stopped anyone wandering in or out without permission. Behind this line there was the customary warning: AUTHORIZED PERSONNEL ONLY!

'What the fuck do you want!' yelled the man with the clipboard.

'We're expecting a delivery of livestock from Belson. Are they here yet?' Raymond asked in a demonically menacing fashion that did not seem to disconcert the Goods In supervisor in the slightest.

'Do they look like they're fucking here? Do they?'

'I don't like your tone. What is your name?' Raymond asked boldly.

'Fuck you, you freak and the horse you rode in on.'

'He hasn't got a horse; he walked here,' Kellor interjected hastily, trying very hard to suppress his amusement.

'Excuse me?' the man replied with sudden and unexpected civility.

'He hasn't got a horse. He walked here,' Kellor repeated.

'Don't get many of those around these days,' replied the man after an extended thought process.

'Many what?' asked Raymond, somewhat confused.

'Comedians who can still walk,' the man answered.

Now the man invaded Raymond's and the Major's personal space. He was as close as he could possibly be while still standing on the authorised side of the yellow line.

'Look, what's your name? I can't call you asshole now can I?' Kellor asked with deliberate rudeness.

'You...' began the storeman and then found he was completely lost for words.

Kellor grinned ruefully, looking alternately between the two men, waiting for some form of support from Raymond. The electronic clipboard clattered to the floor and, uncharacteristically, Kellor was momentarily distracted. He glanced up in time to see the large plump fist heading towards his premature grin. Raymond had long since registered the impending punch and took a diplomatic step backwards. The fist made contact, but Kellor rolled with the heavy blow to some extent and he remained standing, albeit with blood dripping from his lip. Kellor began to think that taking his pent-up frustration out on this mentally deficient ape was probably not such a good idea after all. Unfortunately, his actions had so incensed his assailant that there would not be any peace until one of them had paid a painful price.

The ape began to move forwards more nimbly then Kellor had anticipated and it was not long before the next punch landed with greater force than the first, knocking him this time to the spotlessly clean floor. Kellor lay there, hoping that the fact that he was obviously in no position to retaliate would be sufficient reason for the attack to cease. This was not the case - now a large polished boot played havoc with Kellor's ribs. He groaned in pain and tried to roll from striking distance. While doing so, there was a buzz from the exterior intercom, to the control panel in the corner next to the large service elevator. Raymond crossed the notorious yellow line and trotted over to where the intercom was buzzing furiously: someone was impatient at the slow response.

'Yes, can I help you?' said Raymond, still watching the fight.

Kellor sprang to his feet and sucked in his breath with difficulty. The ape walked forward again and Kellor saw in his attacker's face that ultimately he was not going to be happy with only a little blood being spilt.

'Where's Ben?' inquired the voice on the intercom.

'He's busy just now, can I help?' replied Raymond.

'I don't see why not. Can you send the elevator up? I have some livestock to deliver.'

'How many men do you have?' Raymond asked inquisitively, as he was only aware that the Colonel hoped to get as many Aryan MkIIs as possible.

'Twenty-one men it says here - but I haven't counted them personally.'

Ben, the ape, now had Kellor in a bear hug from behind; however, Kellor had regained his composure and stamped hard down on Ben's left foot.

'Aaarrrghh!!!' Ben yelled, before swinging his adversary around and then throwing him into the wall that stood well back behind the yellow line.

Kellor's back hit the grey-painted wall violently and he slumped heavily to the concrete floor. Ben looked down at the crumpled toe on his boot and then continued the assault.

'I'm sending the lift up now okay?' Raymond said, enjoying the entertainment that was unfolding around him.

'What's all that noise down there? You trying to kill someone?' inquired the deliveryman on the intercom.

Raymond did not answer. Instead he pressed the 'Up' button on the elevator and the machinery clunked and hummed as the lift began its ascent.

Kellor wearily got to his feet and prepared for Ben's next onslaught.

'Look, I'm behind the line. Don't come any further, or I'll have to resort to violence of the worst kind,' Kellor warned.

'I'm gonna kick your teeth down to the back of your asshole funny man,' Ben proclaimed.

Kellor threw two or three fast combinations at the advancing man and all landed as he had desired. Strangely, most had little or no effect and it was not long before Ben got his revenge. The left hook sliced through the air and put a deep gouge in Kellor's eyebrow, from which blood oozed down onto his cheek.

The elevator machinery fell silent as the lift reached its destination. Raymond heard the sound of footsteps clattering on the sheet metal floor above while the altercation proceeded.

Kellor was now drained and exasperated that this man would neither stop coming at him, nor be swayed by his best shots at putting him down. Wiping the blood away from his cheek, he found it was immediately replaced by the constant flow from the wound above his eye. He had run out of things to throw at Ben in a vain attempt to keep him at bay and he was now hopelessly cornered. Kellor had tried to reason with him. That had not worked and Raymond had been of no help at all during the conflict. Finally, Kellor took a sideways stance towards the ape and as he came within striking distance, he powerfully thrust his leading leg up as high as it would go with surprising speed. Normally, Kellor would hit the intended target square in the face but, due to Ben's size; he only managed to hit the man forcibly under the jaw.

The elevator's descent was as noisy as its earlier ascent and Raymond waited in front of the steel shutters in anticipation of some like-minded company It ground to a halt and the internal shutter doors flew open just as Raymond pulled the outer one back. In front of him stood ten blond, blue-eyed men and he at once felt the comfort of silent noises filling his head.

'Gentlemen, please come in. My name is Raymond but you can call me Sir.'

The men walked from the lift slightly bemused about the strangely choreographed scene that they were entering. The fight was still in full swing and articles of hardware were flying artistically through the air. All the new livestock looked similar but they were by no means identical, physical dimensions varied and so did their aggression levels - the result of a far from perfect clandestine breeding programme.

Kellor had finally managed to get the upper hand with his aggressor and one accurately placed elbow to Ben's rib cage finished the disagreement. As his ribs cracked agonisingly and the pain became intolerable, he fell backwards into a convenient pile of arctic sleeping bags while Kellor placed his raw hands on his knees and took a well-earned breather.

'Took your time Major. Now I thought a man of your calibre would have sorted that mess out in just a couple of minutes,' Raymond said as he sent the lift back up to the surface to collect the rest of the waiting livestock.

'Thanks for the vote of confidence, although I could have done with a little bit of help!'

'I may intervene in your business at some stage, but not at this moment in time,' Raymond said cryptically.

Kellor decided not to push the conversation any further. The last thing he needed now was a fight with someone who had been specifically bred to be stronger and more powerful than himself. In fact, the last thing he needed now was another fight full stop.

'Is there a first aid box over there Raymond?' Kellor inquired.

Raymond did not answer; instead, Kellor suddenly became aware of a first aid container flying through the air towards him. Kellor caught the green projectile just in time to stop it sailing over his head and then set about cleaning his wounds and patching them with the liberated flesh glue.

The lift stopped and Kellor wobbled towards Raymond, after weaving his way through the rank of ten bright and shiny young men, all stood to attention. He handed the first aid box back. Raymond just threw it nonchalantly over his shoulder and began to open the lift shutter again.

'Everybody out of the lift and fall in with the rest of your unit, NOW!' Raymond snapped.

It was as though Raymond had turned a switch. He was laying the ground rules down to the young recruits and Kellor could see it clearly. What Kellor did not know, was that the MkIIs could not shout telepathically. Hence, displays of authority had to be performed aloud and this new group appeared very inexperienced in the attributes of their breed.

Raymond walked around the outskirts of the troop, eyeing them from head to toe and conversing silently with them. He did not have anything particularly private to say, but he sought to assess their telepathic abilities. In the meantime, Kellor had sat down at the small table in 'Goods In' and was busy checking himself over for any injuries that he had overlooked.

'Okay gentlemen, if you'd like to follow the rather sad-looking man sat at the desk, our commanding officer, he'll escort you to the operations planning room and I'll be along in just a minute,' Raymond said silently to the new recruits. He turned and marched over to Kellor who was still immersed in his own world.

'Major would you take these men down to the operations planning room and I'll join you in a moment?'

'Sure, where's that?' replied Kellor, still pulling and pushing at his bruised face.

'Down the corridor and it's the fifth door on your left. You can't miss it.'

Kellor stood up and bellowed at the group of beautiful blonde men, 'SINGLE FILE, FORWARD MARCH!'

The men fell in one by one behind Kellor, who was now a picture of military correctness. Raymond smiled as all the little ducklings began to follow 'Papa Duck' and as soon as the last recruit had shuffled his way out of goods in, he walked over to the prostrate 'Goods In' man.

'Let me help you up,' Raymond said, shaking his head.

'Arrggh, ouch, shit that hurts,' Ben said as he rose to his feet, eventually towering over Raymond.

'Where's my money?' asked Ben still wincing from his broken ribs.

'I thought I said you had to work him over to get paid,' argued Raymond.

'I did and you also told me he'd be a pussy!'

'Take it anyhow. By the state of you I think you earned it,' Raymond conceded. He then delved into one of the many pockets on his combat trousers and withdrew fifty Euros. Raymond thrust them into Ben's hand, who at once began to count the cash lovingly.

'Not a word of this to anyone, right?' he added as an afterthought.

'Whatever you say,' said Ben, walking back towards his desk, still counting the money and unconcernedly caressing his broken ribcage.

Raymond turned, exited the Goods In area and quickly proceeded down the passageway down which the Major had disappeared with his new team. As he entered the operations room, all twenty-one MkIIs were standing to attention in the auditorium. He glanced around the room and silently they sat down *en masse*.

'I didn't hear anybody to tell you to fucking sit down!' Kellor bellowed.

Raymond looked at Kellor and gently shook his head in disbelief.

'Oh I see, it was you who told them to sit. Apologies. It may take a while for me to get used to all this E.S.P. stuff,' Kellor said, feeling slightly stupid and a very isolated by Raymond's actions.

Turning to the mute audience, Raymond began to speak, this time audibly, 'Welcome to what will be your new home; for a few days at least. This, by the way, is Major Kellor, our

Commanding Officer as I explained previously. Major Kellor will lead us and, if he should get killed, I'm the one you must take your orders from henceforth - and by the way, he's not one of us as you may have noticed. So ultimately you answer to me.'

Raymond continued to speak vocally for the next thirty minutes while he briefed the assembled men on the current situation and the proposed plan of attack. Finally, he invited the Major to address the new recruits.

'Thank you Raymond. Can you ascertain the abilities of each man and report back to me. Do they have names at the moment? If not arrange for them to be named and label their tunics as such - they all look the same to me,' Kellor said, less than diplomatically.

'Whatever you say Major, but are you sure you don't want to evaluate them yourself?' Raymond mocked.

'No. I think you will be able to make a better job of it than me. I'll be back as soon as I can. I just have to go and make contact with someone before I do anything else.'

He left the room before the discussion went any deeper, having decided that now was the right time to make contact with Daniels - though he was not sure exactly what he was going to say. He made his solitary way to the main control room and entered after receiving the all-clear. Kellor sat down at a free communications console. The Colonel lurched from one of the small private cubicles over in the right hand corner and as soon as he spotted Kellor he made a beeline for him.

'Your new recruits are here Major,' informed the unhappy Colonel.

'I know sir. I've just left them with Raymond. I thought that it was about time I contacted Daniels, before he starts to panic you know.'

'I'll just listen in, if I may. Then there are some urgent things I need to discus with you Major.'

Kellor nodded, then turned fully in his seat to face the console and began to fiddle with the controls and keyboard that lay inset on the desk. After an anxious wait, the operator's voice boomed from the earphones that they were now wearing.

'Eurostate HQ how can I help you?'

'This is Major Rob Kellor. I need to speak to Mr Daniels please,' Kellor asked.

'Putting you through to his office now Major Kellor,' the operator replied instantly.

'Hello, Mr Daniel's PA speaking. How can I help you?'

'Yes I do hope you can. I need to speak to Mr Daniels. This is Major Kellor.'

'Ah the illustrious Major Kellor. He's been waiting for your call. I'll see if Mr. Daniels is free for you Major.'

The line went dead for a short while before the PA came back on line, 'Just putting you through Major.'

'Kellor. How very nice of you to call. How did you manage to find time in your busy schedule to contact me?' Daniels asked sardonically.

'Yeah. I'm sorry for the delay but it's been rather hectic. As you probably know, we got a little bit out of our depth a few nights ago and Beta was injured. We took one Femorist hostage and I'm following up on some leads that I managed to extract from her under interrogation, although they're not worth going into now. As soon as I've completed my investigations I'll come in and brief you on what we've got Sir,' Kellor blurted out his explanation without so much as a pause for breath. His pulse raced as he tried to be as vague as possible while still trying to placate Daniels' insatiable appetite for information.

'Where is Beta now?' Daniels probed.

'She's safe and recuperating from her injuries,' Kellor replied evasively.

'That's not what I asked Major. Where is Beta now?' Daniels repeated unmistakably.

'Last time I saw her she was at the Woodlands Medical Facility being treated in the regeneration unit there,' lied Kellor.

'So what you're saying is, that you don't know where Beta is at this precise moment?'

'Not for sure no.'

Kellor felt the increasing pressure and wondered childishly if he could just hang up without another word. He thought better of the impulse and remained silent, waiting for the next probing question.

'Have you had any contact with the Colonel since we last spoke to each other?' Daniels asked with a mildness that belied his true feelings.

'No sir. It seems he's happy with you giving the orders.'

'Okay Major. I'd better let you get on. Call me when you have something more substantial to report. Goodbye,'

'Yes I will. Goodbye…' Kellor whispered, stunned by the lack of an inquisition.

'What the hell was that all about?' Kellor said finally, when he knew the connection had been severed.

'Seems Mr Daniels has other things on his mind. Conniving bastard that he is,' said the equally confused and suspicious Colonel.

'Why did you give me to Daniels in the first place to do his bidding?' Kellor said, feeling the Colonel's gaze searching for any duplicity.

'I wanted to put someone close to him who I thought I could trust. At the time I was unsure who the Feman spy was within the Government or its associated infrastructure. In fact, to be completely truthful, I'm still unsure.'

'So why've you tried to shut McGeady down if you don't know for sure who the spy is?'

'Fifty-fifty chance. There was no way Wells would have let me arrest Daniels without substantiation of the facts. Something that I don't have, I might add. The final straw came when Daniels ordered McGeady to keep tabs on my movements and at this stage of events, I couldn't take any chances on McGeady finding out anything incriminating. So, I convinced Wells that McGeady was the spy that we were looking for and he went for it. Bloody thing was, we missed our chance to take McGeady out some days ago, so he's still a player,' the Colonel said, opening up for the first time since Kellor had joined the organisation.

'Why the obscure reference to the Greenland Siege then?'

'The obvious. I knew you'd look into it and keep an eye out for any connections to Daniels and the Femorists. Do I really need to spell it out?' said the Colonel becoming a little frustrated at Kellor's ostensible ingenuousness.

'No not really. I just wanted to hear it from your mouth sir.'

'It's all irrelevant now anyway. Once we find the female base and destroy it we can set about using the eggs you retrieve to bring down the government. Just as a matter of interest, did you notice anything suspicious about Daniels?'

'No nothing. He's high on his own power but seems to have the welfare of the Eurostate at heart. One question though, why did he agree to my taking the job of investigating the Stablinka raid? Why not use one his own men and avoid any possibility of a double cross?'

'President Wells is no fool. He makes sure no single man in his government has overwhelming authority and power. Call it self-regulation - we're all encouraged to report on each other and that suits him just fine. Placing one of my men under his control was meant to ensure that any disloyalty would be flagged and then dealt with.'

'So what do you think Daniels is up to now? He seemed different just now, lacking in intensity somehow.'

'He's a smart man. I don't think he'd give it up so easily, but putting you close to him was worth a go. I'm sure he's up to something, but I can't worry about that now. We have our own agenda to complete. By the way, where's the MkII he asked you about?' the Colonel probed.

'Like I told Daniels, last time I saw her she was in the hospital,' Kellor lied.

'Shame. The guard in Chapel's room could remember nothing. Still, must have been Chapel's doing, her disappearing like that,' commented the Colonel, still probing for any signs of deception, but Kellor was having none of it, even though he was feeling at ease with his renewed rapport with the Colonel. No, once you had spun a yarn you had to stick to it, whatever the consequences, Kellor thought.

'Yeah must have been...' Kellor agreed offhandedly.

'If we are done here Major, I'd like you to follow me to the tracking station inside the far cubicle. It seems we have a problem. The female that we are tracking back to her base has...Well let's just go and see shall we?'

'No time like the present.'

They walked to the cubicle side by side, crossing four or five pools of light as they skirted past the other comms stations in the main control room. The Colonel opened the door warily and then squeezed into the tiny space where the operator sat monitoring McDowell's signal. Kellor just managed to push inside as well, but he was unable to close the door behind himself. The cubicle was dim and the tracking display supplied most of what little ambient light was available inside. The flat panel screen was fixed into a slate-grey console at which the operator sat uncomfortably hunched over, analyzing every movement of the small flashing beacon.

'Klaus, tell Major Kellor what you told me earlier about this fucking signal,' the Colonel said irritably.

'Yes Colonel. Well it seems that the commune is further away than we at first reckoned. Either that or the tagged target has gone on vacation. You see this region here - Chernobyl's at the centre. Now, we thought the Femorist base was somewhere in this area, but the signal skirted it for the most part and stopped just there, near the regional border. It remained there for thirty-six hours and then it moved again. She then rode for two twelve-hour stints, with a six-hour break in the middle and now the signal has been stationary for around another six hours. As you can see though, it's another four hundred miles north of this area here that we were focusing in on at first. As you can appreciate there is a little bit of uncertainty as to whether or not she's at her final destination,' reported the operator, poring over the display map.

Klaus looked up as he completed his last sentence and offered a blank, rhetorical expression. Kellor in turn looked across to the Colonel with the same look, not knowing exactly what he was expected to say.

'Before you ask Major. Yes I would like you to take your newly assembled team on a reconnaissance mission. I want you to get as close to the signal source as possible without making contact. If it moves on, follow it and when it finally gets to its destination sit on it and just observe. Lock and I will doubtless join you as soon as you're happy it's reached its final destination. By then, we should be in a position to bring re-enforcements for when we attack the female base,' the Colonel ordered.

'I'll take the aircraft Daniels supplied but I'll need a small troop carrier as well, preferably an airborne one.'

'I'll have one for you by this evening.'

'What about the state air traffic monitoring stations? They'll pick up your movements soon enough Sir and the air force will send out fighters to investigate,' Klaus advised.

'Don't worry. I have several cloaking units available for immediate use. Your AFVE MK12 should be stealthy enough to operate without a cloaking device, but the troop carrier will most definitely need one,' the Colonel explained.

'I suppose I'd better get back to my new recruits then. I'd like to leave as soon as possible, with your permission of course?' Kellor said, standing to attention as best he could in the space available.

'I'd like you to leave as soon as possible too Major. So we're agreed then,' the Colonel said forcefully, his body language clearly indicating that Kellor should be gone already.

'I'll get going then - and don't worry Colonel. I'll more than justify your faith in me. I promise you,' Kellor said awkwardly.

Backing out of the cubicle, Kellor turned immediately as soon as the space allowed and left the main control room without further debate. Walking slowly back to the operations room, he contemplated the vast region that they would have to search for the elusive female base. What if the bike was nowhere near? Then they really would be searching for a needle in a haystack, he thought. That was unless they managed to capture the female who had been riding the bike. Before Kellor had managed to arrive at any useful conclusions he found himself back at the 'operations planning room' and walking into what seemed like a scene from a low budget sitcom. Having lined up the new soldiers in three rows of seven; Raymond had stuck name badges to the front of their tunics. The first row were labelled as Henry 1, Henry 2 and Henry 3, all the way up to seven; the second row were all called Hans and finally the third row were all called Frank.

'What the fuck have you done Raymond?' Kellor said visibly amused by the total lack of imagination.

'I thought you wanted me to name them all! Well I have!' an offended Raymond replied.

'Perhaps you should let me do it and you can concentrate on the evaluations?'

'I've done what you asked concerning the evaluation. They're all of a higher quality than the normally bred soldiers,' said Raymond. For the first time his cool, one dimensional exterior showed a modicum of depth and feeling. Kellor savoured the moment.

'Have you more name badges?'

'Sure, on the table over there,'

'Okay let's start again,' Kellor said, quickly walking between the soldiers before taking the spare labels from the desk and the marker pen beside them.

'Raymond who in your opinion is the best soldier here?'

'Best? In what way?'

'Intellect, aggression, whatever. It doesn't really matter.'

'Henry Two seems very gifted compared with the rest,' answered Raymond dispassionately.

'Okay, now we're getting somewhere. Here you go Henry Two - your new name: John Wayne!' As Kellor spoke he wrote the new name on a fresh label, ripped the old one off and slapped the new label onto the former Henry Two's chest with a thump and a smile.

'Why must he have a surname?' asked a jealous Raymond.

'You want a surname. You can have a surname. Right let's see, Raymond what? Raymond Burr, that's a fine and distinguished surname,' Kellor said enthusiastically and slapped the label onto Raymond's chest.

'There you go, Sergeant Raymond Burr - and just for good measure I'll put my name on my lapel too,' continued Kellor.

Kellor was now enjoying himself greatly and, using Raymond's observations of the new recruits; he named them one by one. During this process Raymond kept looking down at his sticky label and for once smiled in admiration at his brand new surname. By the time Kellor had started on the ninth soldier, it did not matter what attributes the soldier possessed; he just gave him the first name that came into his head. Kellor had used many of his own heroes' names. Hence, amongst the new unit there was a John Wayne, William Bonnie, Robin Hood, Oliver Cromwell, Bruce Willis, Michael Jackson and last but by no means least Raymond Burr.

28 THE FINAL STRAW

Daniels delicately reset his receiver as if any untoward jolt would cause it to detonate. The call from Kellor had revealed enough for him to know that he could no longer rely on the Major's support and he anxiously surveyed the three expectant people in front of him. McGeady sat waiting for Daniels to speak, not daring to break his train of thought while Chapel and Beta stood silently behind McGeady. Daniels jumped up from his seat and strode to the end of his office and back again, gently massaging his temples in a slow circular motion. Daniels paused at the end of his desk and he let out a colossal roar of frustration. Retaking his seat, Daniels looked to McGeady who returned the look without flinching at the public display of dissatisfaction.

'You have no idea as to the whereabouts of Major Kellor?' Daniels asked.

'No none at all - or for that matter the Colonel and Nigel Lock. What we do know though is that they're all together in one place,'

'Kellor's gone native. I'm sure the Colonel's turned him - that's if Kellor was to be trusted in the first place'

'What makes you so sure? He put his life on the line for us,' Chapel interjected over McGeady's head, addressing to the MkII at the same time.

McGeady launched a scolding look towards Chapel over his shoulder, as if admonishing a naughty child, but Chapel had long since cast aside any fears about speaking out of turn to people of authority.

'Chapel isn't it?' Daniels asked, as if he didn't know that was indeed his name.

'Apparently the last time the Major Kellor saw Beta she was being treated in the Woodlands Medical Facility and, as we know from what you have told me, that was a complete lie. No, I think it's safe to say that Major Kellor's now working against us - or at best under duress. Either way, we can no longer rely on him to fulfil his mission. At least not for our benefit anyway,' Daniels continued.

'We don't need him anyway, I thought that's what you said Callum?' McGeady interjected, halting the minor squabble.

'That's not the point. I don't like being double crossed and having those traitors thinking they've gotten away with it. If any of your men cross paths with Major Kellor on their travels, make sure they execute him and make sure he knows it was me who ordered it.'

'So, plan B. It looks like we're dependent on "Doberman" to find the female base. I'm sure we'll not see the Colonel back in official circles until this whole thing's resolved, one way or another. As for Lock, I think we'll be even luckier to catch up with him. One thing I've learnt from the recent surveillance is that they're very careful, very careful indeed,' explained McGeady.

'Agent Chapel, would you escort Beta to the outer office. I wish to speak to your Director, alone…'

Chapel turned smartly and walked straight for the door. Beta followed at a more leisurely pace, seemingly a little lost in the proceedings. The door closed behind them and Daniels turned to McGeady sharply.

'McGeady, if you ever mention Doberman in front of a third party, by name or not, I'll kill you. Got that?'

'I'm sorry, but Chapel is loyal and after what the Colonel's men were going to do to him I'm sure he would never betray us.'

'You could be right but I'll still kill you anyway. We do not have the luxury of complacency at this time,' replied Daniels unswayed by McGeady's reasoning.

'I've now recruited all the mercenaries we need; with Chapel and the female MkII along for the ride we're about ready to go. That's of course when you get the final location of the base,' McGeady advised, emphasising his importance to the operation.

'I'd accept nothing less from you Alec. Anyway, we'll have the location soon enough. I spoke to Doberman the other day, before my meeting with the President and the heads of the armed forces. He was happy to give me the transmitting frequency of the bike that the female's riding, now that the money has cleared into his account of course. So, now I've got two tracking specialists working around the clock on the signal.'

'What if he's double crossed you?' McGeady asked cynically.

'It doesn't matter. it's only Eurostate money and it's a chance we have to take. Besides, there is no more honest form of betrayal than that which is carried out in the pursuit of financial gain.'

'I do hope you're right.'

'So do I Alec, the alternative and its consequences are unthinkable.'

'So, did you get what you wanted from the meeting with the President? I suppose you did; you're still here aren't you,' McGeady asked inquisitively.

'Yes, I did get what I wanted. The airborne troop carriers are ready for you whenever you need them and I have a dozen fighters to provide an escort,' confirmed Daniels.

'With a fighting unit of that size, I'll have to keep clear of the target area until the very last moment. We don't want them getting wind of the fact that they're about to be wiped out, do we?' McGeady said thoughtfully.

'No, indeed we don't. I want you to permanently remove both rebellious parties as completely as you can. Preferably no survivors if possible. Then when you return, I'll pay your hired help and you can look forward to a promotion of sorts.'

Daniels buzzed through to his PA and asked him to come immediately into his office. Quickly, Brad opened the door and closed it quietly behind himself.

'Yes Mr Daniels. What can I do for you?'

'I'd like you to take Alec up to the tracking department labs and introduce him to Luke and David; they'll take it from there. They know he's coming. When you come back, take Agent Chapel and Beta for some lunch, okay?' Daniels asked politely.

'No problem Mr Daniels, it will be done. Alec, if you'd like to follow me,' obeyed Brad.

Daniels waited for the door to close behind McGeady before he picked up the antique telephone.

'Operator, put me through to Military Ordnance right away,' Daniels requested.

Daniels tapped his free hand on the glass desk to an obscure beat as he waited for the connection. He never used a videophone from his office, preferring not to display his body language for all to see while conducting a conversation.

'Military Ordnance, Corporal Jones speaking,' identified the hoarse voice.

'Can I speak to Colonel Hakkinen right away? It's Callum Daniels calling.'

The earpiece rang without another word from Corporal Jones and after a few supplementary rings Colonel Hakkinen answered.

'Mr Daniels, what can I do for you?' Hakkinen asked knowingly.

'Is my warhead ready?' Daniels asked nonchalantly, as if inquiring about a dry-cleaned suit.

'Two days and it will be,' answered Hakkinen, equally unfazed.

'Make it a day,' Daniels stated and hung up immediately.

29 THE CLOSING SNARE

The Cobra AFVE flashed across the skyline, embracing the contours of the land effortlessly. Kellor was beginning to enjoy himself after days of being held as a 'guest' in the underground bunker. He and his small unit had set out in the early hours, tracking the signal, which had not moved since he had first observed the flashing beacon on the tracking screen at the Colonel's base. Kellor was flying at less than half the full speed available to him. Nevertheless, every so often he was forced to double back to rendezvous with the painfully slow troop carrier that followed. Raymond was at its helm, giving Kellor a much-needed break from what felt like the constant monitoring of his behaviour. In the cockpit with Kellor was the MkII called John Wayne. Kellor had decided to use his idol's namesake to keep an eye on the flashing beacon as they approached. It had been a few hours since Kellor had inquired about the target and he felt it was now time to check, even though he knew that the MkII would have alerted him to at the first sign of any movement.

'John, are we still on course? The target hasn't moved has it?'

'No Sir. The target hasn't moved and we're dead on course.'

'Is the troop carrier still on the correct heading?' said Kellor, trying to break the monotony of silence.

'They've drifted slightly to the west. I'll download the corrective heading to their navigation system now Sir,' John said efficiently.

John was as deadpan as Raymond and Kellor wondered if he personally had been that shallow when he was first matured.

'What's our ETA at the signal source?' Kellor requested after another bout of irritating silence.

'Thirty-five minutes Sir. It's just over two-hundred and fifty K's till we reach the signal source,' answered John, quickly calculating the troop carrier's speed against distance, although the ETA was already showing clearly on his virtual reality display panel.

'Tell me when we're approaching fifty K's from the target. We need to set down at that point; I don't want to get too close and spoil the surprise,' ordered Kellor.

'Yes Sir, fifty K's is approximately twenty-eight minutes away,' said John without being asked.

Kellor decided to turn his attention to the troop carrier and spoke to Raymond over the secure communications band between the two craft.

'Raymond can you hear me?' Kellor asked in an unmilitary fashion, deciding not to use the virtual imaging for the exchange.

'I'm reading you loud and clear Major. Over.'

'In around twenty-five minutes we're going to land. Then it's all the way to the target on foot, over,' Kellor replied professionally, taking up Raymond's lead.

'I'll get the men ready. You'll want to hit the ground running. Over.'

'Yes, you're right. However, a slight change of plan. I'll set off first and you can bring up the rear, just in case there's an ambush. I'm going to take John here with me - Privates Jackson and Willis as well. You'll follow my lead with the rest of the unit say, two K's at our rear and if we do get into any difficulties you can come to our assistance,' ordered Kellor, wanting to keep a respectable distance between himself and Raymond's prying eyes.

'I don't think that's a good idea Major. You'll need my experience with the MkIIs. Private Hood can lead the following group. He's more than capable. Over.'

'No. That's an order Raymond. I want someone of your ability backing me up if I get into trouble,' Kellor said, trying to buy Raymond off with praise.

The airwaves fell silent for the next twenty minutes as Raymond accepted the inevitable. Both aircraft continued to skim the ever-thicker carpet of treetops that coated the earth below, silhouetted gracefully against the weird blood-red dawn skyline. Raymond had silently ordered the men in the troop carrier to prepare for a hot landing and they went about their orders quickly and efficiently. The MkIIs wore white combat fatigues with laser body armour underneath their tunics. The armour was more advanced than the jacket that Kellor was wearing, but was also a great deal heavier. Any conventional soldier made to march fifty kilometres wearing the advanced armour would have been exhausted by the time they had reached their destination and unlikely to be in any fit state to fight.

The engines slowed to a muffled hum and Kellor observed the intense concentration on John's face. Strangely, John did not appear to be focused visually on any of the instruments in front of him and Kellor assumed that Raymond must have been instructing John on his responsibilities - namely that he should keep the Major under close scrutiny during Raymond's absence. Unconcerned, Kellor studied the passing terrain through the virtual reality windshield and began to look for a secluded place to set the aircraft down. A break in the trees signalled that it was time to land and the unblemished ground appeared deathly pallid in comparison to the green and white pine trees that surrounded the landing area. The snow curled rapidly upwards below the Cobra while it slowly swallowed up the space between its undercarriage and the white frosty ground. The aircraft touched down just before the troop carrier and the displaced snow gently floated back down to rejoin the displaced surface. Silence descended in the clearing as both aircraft engines whistled to a stop before Kellor's cockpit hatch hissed open. A large triangular section of the troop ship whined mechanically as it lowered to provide an exit ramp for the disembarking soldiers. The two craft were set at right angles to each other and it was at their intersection that the improvised unit assembled for the team briefing.

'Okay gentlemen, I'll be leading the advance party towards the target signal. Privates Wayne, Jackson and Willis will accompany me, while Sergeant Burr will lead the remainder of the unit. Sergeant, you and your team will follow at approximately two K's behind my unit. Your radio call sign will be "All Stars" and ours will be "Target One". Try to maintain radio silence at all times. Once I've located and eyeballed the target, we'll sit on it until you arrive and then re-evaluate the situation. Any questions?' Kellor said in a whisper, his voice muffled by the snow-laden trees and barely audible.

There were no questions from the assembled soldiers. Raymond watched discontentedly as Kellor and his team of three marched out of the landing area. The four men were consumed by the enveloping woods within moments. Raymond looked at his watch; it read 06:35. He began to calculate in his head that if the 'Target One' team marched at say fifteen kilometres per hour, then in eight minutes they would be the desired distance in front, as long as the Major could keep up. Raymond had also worked out that his team of MkIIs could cover the two K's in under four minutes without breaking into a sweat and he relaxed a little.

At 08:03, five airborne troop carriers and twelve fighter aircraft landed at a site eighty Kilometres east of where Kellor and his team had touched down. McGeady had chosen this area because it was well known for the large flat clearings that dotted the pine forests - and the sheer size of the unit moving in to cover the attack on the female base demanded a large landing site. McGeady was unsure of the exact movements of the Colonel's men, but he planned to surround the rebels and the signal source at a safe distance and wait for the action to start before moving in at the last moment for the kill. Recruiting far and wide from within the Eurostate, he had hired a hundred or so mercenaries to make up the expendable division. Controlling this motley crew of men would be a major accomplishment in itself - so McGeady had also ensured that he had five very experienced and extremely loathsome mercenaries to lead the five groups that were to encircle the target.

McGeady summoned the group leaders together and they huddled closely around a map of the general area. The five veteran mercenaries wore dissimilar clothing, although most of their attire was something resembling white. McGeady approached wearing official military arctic clothing and looked positively bureaucratic compared with the rogue's gallery in front of him. He felt intimidated by the assembled group of mindless killers but was determined to keep control of the operation at any cost.

'Gentlemen, I'd like to get one thing straight before we start. This is an unofficial operation as you all know, but I'll not stand for any insubordination from any member of this group. If you don't follow my orders your services will no longer be required and any due payment withheld,' McGeady said firmly, pausing only for the group of men around him to acknowledge the terms he had just set out.

The five men were aware that the real meaning of McGeady's euphemism was that the dissenting member would be executed. None were particularly concerned though; they all felt comfortable that if and when such an occasion arose, then they would be able to resist this ageing Government puppet without too many problems.

'Good lets move on quickly. You all have your signal trackers and we all need to work together to place a three hundred and sixty degree net around the signal source. Three teams will all march the twenty-five kilometres to this point, sixty-five kilometres south of the signal. Greg Tomas, Sasha Curic and Andre Turan will lead the three teams. Greg, your team will go to ground at this point and wait for the other teams to arrive at their springboard camps. Sasha you need to march to the west and Andre you to the east. Ensure that you maintain the agreed distance from the target, no more, no less. Or you may run into opposition earlier than we need you to. Sasha and Andre you're to go to ground at these points here and here respectively,' McGeady ordered, pointing at the map displayed on a military laptop.

'Any questions so far?' McGeady asked tentatively.

'How many women are there in this base?' asked Andre, thinking far ahead.

'I'll come to that in just a moment. If there are no questions about what I've just told you then I'd like to turn my attention to the other two teams. Okay?' McGeady said, brushing aside Andre's question.

'Ivan Dimansk and Patrick Guest are the remaining two team leaders and they'll fly out from here immediately after this briefing. They'll land at this location, one hundred and eighty kilometres directly north of here and they will then march the twenty-five kilometres to the split-up point, here. Ivan, you'll take up position and go to ground to the east here and Patrick you'll go to ground here, to the west. When, and only when, all teams are in position, will we begin as covertly as possible to close in on the signal source. Ivan and Patrick, you must ensure you don't over-fly the theatre of operations. The fighter pilots are aware of this but it's your responsibility to make sure that the order's followed to the letter.' McGeady paused again and waited for any questions before returning to the one raised by Andre.

'Andre, in answer your earlier question, we don't know exactly how many women reside in the commune, but that's of no real significance anyway. Our orders are to wipe out the male anti-government forces after they've taken the commune,'

'So how many men are we going to be up against and what support do they have?' asked Andre, frustrated by the lack of intelligence.

'Again that is unclear, but Mr Daniels assures me that they won't have anywhere near the level of back-up that we've been promised - if we need it of course. The situation's fluid and when the action begins we'll need to assess our requirements at that time,' continued McGeady vaguely.

'If that's the case, why are you staying here while we put our arses into the firing line?' asked Greg Tomas.

'Yeah, exactly. I've never met a trustworthy politician yet!' Ivan Dimansk added before McGeady could reply.

'Gentlemen, Gentlemen. I know we've not had any real time to get to know each other but I can assure you that I'm no politician and can be trusted completely. I will remain here to co-ordinate the operation. I'd like to remind you all that you're being paid a large sum of money to put your "arses in the firing line", as you so eloquently put it Mr. Tomas,' McGeady said firmly.

'Well, we know where to find you if you *can't* be trusted completely,' Patrick Guest interjected, polishing his murderous-looking hunting knife.

'I'm not going anywhere - if that's what you're suggesting,' replied McGeady calmly.

The group fell silent and it began to snow gently. From his tunic, McGeady took a wad of photos of Lock and the Colonel, before passing them around the gathered mercenaries.

'In these pictures are the two main players in the male anti-government force. It is a must that if you identify them at or around the signal source, you inform me. If you do nothing else, you must kill these two men. The good news is, there's a bonus for all if you bring me their heads! Hopefully this will offer a major incentive for you all to work together as a team and get the job done to our satisfaction,' McGeady paused once again, as the offer of a bonus had caused some deadly interest amongst the group.

'If there's nothing else; then I suggest we make a start,' he concluded.

McGeady turned hesitantly and walked back to the troop carrier that contained his command centre. As he walked, he nodded to the group of four fighter pilots who were to provide escort to the two troop carriers travelling north. The pilots were in their cockpits and firing into life their Cobra Mk10 engines before McGeady had made it to the troop carrier and snow began to swirl around him as he passed Beta. She had been seconded to Andre's team, much to Andre's disgust. Her team for the most part had shunned her, apart from one of the more mature mercenaries, Healy Nelson. Nelson had no hang-ups whatsoever about pitching in with a female, even if it was only the shell of one with a male constitution. McGeady watched patiently from the hull door as the three teams marched in a long line away from the makeshift landing site and the two troop carriers disappeared over the skyline, closely followed by the four Cobra fighters.

Just over five hours had passed before Raymond and his team had finally met up with Kellor two K's away from the signal source. They were undercover, high up on a ridge that looked down and across the two aerial kilometres from where the beacon was transmitting. The bike could be clearly seen using field glasses. It had been abandoned out in the open, on a flat area that overlooked the bottom of a valley where, a large but mainly calm river flowed. There were other vehicles parked around the vicinity of the bike, but all were of the four-wheeled type and Kellor seemed certain that they had arrived at their final destination. Crude buildings were set back inside a recess in the valley wall and Kellor could see a road that seemed to wind its way forever up the side of the valley and on to the outside world. Kellor assumed that there must be some underground element to the settlement laid out below, as there appeared to be only a limited amount of shelter on the surface. What he could not see was the cave blasted out from the valley wall. It was shrouded by a large natural stone canopy, which was draped in a thick layer of snow. The snow had drifted high up at the main entrance and concealed the small access hole being used as a doorway.

Kellor ascertained that the clever thing about the base was that it could not be seen from the air, or for that matter from Earth orbit, where most satellites could observe every detail on the *terra firma* with ease. The overhanging ridge made the base vulnerable to avalanches, but very secure against an all-out assault. Any attacking force had to come in from one way only and that was the front.

After a patient hour of surveillance, Kellor could clearly see the movement of various individuals scuttling around by the entrance. It was nearly 13:00 hours and the clouds deepened above them, causing the sunlight to become almost non-existent. In the dwindling light, Kellor could not make out whether the bodies moving around were male or female and he wondered how many more there were tucked up safely inside their shelter.

'Raymond, can you and two or three men get down there and get a closer look and see if you can find the entrance? There must be one,' Kellor asked as he started to feel the cold after the last hour of inactivity.

'Will it wait an hour? It should be really dark then. We can set off now and time it for optimum darkness cover.'

'I don't see why not. Pick your team and make your way down to that rock face to the left of the bike. The trees will also give you cover until you get there safely. Recon the area once again and when you are ready, flash me with your torch. Then you can abseil into the heart of the camp. We can give you cover from here if things get out of hand, okay?' Kellor said in a deadly serious manner bereft of the joviality of his earlier exchanges with Raymond.

'It'll take me at least an hour to get there Major. I'll have to trek back up the valley and go across that rope bridge we passed. Yes we'll have to abseil down the rock face, but I can do better than flash a torch at you. Keep Private Wayne close to you and I'll contact him when I want you to provide cover,' Raymond replied as he felt a knot of tension tie itself in his stomach.

'Can you communicate over that sort of distance?'

'Not with the entire group - some have a shorter telepathic range - but Wayne here has quite an exceptional reception range, especially for one so young.'

'Signal with a torch as well. It's essential we get a fix on your position if we do have to cover you, I don't want any blue on blue fuck ups!'

Kellor thought that maybe Raymond just wanted John to keep a close eye on his actions while he was not around to monitor the situation. But he decided to give him the benefit of the doubt and in next to no time the advance scouting party had left the rear observation point without fanfare or ceremony.

The three men silently marched to the top of the ridge but remained in constant touch with each other. The crunch of the snow beneath their feet was the only indicator of their presence, since ordinary livestock could not see in the absolute darkness among the pine trees. The MkII unit had passed the rope bridge earlier on in the day, around two kilometres back, and Raymond was convinced that it would be the easiest way to negotiate their passage across to the opposite side of the valley. There were a handful of boats bobbing down at the edge of the river, but they were all moored beyond reach on the far side. Raymond thought that maybe they could use them later to bring the rest of the unit across, depending on the outcome of their reconnaissance.

Raymond and his two subordinates approached the foot-bridge from high up on the ridge and they could see now that the crossing entrance, unlike before, was guarded. Even without night vision goggles, Raymond and his men could clearly make out the heavily clothed body of the standing guard, although they struggled to define its gender. Raymond spoke hurriedly and without a sound to his men, sending one to the left and the other to the right of the bridge entrance. After ten minutes of painfully slow progress, the three MkIIs were in place, surrounding the unsuspecting guard in a half-circle trap with his rear hemmed in by the vast drop of the valley elevation. Raymond had crawled most of the way down towards the guard on his belly and even with his heated inner suit he had begun to feel the bite of cold from the icy ground.

'Wait, knives only. No pistols, understood? Over,' Raymond's orders instantaneously resounded within the two soldiers' minds.

Privates Eastwood and Reeves holstered their laser pistols instantly and removed from their sheaths the hunting knives with which they had been issued. The guard stood smoking, blissfully unaware that fifty metres in either direction, forward from the bridge entrance, loomed certain death.

'Private Eastwood, approach the guard now - don't try and hide yourself. Private Reeves, approach the guard from his rear and take him down. I'll cover you both from here, over.'

The two soldiers silently acknowledged the message and Raymond watched the order that he had just given unfold in real time. Eastwood stood up and strolled towards the guard, while Reeves waited for the lone sentinel to turn towards the planned distraction. As soon as Eastwood had gained the guard's undivided attention, Reeves began, as quietly as possible, to close the gap between them.

'Who's out there?' shouted the guard, squinting into the darkness, desperately trying to pick out the undefined threat with a small and rather dim torch.

Private Eastwood could now tell that this was definitely a male that they were dealing with and responded appropriately after hurried advice from his Sergeant.

'I'm lost. I was told that a man could find sanctuary around here?'

The torch beam eventually blundered across it's much sought after target. But it barely managed to illuminate the soldier as he moved ever nearer. The guard began to speak, but was instantaneously cut short as Private Reeves wiped the blade of his knife across the victim's throat. Not satisfied with his first effort to disable the guard, he then plunged the knife up to the hilt in his victim's back. The body dropped to the ground as Raymond hurriedly approached from his vantage point and although the three of them were now standing next to each other, still no audible words were exchanged. Raymond ordered Eastwood to bury the body, while Reeves began to cross the bridge to establish whether another unfortunate guard waited at the other end, as they thought there would be.

Reeves slid over the side of the precarious rope bridge and swung himself to the lowest part. He held only the single base rope of the bridge, the one that people crossing used to step on as they traversed the vast drop below. Private Reeves did not look down; he focused only on reaching the other side of the valley in one piece. Raymond had taken his equipment before he'd set out and all that remained on Reeves' person was his pistol and knife as he began to swing arm to arm along the base rope. The wind flooded up the valley and caused the bridge to swing wildly just as Reeves almost casually made it to the middle. The concealed guard on the other side of the expanse became aware of sudden oscillation of the previously semi-static ropes and moved out of his hide to take a closer look. He struggled to scan the length of the bridge but could only see around twenty feet of it before its image trailed into the black mist of darkness. Abruptly, a blast of wind caught him by surprise as he wandered further from his meagre shelter and this seemed to satisfy his suspicions that the sporadic gusts were the cause of the bridge's swinging. Raymond saw the movement from the far side and raised the laser rifle's sight to his eye. The change in magnification caused him to lose track of the heavily clothed figure for a split second. Just as he regained the desired vision and homed in for the killer shot, the figure disappeared from sight.

'Shit!' Raymond cursed quietly.

Private Reeves clearly heard the whispered profanity and began to look around frantically for any impending threat.

'Sir, what's up?' Reeves asked, swinging precariously by one hand. The strength to hold on was not a problem for the MkII, although the grip through the thick arctic gloves was a cause for concern.

'Sorry, false alarm. There's a guard on the other side but I missed the chance to take him out. He's up on the right hand side of the bridge exit, sheltering in some sort of camouflaged hide,' Raymond replied, intently scanning the far side of the valley with his electronic binoculars.

'Okay Sir, I'll tell you when it's all clear,' he said, swinging his free arm dynamically and regaining his forward momentum.

Within five minutes, Reeves had reached the far side and he was extremely relieved to be able to stand on a rocky ledge under last metre or so of bridge. He swung his lower body forward and placed both feet firmly on the rocks in front of him. Then he walked his hands up the rope and regained his vertical posture before crouching down for a time to replenish his breathless lungs.

Forty-five minutes had now passed and Kellor was growing impatient. He had been watching John almost non-stop for the last fifteen minutes, waiting for some indication that Raymond was in touch with him. John, for his part, was curled up underneath a tree and trying to rest. He had heard a few stray thoughts, but nothing that had been directed at him personally. As he lay there, John could feel Kellor's gaze scrutinize him and every so often he opened his eyes and shook his head, just to confirm that he had received no contact from the Sergeant. The remnants of the MkII unit that had stayed behind at the rear observation point were busy, eating, sleeping or playing a mental game of cards. The object of the game was to read the other player's mind and see what cards he was holding mentally. This completely confused Kellor, as he watched four MkIIs sitting in a circle with no more than a pious grin on their faces. Kellor, exasperated, finally looked back at John who by now, annoyingly, was fast asleep.

Reeves had slid over the cold rocks, silently edging his way towards the camouflaged hide in which the guard was trying to keep warm. After his exertions from crossing the valley he was perspiring liberally and he could feel the cool sweat escape from his brow to run icily down his neck. On closer inspection, the camouflaged hide was nothing more than a modified packing crate that had been smothered in leaves and snow. Reeves lay next to the hide and watched the dull flicker of a candle or oil lamp burning from inside the guard's lair.

'What's happening Private Reeves? I can't see you anymore?' Raymond enquired.

'Sir, I'm nearly done.'

Reeves was now convinced that there was one only guard. He stood up noisily and waited. The guard heard the noise from outside the shelter and dragged himself back to his feet assuming it was another false alarm. Pulling to one side a wooden panel that served as an improvised door, the guard poked his head outside, just enough to crane his head in the direction of the sound that he had heard. Reeves had removed his gloves to obtain a better grip and gratefully seized the cloth-covered head that had just thrust out of the doorway. He had trouble locating the jaw with his right hand but clamped the head as tightly as he could and span it sideways through a generous ninety degrees till it clicked like a ratchet and death rattled in its throat. The body fell from the entrance at his feet, taking with it the sheet of wood that doubled as the hide doorway. Bending down, Reeves grabbed the dead guard's arm and then effortlessly swung it over his shoulder like a rag doll before hurling it in the general direction of the precipice. The body tumbled down into the valley, end over end as Reeves contacted his comrades to give them the all-clear. He watched while the guard's dead limbs took on a rubberised life of their own, as the deceased body ricocheted off the many snow covered rocks it encountered and then finally came to rest in the spiny arms of one of the pine trees that dotted the lower slopes.

John stirred from his imperceptible slumber, tugged off his winter hood and began to knead the cropped blond hair on his head. He stretched and yawned in one frantic action and Kellor watched eagerly for the sign of any news.

'Major, Sergeant Burr has just advised me that they're all on the far side of the valley and are now making ready to abseil down the agreed rock face to the left of the bike. He'd like the men to provide cover for him and his team in around five-minutes,' John said, still lying in his shallow trench.

'John, pass the order around to make ready for covering fire. Ensure they all understand that they fire only on my order and no other,' Kellor ordered.

John fell silent and the surrounding MkIIs began to spread out around the observation point. They found what little shelter there was to be had from the freezing wind and began to get themselves set for the potential action. Within a minute or so peace and quiet was restored once again as their collective firepower was now trained down towards the calm settlement on the other side of the valley. Kellor checked around with one last glance and then crawled stiffly over next to John.

'Tell the Sergeant we're ready if he is; just make sure he flashes the torch to give us a fix on his location,' Kellor said anxiously.

John paused and then replied, 'Sergeant Burr says they are on the way down now. There they are. They have IR beacons attached to their lapels.'

'I take it there won't be any torch then. Where's my NVG's? I don't have the luxury of your eyes Private Wayne,'

Kellor peered at his watch. It was 14:35 - later than they had planned, but not a problem, he surmised. Kellor hated this part of the Eurostate, especially at this time of the year. It was very cold and extremely dark almost all of the time; save for a few hours in the late morning and very early afternoon. Looking up, he began to feel somewhat inferior to the other men in the squad, as he was the only one whose physical limitations forced him to wear night vision goggles, which enabled him to see the settlement clearly and track the IR markers. The MkIIs were not entirely super-human though - they did use night scopes on their laser rifles, more as a luxury than a necessity he thought. Kellor watched the rock face intently and soon made out the three men emerging reluctantly from the tree line above the target bike. Their abseil lines were held in bags, slung beneath them so as not give the game away with trailing ropes. The three white-clad men bounced with impressive agility away from the rock face and eased themselves to the comparative safety of the ground.

Detaching themselves from their abseil ropes the instant their boots sank into the mud-streaked snow, they took immediate shelter behind one of the many four-wheeled vehicles nearby. The camp looked completely desolate as Raymond checked for fresh footprints in the thicker crisp snow outside the vehicle cordon. From this vantage point they could now see under the stone canopy, where the tiny entrance was now clearly visible. Inching their way forward, the three soldiers fanned out; pistols at the ready. The improvised buildings carved into the side of the rock face were completely vacant. Privates Eastwood and Reeves worked their way painstakingly through the first before deciding to skirt around the remaining dwellings. Cowering within fifty metres of the cave exit, Raymond examined the abandoned bike. It was definitely the one that they were looking for. But where was the target woman? And the two guards that they had previously encountered - why were they both men? Undecided, he turned his frayed attention to attaching a set of pulley wheels to the large troop carrier truck parked next to the bike. Raymond had decided this was as good a time as any to bring the rest of the unit down to the settlement by means of a transverse wire fired from the observation point, to which they would attach the pulleys now fitted onto the truck.

Raymond rejoined Privates Eastwood and Reeves by the entrance to the main cave dwelling that had been blasted out of the rock face. There was obviously a guard on the inside but the inhabitants had no cause to expect trouble. They had been isolated in the contaminated landscape for as long as they could remember and an attack was the last thing for which they were prepared.

Private Reeves slid inside the cave opening and the guard stood to face him. Unlike the others, he had no facial hood and Reeves was visibly shaken at the Orger's gruesome appearance. Reeves was momentarily paralysed by a mixture of horror and pity at the grotesque vision before him - and before he had a chance to snap out of it, the mutant raised his laser pistol. Close enough to catch the Orger's wrist with his left hand, Reeves slammed his right palm into the noseless face. The mutant involuntarily fired the pistol and shrieked out in pain as the fleshless nasal bone shattered under the weight of the blow. Realising that things were not going to plan, Raymond and Eastwood came scurrying through the entrance, only to find Private Reeves finishing off the guard with his knife. Raymond shot a telepathic rebuke at his subordinate for having failed to deal with the guard silently and the Private began to apologise vocally.

'Sorry Sir, but his appearance took me by surprise...'

'Shut up. We've no time for this. You, follow me now. We'll hold them until Private Eastwood can get the line set up to bring the others down. Eastwood, get outside and attach the cable to the pulley system on the truck. I'll get Private Wayne to fire the cable down now,' Raymond's orders rang out inside his two fledgling soldiers' heads.

Raymond was aware that the element of surprise might have passed and it was now or never if they were going to bring the rest of the unit down while the immediate area was still quiet. The spot where the guard had been sitting looked as if it might have been a naturally occurring cave, whereas the three shafts that led from it looked distinctly man-made. Raymond looked down towards the grey stone cave floor and spoke to Private Wayne back at the rear observation point. Meanwhile, Eastwood was already outside and waiting for the cable to be fired down from high up on the opposite side of the valley.

The fiery tracer arced across the black gulf between the observation point and the area where the truck sat silently. Private Eastwood waited patiently as the cables' spearhead seemed to take an age to find its way down to the ground in front of him. Finally, earth and snow exploded into the air as the aerodynamic cable end thumped into the soft ground like a mortar shell. The propellant had long since burned out but the metal around its head was still extremely hot - as Eastwood found out the hard way. He immediately dropped the burning hot cable and gave a low whimper of pain as he studied his right palm. Painfully he put his gloves back on and began to shovel snow over the hot part of the cable. He did not wait a second longer than he had to before retrieving the now-cooled cable head and hastening to the pulley system attached to the truck. As Eastwood began to attach the metal cable, his hand began to throb in earnest and the sound of gunfire erupted from within the cave.

Inside the cave, Sergeant Burr and Private Reeves sank beneath what cover they could find, just in front of the spot where the guard had been taken down, anticipating an onslaught of Orgers arriving to see exactly what all the noise had been about. A solitary torch on the wall burned dimly and was soon extinguished when Raymond quickly threw it from the cave wall into the slush at the entrance. Now shrouded in darkness, the chamber was just the cover they needed. Apprehensively though, they watched the openings to the three tunnels that snaked away through the solid rock away. It was the sudden warm glow that radiated from two of the tunnels that alerted them of the impending arrival of more of the cave's inhabitants. The first target ran haphazardly into the cavern area. The flaming torch he held aloft hardly penetrated the all-pervading gloom before the brilliance of the laser bolt burst from Raymond's rifle.

The flare that exploded into the night sky gave Kellor the sign that he was waiting for. Immediately he began sending the MkIIs rapidly down the high tensile metal alloy cable strung between the observation point and the enemy camp below. One man at a time sailed down the half-mile of wire, just to keep the chances of it breaking to a minimum. Towards the end of the crossing, each soldier accelerated to a terrifying and deadly speed, but as the ground hurtled up to meet or break them, they skilfully applied the brake mechanism to slow down enough to hit the ground in one piece. Private Eastwood waited anxiously below to catch and steady the men as they ground to a dizzying halt ten feet above him and then dropped to the earth. Kellor was the last to feel the adrenaline rush of racing across the valley held up only by his wrists. By the time he stopped at the bottom, he was struggling to regain the breath that he had lost halfway down the rapid descent. Kellor looked up at Eastwood and he sprawled in the snow.

'Jeeessuss, that's some kinda buzz!' Kellor exclaimed breathlessly.

'Where's the action at soldier?' he continued, unable to put a name to one of the many virtually identical faces in the unit.

'Over inside the entrance hole there,' Eastwood said, pointing into the featureless darkness that enveloped them as if there were anything to see.

Kellor could not see any hole, let alone the fact that the soldier was pointing directly at it. There was no moon for him to see by and again he felt inferior to these new recruits.

'Take me to your leader,' Kellor said, joking edgily as more gunfire bellowed from the cave exit.

'Excuse me Sir, but you are our leader,' he replied, clearly not getting the joke and thus underlining his alien nature.

'Forget it soldier. Just get me to Sergeant Burr's location,' he ordered, putting on his night vision goggles once again in desperation.

'Follow me Sir,' Eastwood replied briskly.

As they entered the cave, another salvo erupted ahead of them. The entrance area was now empty, Raymond having decided to go on the offensive once they had sufficient numbers on the ground.

'Choice of three Sir?' Private Eastwood said, referring to the tunnels in front of them.

Gunfire crackled and flared from one of the tunnels and Kellor smiled from behind his NVG's as the laser bolt's audible crack followed after a short delay.

'I think we'll take this one soldier - sounds like a party going on at the end of it,' Kellor replied as he led the way down the left-hand shaft.

Both men had their rifles slung over their backs and were brandishing pistols in front of them as they went. In the face of the obvious danger ahead, they stole down the tunnel with the utmost caution. Occasionally, they stopped to check and clear the small cell-like rooms that lay off the main passageway that they were negotiating. The dead bodies littering their path told their own story: Raymond and his men were evidently systematically cleansing the dwelling of all of its inhabitants, regardless of whether or not they were women. The boom of rifle fire resounded around the solid stone walls, now closer than ever. Kellor and Eastwood entered a cavernous chamber at the end of the tunnel that they had taken. It seemed at first glance to Kellor that all the tunnels issuing from the main entrance cave converged in this massive cathedral-like atrium. Yet above and ahead, there were still more convoluted passageways leading away from the echoing subterranean dome. Nonetheless, this was where the enemy had make their stand, maximising their height advantage and raining shots down on the unit of MkIIs who had so ruthlessly fought so far only to find themselves faced with this impasse. Kellor could see a stairwell, carved into the rocky basin where the unit were now corralled and he could also make out a walkway that ran completely around the upper tier of the cool dark atrium. The walkway was about twenty metres above their heads and the Orgers ringed almost the entire ledge, surrounding the pinned-down soldiers. Kellor looked around frenetically for the Sergeant, finally spotting him huddled behind a huge stalagmite with two other soldiers, one of whom looked distinctly dead.

'Private, lay down some covering fire. I need to get across to Sergeant Burr,' ordered Kellor, wiping the sweat from his brow.

'No need Major. I can speak to him from here Sir,' Private Jackson shouted as multiple rounds were exchanged back and forth across the no man's land between the fighting parties.

'No. I'm afraid that's not good enough. This time I need to look him in the eyes. So, on the count of three start firing,' replied Kellor, tiring of all the telepathic conversations.

'One, two, THREE!!!!' exclaimed Kellor as he bolted across the deadly space towards Raymond.

Unfortunately, what little light there was lit up the white arctic suits of the Major and his men like flares. They could not have given the enemy a better set of targets if they'd tried. As the enemy took advantage of this gift and volley after volley of lead and laser rain fell, Kellor dived the last few feet for the sanctuary of Raymond's stalagmite. A melée of conventional bullets and laser bolts sliced past his tumbling body before Kellor hit the ground with an unyielding thud at Raymond's feet and he saw the face of a dead soldier looking down at him.

'Raymond where the fuck are you?' Kellor shouted.

'I'm behind you Major,' he said and powerfully lifted him into a sitting position.

Kellor sat with his back to the rock formation, which was giving them the protection that they so desperately needed. He removed his night vision goggles and looked Raymond up and down for signs of injury.

'You okay?' Kellor inquired, concerned.

'Not a scratch until you arrived, but we're two men down. They were waiting for us up there when we came in. We can't get the angle of fire to hurt them, or even pin them down for that matter. Any suggestions Major?' replied Raymond briskly.

'Flares - you got any on you?' asked Kellor confidently.

'No; but he has next to you,' Raymond replied and began to rifle through the dead soldier's equipment.

Raymond liberated the flares from the dead soldier and a silence fell temporarily in the cavern, broken only by the echoing of their laboured breathing. Quickly, Kellor grabbed the flares and prepared to fire one.

'Tell the men to keep well down until this flare burns itself out. We don't need any more casualties,' Kellor ordered as he raised the flare above his head ready to fire.

In the soiled damp basin area, the MkII soldiers began to take extra cover. When Raymond gave the nod, Kellor pulled the firing cord on the flare. The green light swamped the cavern. It took only a fraction of a second for the flare to smash into the ceiling and then plummet back down to the ground, where still its restricted illumination exposed the stalactite-covered ceiling.

'Sergeant, get your men ready to storm the stairs when I give the word,' Kellor said, with renewed enthusiasm.

'Sir, if you'll excuse me for saying so, you've lost your mind. If they get to the first step they'll be lucky,' Raymond said dismissively.

'Trust me Sergeant. Follow my lead and concentrate your fire at the roof in the general area that I fire at and then, when I think it's safe to do so, I'll give you the signal for the men to advance. If they're as quick as you say they are there'll be no problems and we'll be out in time for tea!'

Kellor turned to face the walkway, where the enemy were continuing to rain gunfire down onto the MkII unit. Without further deliberation, he began to rapidly fire into the ceiling just after the flare finally expired and Raymond almost instantaneously joined him in the continuous and seemingly pointless assault on the roof. The response from the enemy, below the area of the roof where the laser bolts were impacting was immediate. The large stalactites that had been attached to the ceiling for thousand of years began to fall gracefully like giant arrows raining death upon their helpless victims below. Kellor waited for the panic to grow in the enemy, to an extent where he reasoned that it was safe for his men to mount an attack on the walkway.

'Sergeant, tell them to get moving up those fucking stairs, NOW!' Kellor shouted at the top of his voice in an effort to be heard above the cacophony of laser fire and crashing of stone on stone.

Raymond continued to fire while he ordered the previously trapped MkII soldiers forward and up the stone staircase. As the first beleaguered soldier reached the top of the stairs, the firing ceased into the now black and charred ceiling. The advancing troops began to pick off the fleeing enemy ruthlessly. With the way now clear ahead of them, Kellor and Raymond followed the MkIIs up the stairs and down one of the four tunnels that led away from the Cathedral cavern, deeper into the mountainside. This time though, there was no secure fall-back position for the enemy. Kellor and his men methodically worked their way through the remaining areas of uncovered tunnel and hollows. As the time passed, the sporadic gunfire became less frequent. Within two hours, the MkII unit had killed all but a handful of the inhabitants and those who were not dead were being held prisoner in the now artificially illuminated cathedral cavern. Raymond was the last to return to where the prisoners were being held and with him he dragged a forlorn-looking Corporal McDowell.

'Look what I've found Major?' Raymond said to the Major who had his back to him.

While inspecting the five prisoners that they had captured Kellor turned to see McDowell with her arms restrained behind her back.

'I don't think there's any need for the handcuffs Sergeant. I'm sure we have her safely outnumbered,' Kellor said, looking McDowell up and down.

'Not my doing Major. The female was bound and gagged when we found her. I took off the gag and just brought back here.'

'Well remove them anyway. I need to have a serious conversation with this woman. It seems quite obvious that she's not a paying guest here and unless we find out where home is for her, we might as well go now and report that we have failed in our mission,' Kellor said, standing dominantly over the weary Femorist.

McDowell did not recognise him from the drug store fracas. Kellor, on the other hand, knew exactly whom he had in front of him and without warning sadistically butted McDowell, causing her to collapse in a heap on the floor.

'I bet you don't remember me my love, do you?' Kellor asked with a wicked chauvinistic leer unseen since the days before the gender war began in earnest.

He walked swiftly forward and stood once again within striking distance of McDowell.

'One scumbag looks the same as another to me. Those men over there have had their features disfigured by radiation; what's your excuse for being so fucking ugly?' she said, scrambling to her knees with difficulty as her hands were still bound, despite Raymond's recent orders.

McDowell spotted Kellor's boot heading towards her unprotected head and at the last possible moment she managed to swivel on her knees so the vicious kick made agonising contact with her right shoulder rather than her fragile face. McDowell rolled with the blow, avoiding most of its force and she lay there, face down, waiting for the next assault.

Raymond seized the short lull in the attack and began to speak, 'Major do you still want me to cut her hands free?'

'Maybe not… Leave her bound for a moment, at least until she tells us where her base is located.'

Suddenly a breathless Private Wayne entered the cavern after evaluating the external defences and placing four guards around the entrance area.

'What's it like top side Private Wayne?' asked Kellor without taking his eyes from McDowell.

'Blizzard conditions, Sir, and pitch black too. I doubt anything will be on the move until it subsides and the morning arrives, whichever is last,' he replied deferentially.

'Okay, we'll make camp here tonight. Eastwood, secure those prisoners and keep two guards on them round the clock. Sergeant I want you and him?' Kellor began to order and then waited for Raymond to supply him with the soldier's name.

'His name is Private Hood Sir,' Raymond replied dutifully.

'Okay you and Hood follow me - bring the woman with you. I think we should find a nice quiet room somewhere so I can resume my interrogation,' he continued with an air of anticipation, like a man about to wreak revenge for McDowell's earlier performance at the drug store.

Kellor looked around the cavern trying to decide which tunnel to take. In the end, he chose the one nearest to him, one of the three that led towards the valley outside. The first few hollows they came to had obviously been used as sleeping accommodation and were too small for the four of them to comfortably fit into. Finally, the fourth hollow provided just enough room and, by the time Private Hood had ejected the former resident's belongings, it had become positively spacious.

McDowell had originally been no more concerned at being held by what she assumed were government soldiers than by the mutant Orgers who had ambushed her so near the safety of the decoy commune. Now though, she was becoming deeply worried by Kellor's cold intent, by the horror of whatever he was going to do to her before she gave him the information he wanted or died in the process. The long cold walk back to the hastily arranged interrogation room was completed in utter darkness. Kellor wore his NVG's, though of course Raymond and Private Hood could see perfectly well without them. Kellor wanted it that way, just so that McDowell could not see the environment in which she was going to be interrogated. If she could not see, then that would feed her neurosis. Her paranoia would build, not knowing who or what was going on around her and this time Kellor wanted to succeed where he had failed before with Langton.

'Corporal McDowell isn't it?' asked Kellor from behind her.

Standing in the middle of the room, McDowell flinched as Kellor spoke into her ear. She knew he was close, she could feel the warm damp breath on her ear and she turned pathetically away from the voice. Kellor followed the movement of her head and manoeuvred himself around the room to face her directly.

'I hope you put up a little bit more of an effort to resist me than your bitch of a senior officer. She rolled over as soon as I started to get serious,' Kellor continued.

McDowell raised her head tentatively, like a rodent sniffing the air for food, and searched the darkness for any scrap of an image to which she could cling. Days spent tied up in the cold moist air had made her clothes damp to the bone. She had been captured two days earlier and been held prisoner without food or water. McDowell did not know what the Orgers had planned for her but that would probably have been a walk in the park compared to what Kellor had in store for her...

'Sergeant remove her clothes. See how she likes that for starters and Private Hood can you get me some snow or ice,' Kellor said, walking over to the bunk, the only thing that Hood had not thrown out earlier. Kellor lay down while Raymond pushed McDowell hard up against one of the cell's slimy walls.

'Don't move while I do this. It wouldn't take much to turn this knife on you,' Raymond said as he skilfully set about slicing her clothes away from her lithe white female body.

Eventually, McDowell stood there in nothing more than her thermal socks. The Orgers had already taken her boots and the pile of sliced clothing now lay useless at her feet. Her nipples had become erect at the sudden drop in her body temperature and Kellor stood up again. He moved in closer to the female frame and then pushed McDowell's head almost gently against the rock wall to the front of her. He then began to kick violently at her shins, so that they were forced in the opposite direction to her head. Finally, he ceased kicking once McDowell had no other option than to use her head and neck to stop herself from falling to the floor.

'Comfortable?' Kellor asked sadistically.

McDowell failed to answer as panic stifled her responses. Instead she began to cough just as Private Hood returned with a plastic container full of ice and snow.

'Ahh! The refreshments are here Corporal McDowell. Ready for some?' Kellor said taking the container from Hood and placing it on the floor directly behind her.

Kellor removed his Gore-Tex gloves and tucked them safely inside his tunic pocket, before scooping up with two hands some of the slushy ice and snow.

'I only want to know one thing Corporal. So it shouldn't take us long before we part company; with you still alive I hope. Now, if you would, tell where your base is. Then we can get some nice warm clothes on you,' he said, still holding the freezing cocktail in his hands.

'Base? What fucking base? I don't know what you're talking about. You... Arrrggghhhhh!' she screamed out before she could finish her sentence as Kellor slopped the contents of his hands onto her bare shoulders.

If McDowell thought she had been cold before her slushy snow rub down, she was wrong. She felt at this moment that ice had seeped into every pore in her desolate skin. Her teeth began to hammer rapidly together in Morse code style and her every muscle seemed to shiver and spasm with a life of its own.

'Enjoy that did you? I thought I'd stop you before you gave me any more of your bullshit. Now you only have two or three more lies before I stop the snow treatment and move on to some more serious interrogation techniques. So; let's put it another way. Where's the Femorist headquarters that you come from? The place you were probably heading to before this lot of ugly scum captured you,' Kellor said, striving to warm his fingers by blowing vigorously into them.

'I have been with this lot of scum as you call them for many years. This is my home and the only reason that my fellow scum have me bound is that I got caught stealing,' McDowell replied unconvincingly. She had offered the first thing that she could think of to delay the interrogation, but realised that it would not stop the inevitable.

'Nice story Corporal, but I know for a fact that it's not true. So I'll just have to get my hands cold again,' Kellor said and scooped up another two handfuls of freezing cold snow and ice.

She did not scream this time. Instead she gave a sharp intake of breath, her back arched, her numb face skidded down the rock wall and she fell hopelessly to her knees. As she knelt, sucking in her stertorous breath and shivering uncontrollably, Kellor bellowed at the top of his voice.

'What the fucking hell do you think you are doing Corporal? Get to your feet now! We've only just fucking started!'

Kellor continued to shout as he dragged McDowell painfully back to her feet by the bound wrists that hung limply behind her. Kellor pushed her head back against the rock wall and again kicked viciously with his combat boots at her delicate shins, this time drawing gobs of blood.

'If you fall over again I won't be so delicate with you. Answer my question now. Where is the Femorist base from which you come?'

This time Kellor did not wait for an answer before he picked up the container and emptied the contents over McDowell's head and he spoke without waiting for any response.

'That's it; your easy ride is over. Now for some serious stuff.'

'You bastard! You didn't give me time to answer your question,' McDowell said marshalling what diminishing composure she had left.

As brazen and hard talking as she was, McDowell had never been conditioned to cope with even the mildest forms of torture and she was unsure if she could last the distance.

'Excuse me Corporal, but being a bastard is one thing you cannot accuse me of,' Kellor said as he hit McDowell with a single punch to one of her kidneys.

McDowell buckled but did not fall to the ground. By now, her head and neck were throbbing painfully as she used all her strength trying to stay vertical.

'Not bad. I thought you'd have gone down with that last punch. Your boss couldn't take it - she squealed like a bitch before she died. Mind you though, Langton saw it coming. We sorted her out in the basement of the drug store;

that was after you decided to leave the party early of course. Unfortunately, you won't have that luxury this time around,' he continued.

Talking slowly and deliberately as he walked up and down behind McDowell, she began to fear the next assault. Inexplicably all activity ceased suddenly.

The fear welled up as they stood silently for what seemed an eternity. The minutes felt like hours as they dragged agonisingly, until finally she began to shake violently with muscle spasms and collapsed in a writhing heap on the floor. McDowell quickly curled up into a ball in preparation for the next physical onslaught from her interrogators but it did not materialise. Again the minutes ticked by and McDowell began to wonder if there was anybody still left in the room with her. She raised her head to look around but could see nothing. Then, as McDowell tried to sit up, she heard the rustle of clothing before she felt the clenched fist strike her mouth. She yelped in pain as the healing gash inside her mouth tore open again and blood spurted from her thin and drawn lips. The room fell silent almost instantly and her mind raced with visions of what was being done above her in the pitch-black room. Before long, she began to sob, quietly at first, but then almost violently and Kellor seized his chance. Picking her up gently, as if he were about to carry her across the threshold, he sat her down safely on the bunk.

'I'm sorry I don't mean to be so nasty. You see I have to obtain answers for my superiors and if I don't find out what they want to know it'll be me for the chop. You understand don't you?' Kellor said softly, as he sat next to her on the bunk.

'I can't tell you... I can't!' McDowell said between sobs and Kellor placed his arm around her, almost as if they were at the cinema on a date.

'Shame. I don't want to lose my temper again but you give me little choice Rachel. You see I don't work for the government anymore, unlike the first time that we met. I work for men that are utterly callous. Mean bastards all of them and as such, I can do anything I want and I don't have to answer to some over-inflated government official. So let's have no more of "I can't" and "I won't". Let's get this over with before I have to hurt you seriously,' Kellor stood as he finished his final sentence and looked down upon the naked woman sitting crumpled below him.

'You're gonna kill me anyway... aren't you... Whatever I do,' McDowell stuttered and she began to summon new courage from the pain-free numbness of her stripped and freezing body.

'Have you ever had sexual intercourse Corporal?' Kellor asked curiously.

'No I have not. You know we are all biologically pro-grammed to detest physical intimacy of any kind - and besides who's gonna screw me? I never seem to meet the right men these days,' she replied, pleased with herself at finding the strength to answer with a defiant sarcastic gesture, futile as it was.

'If you ask Sergeant Burr over there...Oh I'm sorry, you can't see him can you. Well be assured he's very close. Anyway, if you ask the Sergeant nicely, I think he'll be able to find someone to "screw" you. Perhaps one of those good-looking Orger types would do the honours and be your first?'

'You've got no chance. You men haven't had a proper erection in three hundred years! Are you gonna pluck one out of thin air big boy?'

'You've heard of "Orgasma" surely. Even in your bitches' nest they must have known about it. Gives a man the tools he needs for just such an occasion; even if he's not sure exactly to do with them - or it, to be more precise.'

Kellor knew the rudiments of sex, but had never used it as an interrogation method. This was mainly because he had never had the right equipment to start with and those above him would have frowned upon use of 'Orgasma', especially to perpetrate such a repulsive deed. In fact, he was unsure if he could carry out such a procedure without feeling remorse. This girl was well out of her league and in a desperate position and after his experiences with Beta his animosity towards women had subliminally softened.

'Sergeant, pick the Corporal here a couple of handsome men from the prisoners. Private Hood, obtain some 'Orgasma' from their personal stash, if you would. They must have some around here. We'll all meet back here in ten minutes. It will give the Corporal a chance to reflect and evaluate her situation.' Kellor finished speaking and nodded at his subordinates. The two men immediately set off for the Cathedral cavern and Kellor sat back down next to McDowell.

'Why don't you just tell me the location now, while we're on our own. Then I can find you something nice and warm to wear. You can sit the rest out - they'll never know it was you who gave us the precise location.'

While waiting for a reply, Kellor walked over to the kerosene lamp in the corner of the room and lit it. McDowell was surprised as the grip of darkness receded into the rock walls. She glanced around the room and saw Kellor removing his NVG's.

'Thought you might like some light so you can look your partner in the eye?' Kellor said, tired of waiting for a response.

'What's your problem? Why couldn't you leave us alone? You bloody men ran the show but you still had to take it that bit further. Was it too much to expect to be satisfied with making us cook and clean for you arseholes? No even that was unacceptable; you had to wipe us out completely.' McDowell said, staring Kellor directly in the eye. To her surprise, he averted his eyes from her abject face, as her hollow gaze stoked his smouldering sense of empathy.

'This isn't about us, you and me. Personally, I couldn't give a damn about you and your comrades existing somewhere outside of civilised society. But you entered our world and attacked everything we hold sacred. That's why society couldn't go on with the divisiveness of heterosexual relationships - they caused more pain and suffering than this phoney war ever did.'

Kellor knew she had got to him and that though he should not be answering her questions, he felt compelled to try to justify the ever-dwindling morality of the Eurostate.

'That a standard answer, or did you think of it all by yourself?' McDowell quipped.

'You don't understand. We don't do this because we like it. We do it because we...' Kellor stopped mid-sentence, losing the will to defend his position, one in which he seemed completely lost lately.

After a moment searching for his thoughts Kellor continued, 'It doesn't mean anything anyway. I can't change it so I'll just have to make it work for me. Just like you would if you were in my position,' he said unconvincingly.

'Fuck you too!' McDowell replied bluntly.

As he was about to reply, Raymond and two prisoners entered the room, closely followed by Private Hood, putting an end to the morality conversation. Raymond sensed the Major's loss of appetite for what he had started earlier and he stood silently, absorbing Kellor's every twitch and mannerism.

'Private, do you have the 'Orgasma'?' Kellor asked, feeling his Sergeant scrutinizing every move he made.

'Yes Sir. Do you want me to administer the first dose now?'

'Pick one and give him the first dose. Get him started on the prisoner and then give the other Orger his fix. Rotate them as the need arises...'

The room fell silent and Private Hood carried out his orders with Raymond's assistance before they began the short wait for the 'Orgasma' to take effect on the first male prisoner.

In due course, Kellor observed the Orger beginning to exhibit the first stages of the drug-induced high and, breaking the extended period of quiet, he whispered to Raymond, 'Take over here Sergeant. You know what to do. Come and find me when you have the location - or when the Orgasma runs out. Whichever is first,'

Unable to make out any of the words being whispered McDowell continued to stare directly at the soldiers. Raymond returned her glacial gaze, unimpressed by her futile display of defiance.

'Where are you going to be Sir? If you don't mind me asking...'

'I'm going to report to the Colonel, from the cavern. Private Wayne has the microwave radio transmitter. Where he is, I'll be - okay?' Kellor said, annoyed at the intrusion and all the time wondering if Raymond was quietly picking up his thoughts and feelings.

McDowell felt the room grow darker after Kellor's departure, though the lamp was burning brighter than ever before. Raymond continued to stare until finally she looked away and studied her sopping wet socks. McDowell wriggled her toes and watched the excess fluid run out of the socks, producing a small puddle around her feet. Her toes felt no better but she knew she had to busy her senses elsewhere, before and during the imminent sexual torture.

'Hood, give the other Orger his tablet now and then after the first session is concluded give the first one a second dose.. Let's get on with this,' Raymond said, cutting the first Orger's hands free.

Kellor stood some distance away, still within the connecting tunnel. He was close enough to hear the hard tones of Raymond's voice, but far enough away not to see the hideous shadows of light that drained from the lamp in the room. Kellor lingered thoughtfully, as long as he could possibly bear before returning to the cavern to find Private Wayne. He knew he would hear the cries even from there, but that was the price of his betrayal, he was sure, and he no longer understood why he was forcing himself to play this meaningless game.

30 SOFTLY SOFTLY

'Callum, its McGeady here. I've just intercepted some interesting information,' he said smugly

'Firstly, where are you? Daniels asked.

'I'm at the base camp still. The five attacking groups are closing in as we speak. Currently they're about forty Ks from the signal source. Now for the good news. We intercepted a report transmitted on standard military wavebands. The Colonel or his men must've thought it safe to use this band. It probably didn't occur to them that anybody would be monitoring them and nobody would suspect a military band communication in the first place,' McGeady said, trying to cover every detail neatly.

'Get on with it McGeady. Give me the facts, not your embroidering on them.'

'The Colonel's men have located the Femorist Commune and they intend to attack at first light. The signal that we all have been tracking was located at an Orger camp. It seems Corporal McDowell, 'the rabbit' as the Colonel's men call her, was intercepted by the Orgers and taken captive by them.'

'So how do they know where the female base is if they didn't track the signal directly to it?'

'The Colonel's men overran the camp and got hold of McDowell. One way or another they managed to extract the base location from her.'

'I don't see it myself. It all seems a little bit too convenient for my liking,' Daniels paused. 'I want you to inform me as soon as you are sure that it is indeed the female base that they're heading towards and not just an elaborate smoke screen,' he continued thoughtfully.

'You have my word on it. Now, can I assume that the financial transactions for the mercenaries will be made as soon as the operation is completed? I don't think they'll want to wait around for too long afterwards to get paid. In fact, I am sure that they won't and I don't fancy being around if the payment's delayed!'

'Don't you worry about that Alec. I can give you my personal guarantee that they won't do you any harm - it's all in hand,' Daniels replied confidently.

McGeady thought it strange that Daniels should assure him that the mercenaries would not harm him. There was no way of guarantying his safety at the hands of these loathsome men. The moment passed as quickly as it arrived and Daniels spoke again.

'Before you go McGeady...Remember, when you call in with confirmation that the Colonel's men inside the Femorist base have been wiped out, that I also need to know two specific pieces of information. Firstly, if Nigel Lock and Colonel Johnson are there and secondly, your precise location - just so I can get support units to you as soon as possible,'

'Okay, understood. I gotta go now. I'm about to advance to where one of the five groups is maintaining the cordon around the Colonel's men.'

'Go on then. Call me as soon as you can.'

McGeady placed the radio mike on the console before him. His mind drifted back to Daniels' promise - the one assuring his safety - but he had no time to waste mulling it over before setting off to join in the hunt.

Kellor had decided not to wait for the snowstorm to relinquish its life-extinguishing grip on the area before taking the unit he commanded on the twenty-kilometre march to the female base. Neither had he waited for first morning light - the Orger's base had become far too depraved and claustrophobic for his liking. Raymond had been the one who had ultimately obtained the all-important information from McDowell. He had lost count of the number of times she had been violated before she unexpectedly screamed out the location of her base. When the ordeal had ended she sobbed quietly, huddled on the floor. By the time Raymond reported the success to his superior, two hours had passed since Kellor himself had instigated the interrogation method and all seven of the mutant prisoners were dead from 'Orgasma' overdoses. A fierce argument had begun between Raymond and Kellor as to whether it was practical to push on towards the Femorist base or if they should stay put, waiting for the storm to blow over. Kellor had argued that if he, a mere Mk I breed, could make the march, then the enhanced MkIIs should quite easily cope with the task. Raymond did not have the type of ego to let the challenge from an inferior breed pass unchecked. At 03:00 hours they set off towards the Femorist base, leaving McDowell behind. On Kellor's express orders, she had been dressed and left alive to fend for herself.

Progress was slow, somewhere between six or seven kilometres per hour, though that was pretty good considering the conditions and terrain. At 06:15 hours, the lead party in Kellor's unit had made visual contact with various landmarks that told them that they had arrived at their final destination. Kellor caught up with the lead group, forty-five minutes after they had arrived at their new forward observation point. He was quietly impressed that he had indeed made the march in the atrocious weather conditions and was still alive to prove Raymond wrong. Kellor had not particularly cared whether he survived the forced march or not - in fact it appeared to be the only permanent way out of the position in which he found himself. As he collapsed in what little shelter he could be bothered to find, Raymond came to him with a full head of steam, even after all the exertions of the twenty-kilometre march.

'So what now Major?' Raymond asked abrasively.

'I don't want to fight you Raymond. I have neither the energy, nor the inclination,' Kellor said, exhausted.

'It's going to be light soon, but I don't think we'll see much of it. Do we attack now or when it is certain to be dark in five or six hours?' Raymond asked, ignoring Kellor's plea to be left alone.

'If I must make that decision now, then the answer is that we will attack at first dark, happy?' Kellor replied as he closed his eyes and lay back behind the deepening snowdrift.

'Right. I'll tell the men. The attack will begin at around 13:00-hours.'

'Whatever. Wake me at noon and we'll construct a plan - that's if you don't already have one by then Raymond,' Kellor said carelessly, just before he rolled over and effortlessly sank into a disturbed sleep.

Raymond continued to stand above Kellor waiting. For what he did not know exactly - but whatever it was it did not come. He eventually stomped away at the first sign of a snore from the Major, with the feeling that he had somehow missed the point somewhere along the way.

McGeady had taken a low-level flight to the rendezvous point with Andre Turan's team. He was about to use a jet pack to travel from the wind-buffeted aircraft down to a very small clearing highlighted by a flare lit by Andre himself. McGeady had decided to join up with Andre's team for two reasons. Firstly, now that the target location had moved, Andre's team would arrive in the vicinity before the rest. And secondly, after having to dispose of Agent Chapel since Kellor had sowed seeds of doubt within him, he wanted to keep an eye on Beta, who had so far seemed unaffected by Kellor's betrayal.

McGeady hit the ground harder than he would have liked; it rushed up to meet him unseen, thanks to the blizzard that had engulfed the whole area. Andre's team had lost three mercenaries because of the weather and he was far from happy as he helped the ageing man to his feet.

'Good of you to join us Alec,' Andre shouted above the blast of the wind.

McGeady was unsure whether Andre's comment had been one of sarcastic insubordination or indeed a show of gratitude. However insignificant it appeared, the comment concerned him.

'Pretty poor conditions,' McGeady empathised.

'Tell me about it. Still, we only have eight Ks to negotiate, not as bad as the other four groups. I hope we're not left short of men by the time we have to attack. I've lost three so far. God knows how the other groups will fare,' Andre said, frowning behind his blizzard mask.

The two men made their way into one of the arctic survival tents that littered the wooded area where Andre's unit had made camp and they were grateful for the respite it provided from the storm. There was just enough room inside for the two of them, although both had to lie down on the cold hard groundsheet as they continued their conversation.

'What's the plan from this point on?' asked Andre, removing his blizzard mask.

'It's hard to judge. The Colonel's men were going to march to the target location immediately, but who knows when they'll attack. It's irrelevant whether they attack with the sun up or down, because most of the fighting will be done inside the Femorist base and not top side,' McGeady replied as he sat up.

'We must get in close. Just my unit to start with so we don't lose the element of surprise and then when we are sure that the attack is under way we can bring the other units up in support.'

'We don't want to run into the Colonel's men though - that wouldn't do,' McGeady stated, as he anxiously removed his gloves and blew vigorously on to his freezing fingers.

'We won't. Look,' Andre said, producing a map from his jacket and spreading it flat on the bare groundsheet that lay between them.

'The Colonel's men started out from here, where the tracked signal was radiating from. Their revised target location is here. Due to the terrain that they must travel across, they'll approach the Femorist base from this direction. If it were me, I'd use these low hills surrounding the base to assess the situation. So assuming all of that, we're currently located here, to the west of the Femorist base. If we take this route and set up an observation point here, we'll look down on not only the Femorist camp, but also the Colonel's men and their observation point,' Andre said, as he lay back, satisfied with his deductions.

'Not bad. But we definitely don't want to get drawn into a fight below ground if we can avoid it... Anyhow, when do you propose we set out?' McGeady asked, content to follow Andre's intuition.

'We have a few to spare hours I think. It will take us two or three hours to travel the distance to the observation point. If we set off at 03:00 hours, we should make it comfortably before first light,' replied Andre.

'Better get some sleep then,' McGeady said.

Andre rolled over and turned the small laser lamp to the setting marked 'dim' and McGeady took this to mean that Andre was happy for him to share the two-man tent. Turning up the heat setting on his artic suit, McGeady lay there trying to sleep - but his mind was full of anxiety about the immediate future. Apart from the stress of trying to anticipate Daniels' forthcoming moves, there was the concern about the location of the Femorist base, or rather the fact that it had inexplicably moved by hundreds of kilometres. It had been a long, long time since McGeady had been there. Perhaps they had moved during the time he had been out of contact. Somehow, he doubted it.

The small white civilian aircraft flew precariously down the valley like a plastic model bobbing on a string, well below the top of the valley's steep white sides. It took all the pilot's well-honed flying skills to keep from spreading himself across the terrain while tracking the bike's signal at the same time. Experienced pilot that he was, he still had difficulty in controlling the aircraft due to the vicious cross wind and, in an ideal world, he would have kept his feet firmly on the ground in such weather. Unfortunately, time was not on his side and if he was to save McDowell, he knew he would have to hasten the proceedings.

The aircraft blundered into touchdown not twenty feet from the cave entrance and Hanner was out of the craft before the single engine had stopped whistling. Dressed in light summer clothing more suitable for a visit to the beach than the current arctic storm he struggled against the howling wind, his Hawaiian shirt collar pulled close around his neck. He had been about to leave for his retirement destination when, inexplicably; he had been consumed with an almost paternal sense of concern for McDowell's well being. William could not explain the feeling, but he felt compelled to ensure that McDowell was okay before he finally went his own merry way. Marching swiftly to the cave entrance, he felt a severe chill in his soul and he prayed he was not too late. He entered the cave dwelling with some apprehension, carrying the pump action shotgun warily before him; he knew the area was going to be full of brainwashed livestock, looking to spill each other's manufactured blood. The howl of the storm outside dwindled to a remote whimper as he systematically made his way through the labyrinth of tunnels and chambers, all the while meticulously checking the bodies that were neatly stacked in various areas of the dwelling to ensure that McDowell was not amongst their number. And, as William eliminated the latest pile of cadavers at his feet, he heard McDowell's child-like cry.

'Rachel? Is that you Rachel?' William whispered.

The crying continued and his question went unanswered.

'Rachel? It's me William.'

The room swayed with darkness, as the scythe of light from William's laser torch cut through the black, before it eventually illuminated the fully clothed Corporal McDowell. She sat on the floor, knees drawn up to her chin, her gaze fixed on the open air between them.

'What has happened here Rachel? Have all the men gone? How long have you been here?' William blurted out.

Rachel began to sob and William attempted to get her to her feet, only to be met with a barrage of frantic kicking and slapping. He stood back as the involuntary fit of anger subsided within her and he stood there trying to find the key to release McDowell from her grief-stricken mental cell.

'Do you fancy that drink now? The one that you thought we'd never have?' William finally asked.

Slowly, McDowell lifted her head and then raised her defiled body to its feet.

'Are you buying?' McDowell asked plainly.

'I'm buying,' he concurred, finally smiling for the first time in days.

William left the shotgun behind in the interrogation room and led McDowell back to the waiting aircraft. He did not return for the weapon - he hoped he would have no need for it in their new life.

Raymond gently shook Kellor, in an effort to wake him from his deep sleep.

'Major wake up. We have movement down at the target area,' whispered Raymond.

'Major wake up now!' he said, raising his voice as much as he dare despite the storm still raging around them.

Before he could open his heavy eyelids, Raymond scooped up a handful of the surrounding snow and slapped it hard into Kellor's peaceful face. Kellor grimaced, more from the slap than the shock of the cold snow.

'What's the matter Sergeant? What's the time?' Kellor mumbled.

'It's 13:15 hours sir and if you don't wake up now I'll cut your throat and take charge myself,' Raymond replied irritably.

'Okay, okay, I'm awake. Now tell me again. What the hell is going on?' Kellor said, sitting bolt upright and yawning directly into Raymond's expectant face, much to Raymond's disgust.

'There's movement down at the entrance to the base. At first, there were just a few women. Then a military unit arrived,'

'How many women?'

'Fifteen or so. Visibility is still poor, but that's not the most interesting fact,' Raymond said and paused for effect.

'Don't get all theatrical on me Sergeant. What is this "most interesting fact" you refer to?' Kellor said, short of fortitude.

'They all have a similar appearance. So it probably means...' Raymond said, but before he could finish Kellor butted in.

'They're another lot of freaks.'

The MkIIs within earshot of Kellor stopped what they were doing and turned to face him. Kellor ignored the pressure of their glares and continued undiplomatically.

'They must have taken the risk and developed some of the eggs that they stole from the breeding farm. Let's hope that's the sum total of their freak development programme. Otherwise we may well have our arses whipped by a bunch of well-hung girlies,' he continued.

'So Major?' Raymond said, hoping to spark some coherent leadership.

'So fucking what?' replied Kellor uninterested.

'When do we attack?' Raymond persevered.

'Oh that! Well let's go and kick their little butts now shall we. Perhaps we will all find a merciful release,' Kellor replied strangely.

Raymond raised himself from his haunches and took Kellor's last statement to be an order, for he knew no other way of interpreting it. On all sides the MkIIs gathered themselves and their equipment without a thought passing between them and Kellor sat on his *al fresco* bed, scratching his head.

The route down towards the silo entrance was far from straightforward. Even with the poor visibility, any watchful female would be able to spot their initial advance at distance. Kellor was unconcerned. He was sure that if his team did not finish the job in hand, then it would not take the Colonel long to blitz the area with more men and hardware than was really needed for the job - and anyway, who cared about the ultimate outcome!

At long last Kellor got to his feet and for the first time became conscious of the men around him. He gazed at their young faces and knew that most of them would be dead before he got to know them. That had been the norm for the Eurostate population for many years: inexpressive isolation. The deep grip of despondency had at last breached Kellor's former clarity of purpose. He knew that he had somehow lost his way in life without ever having had the definitive route in the first place. On the other hand, he thought, had he simply exposed the fact that it had had little meaning all along?

Raymond hovered, waiting for his superior to head the advance *en route* for the Femorist base. Kellor had become impervious to his Sergeant's facial expressions, which were intended to intimidate him, and without even a cursory glance in Raymond's direction Kellor led the stream of soldiers from the camp.

Through his electronic image enhancers, Andre peered down upon Kellor's unit as they made their way precariously over the rough terrain down towards the silo entrance. He gently shook his head in disbelief until he finally lifted the enhancers away from his eyes as compassion for their certain fate overwhelmed him.

'He's gone insane. If the women spot them before they get to that tree cover below then, well; they'll be cut to pieces,' Andre said to McGeady.

'Either way, it doesn't matter to us in the long run. We have to take out one group or another, or maybe just mop up whoever is left,' McGeady replied happily.

'But why? You told me this man Kellor was an experienced soldier,' asked Andre, still concerned about the unfolding events.

'Don't worry yourself unnecessarily. In twenty-four hours you'll be out of here and counting your hard-earned money in some bar,' McGeady replied dismissively.

'Where are the other teams? Close by I hope,' asked Andre, ignoring McGeady's complacency.

'You worry too much! But in answer to your question, all four teams are within an hour of here. What state they'll been in when they get here is another matter!'

'And the fighter escort we had earlier? Do we still have use of them now?' persisted Andre, thinking fast.

'Of course. I just have to call them in when we need them. Hopefully we won't.'

Andre scanned the crude encampment that his team of mercenaries had hastily erected on the high peak. He was looking for Beta and his eyes finally settled on her huddled frame, far away from the boisterous group of men.

'This woman - is she any good?' he asked without taking his eyes off her.

'The best; so I'm told,' McGeady replied as he followed Andre's gaze towards Beta.

'What's the deal with her anyway?' Andre quizzed.

'It seems a few modified genes, a cocktail of enhanced data input and hey presto, one male in a female body. More than a match for any of your big tough mercenaries.'

While the two men continued to talk over the attributes of the Female MkII, Healy Nelson walked across towards the forlorn figure. Nelson carried a plate of food that the group of men had just prepared and offered the steaming stew to Beta. Before she could accept the friendly gesture, a less broad-minded mercenary took exception to his kindness, followed Nelson's footsteps in the snow and began taking them both to task.

'What the fuck are you feeding her for Nelson? She's a woman - she can cook for herself,' snapped the irritated mercenary.

'We don't need any problems over here Pierce. There's more than enough food for everyone. Just let her be. She doesn't want to fight you,' Nelson replied.

Beta did not move from her kneeling position as she hungrily grabbed the plate of stew. Nelson faced Pierce as he stood antagonistically over the famished MkII. Pierce was an extraordinarily large man, six feet seven and 500 kilos, but smart and vicious with it. Andre watched with increasing interest as the potential violence loomed.

'Nelson fuck off! I want to talk to the lady, alone,' Pierce said without taking his eyes from Beta.

'She's gonna kick your arse Pierce. Mark my words,' Nelson said shaking his head.

Nelson did not know this for a fact, but he was sure that the government did not allow just any old female livestock on a trip such as theirs.

'She's all yours Pierce,' Nelson said as the tense stand-off continued.

Pierce bent down and buried his face in the plate of untouched stew that Beta was holding. He raised his head quickly and chewed for all to see what little food that had gone into his mouth. Dark brown gravy covered his petit facial features and then Pierce slapped the plate from Beta's hand and began to walk away laughing, wiping the sticky mess from his unshaven bristles. Beta sat down placidly and closed her eyes.

'I'm taking her down to the base with me,' Andre said, still observing the remarkable woman.

'What?' McGeady asked, slightly surprised.

'She and I will go down now and get a closer look as to what is going on. When the other groups arrive, make your way down and join us,' Andre replied.

'Why her? Why not one of the men?' asked McGeady perplexed.

'She has control. Not like these hot heads. I don't want someone dropping me in the shit when we're inside the base. It also means that they won't know for sure if I'm her prisoner or she's mine. It should buy us some time until we can take control of any situation that we may have to face,' Andre said, as sure of himself as he had ever been.

Kellor and his unit had arrived at the safety of the tree line, which was close to the entrance of the silos. Raymond had stayed very close to the Major, unsure of his state of mind. His limited military training had meant that he was blissfully unaware of the potential danger in which their commanding officer had placed them. So, like the rest of the unit, he had marched side by side with the Major. Kellor was in no mood to delay the attack and after only ten minutes was ready to move forwards and away from the safe haven of the trees. Ahead were half a dozen disused silos, fully contained underground and all that was visible from the surface were six massive circular indents in the snow-covered ground. The only part of the base that showed was two solid steel doors set into a reinforced concrete dome. To Kellor's amazement the doors stood ajar, as if someone had been putting the cat out and had forgotten to close them. Even in Kellor's careless state of mind, he was dubious about this ostensibly open invitation to him and his team.

'Sergeant, one way in only. I'll take three men and get inside. If you hear shots we're dead, so don't follow,' Kellor smiled as he stated the obvious and continued. 'If you hear nothing after fifteen minutes follow us in. We'll secure an area to re-group and then go walkabout,' Kellor finished his order.

Raymond nodded and the soldiers that Kellor had requested stepped forward to join him. The four men immediately scampered across the fifty metres of open expanse between the tree line and the silo entrance. Kellor was the last to reach the open doors and ran past the MkIIs who were nervously peering into the darkened portals, checking for threats. The silo entrance gave the impression of being completely disused. But Raymond had seen women enter the base, so Kellor assumed that it must be inhabited to some degree. His eyes grew accustomed slowly to the gloom but he sensed that there were no traps in the immediate vicinity. The three MkIIs entered cautiously and joined the Major by the old steel cage lift. Kellor placed his hand on the elevator motor next to the entrance and lovingly caressed its warmth with his bare hands.

'I'm going to call the service elevator. You two stay here and secure this area. You, come with me. We'll take a chance that they're expecting more residents to arrive,' Kellor whispered to the three men stood in front of him.

'Are you sure about this Sir?' asked one of the fearful soldiers.

'Did they teach you to question orders during your training soldier or do you want to be put up on a charge?' Kellor asked seriously.

'No Sir!' replied the soldier, far too loudly for Kellor's liking.

'Now you're trying give the game away. I'll tell you what soldier, address me as you would another one of your breed, okay?' ordered Kellor.

'But you won't hear me Sir,' replied the soldier, failing to comprehend the Major's reasoning.

Kellor smiled back at the soldier and shook his head. No more was said, as the confused MkII followed his commanding officer into the cage-like elevator. The motor began to hum as they descended to the only floor that they could reach from the service elevator.

Raymond watched the digits on his watch count down towards the completion of the fifteen minutes' head start afforded to Kellor. 'It's too long,' Raymond thought to himself and without further ado all but two of the unit headed for the silo entrance. The two MkII's already guarding the uppermost entrance area of the silo sighed with relief as their companions swelled their numbers.

'Where's Major Kellor?' Raymond silently asked the two men by the lift shaft.

Both men replied obediently and Raymond had to separate the differently worded answers as the thoughts entwined themselves within his head.

'The Major and Private Willis have gone down to check out and secure the area below us. Is that correct?' the Sergeant queried, in an effort to disentangle the scrambled replies.

Raymond held his thoughts back, trying not to alarm the men around him, but they sensed the rage and panic within his mind.

Lieutenant Jenny Stroud spoke calmly to the thirty or so women assembled in the disused operations room. All were dressed as normal combat personnel. Though, in one corner of the room stood fifteen women carefully made up to look identical.

'I've called this meeting just to let everyone know that the first group of men have arrived and are now entering the silo complex. We don't have a fix on where the other group is, but you can be sure that they won't be far behind. If you could all take up your operating stations immediately after we leave this room, I'd be grateful. You should all know by now what you're supposed to be doing. Kathy Taylor, our resident explosives expert, tells me that all charges in the silo have been set. If we survive the attack it'll be a miracle, frankly, and every one of us has accepted the consequences for the sake of our Chernobyl commune's continued survival. For your sacrifice, Commune Leader Kefelnikov sends her heartfelt thanks. Especially that is, to Corporal McDowell who, unfortunately, seems to have disappeared somewhere between where we intercepted her as she returned to the commune and making her way to the silo base here. This will probably be the last time that we speak as a group. So it just remains to say good luck and good hunting,' Stroud said, as she at last raised a desperate smile to signal the end of her team briefing.

Privates Jackson and Eastwood had been ordered to remain topside by their Sergeant and were busy digging a shallow snow trench in which to shelter from the biting wind. Both were relaxed; they knew there would be plenty of warning before they would have to face any action. Thoughts passed between them freely until the interference of a third party's brain waves interrupted their conversation, just as if someone had turned on a poorly tuned radio and begun to drown their voices out in a babble of static. Despite not recognising the thought patterns, both soldiers assumed that the interference was emanating from the silo and so trained their eyes on the open entrance. Crouching down and taking a defensive firing position, the soldiers began to relax again, feeling that everything was in hand. As they waited, the interference in their minds gradually increased in volume and intensity, until finally Jackson began to panic and turned to look away from the inactive silo entrance. Beta and Andre stood side by side, pointing their pistols directly at the stunned soldiers. Their female sibling smiled gently down upon them. Andre was less understanding for he scowled at the soldiers as he fired two stun laser bolts into their white-clad bodies.

'Why don't you kill them?' Beta asked as the noise in her head abated to a low hum.

'Never kill unless you have to. You never know when you may be in need of a little reciprocal mercy and I may be able to use them for my own purposes if we get out of this alive,' Andre replied.

'Shall I tie them up Sir?' Beta inquired.

'Of course. I'm not that charitable. Once you've done that, gag them and take them over there behind those trees. Then cover them in snow so that they can't be seen,' ordered Andre.

'Yes Sir,' Beta replied as she went about her orders.

Andre moved forward to the edge of the tree line and scanned the peaceful silo entrance for himself. He was ready to move on before Beta had finished her tasks and he waited impatiently for her to join him. Finally, as they set off side by side towards the open doors, Andre pulled the lucky coin up from his neck chain on which it hung. He kissed the well-worn dollar; it had been one of many that Andre had been paid as part of his first mercenary earnings and it had kept him safe ever since.

Raymond and his men had entered the large service elevator and set off in pursuit of the maverick Major Kellor. The elevator seemed to have been recently serviced, for it descended quietly. Raymond needed space to think but he had no time to evaluate the situation thoroughly, besides, extensions of his mind surrounded him and his alarm would have spread rapidly rendering the situation unsalvageable.

The men close to the Sergeant sensed his anxiety as the elevator stopped at the only floor. The doors were pulled back rapidly and the MkII soldiers assumed defensive positions in the dank and musty hallway ahead of them. The soldiers scurried amongst the rats as they grew more confident that the probable ambush was a mere figment of Raymond's imagination. There was the annoying sound of dripping water, echoing around the seemingly derelict base and more than one soldier conveyed his telepathic annoyance at the sound. Most, however, went about their business too terrified to contemplate the irrelevant cause of the dripping sound. For the time being, they seemed safe but Raymond could find little sign of Major Kellor's whereabouts.

Organised into small groups, the unit began to edge its way out from their secure foothold. Gradually it began to dawn on Raymond, judging by the state of the silo base, that it must have been previously uninhabited. But if so, why the earlier influx of women? Why the beautifully repaired and restored elevator? The odds were stacking up in his mind and he was sure now that he and his team were sitting in the middle of an extremely elaborate deception. The final clue arrived when the lights were suddenly and completely extinguished. No longer making headway into the unknown, Raymond stopped and contemplated their next course of action.

Andre stood in the centre of the elevator with a gun to Beta's head. He opened the grille-style doors with his free hand and slowly moved forward. The two MkII soldiers waited patiently outside for the occupants of the elevator to show themselves. Andre could smell them in the darkness and he calmly switched on the NVG's that he had placed upon his head earlier. Again the soldiers heard interference in their minds as the occupants edged from the protection of the elevator and into full view. Unaware that he was being bombarded with questions from the two soldiers, Andre began to speak.

'I found this bitch in the forest. I thought I should find out what I'm to do with her?' he said, looking around trying to gain a clear shot at both targets.

'You take the one on the left. I'll take the man to the right,' Andre whispered into the Beta's ear.

'Is that Eastwood?' one of the soldiers inquired verbally, exasperated at the lack of a lucid extrasensory reply.

'Of course it's me, who else would it be?' replied Andre unconvincingly and he knew he would have to make his move now.

Beta felt the mock pressure of the laser pistol being removed from her back and knew it was time to carry out Andre's order. Launching herself over the worthless barrier that stood between her and the soldier on the left hand side, Beta threw herself down with her full weight upon the man's chest. Surprised by the instant attack on the soldier, Andre only managed to wing his target with his first shot. The soldier was not so lucky the second time around and fell instantly dead in a heap behind the improvised defences. Turning quickly, Andre caught sight of the ensuing fight between the two MkIIs. The two bodies rolling around on the floor merged into one and he tried to pick his shot to no avail. Giving up all hope of visually distinguishing Beta amongst the roiling mass of human limbs, Andre decided to take the fifty-fifty chance offered to him and set his pistol to stun. As the two bodies rolled unchecked, he fired multiple bolts at the first torso he managed to get a clear shot at. A single lifeless body fell limp and the indistinguishable person below began to thrash about, trying to free themselves from beneath its flaccid weight. The body eventually slumped to one side and the dark haired soldier stood up confused and terrified.

'Sorry. I can't risk having you regain consciousness,' Andre said altering the pistol setting and shooting dead the young MkII soldier cowering in front of him.

Bending down to attend to Beta, Andre hoped that she was only momentarily stunned and would soon be able to fight on beside him.

'Shit!' he cursed realising that she was out cold and he began dragging the body towards the nearest door.

By the time Andre was ready to move on down through the dark corridors, Beta was safely bundled into one of the small disused storerooms to recover, if she was able.

'Hopefully I'll see you later my sweet,' Andre said, closing the squealing door behind him before assessing in which direction he should head.

The explosion threw Andre across the narrow passageway where he was pinned to the rancid and sodden floor, crushed by the fallen masonry and elevator machinery. The silence gradually returned and the dust began to settle over the wreckage.

It was no more than ten minutes before Andre was extricated from beneath the twisted remains of the collapsed lift shaft. However, both his legs had been severed just above the knees. Beta held him firmly while she carried his broken body back to the storeroom, where she had woken. Earlier, she had regained consciousness and, bewildered by the realisation that she had been abandoned once more; she had set out to find Andre.

'Don't leave me here to die alone,' Andre pleaded breathlessly.

Beta looked down upon him impassively showing only a faint trace of a smile.

'You shot me and then left me on my own,' she said accusingly.

Andre raised his tremulous hand, groped for the dollar that hung around his neck and found it had gone.

'Where's my lucky charm? You must find it or I will certainly die...'

Beta caressed the bloodstained neck from where the lucky charm had gone missing and squeezed firmly. Andre gripped the delicate female wrists that clutched his throat but the blood loss from his severed legs had plundered his strength. Still he tried to release the pressure that was choking the life from his body but without success. The instant that Andre ceased to live, Beta released her grip and gazed upon the well-worn silver dollar nestling in the palm of her left hand.

The mercenaries, or rather what was left of them after their exhausting trek in atrocious weather conditions, had regrouped and now marched cautiously towards the devastated silo entrance. Carrying an anti-personnel grenade launcher, McGeady brought up the rear of the fifty or so men that had survived. Andre was trapped, McGeady knew that for a fact, and he was pleased that the other mercenary leaders who were left alive had little fight left in them. Up ahead, the column of men stopped to take stock of the situation and McGeady began to whistle silently in his head. He did not pay too much attention to the cursing and planning he could hear up ahead. Instead, he wandered aimlessly deeper into the wooded area that surrounded the shambolic group of men, as if he was going to relieve himself. Playing with his clothing for a few brief moments McGeady initialised his grenade launcher and then, to complete the charade, urinated up a tree. When he had finished, McGeady raised the anti-personnel weapon to the top of his shoulder and took aim with his left eye. Gradually he began to edge backwards away from the group of shattered men while the launcher continually advised him of its safe discharge distance. The visual display on the weapon acknowledged that a safe distance from the target had been reached and without hesitation, McGeady fired.

Kellor and the MkII were held in the clutches of the first female trap that they had stumbled upon. They crouched amongst old provision boxes, which had been abandoned when the silo had been last used many years before. Hoping to avoid detection by his arctic fatigues, Kellor stripped off the white outer layers of his clothing, which seemed to positively glow in the dark, and he gestured for his subordinate to do the same. They both had felt the large explosion and Kellor feared the worst. It was at that precise moment that they had been attacked by persons unknown and unseen. Private Willis was Kellor's main concern. He needed him alive, for alone he knew he would be helpless.

'Keep very close to me Private. We're going to backtrack our way out of here very carefully,' Kellor ordered.

'Sir, I can hear Raymond. Do you want me to ask for assistance?' Private Willis reported.

'What are you waiting for? Call him or do whatever you do and tell him to get his arse in here now,' Kellor said glancing circumspectly over the crate that they were hiding behind.

The laser bolt grazed the darkness, before blasting splintered and fiery wood in all directions. Kellor instantly rolled to one side of the crate and fired multiple rounds in the general direction of the enemy. His was met with a robust reaction. Around a dozen lines of tracer threaded their way towards the crate, like horizontal strands of brilliant red wool dancing in the wind and in moments the solid wooden structure began to burn wildly out of control.

'So that did the trick!' said Kellor, unamused by the enemies' response.

He turned, slowly backing away from the searing heat that was radiating from the burning crate. He looked for Private Willis and saw him slumped over into his own lap.

'Do you always assume that strange position when you're talking to Raymond,' Kellor joked hopefully.

The lack of reaction from Private Willis told Kellor what he had dreaded most. He crawled in close to the lifeless body and pulled Private Willis over onto his side. A large piece of packing crate had viciously splintered and plunged all the way through the young soldier's chest. Sadness filled Kellor again. It seemed to him that recently, every time he had managed to re-motivate himself, something brought him back down to earth with a crash. Kellor sat miserably, feeling the warmth of the flames loosen the tension stored within his muscles and he wondered if Private Willis had managed to get a message through to Raymond before his untimely death. The Major's flamed silhouette made an inviting target for the unseen enemy, but for some reason the bolt never arrived. Kellor waited for something to transpire, exactly what he did not know, before unexpectedly he was grabbed from behind and manhandled to the relative safety of the adjoining corridor.

'Major, is that you?' Beta whispered while holding Kellor in a delicate embrace that left him unable to move.

'Beta. How the hell did you get here?' he said stunned.

'With some men.'

'What men?'

'Just men. Mr Daniels sent me with them. Where have you been? They said that you're a traitor,' Beta explained simply.

The flames flickered unseen beyond the safety of the metal door and Kellor picked out Beta's image in its tarnished steel surface. The firm embrace in which he was held did not relax and he began to panic without really comprehending why.

'Beta, let me go,' ordered Kellor without success.

Before she could reply, numerous footsteps echoed from the corridor behind them. Beta span rapidly and caught a glimpse of the advancing men. She backed into the storeroom behind her and dragged Kellor along on his heels.

'Beta let me go and I'll protect you. Those men they work for me. You have nothing to fear. Let me go now!' Kellor screamed.

The bear hug relaxed and he seized the opportunity to turn and interrogate Beta's eyes. Confusion flooded from her features and Kellor was, for just one instant, transported far away from the time and place in which he was lost.

The remaining soldiers of the MkII unit approached the open door, firing as they advanced, unable to identify the retreating targets clearly. Distracted, Beta glanced quickly over the Major's shoulder and saw the streaking laser bolts bearing down upon them and threw herself to the ground to the rear of the door. Kellor spun on his heels in an effort to halt the rapid advance of the unit he commanded, however, he only managed a few short steps before the full weight of their firepower began to flay his discharged and powerless flak jacket. Beta regained her feet and, still skulking behind the safety of the steel door, she heard

Kellor's cry for help as he lay mortally wounded. The Femorists, on hearing the gunfire, had decided to reinforce the position above the burning crate. Lieutenant Jenny Stroud could barely identify the target silhouetted by the burning packing crate's glare and ordered the women around her to pepper the general area with as much firepower as they could muster. The gunfire drew an immediate response from the advancing MkII unit and they began laying down a barrage of shots in an effort to ward off any impending attack. The lethal standoff continued for what seemed an age before the shooting relented and a hush descended and the dripping could be heard once again.

The two frayed bodies now lay either side of the steel door, choking for breath and groping for some unattainable comfort in the darkness that bounded them both.

'I always knew it,' Raymond said, running towards the Major and kicking him full in the face.

The weight of the kick halted what little progress Kellor was making towards the doorway as he tried to reach Beta before she died alone. Kellor had no strength left even to cry out in pain; he lay on his back, gazing up at Raymond who was staring accusingly. Blood ran into Kellor's eyes and he began to blink furiously, trying to clear the stinging red mist from his sight. Beta had given up her fight for life without any further intervention from Raymond or his men. The fire that now raged through most of the storeroom was licking its way towards her withered body and eventually the flames began to turn Beta's white arctic suit, little by little, to powder black. Raymond could see that there was no way of pursuing the enemy through the furious fire and so he turned his attentions yet again towards Major Kellor.

'Major. Can you hear me?' Raymond shouted.

'Are you "the" spy, or just "a" spy?' continued Raymond, enjoying the power he now held over his superior.

Kellor moved his mouth, but no words issued from the willing lips as he battled to maintain his brittle grasp on life. Perplexing thoughts of Corporal McDowell and the vile acts committed against her seeped through his brain.

'Shall I shoot him Sir?' thought one of the remaining MkII soldiers next to Raymond.

'Waste of a bolt,' replied Raymond, convinced of Kellor's impending demise.

'Let's get out of here. Back up to the tunnel that led towards the air purifying system. There must be some way out through there,' Raymond ordered.

'What about the men down at the lift exit Sir?' another soldier's thought permeated Raymond's head.

'They're both dead. I've been trying to contact them for the last half an hour without success. I can't get through to the men on the surface either. Radio communications are useless unless we find the comms room for the silo base. I'd say we're in deep shit,' Raymond explained, now unconcerned that he might alarm the MkII soldiers around him.

Raymond doubled back in the direction from which he and his men had come and returned to the air-ducting tunnel. They had been heading that way originally, that was until Private Willis had managed to request their assistance before he died. Resigned to their fate, Raymond's thoughts darted. He did not particularly care what goal Kellor was working towards. He was just happy that he no longer had to take orders from a man who had been born of an inferior breed of livestock. The remaining soldiers shuffled along anxiously behind Raymond, most too scared to contemplate the hopelessness of their situation.

McGeady scanned the dead bodies strewn across the ravaged landscape in front of him, searching for any signs of life to be extinguished. He began to walk amongst the minced carcasses, shooting anything that looked remotely alive. While continuing to wander around almost aimlessly, he pulled the communications unit from his pocket and called in one of the seconded fighters to pick him up. The vast explosion cast McGeady to the charcoal soil, where the odour of burning flesh from the exterminated mercenaries summoned the contents of his stomach. The area surrounding the silo entrance dropped in an instant, some sixty feet with the second and third implosions. By now, McGeady was desperately wishing that he had not hung around to ensure that there were no witnesses to his act of treason. Using the bodies as leverage, he began to climb his way out from the crater, which now had developed several cavities that plummeted into a lethal abyss. Fire spewed from two of the openings like a pair of duelling dragons, instantly melting the snow around their death trap. McGeady slowly slunk his way to the undefined rim above, being careful not to lose his grip and roll down to what would have been certain death. He saw the swirl of snow first and then realised that the fighter engines had been audible for some time. But he had been too engrossed in escaping the potentially fatal earth subsidence to take any conscious notice of them. Under his own effort he was almost free of the crater when the cable that the pilot had thrown down hit him square on the head. McGeady attached the cable around his waist and with its assistance he crawled his way to the crater's edge.

'Looks a bit of a mess Sir,' the pilot said, helping McGeady to his feet.

Although the vicious storm had subsided significantly, McGeady could not see a great deal, as it was getting darker by the minute.

'Yes. We were attacked from all fronts and then the ground fucking dropped from under our feet,' McGeady answered agitatedly.

'You look unscathed though? Are you sure you're okay Sir?'

'What's your problem? Is that so hard to believe? You've seen nothing right! You flew in and landed some distance from here and you saw nothing,' McGeady barked at the naive young pilot.

Before he could conclude his threat, laser fire began to explode around them. The instinct for survival was still as strong as ever in McGeady. He grabbed the pilot and rapidly made his way to the fighter cockpit. The kid finally came to his senses and shrugged off McGeady's grip before they both climbed into the open cockpit, one after the other. Within a few short moments, the fighter was airborne and McGeady began to puzzle over not only where the laser fire had come from, but also at its lack of accuracy.

'Make a pass over the general area of the silo base,' McGeady ordered when he realised the pilot was trying to get away as fast as the aircraft could manage.

'Yes Sir. Just one thing though Sir, if they have laser surface to air weapons we won't stand a chance at that altitude,' replied the fraught pilot.

'Just do it son and I'll ensure you get decorated for it,' McGeady replied confidently.

The aircraft sharply swung around and dipped down low, so as to embrace the contours of the terrain below. Even McGeady was impressed at the precision and verve with which the pilot negotiated his way back to the area where they had been attacked. Before they reached the immediate vicinity of the silo base, the heat sensors picked up the traces of ten men making their way down towards the devastated epicentre of the large underground explosions. McGeady thought it unlikely that the government forces had managed to climb their way out of the demolished missile base. Or for that matter any of the women, who had so bravely sacrificed their lives to ensure survival of the majority back at the commune. No, he was sure there was more to these blips of scanned heat on the screen in front of him and so the aircraft once again swooped low over the signal sources. McGeady calmly activated every sensor available to him on the virtual reality flight deck and began to download the biological profiles of Nigel Lock and the Colonel.

'Get out of here. Now!' McGeady ordered as the pilot finished the fourth pass without a shot being fired in anger.

'Whatever you say Sir,' replied the confused but relieved pilot.

The screen flashed before McGeady with possible biological matches for Nigel Lock and Colonel Johnson, just as he patched himself through to Daniels on the secure microwave radio link.

'Daniels. It's done. Lock and the Colonel are at the conflict site. Looking for the eggs I suppose. Over,' McGeady said triumphantly, unaware that his assumption had already cost him his life.

'And the base, was it the female commune that we have been searching for, over?' Daniels replied nervously, having waited many hours for the call.

The long pause made for painful listening and Daniels began to think that the microwave link had been broken.

'Yes Sir. I can confirm that the Femorist commune is indeed located at the area previously earmarked for surveillance and that the commune is destroyed as ordered. I can also confirm that the biological traces of Nigel Lock and Colonel Martin Johnson have within the last few minutes been picked up at the site. Over,' McGeady reported in a well-rehearsed manner.

'Good work McGeady. See you when you get back to Berlin,' Daniels replied smiling.

McGeady did not reply. Instead he broke the comms link and yelled at the pilot.

31 DESTRUCTION

The missile flew straight and true despite its mothballed years spent hidden from the Americans. The twentieth century technology worked perfectly as the small but powerful nuclear warhead tracked its way to the silo base some four hundred miles away. The device was miniscule in comparison to the nation-threatening missiles developed by the Russians and the Americans at around the start of the cold war, but this was exactly what Daniels needed. He hoped that the initial explosion and the resulting nuclear fallout would disinfect the silo base and a surrounding area for a radius of about 200 kilometres. Anybody caught below the surface would be trapped at best and the people above ground would be incinerated instantly. The radar display in McGeady's fighter picked up the supersonic ICBM (Inter-Continental Ballistic Missile) clearly and the pilot turned to McGeady with panic slicing lines of trepidation across his juvenile face.

'Sir, I've picked up a fast moving signal on one of my screens,' reported the pilot.

'Aircraft or what?' asked a concerned McGeady.

'I can't tell Sir,' answered the pilot uneasily.

'Best guess son and make it quick. Our lives could depend on it.'

'Missile of some sort. Not moving fast enough to be one of our latest but, still a missile all the same. It's not targeting us it would seem, but it is heading for the area that we have just evacuated from Sir.'

'Daniels you bastard!' McGeady cursed gently.

'Excuse me Sir?'

'Don't you worry about it son. Just get us out of the area as quickly as possible. I've got the feeling there's going to be a very big bang soon and we don't want to be hanging around here when it goes off.'

The pilot took the aircraft into a steep climb, draining every last drip of thrust from the engines and both occupants were thrown back ferociously into their seats as a result.

'Where we heading son, the sun?' McGeady said somehow finding his last modicum of morbid humour.

'Sir, if we get high enough we'll be okay. Most nuclear missiles direct their full force horizontally not vertically. It's as good a chance as we've got Sir.'

'Who said anything about nuclear missiles...'

'Would you want to get out of here so fast if it wasn't?' replied the pilot straining every muscle to keep control of the violently shaking aircraft.

The missile signature on the radar screen intersected the co-ordinates of where the silo base was located, before disappearing instantly. The dark clouds that enveloped the Cobra immediately blazed with an explosive deadly white light as the aircraft disintegrated before McGeady's very eyes and he knew that he was going to die.

State television devoted barely a minute of airtime to the massive explosion, which had occurred on the previous day. The initial news blackout had only been replaced with a few dubious and sketchy details and Daniels watched with some amusement as the newsreader told one lie after another.

'Yesterday in an area eight hundred kilometres north of the Chernobyl nuclear disaster site, Femorists unintentionally exploded a nuclear device that had been intended to hold the Eurostate to ransom. The explosion devastated an area of approximately two hundred square kilometres but there are no reports of any male victims as the location is thought to be completely unpopulated. The area is already well known for the contamination generated by the Chernobyl meltdown, which occurred in the late 20th century. It is thought that the fallout from yesterday's explosion will cause few further problems to the Eurostate as a whole. Now for the weather,' reported the newsreader.

Daniels sat contentedly, holding the thought that most, if not all of his enemies had been wiped out in one single manoeuvre.

The Colonel and Nigel Lock huddled in the small underground office, satisfied that they had escaped with their lives. The now muted broadcast played out on the small computer screen and Lock frowned further as he saw from the weather report that it was going to snow again.

'Good job I still had access to my contacts in Military Ordnance. We might have been there amongst that mess if it hadn't been for the tip off from Hakinen,' Colonel Johnson advised.

'The clones we sent won't throw them off the scent for long though. Daniels will wallow in the glory for a while and then he'll pick up where he left off,' Lock warned.

'Now that the eggs are gone and our power base has been undermined we may as well leave here and set up elsewhere, away from Daniels' reach,' the Colonel suggested.

'Far East? We have some sympathisers there that we can meet up with and re-group,' suggested Lock.

The door to Lock's office slammed shut precisely at the same time that Olga Kefelnikov opened hers and set out for the IVF Lab to see Dr Oliver. The weatherman's voice faded behind her as she jauntily made her way along the corridor and entered the elevator. It did not take Kefelnikov long to find Dr Oliver, who was engaged in deep conversation with one of the lab technicians.

'Dr Oliver, how are things?' Kefelnikov asked excitedly.

'Fine. It may be some time though before you have your army. You see we can only breed in batches of twenty. So I think it may be as well to place fully developed livestock with other communes around the Eurostate until we are ready to re-group. If we keep them all here until then we'll all starve,' Dr Oliver stated.

'That's fine Doctor. It seems we may have inadvertently been supplied with all the time that we need now,' Kefelnikov said smiling.

❖ ❖ ❖ THE END ❖ ❖ ❖

ACKNOWLEDGEMENTS

I've dreamt of writing this part of Extinction for many years - I suppose it reminds me of all those cheesy acceptance speeches at award ceremonies (although I've not won anything)- I'd like to thank my cat, my dog, but most of all everyone who believed in me blah blah blah!

Still, there are people to thank, who without their influence, this novel would not have been written. It started with Elise, my special needs daughter just after she was born in 1998. She was diagnosed with Williams Syndrome at about four weeks old, devastating is the only way to describe it. Unfortunately, one of the symptoms of WS is a lack of restful sleep, which obviously means parents endure difficult nights, these being more pronounced than that of a healthy child.

I started to write as Elise slept fretfully through the night and into the early hours - choosing to avoid hours of broken sleep and just crack on and write Extinction. However, this was not her only influence on the book, I got to thinking how the Nazi's had abhorrently murdered special needs children during the war after one particular father had written to one of Hilter's ministries to ask if he could unconditionally euthanize his handicapped son?! I then wondered how certain people aspire for the perfect child in terms of eye and hair colour, sex, etc - where does this stop, now that our wonderful scientific community can manipulate our genes and produce children to order, a commodity to be traded like some pedigree dog.

Don't get me wrong - if I could wave a magic wand and give my daughter a normal healthy life then I would. But this transformation would be for her fulfilment and not due to any selfish or futile quest for perfection on my part. When we first found out about Elise's condition another WS parent said to me "parents are devastated that their child will never play the piano or speak a foreign language - but remember a healthy child might not do these things either...". Now in a strange way I found this extremely annoying - assuming my sadness and pain for my daughter's condition was due to me not being proud of her - as if my needs and feelings were more important than hers! My sadness for Elise's condition comes from how she will cope with her disabilities and how she will be treated throughout her life and has nothing to do with my position as the *'proud father'* who hopes to see his child excel in life - I could not be prouder of my beautiful daughter even if she was a child protégée.

I would also like to say a big thanks to Mindy Lou (you know who you are!). In 2004/05 my life to fell apart, leaving the martial home, finding my corporate job and corporate arseholes too much to bear after my split. Wandering in the wilderness for many months I finally met Mindy Lou and she has been a source of inspiration and support and truly I am not quite sure where I would be now without her influence and love.

During the last two years my parents have been a major support and have encouraged me to pursue my aspirations as an author, never once saying 'don't be silly son - go back to a steady job and live an unfulfilled life...' Thank you!

Finally, I'd also like to thank the wonderful M-Y Books for helping me achieve the publication of 'Extinction', thank you Jonathan and Kevin for all of your help and patience.

P G McKenzie